The Cuckoo Child

Katie Flynn has lived for many years in the north-west. A compulsive writer, she started with short stories and articles and many of her early stories were broadcast on Radio Merseyside. She decided to write her Liverpool series after hearing the reminiscences of family members about life in the city in the early years of the twentieth century. She also writes as Judith Saxton. For the past few years, she has had to cope with ME but has continued to write.

Also available by Katie Flynn

KATIE FLYNN

The Cuckoo Child

arrow books

5 7 9 10 8 6

Arrow Books
20 Vauxhall Bridge Road
London SW1V 2SA

Arrow Books is part of the Penguin Random House group of companies
whose addresses can be found at global.penguinrandomhouse.com.

Copyright © Katie Flynn 2005

Katie Flynn has asserted her right to be identified as the
author of this Work in accordance with the Copyright,
Designs and Patents Act 1988.

First published in Great Britain by William Heinemann in 2005
First published in paperback by Arrow Books in 2005
This edition reissued by Arrow Books in 2018

www.penguin.co.uk

A CIP catalogue record for this book is available from the British Library.

Typeset by Palimpsest Book Production Limited, Falkirk, Stirlingshire

Penguin Random House is committed to a sustainable future for
our business, our readers and our planet. This book is made from
Forest Stewardship Council® certified paper.

Printed and bound in Great Britain by Clays Ltd, Elcograf S.p.A.

For Maisie Latto, whose memories of the
Buster Stalls and their chips and peas
took me straight back to my own childhood.

Acknowledgements

Many thanks to Fred Prince for putting me right on cockney rhyming slang and conditions in the East End pre the Second World War – thanks Fred!

Chapter One

March 1928

'Dot! Aw, c'mon, Dot, I knows you're there!'

The shout came clearly to Dot's ears, echoing slightly through the tin lid of the dustbin in which she was hiding. She could tell that Fizz was in the jigger which ran along behind these yards, but she could also tell that he hadn't got a clue as to where she was. How could he? Everyone was scared of old Rathbone, the butcher, in whose bin she thought she crouched, so the last place Fizz would think of looking would be in Rathbone's yard. She had only gone in there herself because she knew Fizz was hot on her heels.

She cocked her head, listening intently, and heard the patter of Fizz's plimsolls as he trotted along the jigger. She grinned delightedly, hugging herself at the success of her ploy. She had climbed over the wall which separated the yard from the jigger and had dropped down on to the weedy paving stones, meaning to find somewhere to hide, expecting to see a shed or a handcart, or even a pile of old boxes. Instead, she had seen three large galvanised dustbins. She had raised the lid of the foremost of these and had realised at once that it would make an excellent hiding place – if one was not too fussy, that was. But now that she was in the yard, she did not have much choice. Both the other bins were full to bursting, their lids not fitting properly over the mess of refuse within, but the third bin was almost empty. Then, whilst she had hesitated, she had heard a voice, sounding as though it came from the vicinity of Mr Rathbone's back door. It was unbelievably bad luck in one way, because she had thought that the butcher, if this was his bin, would be safely ensconced in his flat above the shop, but it appeared she was wrong.

So she had hopped into the bin, pulled the lid into position as silently as she could, and now waited in the noisome dark for silence to come once more. Then, and only then, would she get out of the bin, scramble over the wall and make for 'home' which, in this particular game of relievio, was the yard of the Old Campfield public house.

Unfortunately, as the sound of Fizz's flapping plimsolls faded, Dot heard the back door of the shop squeak open and footsteps entering the yard. She felt the hair rise up on the back of her neck; oh, Gawd, if old Rathbone caught her here there would be hell to pay. He hated kids and had a sharp way with them. When Dot's Aunt Myrtle sent her to get the messages, she never bought meat off old Rathbone if she could possibly help it, even though he was the nearest butcher to Lavender Court. Aunt Myrtle said he gave short weight on the cheaper cuts and his better stuff was too expensive, but Dot would not have gone to him in any case. She hated his big square red face, the large yellow teeth which showed on the rare occasions when he smiled, and the mean little eyes, almost hidden in rolls of fat. He was spiteful, too; he would deliberately bang your parcel of meat down on your fingers if you were unwise enough to have a hand on the counter, and if you dared ask for a free bone, or a bit of suet for a pudding, he had been known to grab a child by the shoulders and run it out of the shop, saying as he did so that he weren't a charitable institution and didn't mean to keep bleedin' slummies in luxury, not he.

However, the footsteps stopped just short of the dustbins and Dot heard someone inhale deeply, and then begin to speak. 'Ker-rist, that were a narrow squeak, me old pal. Still, it were a bloody good haul; the best so far, I reckon. We can't do nothing immediate, of course, 'cos the scuffers will be turnin' over every fence for miles around – every known villain, too – but they ain't likely to come to a butcher's shop in search of a grosh of jewellery.' Dot, listening intently, was pretty sure that the speaker was Mr Rathbone himself – so she had been right, this was his yard – and crouched even lower in the bin. 'Yeah, I reckon we done pretty well for ourselves.'

'Keep yer voice down,' his companion urged. It was a thin, whiny voice, one which Dot did not recognise, but she could imagine the owner. He would be small, skinny and weaselly, with watery eyes and a loose slobbery mouth. In her mind, she could see him clearly: thinning hair, a pink and whiffling nose, and a tiny, sandy moustache. But now the butcher was speaking again.

'Don't be such a fool; who's to hear me? All the other shopkeepers will be in their flats and not hovering about in their yards.' Nevertheless, he dropped his voice. 'No, we're safe enough here, and we can't talk in the flat. It's sheer rotten luck that me old mam came calling. I can't get shot of her before ten or so, or she'll get suspicious. She's not seen you, since she came in through the shop, and that's just as well an' all! She's a rare gossip, so I don't tell her that I've got me fingers in more'n one pie. You know women; she'd blab to some pal or other, an' our goose 'ud be cooked. No, this is strictly between you an' me, Ollie old pal. We both teks the risk an' we teks a half share in the profits an' all. That's what we agreed, ain't it?'

'Oh aye, I reckon you're right; least said, soonest mended,' the whiner called Ollie said. 'How soon will it be safe to sell 'em on, d'you suppose?'

'If I could take 'em to London, like I means to do, mebbe we'd get away wi' a few weeks,' the butcher said reflectively. 'But mebbe longer if the old feller croaks; you're a might too handy wi' that stick o' yours, Ollie. There was no need to hit him twice, you know.'

The other man gave a whicker of laughter. 'I 'ardly touched 'im,' he protested. 'Skull like bloody paper, that one, but he were comin' round afore

4

we were out the door. You don't want to worry about him; he'll be tellin' everyone how he scared us off before we'd found the safe.'

'I reckon you're right,' the butcher said grudgingly. 'Tell you what, though, we'll have to get rid o' that emerald necklace. It's been the centrepiece of that window ever since I can remember, so everyone who's ever glanced into the shop will reckernise it at once. Besides, it's gorra be paste; stands to reason. If it were real it 'ud be worth a king's ransom an' no insurance company would cover it. I didn't mean to tek it, but then I didn't expect the old feller to pop up from behind the counter like a bleedin' jack-in-the-box. I shoved the rings, the gold chains and the earrings an' that into me pockets when he started to speak and the bleedin' necklace must ha' got snagged on somethin' in me hand, so I just shovelled the whole lot away an' legged it.'

'Yeah, I reckon you're right,' Ollie said, after a thoughtful moment. 'Pity, 'cos it 'ud look good on any woman's neck – 'twouldn't matter if it were paste. I don't see why we need to tek the other stuff to London, when there's fences a lot nearer home, but s'pose you took the necklace down there, though? It 'ud be worth a few quid, I reckon.'

'Didn't you hear what I said?' the butcher snapped, almost crossly. 'Wharr'ave you got for a brain, Ollie? Lard? The scuffers will issue a description of everything we took an' the only thing which really stands out is that bleedin' necklace. Diamond rings, gold chains an' fancy earrings are common to every jeweller in the land, pretty well. Give 'em six months an' they'll sell like hot cakes an' not a question asked. I know what you mean, but we might as well write "robbers" on our foreheads in red ink as try to sell the emerald necklace. It's gorra go, and it's gorra go tonight. And I ain't doin' nothin' clever, like takin' it down to the Mersey, 'cos if I did, some interferin' scuffer would either stop me on the way an' search me pockets, or some kid might fish it out o' the mud an' run after me to tell me I'd dropped it.'

'I could take it,' the other said eagerly. 'No scuffer 'ud stop me.'

But the butcher cut across this remark, his voice menacing. 'No you don't, Ollie my son. It ain't that I don't trust you, but wharrever we do, we'll do together. This is goin' in the dustbin. Tomorrer's collection day, and when I dumps the old newspapers in the mornin' I'll put a match to the bin an' the whole lot will go up like a bonfire on Guy Fawkes night. I'll be in the shop early, afore anyone else is about, an' after the fire in the bin has died down I'll rake through the ashes, make sure there's nothin' left to give us away.'

Dot's skin crawled with apprehension, but she stayed still as death; they were, after all, the width of the yard away, which she judged to be about twenty feet. It was only when she heard footsteps coming across the yard towards her, and realised that the butcher must mean to jettison the necklace

6

right away, that she was unable to prevent herself making a quick, involuntary movement, ducking even lower in the bin so that her elbow struck the side with a soft – though quite painful – clunk.

The footsteps stopped abruptly. 'What were that?' the man called Ollie asked suspiciously. 'I reckon someone's hiding behind them bins, for all you said—'

'No one but a midget could hide behind them bins. It were likely a bleedin' rat,' the butcher said dismissively. And as if to prove him right, there was a scuffling, a muffled squeak, and then the butcher's voice, triumphant. 'Told you so. Them bleedin' rats is everywhere. Bloody things is a menace to a butcher. I've had the Public Health round many a time, sayin' me premises ain't clean, but if I gets cats in they grumble about them an' all.' The footsteps began to approach the bin once more, but even as he lifted the lid from Dot's hiding place the butcher continued his grumbling monologue. 'They marches in an' out of me shop as if they owned the place; and them rats is strong too. They shove the lids off the bins an' go rootin' round inside, makin' a terrible mess. Looks like I'll have to borrow a couple o' terriers off mad old Jumbo, what keeps the second-hand bookshop further up Heyworth. They're a mangy-looking lot but they can clear a nest of rats in five minutes flat.'

The bin lid clattered back on even as Dot felt something cold and slithery fall down the front of her ragged dress. Fortunately, her gasp was muffled by the closing lid and she realised, with great relief, that the men had turned away from the bins and were returning to the back door of the shop.

'We'll 'ave a quick bevvy in the back of the shop, then you'd best be on your way, 'cos it's better if we ain't seen together tonight,' the butcher decided. 'We'll meet Saturday night in the Elephant, on the corner of Stonewall Street, but for now I'll open a couple o' bottles o' Guinness, then we'll split. I don't want me mam pokin' her nose in an' askin' questions about what I've been doin', because you know—'

The back door shut quietly, cutting the sentence in half, but it was a good ten minutes later before Dot dared to so much as move in her smelly prison. Until then, she continued to crouch in the bin, going over what she had heard. There had been a jewel robbery – that was plain enough. The robbers had taken the necklace by mistake and meant to destroy it in the morning; that was clear, too. What was not so clear was how the man called Ollie would leave the premises. Dot remembered that there was a door in the butcher's back wall leading into the jigger, to which Mr Rathbone held the key. The sensible thing, she realised, would be for the man to leave by that route, and you never knew when that would be, so it behoved her to get out of the bin – and the butcher's yard – in the quickest possible time.

Very, very cautiously, Dot straightened up a bit and began to lift the lid above her head, but at that

8

very moment the back door creaked open again. Terrified, Dot actually considered making a dash for it, then realised that this would be an act of sheer madness. The wall was high, not the sort of thing one could scale in a moment, and there were two men and only one of her. What was more, the bin was very deep; it had been quite difficult to climb in, and would be even more difficult to climb out. She would be caught and dragged into the butcher's shop and, she belatedly realised, they would guess she had been in the bin for some while and must have heard every word they had uttered. With the hair rising up on the back of her neck like a dog's hackles, she imagined herself in the grim and bloodstained room behind the shop, where Mr Rathbone jointed the carcasses of the beasts he bought. He would chop her up into little pieces without a second's hesitation, and boil her into a brawn which he would sell off, cheap, to the customers he disliked most. Without so much as glancing towards the back door, Dot lowered the lid with the utmost caution and ducked down into the bin again, pushing her head between her knees and praying to any deity who might be listening that she would not be discovered.

Whether her prayers were heard, or the men had had no intention of investigating the bins, Dot did not know, but she did know that they went straight past her hiding place. She heard a key rasp in the lock of the door into the jigger, a murmured 'good night', footsteps pass into the cobbled entry, the door shut and a key rasp again. A heavy tread then went back to the shop, a door opened and closed and Dot was alone.

For a moment, Dot's relief was so great that she simply sat there in the dustbin and thanked her stars that her worst nightmare had receded, if not vanished. She was still not out of the wood, but if she waited another ten or fifteen minutes surely she would be safe enough. Once she was certain there was no one in the vicinity, she could climb quietly out of the bin, scale the wall using various footholds in the crumbling bricks, drop down into the jigger and make her way home.

Not that home was truly home, exactly. Dot's father had been washed overboard and drowned during a storm when Dot was only three, so she could scarcely remember him, save as a tall, red-haired man who breezed into the house a couple of times a year, bringing lovely presents for his wife and small daughter. He had laughed a lot, given her shoulder rides and played boisterous games with her. Then he had died and her mam had become quite a different person, no longer fun-loving and full of laughter but edgy, weepy, and difficult. They had moved out of the little house which was all the home that Dot had ever known, and into other houses or flats or even lodgings.

By the time she was of an age to go to school, Dot must have lived in a dozen or more different parts of the city and had grown used to never belonging anywhere. But then her mam was taken ill and they moved into Aunt Myrtle's house in Lavender Court. Temporarily, Dot's mam had said, just until she found a decent job and a little home she could afford.

Only it had not been so easy. Her mam, Letty, was unable to find a decent job in Liverpool and had wandered further afield, promising, on her rare visits, to take Dot away with her just as soon as circumstances allowed. Then she had gone after a live-in job down south and had never returned, and Aunt Myrtle suspected that her sister had died. Aunt Myrtle had continued to house her, though Dot knew her aunt regarded her simply as an extra mouth to feed. The real fly in the ointment was Uncle Rupert, who had resented Dot for as long as she could remember. He was neither a good husband nor a good father, and had several times suggested that they should dispatch Dot to an orphanage, where she belonged. This terrified her; gave her nightmares. A friend had once taken her into such a place and the size of it, the coldness, the great bare rooms and the obvious awe, not to say fear, that the children seemed to feel for the adults in charge of them, had made Dot dread such a fate. But as she grew older the threat had receded, for she was useful, and when her aunt was out she could make a meal for her boy cousins and her uncle, and she helped with domestic tasks and all the household messages.

Clothing was always a problem since Dot could scarcely wear 'hand-me-downs' from her cousins and there was no way the family could afford new clothes, so when she grew out of a garment Aunt Myrtle took her to Paddy's market. Shoes were such a rare commodity that Dot was even now waiting for Fizz to pass on his dreadful, dilapidated plimsolls, and planning how she would nick a pot of glue from Woolworths to attach sole and uppers together once more.

Her uncle would always dislike and resent her but, Dot reflected, he did not even like his own children very much and anyway, he was not often in the house; working in a factory during the day and spending most evenings in one pub or other, only coming home to sleep.

The chief trouble was, Dot knew, that having one girl in a family of boys made life more difficult for her aunt. When she was small she had slept in the boys' room, but two years previously, when she was ten, her aunt had decided this was no longer right, and had made her up a makeshift bed in the kitchen, the front parlour being sacrosanct so far as her aunt and uncle were concerned. Apart from anything else, it was where Uncle Rupert couched down when he came in late, the worse for drink, and though this had begun to happen less than when she had first moved downstairs to sleep, it still meant that Dot could not have a bed in the parlour.

Having a child sleeping in the kitchen, however, was extremely inconvenient. Although she often fell asleep as soon as she climbed on to the old sofa, she was equally often woken by the rows which followed Uncle Rupert's return from the pub. At first, she had tried to placate the combatants, but very soon realised that this was not wise. When in his cups, Uncle Rupert had once slung her right across the kitchen; she had broken her arm and knocked her head against the dresser, and Aunt Myrtle had been as cross with her as though her wounds had been self-inflicted. 'You mind your own business and don't you ever contradict your uncle again,' she had warned grimly. 'When he's drunk, he's real violent; why, you might have been killed. So when they asks you at the hospital how you got hurt, you're to say you ran downstairs to answer a knock at the door, tripped on your nightdress, and tumbled down the flight, otherwise the hospital will tell the scuffers and that'll make real trouble for us all. Is that clear?'

It had been; and now, when her uncle came back from the pub, Dot pretended to be asleep even if she was wide awake, and though she had once been forced to crawl under the sofa when Uncle Rupert and Aunt Myrtle came to blows she supposed that No. 6, Lavender Court, was the nearest thing to a home she was ever likely to know.

Now, Dot straightened up once more and gingerly lifted the lid. It was full dark, but because it had been even darker in the bin she was able to ascertain that the yard was empty. With the lid of the bin still in her hands, she stood up, then realised that she would have to lean over the edge

13

of the bin and prop the lid up against its side, since she would need to have both hands free to extricate herself. Climbing in had been relatively easy because she had not been worried about making a noise. She had known the shop was shut and had assumed – wrongly as it happened – that it was also empty. She had climbed on to a full bin, taken the lid off the almost empty one, jumped down into it and pulled the lid back into position. But now, standing up in the bin, she needed all her strength and ingenuity to get out without knocking it over and making the sort of clatter which might easily bring someone running. However, she managed it. Standing in the yard, she replaced the lid of the bin as quietly as she could, climbed up the wall, and was actually sitting astride it when something made her glance up towards where the jigger joined the road. There was a shadow . . . for a moment Dot froze, then changed her mind and slipped down into the jigger. The man, if it was a man, was still some distance off. She would simply pad past him because she had every right, after all, to be in the jigger. Having made up her mind, Dot strolled, nonchalantly, towards him. He was tall – huge, in fact – and heavily built and it wasn't until he was almost upon her that she realised the reason for his unusual height: he was a scuffer and his helmet added a good six inches to his stature. She would have walked past anyway, but the policeman stopped. For a moment, she thought he was going to hit her, but there was a click, and she found herself staring into the beam of a torch. She ducked her head, beginning to protest, and the light swung away from her face to illumine, instead, her small and skinny body, her ragged and dingy dress, and her bare and dirty feet. 'Nah then, nah then, where did you spring from? One minute I thought I was alone and the next minute I weren't. Bin thieving, have you? C'mon, out with it.'

The light had returned to her face and Dot screwed up her eyes and scowled. 'Course I haven't; there ain't nothin' to thieve round here,' she said. 'We were playin' relievio and I were goin' back to me pal's house for me tea and this is a – a short cut, kind of.'

'Short cut?' the policeman said incredulously. 'This here jigger ain't a short cut to anywhere. C'mon now, where was you going?' He reached out a hand, the fingers big as sausages, no doubt intending to grip her shoulder, but Dot knew a trick worth two of that.

'Look out, mister! Behind you!' she shouted, and even as the man's hand fell back to his side as his head turned she was off, running like the wind, intent upon putting as much distance as possible between herself and the long arm of the law. For a moment, she heard heavily booted feet in pursuit, but then she was on Heyworth Street, with people and traffic, and even a few kids like herself.

Several people stared as she shot out of the alley mouth and one small, weaselly man tried to bar her way, beginning to call her 'another bleedin' little thief', but Dot dodged him easily and flew onwards. She knew that the scuffer would not bother to follow her out here. After all, what was the point? In the bright beam of his torch, he would have known at once that she was not carrying stolen goods; that her skimpy little dress could scarcely hide anything of value. So she made her way back along Heyworth Street towards Lavender Court and was almost at her own door before another thought struck her. A policeman! If she was going to tell anyone about the conversation she'd overheard, it should definitely have been a policeman. What an idiot she was! Her reason told her that the scuffers were unlikely to think that she had carried out a daring robbery . . . but then, suppose the policeman hadn't believed her, had thought she was making it up to try to get horrible old Rathbone into trouble? No, the impulse to confide in anyone was a dangerous one. News got around; a secret shared was no longer a secret. All it needed was one whisper and old Rathbone would be after her, sure as sure. He'd call her a wicked little liar and he would be believed because he was an adult and because no one would connect him with a robbery from a jeweller's shop. No, better by far to keep her own counsel. In fact, best of all, she should forget what she had heard, put the whole incident out of her mind, and not even tell Fizz that when he had run past, shouting her name, she had been just the other side of the wall, hidden away in old Rathbone's dustbin.

Having made up her mind, Dot swerved into Lavender Court and headed for No. 6, then stood for a moment, staring at the house. There was a light on in the kitchen and by squinting across the court she could see movement within, and also catch a glimpse of the clock above the mantel. She was surprised it was not yet eight o'clock, for it felt like midnight. She took two steps towards the door, knowing that Aunt Myrtle would have served the evening meal already, and that she would be lucky to get a bit of bread and a drink of tea, for the boys were always ravenous and someone would have eaten her portion as soon as it was clear that she was going to be late. She could go round to Fizz's house and see if his mam would give her a cut off a loaf and a spread of jam. Fizz's mam was skinny and energetic, and a good deal more efficient in the kitchen than Aunt Myrtle. She baked her own bread, sometimes even made her own jam, and never served shop-bought cakes or pies to her family. Yes, she would visit Fizz, even though she had no intention of discussing the night's adventures with her best pal. She turned decisively away from the brightly lit kitchen window and, as she did so, felt something hard slide round her waist, where the bodice of her dress ended and the skirt began. For a moment, she could not imagine what it could be, and she stuck her hand down her front, her fingers closing at once on the object. Hastily, she let it go again as though it had been red hot. She did not need to produce it to know what it was; it was the bleedin' necklace the two thieves had been so anxious to get rid of, the necklace which was so identifiable that any police force in the whole of the country would be sure to recognise it – and she, Dot McCann, was in possession of it!

For a moment, she was frozen to the spot; what the devil should she do? She dared not simply abandon it because she could remember, all too clearly, what Mr Rathbone had said. If she went and threw it in the Mersey, someone would see her. If she shoved it into one of their bins the dustmen would find it and the householder would be accused of the robbery. Desperately, Dot crossed the yard, one hand clamped to her waist, feeling the stones of the necklace pressing against her ribs. What to do? What to do? There must be somewhere she could hide it, somewhere truly safe, because it was the only evidence she had of the robbery and she felt, vaguely, that some day she might have to prove that she really did know who had done the deed. Yet she did not want to have the wretched thing on her person or anywhere in her vicinity; it was far too dangerous. Once or twice in the past, she had secreted pennies and ha'pennies in a convenient hole beneath the sofa cushions, but on one memorable occasion Aunt Myrtle had had a rare attack of spring cleaning and had swept up Dot's tiny savings as they tumbled out on to the floor. Her aunt had not realised that the money belonged to her niece and Dot had not liked to say, so she had ended up being given it to buy potatoes.

She was still pondering the matter when she realised that she did know a place where the necklace could be hidden. She set off in the direction of one of her favourite spots – the ruined church, with its deserted churchyard, just off Brow Side. For a couple of years now, she had liked to play in this churchyard, examining the closely packed gravestones and reading the epitaphs upon them, though she avoided the ruined church itself, which she knew to be as dangerous as people said. In one corner there was a miniature grave, the resting place of a baby who had died when only two days old, and Dot had sometimes sat by this little grave having imaginary conversations with the tiny inmate, who had been christened Rhiannon Williams. So far as she knew, no one visited the graveyard now, for the iron gates had been padlocked shut for years and the wall was difficult to climb unless one knew where to find a foothold. She knew it as well as she knew her aunt's back yard and now, having first checked that she was unobserved, went over it like a cat.

Most of the graves were very old and overgrown, the weeds and grass knee high in summer though now they did not come halfway up Dot's calf. Little Rhiannon had died a hundred and fifty years ago so it was about as secluded a spot as was possible to find in the area. Without thinking twice, Dot made her way towards the quiet corner, half hidden by ancient yew trees, and squatted down beside the small grave. Fortunately, it had rained the previous day and though chilly, the ground was not frosty. It was the work of a moment for Dot to carefully remove a clump of grass and to make a decent-sized hole beneath it, directly in line with the capital R of the child's name. She glanced around her but the churchyard was deserted. Nothing moved. Dot thrust her hand into the bosom of her dress and produced the necklace. She was too far from the street lights to get any illumination from them and the faint starlight drained the stones of colour, yet even so the sheer beauty of the thing made her catch her breath. She held it over the hole she had just made, swinging it slowly and watching with awe as the faceted stones threw back what little light there was. She would have dropped it into the hole – had intended to do so – but it seemed wrong, almost wicked, to treat something so beautiful with so little respect. Instead, she gathered handfuls of the weedy grass, made a sort of nest, placed the necklace reverently in it, covered it with a little more grass and then, with a sigh, filled in the hole, patted it down and replanted the original clump. Only then did she dust her filthy hands on her dress, stand up and view her handiwork, and find it good. The little granite headstone looked as it always had, innocent and untouched. Quickly, Dot bent and traced the child's name with her fore-finger. 'Take care of my necklace, Rhiannon,' she whispered. 'I'm sorry I haven't been to see you lately. I – I've been kind of busy. But I won't forget you again. I'll come back often, because now you and I have a secret. I can't stop any longer because I'm going to go round to Fizz's house and see if his mam will give me a bite of supper.' She stood for a moment longer, looking down at the small grave, and then slipped out of the graveyard as silently as she had come; a shadow among the shadows.

Chapter Two

When Dot awoke next morning, it was to find Aunt Myrtle already up and filling the big iron kettle from one of the buckets which always stood under the sink. The houses in Lavender Court were all back to backs and had no running water, but there was a tap up by the privies and every evening a queue of boys and girls – and the odd adult – waited patiently for their turn to fill a couple of buckets. For a moment, Dot could not imagine why she had slept so late, nor why she was so extremely tired, but then the events of the previous day came back to her in a rush and she sat up, pushed back her blanket and reached for her clothes, remembering that today was a school day, which meant she would wear what Aunt Myrtle called her 'decent dress', a navy cardigan which her aunt had darned quite neatly and the black plimsolls which Dot donned at eight o'clock on school days and removed at four in the afternoon. Aunt Myrtle was not mean, exactly, but she had four growing sons and a rather feckless husband so, as she frequently informed her family, she could not afford to let the children go shod except when they went to school, and then only because none of the schools would take pupils who arrived barefoot.

So Dot pulled open the bottom drawer of the sideboard, yanked out her good school clothes and her plimsolls, and dressed hurriedly. Then she grabbed an old broken comb and dragged it through her crop of ginger curls. She knew, of course, that one should wash before dressing, but today there was no time for such niceties. All too soon, her cousins would come pounding down the stairs, eager for their breakfast, and her aunt would not be best pleased if Dot was still not ready.

As she finished with the comb, her aunt turned and sniffed suspiciously. 'Dorothy McCann, have you trod in something?' she demanded. 'There's a rare ripe old smell in this kitchen; I noticed it as soon as I come down the stairs.' She advanced a couple of steps towards her niece, then recoiled. 'Wharra pong! I dunno where you was playin' yesterday – you were very late home – but you can just get out into the yard an' swill yourself under the tap. Oh, and fetch me them clothes you was wearin' yesterday an' I'll put 'em through the tub.'

'Thanks, Auntie,' Dot said gratefully, taking her play clothes across to the sink and dumping them on the draining board, where a most unpleasant aroma emanated from them. Then she bolted up the hall and out into the court, heading for the tap and stripping off her cardigan as she did so. It wasn't easy to get clean with no soap and no towel, but Dot did the best she could and presently returned, dripping, to the kitchen, where her aunt tutted, removed the thin roller towel from the back of the door, and gave Dot's hair such a good rub that her niece's eyes watered. But at least by the time she had struggled into her cardigan and plimsolls and was respectable once more she no longer smelt – at least not of dustbins – and she took her place on the bench between Dick, who was seven, and Alan, at five years old the baby of the family. Presently, Aunt Myrtle dished up the porridge and Sammy, who was fourteen and working in the fruit and vegetable market on Cazneau Street, handed round mugs of weak tea. There was never much talk at breakfast, everyone being in a hurry to get either to school or to work. Aunt Myrtle herself had several cleaning jobs, mostly in the big houses on Rodney Street, and she liked to be in work by half past eight. A good many of her clients were doctors and, though they liked their surgeries and waiting rooms to be clean as a whistle, they preferred that the cleaning women they employed should do their work either before their patients arrived or after they had left.

Whilst the rest of the family ate, Aunt Myrtle was cutting up a loaf and smearing each slice with margarine and fish paste, and presently there were five neat parcels wrapped in greaseproof paper ready on the table. There was a drinking fountain in the school playground so no one went thirsty, and Auntie Myrtle's hefty sarnies kept the wolf from the door until teatime.

Lionel, who, at thirteen, was the nearest to Dot's

age, grabbed his carry-out and left, and Dot followed suit, taking her skimpy little coat from the hook on the back of the kitchen door and holding out a hand to Alan. 'C'mon, kiddo,' she said bracingly. 'I'll just walk you up to school, same as usual, but I don't want to be late meself today, so don't you go running off or pretending you'll tag along wi' Dick, because I know you of old, I does.'

It was true that she knew most of Alan's tricks, for when he had first started school he had hated it and sagged off whenever he could. Aunt Myrtle, however, had devised a neat scheme to ensure that her youngest at least arrived at school each day. She made Dot responsible for actually handing him over to his teacher, even if it meant that Dot herself was sometimes late. Though Dot had resented this at first, Alan had grown accustomed to school, even seemed to like it, and now there was no problem in getting him to his class since he had a good many friends in his year and, whilst not the brightest of the family, managed to hold his own, and got on well with his teacher, Miss Collins.

So Alan and Dot set off together at a fair pace and presently emerged on to the main road, where the boys' school and the girls' stood a short distance apart. Passing a newsagent's shop, Dot glanced idly at the fly sheet and saw, emblazoned in black on white, "Jewellery snatch in Church Street – owner left for dead."

Dot was so shocked that, for a moment, she actually stopped short and stared; then common sense reasserted itself and she hurried past. Left for dead sounded bad, but all it really meant was that the thieves had whacked the man and not bothered to stay until he came round. She wondered if this was the robbery committed by Mr Rathbone and his pal. For all she knew, in a big city like Liverpool, they might have a jewel robbery every day of the week. The fly sheet had not given the name of the shop, just the street. Dot did not often venture into the city centre, but when she did she usually walked along Church Street, admiring the wonderful shop windows and the goods displayed therein.

'Why did you stop in front of that newspaper place, our Dot?' Alan said plaintively. 'D'ya have a ha'penny for sweeties? They sell sherbet dips, too.'

'They may sell 'em, but I've no money to buy 'em,' Dot said, beginning to jogtrot along the pavement and pulling Alan with her. 'Come *on*, Alan. I were late twice last week, thanks to you, an' I don't want to be late again today.'

Alan was an agreeable child when handled right, and very soon Dot had handed him over to Miss Collins and turned to make her way back to her own school, which meant passing the newsagent's once more. She wished she could have bought a copy of the paper so that she might learn the full story of the jewel robbery, but comforted herself with the thought that by next day there were bound to be copies of the paper in waste bins, or left on trams all over the city. Yes, if she were patient, she would find out just what Mr Rathbone, and friend, had been and gone and done.

Above her head, the clock over the chemist's shop struck the hour, and Dot broke into a gallop. She had a friend at school, Irene Boycott, whose parents were quite well-to-do and Dot remembered that, occasionally, when she had called at their house to ask if Irene could come out to play, Mr Boycott had been sitting by the fire with a cup of tea and a piece of cake to hand, and the *Echo* spread out before him. As she dived into the school yard, Dot decided that, by hook or by crook, she would go round to the Boycotts' house when school was finished and see if she could get a read of Mr Boycott's paper.

Smiling happily at the thought, she entered her classroom and slid into the desk she shared with Irene.

By four o'clock that afternoon, Dot was sitting comfortably in the Boycotts' kitchen, eating hot Welsh cakes smeared with honey, and listening to a music programme on the Boycotts' large, walnut-veneered wireless set. Unfortunately, she had not realised that her clever plan was unlikely to work until she had actually entered the Boycotts' cosy kitchen, and then it would have looked very odd indeed to simply change her mind and leave.

Not that it was her fault that her plan had gone awry. She and Irene had burst into the kitchen, Irene clamouring for something to eat because it was so cold that she was starving, just about. Mrs

Boycott, cooking Welsh cakes on the griddle, had promised them a good plateful presently, adding that there would only be the two of them to devour the lot since Mr Boycott, who was an accountant in a big block of offices on Exchange Flags, was working on the end of year figures and would not be home till ten or twelve that night.

Dot's heart had sunk, though on the spur of the moment she had suggested that she and Irene might pop along to the newsagent's and buy Mr Boycott a copy of the *Echo*, since otherwise he might miss his evening read. Mrs Boycott had thanked her, but shaken her head. 'Mr Boycott will send the office boy out for a copy, I don't doubt,' she had said. 'Knowing he was going to work late, he took a pile of sandwiches, an apple, some of my fruit cake, and a flask of hot tea to the office with him.' She had chuckled, benignly. 'And you know Mr Boycott; he can't enjoy a meal without he's reading his paper, so he'll make sure of that, whatever else he may miss out on.'

So Dot's lovely plan had crumbled to dust and, though she enjoyed the delicious Welsh cakes and the glass of hot milk which accompanied them, she was quick to suggest that she and Irene might like to play out. Dusk comes early in March and Mrs Boycott looked a little doubtful but Irene, who had a brand new skipping rope, added her pleas to her friend's, and very soon the two girls were strolling along, Irene chatting brightly and twirling her skipping rope whilst Dot kept her eyes peeled for a newsboy. She found one at last but, unfortunately, he was not a boy she knew, which made it a little awkward to ask a favour. However, by now Dot's curiosity was stronger than her fear of a rebuff so she told Irene to skip on to the end of the road whilst she approached the boy, who was sitting on a low wall by a tram stop, looking bored.

''Scuse me,' Dot said politely, 'can I have a look at the front page of the *Echo*? I can't buy one – no pennies – but there's a bit I'd like to just glance over, if you wouldn't mind.'

The boy looked her up and down. 'I'm *sellin'* papers, not givin' 'em away,' he said. 'Go an' get your mam to hand out some money.'

'My mam's dead; I live with me aunt and me cousins,' Dot said, trying to sound pathetic. 'There ain't no money left for things like newspapers after me aunt's bought the food. Anyhow, I don't want to take the paper away. I won't even have to touch it. If you was to spread it out on your knee – just the front page – then I could tell whether the bit I want to read is on it or not.'

The boy still looked unconvinced. 'Yeah, I dare say, but if everyone axed to have a free look at the paper, how many d'you think I'd sell? No, girl, if you can't afford to buy one, wait till tomorrer, when they'll be wrapping up chips or chucked down in the gutter, for anyone to read.'

Dot heard the note of finality in his voice and began to turn away, then turned back. 'Suppose – suppose I swear on the Bible to come back here tomorrow and give you a ha'penny if you'll let me look at the front page right now?' she enquired hopefully. 'You'll get your money, honest to God you will. I've – I've gorra few pence hid away but by the time I've gone back to Lavender Court and rooted around in me secret hidin' place it'll be tomorrer. An' if one of me cousins sees me, then that's me secret hidin' place gone up the spout.' She put all her pleading into the last remark, despite knowing that she had no money hidden anywhere. But a ha'penny was easy enough to earn, she told herself righteously. If the boy were content to wait until the following day, she could certainly give him the ha'penny she had mentioned.

But the boy was looking at her with more interest. 'Lavender Court?' he said slowly. 'I've gorra pal what lives in Lavender Court, Lionel Brewster. D'you know 'im?'

'He's my cousin. After my mam and dad died, his mam took me in; she's me Aunt Myrtle, what I just told you about.'

The boy grinned. 'Well, I'm blowed. Ain't it a small world?' he marvelled. 'So you're Li's cousin? Well, I'm 'is mate, Monkton – Monkey, they call me – so since you're me pal's cousin, I dare say I might let you have a read of one of me papers then. Only try not to muck it up, 'cos when the next tram comes along I'll likely have some customers an' they won't buy damaged goods.'

'Thanks ever so,' Dot said eagerly. She took the newspaper with great care and spread it out on the wall, realising as soon as she looked at it that if she was to keep her secret she would have to be very careful indeed, for the entire front page was taken up by a jewel robbery at Mitchell & Grieves in Church Street. Fortunately, she was a quick reader and was able to assimilate the article in a very few moments before turning to the second page and pretending interest in a story about a boy who had rescued his friend after the younger child had slipped off the chains on the floating road and plunged up to his waist in Mersey mud, just as the tide was beginning to come in.

Dot studied the story with great diligence whilst carefully storing away in her memory every detail of the jewel robbery from the front page. According to the police, old Mr Grieves always worked late in the shop on a Thursday night, though he was not then open for business. Apparently, he was a man who did everything by the book and it was said that one could set one's watch by him, so exactly did he stick to his familiar routine. The police had told the reporter that had this not been the case, the robbery would probably never have occurred, and warned the public that sticking to routine was a gift to any would-be thief. The report went on to say that Mr Grieves always shut the shop at five o'clock on a Thursday, began his various tasks, and at six o'clock on the dot went outside in order to examine his window as a customer might. Having checked, he would return to the shop and it must have been then that the thieves entered, probably close on his heels. Dot knew that this was wrong, however, from what she had overheard whilst in the butcher's yard. The thieves had had a real shock when Mr Grieves had suddenly appeared from behind the counter; that must have been why Ollie had hit him with the stick he carried. But then the butcher had said Ollie had hit the old man a second time; surely there had been no need for that?

'Did you see about the robbery, on the front page? I knows old Grieves; he's a decent old feller. He often buys a paper off of me; never takes his change, neither. It's too bad he were robbed, though there's some as I wouldn't mind robbing meself, from them posh shops down Church Street. Tell you what, turn to the stop press. If they've cotched the buggers, it'll be in there.'

Dot did not know what he meant but watched as he flicked the pages over until he came to a column on the back page, printed in slightly darker ink and headed 'Stop Press'. Together, the two of them read the headline 'Jewel Robbery' and then the paragraph beneath, which announced that Mr Grieves had died shortly after reaching hospital and the police were treating the case as murder.

The two young people stared at one another as Monkey carefully folded the paper into its original shape. 'The poor old gent,' he breathed. 'I hopes they get the buggers, so I do. I can't say I'm a perttickler friend of the scuffers – they's too fond of tellin' me to move on – but I'm with 'em all the way on this one. Just wish I'd been in Church Street last night, but I'll have a chat to the feller who were and see if he noticed anything. You never know. It ain't everyone what bothers to read the stop press.'

'No-o-o, but it'll be headlines by tomorrow,' Dot said shrewdly. 'Thanks ever so, Monkey; I'll tell Li you done me a good turn, but I'd best be gerrin' off now, or they won't save me no tea.'

When the bell rang in his flat over the shop, Archie Rathbone went down the stairs at once, though he opened the door cautiously enough. He held a folded copy of the *Echo* in one hand and, the moment his companion entered the room, stabbed at the stop press announcement with one fat forefinger. 'Have you seen that?' he demanded. 'Wharrever made you do it, Ollie? There weren't no need to hit him twice, an' now look where it's got us . . . or you, rather.'

The other man scowled. 'It ain't murder unless you meant to do it,' he protested. 'It were the excitement of the moment, and him popping up like a jack-in-the-box from behind that bleedin' counter. But that ain't why you axed me to call round, were it? Well, stands to reason it couldn't ha' been, 'cos the paper weren't out when I saw you earlier.'

Mr Rathbone sat down heavily at the table. 'No, it weren't old Grieves's death,' he admitted. 'It's something really strange . . . I don't understand it at all. 'Member me chuckin' that necklace in the bin? Well, next mornin' I went out there with the ash pan and looked into the bin to make sure before I burned the whole thing up, and it weren't there.' As he was speaking, he had stared steadily into the other man's face and now he continued to do so, his round, rather bulging eyes accusatory. 'Did you come back, Ollie? Did you come sneakin' back down the jigger an' climb over the wall and help yourself to that necklace? If you did, you're flamin' mad because the thing's red hot and reckernisable. I told you not to touch it, so what've you done with it, eh?'

The other man took a deep breath. 'I don't have a key to your back gate, Archie, and a man o' my years don't go scramblin' over walls like a kid o' nine or ten. If you ask me . . .' He stopped speaking suddenly. 'Oh my Gawd!'

'What's the matter? What've you remembered?' the butcher said anxiously. 'C'mon, out with it.'

The other hesitated for a long moment, and then he said, slowly: 'I come past the end of the jigger . . . oh, about twenty minutes – maybe less – after you and I had said we'd best go our separate ways. And – and I glanced down it, the way you do, and there were someone talkin' to a young girl. I didn't see him at all really, but I saw her 'cos the feller were flashin' a light in her face. Then, just as I turned away, she broke free of him and rushed past me as if the devil were on her tail. Mind, she weren't carryin' nothin' but, if you ask me, I reckon that feller had caught her comin' down the wall or gettin' into mischief of some sort. An' if the necklace is missin' . . .'

The butcher's breath hissed between his teeth. 'If she's got the necklace, we're dead meat,' he said gloomily. 'Specially you, Ollie. It were you who killed the old feller.'

The other began to protest, then grinned. 'Who's to know that?' he said derisively. 'No one knows who struck the blow, 'cept you and meself, Archie Rathbone, an' if you think you'd be believed above me if I said it were you who hit out . . . well, there's a few round here who know your nasty temper and dead men tell no tales, so old Grievesy ain't likely to speak in your defence.' He leaned across the table and clapped the other man consolingly across the shoulder. 'Don't worry. Even if the kid did prig the necklace, she won't attach no significance to it an' kids don't read the paper. We'll be all right, old feller. The stuff's hid away where no one won't find it until we've got a chance to take it down to your pal, and once he's got it there'll be nothing to connect it with us.'

'I thought you said we needn't bother with a fence in London when there's fellers a lot nearer home,' Archie grumbled. 'I reckon the stop press has changed your mind about it.'

Ollie shrugged. 'Better safe 'n sorry,' he observed. 'Besides, we'll gerra higher price from a London fence, seein' as the stuff has come a long way from his patch. I wonder where that kid will stow the necklace, though – if she took it, that is. If she leaves it lyin' about where her mam or dad could find it, that could bring trouble round our ears. Now what sort o' kid goes scrattin' through dustbins at that hour of the night?'

Archie Rathbone stared down at his huge, meaty hands, then suddenly slammed them down so hard on the table that his companion jumped. 'She were in the bleedin' bin,' he said. 'Yes, I'm sure of it, she were in the bleedin' bin. There weren't much in it when I looked this mornin' but what there was had been trampled flat, like. I had to poke around with a stick to make sure the necklace weren't there. Why, the dirty, thievin' little bitch! If I ever lay hands on her . . . what did she look like? How old were she? What were she wearin'?'

Ollie stared, then shrugged, a trifle helplessly. 'She were just a dirty little kid, around nine or ten I'd say, but I reckon I'd know 'er again,' he said. 'She had long, tangly hair, sort of gingery I think it was, but apart from that I couldn't describe her.'

The butcher snorted. 'Fat lot of good that is, but if she were in the bin she won't have seen nothing and voices is voices. I doubt she can identify either of us, particularly if she simply hopped into the first almost empty bin she come across, because I reckon one bin is very like another. Chances are she'd no idea whose bin it was when she got into it. Only, if she were searchin' the bins for something to steal, why in God's name did she climb inside it? Oh, Gawd, can it have been because she heard us talking? Only – only I don't recall as we said much that would put us behind bars. I dare say we argified a bit about chuckin' the necklace away, but I don't reckon we used names, nor nothin' like that.'

There was a silence while both men cast their minds back until Ollie suddenly spoke. 'Hide 'n' seek,' he said decidedly. 'Slum kids have always played hide 'n' seek and she'd probably tried the odd shed, and a privy or two, before comin' across an almost empty dustbin.'

The butcher's face cleared. 'Aye, you may be right. An' if so, an' she don't know whose yard she were in, then she may not squeal on us,' he said. 'But I'd be a deal happier if we knew who she were so we could tell 'er to keep 'er trap shut or we'd shut it for 'er. You're round and about a good deal, Ollie. Just you keep your eyes open, see if you can spot 'er. Once we know who she is an' where she lives, we can . . . we can . . .'

'We can make sure she's no threat to us,' Ollie said. He spoke quietly and unemphatically but, on the opposite side of the table, the butcher gave a little shiver. He was not fond of children and had few scruples, but something in his companion's face made him say hastily: 'No need to act violent, Ollie; a threat'll do the trick. We don't want two murders on our hands, do we?'

Ollie's eyes opened in mock astonishment. 'Me? Harm a kid?' he said. 'No such thing. When I find her, I'll put the fear o' God into her so she'll hand back the necklace and never say a word to a soul about it.'

'Hand it back? But we've agreed it's red hot, far too dangerous . . .'

Ollie gave a derisive snort. 'Have your brains gone beggin', Archie?' he demanded. 'That necklace is the only proof the kid's got, if she wants to go to the authorities. Otherwise, she's just a kid, lyin' her head off to get attention, an' all you'll have to do is ask what the devil would you be doin' chuckin' a necklace worth a deal o' money into your own rubbish bin. No, without the necklace, she's no sort of proof.'

The butcher sighed, stretched and stood up. He walked over to the fire and pulled the kettle over the flame, then spoke over his shoulder to his companion. 'Gawd, I wish we'd destroyed the necklace then and there, or hung on to it ourselves, for that matter. Still, no good crying over spilt milk. Come to think of it, old pal, who's she likely to tell? She didn't have no right in that bin an' she didn't have no right to take the necklace, either. I don't reckon we've much to worry about in that direction, an' once we've got rid of the other stuff and divvied up the money between us we can put the whole business behind us an' forget it.'

Ollie nodded slowly, and presently accepted a cup of tea and began to talk of how they would travel down to London and visit the fence together. When he left, he had agreed that the child was no threat, even agreed not to bother to keep his eyes peeled for her, but in his small, calculating mind there was one thought which he had not shared with the butcher. His memory of the conversation which had taken place near the bins was a lot sharper than Archie Rathbone's. He had told Archie that no one knew which of them had struck Mr Grieves down, but if the kid had been hiding in the bin she would have heard Archie telling him that he had not needed to hit the old man a second time. She was the only person who knew he was the murderer and could clear Archie of the worst crime, whilst landing himself in it up to the neck. So it stood to reason that she would have to be silenced and he did not mean to do it just by threats. In a big city like Liverpool, swarming with kids, it would be a simple enough matter to get rid of her once he'd found her. The river, the canal, the railway, the roads, were all dangerous places; barefoot urchins were injured or killed often enough for one more to be unremarkable. Just let me find her and then we can get on with planning another job, Ollie told himself. And next time, he'd make certain his face was covered before he entered anyone else's premises; because he'd not bothered to pull up his muffler he had had to hit Mr Grieves a second time since he had had no desire to be iden-tified by the old man.

So now, the only thing he had left to do was find the kid and then get rid of her; knowing kids as he did, he was pretty sure she would have hidden the necklace, but should it come to light it might even be a good thing since it would cast suspicion in the wrong direction. Provided the girl was dead, that was.

For several days after the robbery, Dot lay low. She had thought herself safe enough once she had hidden the necklace, but it had gradually been borne in upon her that Mr Rathbone would expect to find the necklace in the bin when he went to destroy it next morning. He might be all sorts of fool but he must realise, as she did, that stones and metal were unlikely to disappear completely, even when set on fire. Furthermore, she had an uneasy feeling whenever she remembered the weaselly man on Heyworth Street who had tried to bar her way as she shot out of the alley. Suppose, just suppose, that the weaselly man had been Ollie? He had called her a thief but there was nothing to steal in the jigger . . . unless you happened to know that an emerald necklace nestled in one of old Rathbone's dustbins, waiting to be destroyed, or fetched out secretly when Mr Rathbone's back was turned, to be tucked away until everyone had forgotten the robbery, when Weasel Face would be able to dispose of it at his leisure.

It would have been nice to tell herself that Ollie – if indeed it was Ollie – had not had time to notice her during their brief encounter, but the truth was they had stared into each other's faces for a split second and the weaselly man's countenance – narrowed, greenish eyes, a long thin, pink nose, a mouth fringed with raggedy teeth, and sandy hair protruding beneath a filthy old tweed cap – was burned on Dot's brain, so she supposed that the same could be said in reverse.

Dot remembered, however, that someone had once said, 'Know thine enemy,' and this thought was a real comfort. She had dreaded being pursued by a faceless thief but now, at least, she did indeed know her enemy, and could make sure that she was never alone either with Mr Rathbone or with the weaselly Ollie.

Over the course of the next few weeks, she was careful, very careful indeed. She kept away from crowded places, made sure she went to and from school with a gaggle of other children, and actually used a couple of rubber bands, which the postman had dropped on the pavement, to plait her hair into a couple of pigtails. She didn't actually do the plaiting herself, but got Fizz's elder sister, Laura, to do it for her, and was delighted when her teacher complimented her on her tidy appearance and actually gave her a small comb, because Laura had made her parting by guess, and Miss Unsworth showed Dot how much nicer a straight middle parting looked.

Of course her cousins were as delighted with her plaits as Miss Unsworth; they pulled them, tied them into knots, attached them to the back of the kitchen chair whilst she was eating her tea, and generally used them as a means of irritating her. Dot, however, knew that the boys would grow accustomed to the pigtails, so kept doggedly on.

At her teacher's suggestion, she actually held her head under the pump at the end of the yard, and scrubbed away at her hair with a bar of carbolic soap, lightening her locks to a pleasing shade of reddish gold and, she hoped, changing her appearance even more.

The worst part of it was that she still dared tell no one. Fizz was her best friend, but there was no denying he was a gossip. He would not mean to tell, would promise silence to the grave, but then he would forget, mention to his mother, or one of his school friends, that Dot knew more about the robbery than she was letting on, and the fat would be truly in the fire. She had other friends – Irene Boycott, Lizzie Moffat, who lived two doors further along the court, and Phyllis Watson, whose mother owned a corner shop on Heyworth Street. Mrs Watson was a pleasant, easy-going woman, who would never make much money since she allowed customers to buy from her on tick, but Dot was not concerned with that side of the Watsons' life. Mrs Watson let her and Phyllis play in the big storeroom behind the shop, leaping like goats from the sack of rice to the sack of lentils, up on to the box of margarine and down round the boxes of dried fruit. Of course, they were under promise not to spoil – or devour – Mrs Watson's stock, but it was a grand place to play, especially on rainy days when Aunt Myrtle turned her out, regardless, and there was no school. However, fond though she was of all three girls, she could not possibly have admitted to them that she had hidden in a dustbin, let alone eavesdropped on a conversation between two grown men. They would have been shocked and, even if they had not told their own parents, would have insisted that she go to the police. No, she must keep the secret locked in her own heart.

It had been March when the robbery took place, and it was getting on towards the end of May when something extremely worrying occurred, and made Dot long, even more fervently, for a confidante. It was the Saturday morning of the Whit weekend and Fizz's mam had given him a pile of neatly ironed shirts in a large wicker basket, and his fare on the underground railway to Birkenhead. There was a boys' school which sent a great number of shirts to a laundry on Scotland Road, where Fizz's mam worked from time to time. But, apparently, two of the laundry women had fallen sick, and the delivery boy had gone down with the same malaise, so the laundry proprietor had given Mrs Fitzwilliam the shirts and asked her to do them herself, to deliver them and, of course, to keep the money. Mrs Fitzwilliam had been delighted, going along to the communal washhouse, washing and drying the shirts, starching the collars until Dot thought, ruefully, that they were liable to cut the throats of any pupils wearing them, and then packing them into the basket and giving them to Fizz to deliver. 'They'll pay you six and ninepence, and you can keep the ninepence for deliverin' them,' she had said instructively. 'I dare say young Dot will want to keep you company, so I'll give you her fare an' all. Then, if you want to go out on a spree Sat'day afternoon, you'll have a bit o' money to spend.'

'But we'll have missed the penny rush,' Fizz had said, rather dismally; he loved his weekly visit to the picture house, knew the names of all the film stars and intended, he told Dot, to be a cowboy when he grew up.

'But cowboys have to be terrible handsome and – and they all have kinda dangerous faces,' Dot had observed. She had not wanted to insult her friend but his round, rosy, rather flat face, his snub nose and his spiky, straw-coloured hair were unlikely to change greatly, she thought, in the years to come. 'Besides, you can't ride a horse or whirl one of them ropy things and catch a cow or – or use a six-shooter, even.'

Fizz had turned on her a look which had mingled contempt and pity. 'They teaches you to ride a horse and shoot straight, an' stuff like that,' he had said loftily. 'Don't you know nothin', Dot McCann?'

Dot, realising that she had offended her pal, had said meekly that she was sorry for doubting him and had hastily changed the subject, but now, as they walked towards the Central underground station she was unable to prevent herself from giving a little skip of excitement. 'Since we're going over the water, we might as well go a bit further

44

and take ourselves off to New Brighton for the rest of the day,' she suggested hopefully. 'I know you hate missin' the Sat'day rush, but do you know what film's showing? It's *Little Miss Deputy*, what's all about a cow*girl*, not a cowboy, starring that Texas Guinan, the one you thought was such a twerp.'

Fizz's darkening brow lightened considerably. 'Oh, it's *her*, is it?' he said cheerfully. 'To my mind, there ain't no such thing as a cowgirl – girls can be cows, an' I know several of them who are, but a woman dressed up in a Stetson and chaps, and jangly boots, is going agin nature, if you ask me.'

It would have been fun to disagree, to tell Fizz that Texas rode, shot and lassoed better than any man, but Dot realised that she had best hold her tongue, especially if she wanted to go to New Brighton and to have a share in Fizz's ninepence. So, instead, she talked about school, Aunt Myrtle's latest fight with Uncle Rupert and the fact that Fizz's sister, Laura, had just got a job at the dairy on Heyworth Street. This passed the time pleasantly until they dived down the steps of the underground station and found themselves immediately caught up in a large crowd, many of whom seemed to be in a holiday mood. Dot guessed that because it was bright and sunny she was not the only one who had thought of the delights of New Brighton; why, some of these people might be going over for a weekend at the seaside, staying in one of the many boarding houses which offered cheap accommodation to families eager to escape from hot and grimy Liverpool streets.

A train came roaring into the station and the crowd surged forward, even though they must know that they would be unable to board the train until those passengers waiting to alight had done so. She was shouting into Fizz's ear that she doubted if they would be able to get this particular train when the doors opened and people began to descend. Others immediately pressed forward and Dot and Fizz got separated, though by the time the train drew out they were right at the front of the crowd and pretty sure of catching the next one.

Dot guessed that Fizz's laundry basket had come in useful to barge people aside, but also thought that it might impede his getting on the train. She signalled to him over the intervening heads that she would try to join him and was inching towards him on the very edge of the platform when she heard the roar and felt the tidal wave of hot air as the engine of the next train emerged from the tunnel. Prudently, she moved back from the edge, and even as she did so felt a sharp push between her shoulder blades and staggered forward again. Had it not been for the man standing beside her, she might well have fallen on to the line, but he shot out an arm and grabbed her, saying chidingly, in a strong Lancashire accent: 'Hold up, lass! Ee by gum, how they do shove to be first on t' train. You want to be careful when you're in the front.

Someone give you a push, did they? Aye, I felt it meself. That's why I grabbed a hold of you.'

Dot, feeling quite weak with shock, mumbled her thanks and, as she got into the train, turned to look behind her, though she knew that she was unlikely to be able to pick out whoever had pushed her – if indeed anyone had – in the motley crowd. Infuriatingly, there were at least three people now jostling aboard the train with ferrety faces and large caps, but Dot was pretty positive that none of them was Ollie. However, she was also pretty positive that Ollie was far too fly a character to hang around after committing an act of aggression. He would have got away immediately or would simply have moved smartly to his right or left, getting aboard the train through another doorway. For a moment, she hesitated, thinking it might be safer to fight her way off the train and simply go home, but then common sense reasserted itself. *If* she had been deliberately pushed – and she was by no means certain that this was the case – then it simply must have been Ollie because Mr Rathbone, she knew, would be in his shop, particularly on a Saturday morning, with all his customers hurrying in to buy their Sunday joints.

'Hey, Dot!' It was Fizz, sitting comfortably on his laundry basket and grinning conspiratorially at her. 'Wanna seat? There's room for two if you can fight your way down here.'

Dot began to wriggle past strap-hanging passengers as the train started to move, cursing inwardly.

It was just like Fizz to call attention to her when the last thing she wanted was to be noticed, but she sank down on the laundry basket, then glanced furtively round her. To be sure, she was low down, but after a couple of moments of staring she was reasonably certain that the weasel-faced one was not amongst those present and felt her heart, which had been thumping noisily, slow to a steadier pace.

'Dot? Whazzup? You look all hot and bothered.' Her pal grinned at her. 'Someone pinch your bum when you was in the crowd on the platform? I saw you lurch forward, like – give me quite a turn it did.'

Dot stared at him. 'Someone shoved me,' she said in a husky whisper. 'Did you see who done it, Fizz?'

Fizz gave a hoarse guffaw. 'Someone shoved you? I reckon half a dozen shoved me. I near as damn it went down in front of the train. It were only me laundry basket what saved me. You'd think that folk off for a bit of a holiday would be more careful, but not them. Anyroad, what makes you think you're so special?'

Fizz had a loud voice, which he had to raise in order to combat the train's clatter. 'Hush! I don't think I'm special,' Dot said, wincing. 'It were an accident, I'm sure; I just wondered if it were some-one from school, playing a trick on me, like.'

Fizz grunted. 'I didn't see no one I knew, but then I didn't look, pertickler,' he said. 'I wish me mam had something good planned for Monday, but she's a bit short of the ready right now. Wharrabout your Aunt Myrtle? I don't s'pose she's plannin' to take you an' your cousins off for the day, is she?'

Dot made a derisive noise in the back of her throat. 'Poor Aunt Myrtle never has a penny over once we's all fed,' she told her pal. 'And if she had, Uncle Rupert would get it off her, though things are lookin' up a bit now Sammy's earnin'. He told me uncle straight out that if he tried to touch a penny of his wages – Sammy's, I mean – he'd go straight to the nearest scuffer and report he'd been robbed. Uncle Rupert tried to give him a swipe but Sammy punched him on the nose and it bled buckets, so now Aunt Myrtle's made the same threat and I do think me uncle's a bit more careful . . . he asked Aunt Myrtle for a couple of bob last weekend and when she said she hadn't got it he didn't belt her, norreven a little bit.'

Fizz gave her a curious look and Dot realised, with some dismay, that the private life of the Brewster family was something which she had never before revealed to Fizz, knowing his weakness for gossip. Indeed, she would not have done so now had she not been anxious to turn his thoughts away from the shove on the underground platform.

It was at this point that the train stopped at Hamilton Square and everyone began to get out. Fizz and Dot, thanks to the laundry basket, were amongst the first to alight and presently they set off in the direction of the boys' school, chatting

49

amiably as they walked. Dot looked around her with feigned interest but in fact she saw very little of her surroundings since her mind was still preoccupied with what had happened just before the train had come into the station. If Ollie had recognised her and decided to kill her, he must have had a hundred opportunities before now. But, thinking it over, she decided that she was almost certainly making a mountain out of a molehill. Weeks and weeks had passed since the robbery and no one had attempted any sort of aggression against her. Why should it happen now? From the back, with her hair plaited and washed to a far paler shade than it had been on the night of the robbery, it seemed most unlikely that he could have picked her out as the girl running out of the jigger. It was not as though she was wearing the necklace, and though she had visited the graveyard several times she had not once disinterred her prize, though secretly she was longing to do so. She wanted to see it in daylight, to see how the beautiful green stones would glitter as sunshine touched them. But she had resisted temptation and had felt a growing confidence that, if she continued to be careful, she would remain safe. It was only if she tried to inform on the butcher and his pal that she might run into trouble, she concluded; or, of course, if she confided in anyone else regarding the robbery, and the murder which had followed it.

'Here we are; we turn in up that long drive and go round the back, Mam says,' Fizz told her, a trifle breathlessly. 'Once we've got rid of the laundry we can come back to the centre of town and catch a bus up to New Brighton.'

Dot beamed at him. 'So we *are* going to the seaside,' she said gleefully. 'Oh, Fizz, you're a grand feller, so you are! It'll make up for . . .' Her voice trailed away. She thought, guiltily, that she really must watch her tongue; she had very nearly given herself away. Fizz looked at her enquiringly, so she hastened to end the sentence. '. . . for not being able to go to the Saturday rush,' she said glibly. 'Let's hurry!'

Crossing the court that evening, Dot thought, blissfully, that the day just ended had been one of the happiest in her life. The sun had shone. She and Fizz had paddled, made a huge sandcastle, and feasted on chips and fizzy lemonade. They had run races along the hard, wet sand, and when the tide came in they had actually bathed; Dot clad only in her knickers and Fizz in his underpants. Dot had gazed at this garment with awe since none of her cousins owned such things, but Fizz had said, complacently, that his mother had advised the donning of them just in case they should end up at the seaside and want to swim.

Swimming, so far as Dot was concerned, was an activity she could not share with Fizz; boys learned to swim either in the baths on Netherfield Road or in the Leeds and Liverpool Canal, usually up by Tate's. The water there was warm because the factory jettisoned unwanted hot water into that part of the canal, known to the kids as the Scaldy. Girls, however, rarely joined in the sport, so Dot could not swim. But today she had let Fizz hold her up by the chin whilst she did her best to follow his instructions, and for one or two moments had actually kept herself afloat. Naturally, this had made the day even more special, so Dot thanked Fizz fervently for a grand time, waved to him until he disappeared inside his own home and then made her way to No. 6.

She had no means of knowing the time, but dusk was falling and she knew that Aunt Myrtle would have served the evening meal long since. She would not have worried over her niece's absence, because Dot was often out late in the summer when the evenings were long and light, but she would not have saved her anything other than bread and jam. Not that I need it, Dot told herself buoyantly, letting herself into the house and going towards the kitchen. After all those chips and fizzy lemonade she doubted if she could eat another mouthful.

She opened the kitchen door rather cautiously, because you never knew with Uncle Rupert. He got paid on a Friday but liked to do the majority of his drinking on a Saturday, so if he had spent all his money the previous night he would be home and in a bad temper. However, when she poked her head round the door, the kitchen contained only her aunt and her cousins Dick and Alan. She slipped into the room and grinned at her aunt. 'Me and Fizz went to New Brighton to deliver some laundry for his mam,' she said brightly, even though no one had asked her where she had been all day. 'He tried to teach me how to swim – I nearly can – and we mucked around on the sand all day. It's all right, his mam said we could; she give us our bus fares and a penny or two over for chips.' As she spoke, she glanced at the clock above the mantel and saw that it was not yet nine o'clock. Presumably, her uncle was down the pub, and since he never returned till closing time she would be safe enough for a while. She looked, hopefully, at Aunt Myrtle. 'I know I missed supper and I know I had chips, but I'm awful hungry, Aunt Myrtle. Any chance of a mouthful of bread an' cheese? It 'ud go down a treat.'

Aunt Myrtle heaved an exaggerated sigh but went over to the bread crock, got out the loaf and cut a thick slice. Then she took a pot of jam from the cupboard and smeared a small amount over the bread. 'You know my rules,' she said. 'Food's on the table at six an' if you're late, you get nowt. Still, you can fill up on bread and jam. You're norra bad kid.'

Accepting the bread and jam, Dot had the grace to feel guilty. In point of fact, she was not hungry, but had suddenly realised that it would not do to let her aunt think she was being well fed by someone else or next time she came in, having missed a meal, her aunt would not offer bread and jam. So she settled down to eat the food and found, in fact, that she was glad of it and equally glad of the mug of tea which her aunt handed to her presently.

Dick was sitting at the table with a sheet of newspaper spread out in front of him. He had his father's boots on the newspaper and was glumly cleaning them. For this task, he would undoubtedly be paid a ha'penny – if his father would not shell out, then his mother would – because, once a month, the whole family went to early Mass on Sunday morning and Aunt Myrtle insisted that they should go in style. Suits, collars and even ties were redeemed from the pawn shop on Saturday night and usually returned on Monday morning, whilst boots and shoes were polished and hair was neatly brushed back and oiled into flatness with Brylcreem if they were in the money, but otherwise with a smear of anything greasy which would keep it down for the duration of the service.

Dot finished her bread and jam, drained her mug and went over to the sink. They had no running water but she noted with approval that the buckets beneath it were all full; Sam or Li had done their chores before going off to enjoy whatever jaunt they were involved in. Sam liked the pictures and Li was a football player. He and his mates had a much prized football which they had all saved up to buy, and would kick it around in one of the parks until it grew too dark to see properly. Then they would sit around yarning and generally mucking about until just before the pubs closed, when they would rush home, anxious to get into bed before their fathers returned. Dot knew that Uncle Rupert wouldn't even notice whether his sons were home or not, but she supposed other parents might show more interest in their offspring.

Dick seemed to have finished the boots, to his own satisfaction at least, for he got up, placed them side by side with the other footwear and was about to scrumple up the paper when his mother addressed him sharply. 'Don't you go fillin' my rubbish pail up with all that dried mud. Toss it into the court, then fold the newspaper neatly and put it with the others. Then you'd best gerroff to bed, afore your dad comes in. Likely, he'll be in a good enough mood, but just in case . . .'

Even the thought of Uncle Rupert in a temper was enough to shift his sons. Alan, who had been scribbling on a scrap of paper with a stub of pencil and muttering to himself as he did so, got to his feet with alacrity and headed for the door, whilst Dick shot past him with the newspaper held out before him and was back in a trice, folding the sheet as he came and shoving it amongst the other papers, which his mother kept in a pile beside the water buckets. Dot thought that he had probably shed a good deal of the dried mud as he ran to the door, but she said nothing. After all, when Uncle Rupert came back from the pub, he was unlikely to be in any state to wipe his shoes on the mat, and next morning he and his two eldest sons would doubtless be blamed for the state of the hall floor.

'Get into bed, chuck,' her aunt said, as soon as the boys had disappeared. She did not speak unkindly, but there was enough urgency in the remark to make Dot glance up at the clock again. Goodness, it was almost closing time; she and her aunt had best get a move on.

Aunt Myrtle bustled around, clearing the kitchen, putting away anything which her husband might choose to hurl at the wall in a temper, or simply trip over. Then she dipped a large tin mug into one of the buckets of water and set it down in the middle of the kitchen table. Dot was aware that men who have drunk a great deal are astonishingly thirsty after such bouts, and knew that her aunt would fill the enamel jug with water and carry it up to bed with her, just in case her husband made straight for the stairs. Usually, however, he would come into the kitchen first and help himself to a mouthful of cheese, or perhaps an apple, if one of the boys had acquired some fades from the market stalls. He might make a great deal of racket, shout for his wife, and swear at life in general, but, to do him justice, he never deliberately disturbed Dot, and provided she feigned sleep convincingly enough would soon grow tired of the kitchen and lurch out either to sleep on the sofa in the parlour, or to make his stumbling way up the stairs to bed.

It was then, when there had been quiet for ten or fifteen minutes, that Dot would get down from the sofa and extinguish the lamp. With the room in darkness, she would speedily fall asleep, probably not waking until Aunt Myrtle roused her next morning to help get the breakfast. Aunt Myrtle always left the lamp lit in the kitchen because, on the only occasion when she had not done so, Uncle Rupert had lit a newspaper at the fire, meaning to kindle the lamp, and had dropped the paper on the hearthrug, starting a conflagration which had done a good deal of damage to the family's few possessions. That had been when Dot was only seven, however, still sleeping upstairs in the boys' room and learning what had happened only when she came down for breakfast next morning. So naturally she was happy for her aunt to leave the lamp lit, preferring it to finding herself in the middle of a raging fire whilst her uncle tried to douse it with buckets of water, and blamed everyone but himself for what might well have been a fatal accident.

Once or twice, as the minutes ticked by, Dot fell into a light slumber, but she was awoken, fully, by The noise of the front door crashing open. Heartbeat quickening, she pulled her blanket up as far as she could. The fact that her uncle was so late must mean he was even more drunk than usual and, though he always ignored her, you could never tell for certain what would happen. It was best to play safe and keep as out of sight as possible. Dot heard stumbling footsteps approaching and heard, also, the mumble of voices. Uncle Rupert must be drunk indeed if his friends were having to bring him home; she just hoped they would not accompany him right into the kitchen, though she realised this was a strong possibility. After all, they could scarcely abandon him and would assume his wife would be in the kitchen, waiting for him.

The door opened; it would not have been fair to say it crashed open, but it certainly swung pretty wide, knocking into the bottom of the sofa upon which Dot lay. Uncle Rupert's voice, thick with drink, muttered: 'You're welcome as the flowers in May, so you are, and why don't one of you pour us all a li'l d-d-drink, 'cos it's a well know fac' . . . fac' . . . fac' that a hair of a dog is the best cure for . . . aaargh! Aargh!'

Dot's nose wrinkled with distaste; Uncle Rupert was clearly vomiting. She just hoped to God he'd managed to reach the sink because it would be a lot easier to swill it away once he had staggered off if he had done so. If he had been sick on the floor, it would be a mop and bucket job, and even the thought of getting out of her bed to do the work made her tired bones ache.

'You dirty old . . . Look, Rupe, if you're goin' to be sick again . . .'

There were some more ghastly, gurgling noises and Dot heard the scrape of a tin mug as it was lifted off the table. 'Clean out your gob with this,' a man's voice said commandingly. 'My God, what a couple of glasses of gin can do on top of a belly-ful of porter! Look out, Archie – he's going to keel over an' we can't leave 'im face down in that.'

'I don't see why not,' the other man's voice

grumbled. 'We didn't ask him to get drunk as a bleedin' pig. Still, we'll dump him on the sofa, purrout the lamp an' leave 'im to it. I wonder why his missus ain't up, waitin' for 'im?'

The reply was brief and coarse but Dot scarcely heard it. When the man had mentioned the sofa, she had taken a squint at them and was now frozen with horror, unable to move a muscle. Even in her wildest nightmares, she had never dreamed that Butcher Rathbone would visit No. 6, Lavender Court, but here he was, actually suggesting that they should dump Uncle Rupert upon the sofa on which she lay. And the other man . . . ? Desperate though her fear was, she still tried to get a look at him, but he was between her and the lamp, simply a dark shadow bending over her uncle.

'C'mon, get your hands under his armpits, and we'll heave him to his feet,' Archie Rathbone said authoritatively.

But whilst Dot was still wondering whether they would notice her and move away, or simply sling the drunken man on top of her, she heard another voice. 'What the devil's goin' on here? Oh my Gawd, don't say the silly old bugger's been and gone and fallen under a tram. Or is it just the drink, as usual?' It was Aunt Myrtle, who must have heard the racket the men were making and, realising that there were strangers in her home, had come down to sort things out.

Dot burrowed under her covers once more, but listened, with a wild and bumping heart, to Mr

Rathbone's explanation. 'It were just the drink,' Mr Rathbone said. 'The fact is, me and a couple of me pals were celebrating a – a – birthday and old Rupert here joined us and took one over the eight, as they say. Being pals, we brought him home, but we expected his good lady to see to him. So since you're here now, we'd be much obliged if you would take over, so as me and me mate can return to our own homes before dawn breaks.'

'Right. Thanks very much, Mr Rathbone,' Aunt Myrtle said. 'If you'll just bring him through to the parlour – me niece sleeps in here – I'll clean 'im up and see he don't come to no harm.'

The men agreed to this, and presently Dot heard first the parlour door and then the front door slam, and knew that the two men had left and that Uncle Rupert would remain in the parlour until morning. Quick as a flash, she jumped off the sofa and ran to the window. With the utmost caution, she eased back the curtain a tiny way and applied her eye to the crack, but she soon realised she might as well not have bothered. There was only one street lamp in the court and that was at the far end, by the privy. To be sure, there was a sliver of moon high in the dark sky, but all it showed was two figures making their way across the cobbles towards Heyworth Street.

Dot closed the door and was about to return to the kitchen when her aunt came out of the parlour. She was looking furious. 'Trust your bleedin' uncle to go puttin' me under an obligation to the meanest, most expensive butcher on Heyworth Street,' she said crossly. 'All that mumblin' about me best pal . . . and then Mr Rathbone sayin' no doubt he'd be seein' me quite soon when I were after some nice chops, or a bit o' shin for some stew. Still, perhaps now he's gorrin wi' Rupert, he'll put in a few bones for soup, or a nice bit of offal . . . for free like, I mean.' They had reached the kitchen now, and she looked down at the puddle on the floor with deep distaste. 'Put the kettle over the fire, chuck, an' when it boils you can pour it into a bucket, add some bleach and mop this mess up in a trice. I'm goin' back to bed.' She grinned, suddenly, at her niece. 'Wharra good job you wasn't asleep after all. I bet you gorra scare when they said they was goin' to drop 'im on the sofa on top of you. What did you mean to do? Lie doggo until they'd left, or set up a squall to make 'em think the sofa cushions had come alive?'

'I dunno,' Dot said wearily, fetching the bucket and beginning to pour hot water into it. 'I hadn't made up me mind, like. To tell the truth, I were sound asleep when they come in and I was still wonderin' what were goin' on when I heard your voice. I were relieved, I can tell you.' Her aunt chuckled and stood watching as Dot poured the strong bleach into the bucket, then fetched the mop and stirred it vigorously. When she began to mop, Aunt Myrtle turned as if to leave the room, but Dot stopped her and bent an innocent, enquiring gaze on the older woman. 'I know Mr Rathbone, a'course, though we hardly ever gerrour messages from him 'cos he don't like kids, but who were the other one? It weren't Mr Wright, what lives further along the court, and it weren't me uncle's other drinkin' pal Mr Ellis either; I knows their voices and I'm sure it weren't either of them.'

'I dunno meself,' her aunt said, heading for the parlour door. 'Old Rathbone don't usually drink at the Elephant; he's a feller with a deal more money than our Rupert. I guess he an' his pal are from t'other end of the street and don't come this way much.'

'I see. Don't go for a moment, Aunt Myrtle. I – I don't want Uncle Rupe comin' in once I've turned the lamp out; can you take him his water through, do you think?'

'Well, I will say this for you, Dot McCann, you've got your wits about you,' her aunt said, almost approvingly, coming back into the room to pick up the almost full tin mug. 'I'll put it near the head of the sofa, then he can't fail to see it when he wakes up. I never drew the parlour curtains across an' it gets light early at this time o' year, so he won't come blunderin' in to disturb you again.'

Dot breathed a sigh of relief and presently, finishing her task, she rinsed her hands in a little clean water, dried them on the roller towel and returned to the sofa, where she fell into a disturbed sleep.

Chapter Three

'John Cochrane, get back into line at once and don't let me see you turning sideways to gaze at what doesn't concern you again.'

Someone sniggered and Corky twisted round and gave the boy a glare, then turned quickly back again to face the front. The boys were marching in crocodile formation from the untidy, draughty barracks of a house to the playing field, shared by just about every school and institution in the neighbourhood, where they held their once monthly game of punt-about. You could scarcely call it football since there would be fifty boys playing it, but even so it was eagerly anticipated by the boys at the Redwood Grange Orphanage, for it was the closest thing to freedom ever offered by that establishment.

'What's so funny about my name, Tolstein?' Corky muttered, addressing the sniggerer. 'It ain't anywhere near as funny as Tolstein. At least it's an English name . . . or Irish, at any rate.'

The sniggerer looked apologetic. 'I weren't laughin' at you, Corky,' he said humbly. 'I were laughin' at old Blister, 'cos when he shook his fist at you like that, the drop on the end of his nose fell straight on to his knuckles. Wish my name were Cochrane,' he added wistfully. 'What was you lookin' at, anyroad?'

'Dunno as I were lookin' at anything in pertickler,' Corky said vaguely. Old Blister hated him, but then there was constant war between most of the boys and the men in authority over them. There were so many rules, that was the trouble. For instance, no one was supposed to talk when being herded from the orphanage to the playing field and the boys were always warned not to gaze into shop windows, not to lag behind or hurry forward, and never to look at passers-by but to keep their gaze fixed on the back view of the boy in front.

Corky was a foundling, which meant that he had been left on the doorstep of the home fourteen years ago. There had been a note pinned to the thin piece of blanket in which he was wrapped and this had read: *John Cochrane, aged about five weeks. Please take care of him.* Corky had maintained for a long while – still maintained to his friends – that this meant he had not just been abandoned, that his mother had intended to return for him as soon as she could, but something had intervened to prevent her from doing so. However, he had not voiced the theory aloud for some considerable while because what was the point? There were boys there who had simply been dumped and had been named by Mr Burgoine, the head of the orphanage, according to the whim of the moment. There were others who had come here, aged anything from three or four to eleven or twelve, because their parents had died or could no longer cope with the number of children they'd produced. Once, Corky had envied such boys, but he did so no longer. They had memories, to be sure, but they must be wistful memories. Corky had dreams, and in his opinion dreams were much better than memories because you could be anything you liked in a dream.

He had tried to explain this theory to a young reporter, a certain Nicholas Randall, who had come to the orphanage for a couple of days earlier in the week to interview the boys for an article he was writing about one of the largest orphanages in London. He had talked to Corky alone, sitting behind a desk in a small room which was used to interview new members of staff. He had been a nice young fellow and when Corky had told him that he intended to be a great man one day, make piles and piles of money and take over the orphanage himself, he had clapped him on the shoulder and said he was a grand chap, full of grand ideas, and would undoubtedly do something truly worthwhile when he was a man. But as he talked and laughed and listened, Corky had seen that his eyes were sad and had known that this young man was altogether different from the staff who ran the Redwood Grange Orphanage. This young man had the imagination the others lacked; he could put himself into the shoes of a child who had never known love or a home of his own, and he had sincerely pitied the Redwood Grange boys.

But it was something which had happened the day after the interview that Corky was mulling over now. He had been in the punishment cupboard – locked in, to be precise – when the young reporter, and one of the junior masters, had stopped just outside it, presumably for formal farewells. By this time, Corky knew that the reporter was doing a series of articles on children's homes up and down the country and thought, vaguely, that it might be interesting to find out how Redwood Grange compared with other orphanages.

But then the teacher had begun to talk and Corky found himself listening intently. 'I hope you'll give us a good report,' the master had said. 'You must remember we're doing our best against fearful odds; most of these kids are the dregs of society, with scarcely any common sense, let alone brains. But we try to inculcate some rudimentary education, though of course the Board are so parsi-monious that the teacher/pupil ratio is about thirty to one. Still, they're better off in here than roaming the streets, with their bellies empty and their feet bare.'

There had been silence for a moment and then the young reporter had spoken with suppressed violence. 'Better off in here than on the streets? What are you saying, man? I'd rather see a happy, filthy child, with life and mischief in its eyes, even if it had to beg on street corners for a penny or two to buy bread! You may have tried to teach these kids, tried to discipline them, but all you've done is make them see that they're no-hopers. Why, if I had to advise any of your boys, I'd tell 'em to get out, to see how real, honest-to-God grimy people live. And that's what you ought to be doing. Otherwise, how can they survive when they leave here?'

The teacher had laughed, uneasily. 'We've a hundred boys in this place,' he had muttered. 'If there were only fifty, it might be a different story, but there isn't much you can do with that many. The dormitories were intended to hold six and now they hold a dozen. We do our best . . .'

But at this point, the men had moved away, leaving Corky with a good deal of food for thought whilst he waited for release. He had been in the punishment cupboard for being caught coming down from his dormitory after the midday meal. He had gone up to fetch an exercise book which must have fallen from his book bag when he had snatched it up that morning, but this had been no excuse and he had been told by Mr Evans, who had caught him coming down the stairs with the book, that he would not be released from the cupboard until after tea, which meant, of course, that he would miss the meal.

Corky had been annoyed at the time because he looked forward to his tea. There was always a huge plate of bread and marge, though never as much as one would have liked, a tin mug of weak tea and a slice of seed cake. But because of the overheard conversation, he had been glad of the thinking time. The more he considered what the reporter had said, the more determined he became to take the young man's advice. London was full of boys who probably looked a lot like him – oh, they were dirty and he was clean, but he could soon remedy that – and with a hundred boys at Redwood Grange, why should anyone bother to look for him, even after they discovered he was missing? They would probably be downright grateful; there was never enough food to go round, so once he was away he would be one less mouth to feed.

The real obstacle to running away, the one the masters relied upon, was the orphanage uniform. The boys wore brown shirts and brown trousers, made of some strong cotton material which was too hot in summer and much too cold in winter. It was also horribly distinctive, but Corky, glancing at the crocodile of brown-clad boys ahead of him, decided that this was a challenge to ingenuity. If only he had some money, he could buy some sort of garment from someone, he supposed. But the Redwood Grange boys were never given even the smallest sum until they were fifteen, when the powers that be apparently realised that some knowledge of money was essential if they were to survive after leaving the orphanage. Since Corky would not be fifteen for a whole year, he scarcely knew what money looked like, though there were representations of all the coinage, from a farthing to a half-crown, and even pictures of bank notes, in their blue arithmetic books.

So Corky struggled with his problem as the crocodile approached the recreation ground. When they were walking through the narrow streets, fringed on either side by tottering slums, they often saw lines of washing flapping above their heads. Once I'm away, I can nick an old shirt and some grey trousers off one of those lines, Corky told himself. Once I'm away I'll be all right, and this here's my best opportunity because no one, not even old Blister, can keep his eye on fifty boys at once. No use going now, because a gap in the crocodile would stand out like a sore thumb, but when we get to the rec everyone will push forward and fan out and then, if I keep my nerve, I can be away before old Blister's nose has lost its drip.

Corky's partner in the crocodile was a small, wiry boy called Freddie; not a particular friend, merely someone Corky knew vaguely. If Freddie had been a pal, Corky's escape would have been more difficult; it would have meant involving someone else, and this was always dangerous. A friend would search for you, might even set up a hue and cry unless he were in on the secret, and in Corky's view, a secret shared was soon common property.

He was still considering in which direction he should run when they reached the gates and everyone surged forward. Old Blister was at the head of the crocodile and Ratty Evans at the tail, but as they reached the gates Ratty hurried forward, shouting at the boys not to shove, to behave like responsible citizens for once in their lives. Corky glanced around him; no one was even looking in his direction. If he was serious, if he really meant to escape, then now was the time to do it. Without giving himself time to consider, he turned and bent as though searching for something he had dropped, and in this position squiggled against the tide of boys trying to get through the gates, and dived down the nearest alleyway.

If there had been a shout from behind . . . but there was not. No one had noticed his departure, and even had they done so, Corky believed that his fellow pupils would not have snitched on him. Why should they, after all? So he continued to pad along the alleyway until he emerged on to a main road. He crossed the busy street, trying to look both purposeful yet rather aimless, and now glanced behind him. The alleyway down which he had made his escape was empty, the street before him crowded with strangers. Corky stopped short for a moment, feeling the breath catch in his throat. He was alone, in a great city of which he knew absolutely nothing. Boys at the Grange were never alone, except in the punishment cupboard, and sometimes you were not even alone there, only locked in the dark and denied a meal. For a moment, panic gripped him; he had so little knowledge, so few resources. He was running away all right, as the young reporter had advised, but surely one ran away *to* something, or someone – to a family or a friend, somewhere where one would be welcomed. The trouble was, he knew so little! It was essential to get as far away from Redwood Grange as possible if he were not to be ignominiously carted back there by some well-meaning bobby. He knew there were ships in the Port of London and assumed one could stow away upon such a vessel, and he knew there were railway stations whence one could travel to distant parts of the country, but he had no idea in which direction any of these places lay and until he managed to shed his uniform he dared not ask. Any member of the public in these parts would take one look at his brown uniform and know he had no business to be out on the streets alone. His best course, he decided, plodding doggedly along the pavement, was to simply keep walking in as straight a line as he could manage, until it was evening. Then he would be far away from the Isle of Dogs and folk would not be so likely to realise he came from an institution. In fact, if he could just nick a pair of trousers – grey ones – he was pretty sure that he would pass muster as an ordinary street arab and would be accepted as such by anyone he might accost.

Having made up his mind on this point, Corky began to take a little more interest in his surroundings. It was still broad daylight but he fancied the sun was not as hot as it had been and was a good deal further down in the sky than at the start of his adventure. Soon, he thought, the boys would be leaving the recreation ground and forming into a crocodile. He wondered if Blister would count heads or tell them to walk with their original partners, but he knew that both actions were unlikely. To be sure, Blister would shout at them to form into a crocodile but he would walk ahead with Ratty at the tail, occasionally chivvying their charges to walk faster, but taking very little notice of them otherwise. And Corky remembered, with pleasure, that there had been fifty-one boys so the chances were that, lacking a gap in the crocodile, he would not even be missed.

Corky kept on walking. I'm like Felix, the Film Cat, he told himself, for amongst the tattered books in the Redwood Grange playroom was a much loved copy of a Felix annual and most of the younger boys knew every page by heart. Twice a year – sometimes more often – a benefactor of the orphanage paid for all the boys to attend a showing at the local picture house, and was kind enough to ensure that they saw westerns, cartoons, or gangster films, rather than educational ones.

It occurred to Corky that it must be teatime, since his stomach was beginning to rumble suggestively every time he passed a shop with bread or cakes displayed in its window. He would not have been human had he not considered a quick smash and grab, but he knew that this would lead to his eventual capture for the cry of 'Stop thief' would turn every honest man's hand against him, and presently he was glad he had not taken to crime. He was standing outside a baker's, gazing wistfully into the window, when there was a tap on his shoulder. He stiffened, made as if to dart away, and found a bag being held under his nose and giving off the most entrancing, spicy smell. He looked up; the bag was being proffered by a fat little woman in black. She had tiny spectacles perched on a little snub nose, and the expression of her small grey eyes was kindly. 'When I were a kid, I ran away from one of them there orphing places,' she said, her voice very low. 'It didn't do me much good 'cos I were caught next day . . . well, I were that hungry, I were quite glad to be caught . . . but I 'opes as you'll 'ave better luck, lad. I bought four buns; I'll tek two for me tea an' you can 'ave the bag with the other two in it.' She thrust the rustling paper bag into Corky's hands. 'And 'ere's a bit of advice, sunshine. Dirty yourself up a bit; kids rahnd 'ere get mucky soon as they leave their 'omes. Good luck!'

She turned and began to waddle away but Corky caught her up. This was the biggest piece of luck so far, he told himself. Quite by chance, he had met someone who would help him, who would not give him away. He put a hand, timidly, on her sleeve, and she stopped at once and smiled at him. 'Yes, me old china?'

'Thanks for the buns, missus, only – only I'm

more in need of ordinary clothes than food, if you get my meaning,' Corky said.

'Well, I ain't got no spare money, but if you want to come back to my house I could fix you up wi' summat what weren't a uniform. I'm a ragger, if you know what that is,' the old lady said.

Corky was overwhelmed. He said huskily: 'Oh, missus, I'd be that grateful. If there's anything I can do for you then I'd do it like a shot.'

The old woman laughed and handed him the bulging canvas bag she was carrying. It was really heavy and Corky marvelled at the old lady's strength. It must be her week's shopping, he told himself, hefting it on one shoulder. 'Mrs Perkin, that's my monicker, an' who's you, my fine young feller?'

Corky hesitated. He had no desire to tell anyone his real name yet it seemed downright insulting not to do so when Mrs Perkin had already been so good to him. He decided on a sort of halfway house. 'Me pals call me Corky and I'd be right glad if you did the same,' he said. 'I can't shake your hand, Mrs Perkin, on account of both mine being full, but I'm happy to meet you. Well, it were a rare bit of luck for me,' he added honestly. 'Which orphanage were you in? Somewhere local, were it?'

The old woman chuckled, but shook her head. 'Nah. You might not think it 'cos I'm a real Londoner now – a Cockney sparrer you might say. I did get away from the orphanage in the end. It were in Liverpool, what's a big city . . . oh, miles an' miles from London. It were harder for me, bein' a girl, and I was small for thirteen, too – still am, for that matter, though I shan't see seventy agin – but I were determined, you see? I'd met this young feller who were cabin boy on one of the big liners and though I were only young, I wanted to see him again. He give me his address down London, said if I were ever that way I must call in because his ma were a grand old gal and would help me as soon as she knew I were a friend of her Georgie, so I smuggled myself aboard a coaster and after quite a long while I got to London. I made my way to the East End, to Abbot Road in Poplar, and old Mrs Perkin was everything her son had said, and more. She took me in, helped me to find a job, saw me clothed decent an' four years later I married Georgie and we set up house in the very same place I'm taking you back to, this minute.' As she spoke, she had turned into a narrow entry between two rows of houses, and after a few yards she stopped outside a substantial-looking door set in the brickwork. She lifted the latch then waved Corky to go before her. 'Here you are, 'ome, sweet 'ome! Welcome to number twelve Herbee Place, Bethnal Green. It ain't much but no one won't search for you 'ere and the two of us will be snug as bugs in rugs – till you want to move on, of course.' She fished a key from the lintel above the door, turned it in the lock, and the two of them entered a small but cheerful kitchen. A fire burned in the grate, a black iron kettle steamed on the hob and there was a good smell of cooking which seemed to emanate from the round black pot which hung on a chain over the fire. 'Where's you thinkin' of headin' for? Got somewhere in mind, have you?'

Corky shook his head. 'I don't know where's best to go, 'cept that I want to be as far from the Isle of Dogs as possible. I wonder . . . how old do you have to be afore you can become a cabin boy?'

His hostess had sat herself down in a chair, or rather collapsed into it, but now she turned and gestured to the kettle on the hob. 'Pull the kettle over the fire, there's a good lad. I's dead parched, and dyin' for a cup o' char,' she said. 'As for cabin boys, I dunno as there's a pertickler age but I dare say someone might take you on. There's no fishin' fleet out o' the Port o' London but I remember Mr Perkin tellin' me once that his father had sailed with a fishin' fleet out o' Plymouth, in Devonshire, when he were no more than twelve. Ah, kettle's boilin', I'm glad to see.'

She made as if to struggle out of the chair but Corky shook his head at her. 'No you don't,' he said firmly. 'Tell me where you keep the tea and so on and I'll make us both a cuppa.'

The old woman sighed deeply and sat back in her chair. 'Tea's in the cupboard beside the sink and there's a jug of milk on the stone slab under the window,' she said. 'Beside the milk, there's a lump of marge. If you'll split the buns, we'll have a spread of marge on them and eat them with our tea. Can you manage that, d'you think?'

'Course I can,' Corky said, a trifle reproachfully, and then had to ask where she kept her knives, but presently the two of them settled down with tea and buns and Corky told his new friend a good deal about Redwood Grange, most of which caused her to eye him sympathetically and to say that he was clearly best out of it, even if his escape might not lead to an easier life so much as a different one.

After the tea was drunk and the buns eaten, Mrs Perkin showed Corky round the house. She was very proud of the fact that the hot water for baths and washing up came from a gas-powered geyser above the sink. To be sure, one still had to carry cans of water to fill the big tin bath, but only ten years ago she had had to heat the water in a large kettle over her kitchen fire, so the geyser represented a considerable saving in labour, so far as his hostess was concerned. This seemed odd to Corky, since whatever the failings of the orphanage hot water had always gushed forth at the turn of a tap, but he did not comment, realising that it would have been tactless, to say the least.

Downstairs, there was a reasonably sized kitchen and a small scullery which smelt strongly of lye soap and damp. There was also a front parlour, full of what Mrs Perkin considered rare and beautiful pieces of furniture, ornaments, rugs and the like. She explained to Corky that she did not use the room when she was by herself but only on high days and holidays, such as at Christmas, when her two sons and their wives came calling. 'I got a son in the antiques business, that's Wilfred, and another son, Rodney, who's got a coal lorry,' she said. 'Neither of them live far away and they're both doin' very nicely, specially Wilfred. He keeps on at me to give up me work, to settle down to just keepin' my house nice and spendin' a bit more time with them. But, to tell you the truth, young Corky, I loves meetin' people, and as a ragger I'm seein' new faces all the time, so this 'ere quiet life our Wilfred recommends ain't for me. Besides, I likes me independence. Wilfred says he'd make up any shortfall if I agree to give up raggin', but to my mind that's little better'n charity an' I've not sunk that low yet.'

She was leading Corky upstairs as she spoke, on to a small, square landing from which led two doors. 'I sleeps in the front, 'cos I'm of a nosy disposition and when you gets to be over seventy you don't sleep so good,' she explained. 'Besides, it's the bigger room an' I like a bit o' space round me.' She threw open the door, revealing a sizeable bedroom with several thick, expensive-looking rugs upon the floor, an enormous brass bedstead – the bed covered in a colourful patchwork quilt – a heavy marble washstand against one wall and a comfortable cushioned chair pulled up close to the window, which was curtained in red velvet to match the cushions on the chair. It was easily the nicest and most luxurious bedroom Corky had ever seen and he told Mrs Perkin so. The old woman beamed at him.

'Aye, it's a bit of all right,' she agreed. 'My Wilf had the furnishing of it and he were determined it should be real pretty. He knows I don't sleep so well, particularly in summer when dawn comes early, which is why that lovely chair's drawn up to the window. You'd be surprised at what goes on once the light comes at this time o' year, and I sees it all.' She chuckled genially. 'It were Wilf what gave me them binoculars what you can see on the window ledge. Once a week, sometimes more often, Wilf comes on a quick visit an' I tells 'im everything I've see'd. But what am I gabblin' away for when I brung you up here to show you where you can sleep.' She trod heavily across the tiny landing and opened the second door. 'There ain't much room, 'cos Wilfred uses it as a kind o' storehouse for stuff that he can't sell immediate, from one cause or another. But I can bed you down on that there elegant sofy thing – Wilf says it's a Georgian day bed, a chaise-longue by them Frenchies – but if you're stayin' for more than the odd day or two, I'll get you to carry some o' this stuff round to Wilf's shop.'

'Oh . . . but won't he mind, if he wants it stored here for a bit?' Corky asked, rather apprehensively. An antique dealer sounded important; the sort of person who might easily disapprove of a runaway orphan. 'It's all right, missus, honest; I can squeeze in there, snug as a bug in a rug.'

'Truth to tell, lad, I think Wilf would be quite glad to get some of the stuff back. He were sayin' only the other day that stuff what's been here two years oughta be on shelves, 'cept he's so busy he's not had a chance to come and fetch it.'

'But you said he comes visiting every week,' Corky objected. 'If he really wanted the stuff, couldn't he have took it then?'

He happened to be looking at his hostess as he spoke and saw her eyes shift uneasily, but she replied in a matter-of-fact tone: 'It's plain to see you've never met my Wilf! He's a real gent, dresses to kill, you might say. He wouldn't dream of being seen cartin' stuff through the streets like any common carrier, and he wants the stuff a few pieces at a time, see. Otherwise, he could send a handcart, or even a van, for them. It's all a matter o' space. He used to rely on me fetchin' 'em round whenever he needed 'em, but there's no denyin' I'm not what I was. Why, that little walnut table, which is real old – hundreds of years, I dare say – and worth a mint, Wilf tells me, felt heavy as lead when I tried to lift it and the bloody legs got between my old pins an' near as dammit tripped me up, an' I was only movin' it across the room, which were a good thing because if I'd tried to take it downstairs I reckon I'd have broke me neck before ever I reached the front door.' She looked at him anxiously. 'I know Wilf wants the table and the shop ain't difficult to find. Would you take it round to him for me? It ain't very big, it's just awkward, like.'

'Course I will,' Corky said stoutly. He just hoped the antique shop wasn't on a main road or near a police station. It was still broad daylight outside and Mrs Perkin had not yet gone through her rag collection to find him suitable clothing. However, in view of her kindness, it would have been churlish to point this out. Corky went over to the little walnut table and picked it up, discovering that it was indeed heavy.

Mrs Perkin beamed and nodded approval as he carried it carefully down the stairs, but when he took it along the short hallway she called him back, almost sharply. 'No, no, no, not right now. I've got to find you some clothes what won't scream orphanage at every passer-by. Best wait till it's a bit dusky like, too, 'cos you don't want to be recognised, do you? And don't think you're goin' to have to carry it all the way to my Wilf's, because I know – none better – how heavy it is. Agin the privy there's a lean-to shed; I've a sturdy little wheelbarrow in there that you can use. Put the table in the parlour for the time being and we'll deal with it when we've ate our meal – it's shin of beef stew – and found you something to wear.'

Corky thought the shin of beef stew was the nicest food he had ever tasted, even better than the buns, and he was pleased with the clothing Mrs Perkin provided. It was just right; the shirt was much mended and the sort of shade, between grey and blue, which showed that it had not been washed too often. And the strides, both patched and frayed, were still sturdy enough to be useful, and dark grey. So when at last Mrs Perkin began to tell him how to reach her son's shop, he felt pretty confident that he could do her errand without trouble, especially when she cast some filthy old rags over the walnut table, saying that this was the way she had always taken goods to her son, before her strength had failed her. 'No one's likely to try to thieve from a ragger,' she said comfortably. 'But that there table's a little gold mine . . . well, no, it ain't worth that much, but it's a nice piece, all the same. If you get it safe to my son, then you're sure of a home wi' me, so long as you want one. And if you take a few more things out of the back bedroom – Wilf will tell me what an' I'll pass it on to you – then I dare say, when you *do* leave, you'll find yourself the richer by a bob or two.'

This sounded ideal to Corky, who could not believe his luck. Earlier that day, he had been homeless, friendless, hungry and, if he were honest, frightened. Then, out of the blue, Mrs Perkin had recognised him for what he was, a penniless, runaway orphan, and had taken pity on him. Now, he had a home – for a while at least – a good friend and even a job – of sorts – for the back bedroom was crammed from floor to ceiling almost with bits of furniture, rich-looking leatherbound books, ornaments so beautiful that they took Corky's breath away, and many other similar things. Wilfred, Mrs Perkin had implied, would be glad to receive the stuff, a few items at a time. Suppose he gives me threepence every time I take something round, and suppose Mrs Perkin lets me stay with her until the room's empty, Corky dreamed, trundling the wheelbarrow over the uneven flagstones, then I'll be an old man as rich as the king before I have to leave. The thought tickled him and he began to whistle and to glance around him as he pushed, for this was a part of London in which he felt at home, though he had never been here before. In the small side streets, kids played hopscotch, marbles or skipping. Despite the lateness of the hour, some of the small shops were still open, and because it was a warm evening women gathered on their doorsteps, gossiping and calling out to each other as they did so.

It was because he was so interested in his surroundings that the accident happened. The wheelbarrow caught on an uneven flagstone and tipped sideways, depositing the little walnut table upon the pavement. Corky had noticed, vaguely, when he had been wrapping the table in rags, that there was a little drawer beneath it which had been held shut with pieces of tape. It now appeared, however, that the tape was quite old, for the drawer shot open a couple of inches and, as Corky tenderly stood the table on its feet, it opened a little wider, allowing him to see the contents. For a moment, Corky just gaped, then he rammed the drawer shut, lifted the table back into the wheelbarrow and smothered it in rags once more. Jewels! The little drawer had been stuffed with necklaces, brooches and earrings. No wonder the table had seemed so heavy.

Beginning to trudge along the road once more, Corky thought, first, that it was none of his business and, second, that an antique dealer had every right to put jewellery in a reliable hiding place, if he so wished. He rather doubted if Mrs Perkin knew about the jewellery, but again that was neither here nor there. He was sure she would never have poked around, examining her son's property; why should she? He had seen the beautiful ornaments casually displayed in the little room, so Wilfred was not trying to hide anything from his mother. But he would just mention that the drawer had fallen open, when he reached the antique shop, and see what Wilfred said. He realised, belatedly, that had the drawer shot even wider open and had he not noticed it, some of the jewels might easily have got lost. Yes, he would tell Wilfred exactly what had happened so the older man would know that he was honest and had no intention of cheating, or deceiving, either Wilfred himself, or Wilfred's mother.

Presently he reached the shop, which was quite large, though not on the main road, as he had imagined, but down a side street. Over the door, the legend *Wilfred Perkin: Antique Dealer* was painted in gold on a green background, but when he tried the door it was firmly locked and he remembered Mrs Perkin's instructions. 'Me son lives over the shop so if he's already locked up, you'll find a little side passage to the left of the frontage, what leads round the back. There's a cobbled yard and you just cross that and knock as loud as you can on the back door. Wilfred's cautious by nature so he'll mebbe ask who you are before he opens the door, but just you say you've been sent by Mrs Perkin of Herbee Place and he'll have that door open and you inside afore you can say knife.'

It was all exactly as Mrs Perkin had said. Corky trudged across the cobbled yard, knocked on the door, and was asked, in a suspicious voice, to name his business. Corky shouted back that he had come from Mrs Perkin of Herbee Place and waited, listening to what sounded like half a dozen doors being carefully shut before the back door was opened and he was ushered inside. It was a strange room, panelled from floor to ceiling in varnished wood. There was a table and several upright chairs in the middle of the room and, glancing round, Corky realised that the panelling was, in fact, the doors of cupboards where, he presumed, Wilfred Perkin must store a good deal of his stock. None of the cupboards had handles or knobs on – presumably so that burglars would think the room was empty – but, despite his care, one of the cupboard doors had not been completely closed, and through the tiny crack the lamplight revealed something shiny within.

Corky was still thinking what a clever scheme this was, because burglars would have no idea that the room contained hidden treasures, when there was another knock on the back door. Hastily, Mr Wilfred Perkin bundled Corky, the wheelbarrow and the walnut table through another door which led into the darkened shop. 'You're a pal of me mam's so I know you's trustable, but I don't want a peep out of you, understand?' he hissed. 'This'll be some – some customers as I'm expectin' but they – they are very shy and wouldn't want you watchin' while we does our business, so just you keep mum and it'll all be fine and dandy. Awright?'

'Hey, wait a minute, mister, there's something I've got to tell you,' Corky whispered. 'That there table . . . the drawer came undone when I wheeled it over an uneven flagstone and there's stuff inside. It's all right, I didn't lose nothin', but the tape's old and wouldn't stick back again, so . . .'

'Yes, yes, yes, so long as nothin' fell out,' Wilfred Perkin said distractedly, pushing Corky further into the shop and beginning to close the door. 'I shan't be long, so just you stay mum till I calls ya.' And on the words, he pulled the door softly to. Corky heard him cross the room, ask a question and then creak the back door open and usher someone into the stockroom. For a moment he stood in the dark but then, realising that Mr Perkin's business might take some time, he lifted the walnut table carefully out of the barrow, stood it down, noiselessly, on its spindly legs and settled himself, as comfortably as he could, in the place the walnut table had just vacated.

Sitting thus in the dark was rather an eerie experience and Corky soon grew both bored and stiff. He rose quietly to his feet and went over to the door, hoping to hear some indication that the business being conducted on the other side of it would soon be over. However, the voices continued to murmur and he realised that there were at least three people in the stockroom and, obviously, there was haggling going on. Corky knew little about business, but he did know about haggling, since the boys did it all the time. If you had acquired a good big conker and wanted to swap it for half of someone's seed cake at teatime, the seed cake owner would try to retain as much of his booty as he could whilst the conker owner praised his property to the sky, swore it was a tenner when it might really only be a fiver, and eyed the seed cake hopefully.

Having got out of the wheelbarrow, Corky did not much want to get back in. Since he was getting his night eyes in the darkness of the shop, he began to look around him. He saw tables, chairs, sofas and china cabinets, little stools and beautiful ornaments, and realised that he had been wise to remain still. One unguarded move could send a figure on a pedestal crashing to earth, making a huge noise and breaking what might well be a valuable piece. Still looking round, he jumped when he saw a pair of large eyes staring down at him. For a moment, his heart fairly thundered, then he relaxed. It was a model Red Indian, standing almost six foot tall, with a great feathered headdress and a bow and a quiver of arrows slung over one shoulder. Corky had been holding his breath but now he let it out in a long sigh of relief; what a fool he was! The only living thing in the shop was himself.

Even as the thought entered his mind, there was a movement in the shadows and, whilst he was still telling himself that he was imagining it, something soft and warm brushed against his leg.

Corky could not help himself. He gave a squawk of fright and shot through the door into the storeroom, eyes starting and every hair on end. There were three men seated round the table, all of whom turned startled eyes upon him, but Corky was past caring. 'There's – there's a bleedin' Indian. I thought he were a wax one, like, but he's come alive. He grabbed me leg,' he gabbled. 'I dussent stay in there though I know you said not to disturb you. I ain't scared of the dark but I am scared of that there Indian.'

Mr Perkin was looking flustered but he pulled himself together pretty quickly, considering. 'You stupid young bugger, it were only the cat,' he said. 'That there Indian's a cigar store Indian; don't you know nothin', boy?' He turned to his two companions. 'It's all right, fellers, this 'ere's me nephew, Ben, what's been doin' a bit o' fetchin' an' carryin' for me. You needn't be afraid he'll blab.' He turned back to Corky. 'Me an' these gentlemen' – he

waved a hand to indicate his two companions –
'have just concluded a bit of business, so if you
run upstairs to Mrs – to your Aunt Bertha, I mean
– and ask her to give you a bottle an' three glasses,
we'll conclude our deal over a drink.'

Mr Perkin ushered Corky firmly back into the
shop, closing the door behind him. As he did so,
he remarked: 'Young fool! I reckon the cat must
'ave followed you in, 'cos I never let 'im in the
shop. Off with you.' He indicated the stairs behind
the counter which led to the flat above. Then he
returned to the back room, shutting the heavy oak
door.

Corky climbed the stairs and was met at the top
by a good-looking, dark-haired woman in a black
dress. He began to explain his errand and she
nodded, saying in a puzzled tone: 'Aye, I'll fetch
the wine and the glasses, but who the devil are
you? I disremember my husband mentioning there
was a lad involved.'

'I'm not involved; Mrs Perkin of Herbee Place
asked me to deliver a table . . .' Corky began, but
got no further.

'Oh aye, Wilf said she were lookin' for a likely
lad,' the woman said. She put a small round tray,
on which rested three glasses and a squat bottle of
dark brown liquid, into Corky's hand, then accompanied him down the stairs, illuminating the way
with a small lamp. As soon as he reached the storeroom door, she turned and left him. Corky was
wondering how he would open the door without

putting the tray down, when he realised that it was on the latch. He slipped through the doorway and Wilfred immediately got to his feet and took the tray. 'Get back up to your aunt,' he said. 'We've just about done here; I'll be up myself presently.'

Corky was sitting in the kitchen of the Perkins' flat when Wilf came in. 'You nearly landed us all in hot water, young fellow-me-lad,' he said. 'Still an' all, it weren't your fault . . . nor mine, neither, for that matter. What *is* your name, by the by?'

'I'm Corky,' Corky said. 'And if it's all right by you, Mr Perkin, I'll get off now, but I 'spect I'll be seein' you again, 'cos your ma says there's a deal o' stuff to be transported from her spare bedroom to your stockroom; ain't that right?'

'Aye, you're right there,' Wilfred Perkin agreed. 'And you ain't a bad lad; you're a good lad, in fact. My ma does know how to pick 'em, I'll say that for 'er. You never so much as blinked when I called you Ben and said you were me nephew, an' I reckon if I'd been standin' near that Indian in the dark an' the cat had brushed against me, I'd have squawked just as loud as you did.' As he spoke he was ushering Corky down the stairs and across the darkened shop, steering him unerringly back to the wheelbarrow.

'Glad I were OK, Mr Perkin,' Corky said, seizing hold of the handles of the wheelbarrow and beginning to trundle it towards the back door. He was actually in the cobbled yard when Mr Perkin dug his hand in his pocket and produced a handful of coins. He selected one, hesitated, then added another, both of which he handed to Corky. 'There y'are,' he said gruffly. 'It's a bit more than I'd normally pay, but we've had quite a night of it, eh, young feller?'

'Thanks, mister . . . I mean, thanks, Mr Perkin,' Corky said. He did not need to look at the coins to know that he held sixpences in his hand: a veritable fortune!

'You'd best call me Wilf; everyone else does,' the older man said, beginning to close the door. 'G'night, young shaver.'

'G'night, Mr – g'night Wilf, I mean,' Corky said and heard the other chuckle as he closed and bolted the door.

All the way home, Corky pondered over the events of the evening. There was something fishy going on, he was sure of it. It didn't take a genius to see that Wilf was a pretty sharp character, and as for the two men who had visited him, Corky thought he had never seen a more villainous couple. They were large men, respectably dressed, but one had had his back to him, so he had been unable to see his face, only the back of a thick red neck. The man facing him, however, the really fat one, looked familiar; he was sure he had seen him before. A tradesman, perhaps? Or someone working on the railway, or a tram driver? Corky could not remember, but the man had clearly not recognised him, so perhaps it was just his imagination. Yet there was definitely something . . . he could not explain it, even to himself, but he had been glad when the men had left and had found himself hoping he would never meet them again.

If Wilfred had been an honest man, of course, he would not have pushed Corky into the darkened shop when his visitors arrived, nor would he have lied to them, saying that Corky was his nephew Ben. And then there was old Mrs Perkin of Herbee Place, who had been so kind to him. She had pretended to befriend him simply because he was an orphan, as she was, but Mrs Wilfred Perkin had said that her mother-in-law was looking for a 'likely lad', so the old lady's friendliness and generosity had not been spontaneous. She must have known he was an orphan because of his horrible uniform, guessed that he was also a runaway, and thought that someone homeless, friendless and penniless would be an ideal go-between to assist herself and Wilfred in whatever deep game they were playing.

By the time he reached Herbee Place again, Corky had made a difficult decision. He had hoped to stay with Mrs Perkin for weeks and weeks, maybe for months, but he had now decided that this would be dangerous. He was horribly aware that he knew very little of the world outside Redwood Grange, but he had always been an avid reader and knew that there were people in London's underworld who were receivers of stolen goods, and only a little thought had convinced him that Wilfred and his mother were both handling property which was not rightfully theirs.

However, it would not do to let the Perkins realise that he knew what was going on. He would go along with it whilst he had to, but as soon as he had sufficient money to get away, get away he would. He had no intention of informing on the Perkins – it would be far too dangerous – but before he left them, he thought he might leave a note explaining this and pointing out that, if they pursued him, he might be forced to talk to the coppers, simply in his own defence.

When he got back to Herbee Place, Mrs Perkin was waiting up for him. She beamed as he entered the kitchen and cut a big slice off a rich-looking fruit cake, then poured him a mug of hot cocoa. 'I were gettin' right worried,' she told him, wrapping her hands round her own mug. 'Did you get lost? I thought you'd just leave the table with my Wilfred an' come straight back. What kept you?'

Corky thought that her tone was a little sharp and found himself wondering whether she had guessed that he had guessed; but it had been a full and exciting day and he was too tired for much more thought. 'Customers came in while I was unwrapping the table so I had to wait in the shop,' he explained. 'It was all right and I didn't get lost, not goin' or comin' back, and Wilf – he told me to call him Wilf – gave me a bob for me trouble,' he ended.

Mrs Perkin's small eyes widened. 'A shillin' – a whole shillin'!' she breathed. 'Well, I reckon he were pleased with you. I reckon he thought his

old ma knew a thing or two when it come to findin'
a good lad. Now, eat up your cake an' finish your
cocoa an' get yourself up the apples an' pears, and
when you come down in the mornin' I'll 'ave a
cooked breakfast waitin' for you.'

Chapter Four

Corky had not intended to stay indefinitely with Mrs Perkin, but he was sorely tempted to do so when he realised the joys of living in a house with one other person, when that person seemed to enjoy your company and did everything she could to make your stay a pleasant one. Also, Wilf paid Corky well for errands run and it wasn't only gradually emptying old Mrs Perkin's spare bedroom; there were other jobs for which a lad was useful. These jobs were not so well paid because they took place in daylight and were, Corky was sure, legitimate business. A man and his wife would come into the shop, admire a dining table and four upholstered dining chairs, and perhaps agree to pay extra to have these items delivered to their home. Corky would then take a handcart from Wilf's shed in the back yard, help to load the items upon it, and trundle them to their new owners' abode. Wilf paid him for these duties on a distance basis, though once or twice Corky had been forced to point out that half a mile uphill was a deal harder than half a mile down, and though Wilf always laughed, and exclaimed that his new delivery boy could get blood out of a stone and expected money for nothing, he usually paid up. After this had happened half a dozen times, however, Corky began to wonder whether Wilf thought that he was discreetly blackmailing him, which was most certainly not the case. Though Wilf was always genial towards him, Corky was wary of the older man, so he decided to accept the money he was given in future without mentioning hills or heavy traffic.

Almost imperceptibly, the days and the weeks passed, and Corky realised that he was truly happy for the first time in his life. Mrs Perkin might have offered him refuge for her own reasons, but what was wrong with that, after all? She had wanted help of a sort which he could provide, and in return she gave him a roof over his head, food in his belly, a comfortable bed and, above all, the feeling that he was accepted for himself, liked and trusted; that he could turn to her in need as she occasionally turned to him. He often ran errands for her, doing her shopping, accompanying her when she visited relatives in order to give her an arm when she needed one, and generally behaving almost like the 'kind o' nephew' which she sometimes called him.

After he had lived with her for six or seven weeks, Corky knew that she had no nephews, and no nieces either. Her husband had been the youngest of a big family, but death had claimed them all save for two spinsters who lived in Hammersmith, and since she visited them at least once a week, Corky knew the journey across

London quite well. At first, he had demurred over entering their house, had said he would amuse himself in the neighbourhood until Mrs Perkin was ready to return, but she had insisted that he stay with her, and he soon learned to be useful to her sisters-in-law, carrying water, coal, or anything else which was heavy, or laying a fire in a little-used grate. Such small acts were always rewarded, sometimes by an apple, or a piece of cake, or a penny to spend at the shops, but what Corky really valued was the feeling of being one of the family, accepted without question. At first, he had been awkward, shy, afraid to look around him in case his interest was labelled curiosity, and resented. Then he became easier with them, laying the table for a meal, peeling potatoes to save rheumatic hands the task, making a pot of tea as a matter of course the moment they entered the house. The old ladies were fond of a game called Pelmanism, or Pairs, which called for a good memory, and one of the sisters liked another card game, cribbage, and pounced on Corky as soon as he entered the kitchen, demanding that they begin a game at once because she knew 'my dear sister Aggie' would be happy to lay the table and get out the food for high tea.

As summer progressed, Corky settled deeper into the niche he had made for himself and became more and more reluctant to leave. His little store of money was growing nicely and he had no idea how he would earn more if he were to abandon the Perkin family. And of course, every extra day that he stayed, it became harder to leave. He truly felt that the Perkins were his family, that he belonged for the first time in his life. He was even prepared to pretend that there were no stolen goods hidden away in the spare bedroom, and when Wilf began to give him articles to take back to Herbee Place, telling him to put them well to the back of the existing stock and not to return them to the shop until he gave the word, which might not be for many months, he always accepted this without comment and tried to tell himself that there could be a perfectly honest reason for such behaviour, though in his heart he knew otherwise.

One hot summer day at the end of July, he had been told to take a very nice rolltop writing bureau to a house a couple of miles away. Because the sun was shining so brightly, it did not occur to Corky to pick up a dust sheet to cover the well-polished satinwood, but, fortunately, Mrs Wilf was in the shop and ran after him to throw a large dust sheet over the writing desk and say, a trifle breathlessly, that she could smell thunder in the air and was never mistaken over such things. Corky, looking up at the bright blue sky and the brassy gold of the sun, thought that she was wrong this time, but said nothing. He had delivered the desk and was turning for home, sweat streaming down the sides of his face, when it occurred to him that the sun had disappeared, although it was still very hot. What was more, the light was odd. Scarcely had the thought crossed his mind when there was a crack of thunder directly overhead and he saw forked lightning, lilac-coloured against the yellowy sky, plunge to earth. Seconds later, the heavens opened; rain poured down like a river, the drops enormous. Corky grabbed the dust sheet and wrapped himself in it, but it impeded his progress, tangling between his legs, and anyway it was soon completely drenched, so he slung it back on to the handcart and continued on his way. People in light summer clothing – for no one, except Mrs Perkin, had anticipated the dramatic change in the weather – scattered, searching for doorways, shops, anywhere where they might gain shelter, but Corky, of course, could do no such thing. A handcart was a valuable item and not one to be carelessly abandoned, so he grimly pushed on, relieved not to have the added weight of the bureau and anxious to get back to the shop without unnecessary delay. Ahead of him, a carter was trying to persuade an enormous dray horse that the thunder and lightning would not hurt him. But the horse was not convinced; it kept rearing up, rolling its eyes and crashing its hooves on to the cobbles once more. Corky was tempted to help but still dared not let go of the handcart. To be sure, there were scarcely any adults about, but street urchins were everywhere, bright-eyed and sharp-witted, always on the lookout for something to pinch. If he let go of his handcart for one moment, they'd have it, sure as check.

Fortunately, the rain was warm, but even so, Corky had never been happier to turn the corner and see Wilfred Perkin's shop front. He wheeled the handcart down the covered passage and into the yard, shoved it into the shed, and made for the back door at a gallop. He entered the storeroom, water pouring from him, and saw that there was a strange man – a customer, he presumed – in the room. Wilf was sitting at the table with a long list before him, looking up at the man and shaking his head whilst saying earnestly that his shop did not contain any of the items for which the stranger was searching, and certainly not a man's gold hunter watch, set with gems instead of numerals, and inscribed *Charles, from your Caroline*.

Corky gave an exclamation. What was Wilf thinking of? This man wanted such a watch and he, Corky, knew jolly well that they had the item in stock, though he could not recall an inscription. 'Have you forgot, Wilf?' he said, brushing wet hair from his face. 'There's one just like that in the corner cabinet, inside the cigarette box inlaid with mother-of-pearl. I see'd it only last week.'

Wilf looked up at him, his eyes hard. 'What the devil are you talking about, boy?' he said angrily. 'You don't know nothing about my stock. You're just my delivery boy.'

There was something in his glance which warned Corky to back down and he began to do so, but the stranger seized him by the ear and began to push him towards the shop, saying as he did so: 'Out o' the mouths of babes and sucklings, eh, Mr Perkin? C'mon, young feller, show me this 'ere cabinet or I'll give you the 'iding of your life an' chuck you in prison for hobstructin' the law.'

Poor Corky was horrified; this man must be a plain clothes police officer, searching for stolen goods, and he, fool that he was, had thought him merely a customer searching for a very fancy gold hunter watch, either for himself or as a presentation gift for someone in his employ, perhaps.

But it was too late for conjecture. The man dragged him to the corner cabinet and peered inside, then tried to open it, but it was locked. 'This is the wrong one, sir,' Corky squealed, for the man's grip on his ear was painful. 'Lemme go. I made a mistake, honest I did. There ain't no gold hunter watch . . . well, I dare say there is, I seen it somewhere, but now I come to think, I reckon it were in Mr Parish's shop, not this one.'

It was a brave effort – Mr Parish was another antique dealer from whom Wilf sometimes bought goods – but it availed Corky nothing. 'Where's the bleedin' key, youngster?' the policeman growled. 'I've been visitin' this shop for years, knowin' full well that Wilf is a fence, but never able to prove a thing. My inspector is gettin' that fed up with me, actually said I were a pal of half the villains in this manor, so an arrest for receiving stolen goods would go down right nicely.'

'He isn't . . . a villain, I mean . . . and he don't receive no stolen goods,' Corky shouted wildly.

When the strong arm of the law had hold of your ear, truth did not seem particularly important. 'An' I dunno where the key is, mister, honest I don't.'

Still holding him firmly by the ear, the policeman produced a truncheon and smashed a couple of small square panes of glass, then tucked the truncheon back into his belt and reached for the cigarette case. One-handedly, he flicked it open, then beamed. The gold hunter watch nestling within was, unmistakably, the gold hunter watch on the policeman's list.

Wilf had come through from the storeroom and now he peered at the watch and then up into the policeman's face. 'I dunno how it got there, sergeant, but I ain't never set eyes on the bleedin' thing before,' he said in a wondering tone. 'I reckon this lad must 'ave dipped someone in the street and hid the thing away, meaning to sell it to me when it weren't so hot. Aye, that's what must ha' happened; it's plain as the nose on your face.'

The policeman was still holding Corky's ear, though not quite so firmly as before, but he grinned at Wilf's words, then gave a derisive snort. 'Pinched it hisself, did he? Then answer me this, Mr Clever Bloody Perkin. Why did he tell me where it were hid, eh? And how did a little lad like him manage to break into Albemarle Castle, which is pretty well guarded, I might tell you, and get away with a score of valuable oil paintings and half the marquis's collection of snuff boxes, to say nothing of his lady wife's jewels?'

'I'm not sayin' he did a proper robbery,' Wilf said, with all the indignation of a man sadly misunderstood. 'I dare say he prigged it off o' the thief . . . yes, that'll be it. As for paintings, and jewels and snuff boxes . . . well, can you see any about here?'

'No, but I've suspicioned for a long time that you stow stuff away somewhere in your flat upstairs, or in your old mam's place,' the policeman said shrewdly. He put a hand on Wilf's shoulder. 'Wilfred Perkin, I arrest you for receiving stolen property. You'd best come along o' me and make a statement while I put in for a search warrant and whistle up reinforcements.'

Wilf tried to wriggle free, and in order to snap the handcuffs on him the policeman was forced to let go of Corky's ear. The boy did not think twice but made for the shop door, shooting through it on to the road and pelting as hard as he could go in the direction of Herbee Place. The whole thing had been his fault, but how could he know that the man was a policeman and not a customer? He simply had to warn old Mrs Perkin, for she had been kind to him and he could not bear to think of her being cast into prison. If this happened, he did not think she would last very long and he knew that, in the circumstances, her death would be on his conscience for the rest of his life.

It was still raining heavily and though, behind him, he could hear the policeman's whistle and his stentorian shout of 'Stop that kid! He's a thief'

Corky did not think that anyone so much as noticed him, for the rain was like a curtain of water and all the kids he could see were running and keeping their heads down, as he was. No one would saunter in such weather, but nor would they pay attention to a police whistle when all they wanted was to get out of the rain and into shelter.

By the time he reached Herbee Place he was breathless and panting and probably looking extremely wild, for when he burst into the kitchen, beginning to gabble that there was trouble at the shop, Mrs Perkin surged to her feet, looking horrified. 'Did you fall in the river down by the docks, Corky?' she asked, bustling over to the back door and taking the roller towel down from its place. 'Why, if you ain't a drownded rat! You must ha' run a couple o' miles to get in a two an' eight like this. Sit yerself down, an' I'll make a cuppa char whiles you tell me what's up.'

'The coppers is up,' Corky said breathlessly. Tears were beginning to mingle with the water which ran down his face. 'Oh, Mrs Perkin, it were all my fault but I didn't mean no 'arm, honest to God I didn't. I thought the feller were a customer an' I telled 'im we did have a gold watch like the one he wanted, only Mr Wilf said he didn't have no such thing, so I smelled a rat then, only the rozzer had me by the ear . . .'

Mrs Perkin sighed deeply, a puzzled frown creasing her brow. 'Drink yer tea an' slow down,' she said heavily. 'I guess you give the game away without meaning to – I wanted to tell you what were goin' on so's you'd keep mum but Wilf, he wouldn't. Said the fewer folk knew, the safer we'd be. But you never grassed on us? Not deliberate like?'

'No, course I didn't,' Corky said stoutly, but with a wild and beating heart. 'It were like this, Mrs Perkin. I come back from deliverin' the bureau, through all the rain and thunder and lightning, and I sort o' burst into the stockroom with water running from me like a river . . .'

Now that he had calmed down, he told his story well, emphasising that he had tried to put the blame on Mr Parrish, a man he knew Mrs Perkin thoroughly disliked. He ended by telling her that the plain clothes copper had arrested Wilf and gone back to the station to get a search warrant, probably for the shop, the flat above it, and Mrs Perkin's own home.

The last remark caused the colour to drain from the old woman's cheeks and she sat for a moment, gazing sightlessly ahead of her. To Corky's distress, he saw that her lips were trembling and her eyes tear-filled, but then, suddenly, she seemed to come to a decision. She brushed the tears from her eyes and tightened her mouth. 'It weren't just your fault that we're in trouble,' she said briskly. 'Wilf said he had a customer for that watch which is why it weren't stored safely away where no one could set eyes on it. But – but the truth is, a spell in prison would just about kill me . . . so we're goin' to have to shift all the stuff in the back bedroom, 'cept for the bed you sleeps in an' the little washstand what I paid for honest, years ago. Are you game to help me, Corky?'

'Course I am,' Corky said stoutly. 'But it'll take days to shift this lot. And where's we goin' to put it, Mrs Perkin?'

Mrs Perkin winked at him. 'There's more'n one safe house in Bethnal Green,' she told him. 'And I've more'n one friend, young feller-me-lad. Afore you come along, Jim Craddock and his sons, Egbert and Vincent, used to move stuff what were too heavy for meself, and they delivered for Wilf as well. They've a proper motor van, so they was a good deal quicker, but of course, with the three of them at it, they charged a pretty penny. Sometimes, Wilf said it weren't scarcely worth his while to sell some pieces 'cos his profit were all ate up in delivery charges. Howsomever, it'll be all hands to the pump in a crisis like this 'cos all our pals would like to do the rozzers in the eye.' As she spoke, she had been rummaging in the dresser drawer and presently withdrew a pad of lined paper and a stub of pencil. She wrote a brief message which Corky read over her shoulder – it simply said: *Police getting search warrant for my back room. Get the whole gang round here as soon as poss. Aggie.* Then she tore off the page, folded it and wrote a name and address on it. 'If you give this to Jim Craddock, he'll see it does the rounds. Hurry, lad; deliver it then come straight back here. Awright?'

Corky wasted no time. He snatched the note from her hand and sped up the road. By now, he was conversant with most of the small streets surrounding Herbee Place and knew the Craddocks' house particularly well as the van was usually parked in front of it in the evenings. It was a big van, painted blue, with the words *Craddock & Sons, Carriers* written on both sides and on the back, with the legend beneath: *Any time, anywhere, Craddock & Sons will get you there.*

As he ran, Corky began to worry that Mr Craddock might be out and then what would he do? If he left the message with anyone else, say Mrs Craddock, she would be unable to do anything until her husband and sons returned home, and by that time the search warrant might have been obtained and fat rozzer paws might be sifting through the multitude of goods in his hostess's back bedroom.

But he need not have worried; the van stood outside the Craddock house and it was Mr Craddock himself who answered the door to Corky's knocks. Corky handed over the note, beginning a breathless and garbled explanation, but this, too, proved unnecessary. Ignoring him, Mr Craddock turned in the doorway and shouted, and almost immediately his two large sons were at his side. Mr Craddock read the note aloud, then hesitated and read it again. 'Egbert, go and alert the Millers. Tell them the van will be leaving in five minutes so if they wants a lift, they'd best get a move on.' He turned to his other son. 'Vinny, fetch the O'Haras and get your bleedin' skates on 'cos Terry's too fond of the ale and once the pubs is open . . . besides, he's no use to us if he's had a tankful.' He turned back to Corky, hovering uncertainly on the doorstep. 'Got any other notes?' he demanded. 'If not, an' you're comin' back to Herbee Place, you'd best jump in the back of the van.'

It was amazing how fast everything happened after that. Not only the Craddocks, but a crowd of men, many of whom Corky had never set eyes on before, turned up in Herbee Place. They formed a human chain and stuff came down from the back bedroom with amazing speed, though everything was prudently covered in dust sheets. The Craddock van was filled three times before the room was empty and it was all done in the space of an hour, though Corky had no idea where the goods had gone and found he did not want to know either. He who knows nothing can tell nothing, he thought, though he did point out to Mrs Perkin that behind every twitching curtain in Herbee Place was a pair of interested eyes, and in the nature of things those eyes would possess a nose which could smell out trouble and a mouth which could gabble to the rozzers about it.

Mrs Perkin, however, gave a contemptuous laugh. 'They won't grass,' she assured him. 'For one thing, they're all my friends, and for another, the rozzers is everyone's enemy. Everyone's hand is against 'em. Besides, our neighbours don't want to get up one morning and find their house has been burned to the ground, or their winders have been knocked out, and my Wilf's a man of influence.'

Corky was forced to agree that she was probably right, but then another thought struck him. 'My room's too empty,' he said. 'Them chaps took everything and that ain't natural, missus, honest it ain't. Wouldn't it be better if we could get a few things from the shop – things that are legal, like – so that the rozzers could see that the room had been used for storage? It 'ud look more – more natural with a few things scattered around, things which are really kosher.'

Mrs Perkin stared at Corky whilst a slow smile spread over her face. 'Corky, you're worth your weight in perishin' gold,' she said, almost reverently. 'Go down to the parlour and fetch up a few items. They're all legit.'

When he had finished, Corky came down to find Mrs Perkin with a small carpet bag in one hand, awaiting him. She hustled him towards the back door, saying as she did so: 'And now you'd best be off, lad. I dunno where you're going but it 'ad better be as far away from 'ere as you can get. Don't go thinkin' you can stay in London, because the rozzers will winkle you out to give evidence against my boy, and of course they'll guess I were warned when they see the back bedroom so I reckon you'd be done for aidin' and abettin', if not worse. You didn't like that there orphanage you was in but I reckon you'd find Borstal a good deal worse.'

Corky had guessed that he would not be able to stay with the Perkins, would have to move on, but had managed to put it to the back of his mind whilst so much was happening. Now, he took the carpet bag from his hostess and tried to grin, though he guessed it must be a pretty wobbly effort. ' 'S awright, Mrs Perkin, I always meant to move on one of these days,' he muttered. 'But I don't know as I can get out o' London today, an' – an' – I dunno where I can sleep, unless I can kip down on the Underground, of course. 'Cos it's still raining cats and dogs and I don't want to die of pewmonia.'

Mrs Perkin laughed and pinched his cheek. 'You've saved us Perkins from an 'orrible fate an' I mean to see you don't suffer from it,' she said firmly. 'I packed all your stuff in this carpet bag – there weren't much – and I added a nice little sum to that purse of money you've been saving. What's more, there's a packet of ham sandwiches, an' a packet of cheese ones, three apples and a wedge o' my rich fruit cake. So I reckon you won't starve for a day or two. You'd best make your way to one of the main line stations and buy a ticket . . . oh, to anywhere you fancy. Liverpool Street's the nearest; can you remember how to get there? But if you can't, anyone will tell you the way.' By this time they were in the cobbled yard and Corky saw that his old friend's lip was trembling and that there were tears in her eyes. 'You've been like a son to me . . . well, mebbe more like a grandson,' she said huskily. 'I'll never forget you, young Corky, but – but you can't stay. You do understand that, don't you?'

Corky nodded dumbly, not trusting himself to speak. It won't do for the pair of us to stand here crying our eyes out, he told himself, and even as the thought entered his head the rain, which had slowed to a light drizzle, started in earnest once more. He was just thinking it was as well, since it made the parting easier, when he heard a thundering knock on the front door. Hastily, Mrs Perkin gave his hand a squeeze and turned towards the house. 'Off wi' you, and don't linger,' she hissed. 'Write me a letter so's I know you got away okay. Don't forget, Liverpool Street's the nearest.' And with that she disappeared inside the house and Corky could hear her muttering as she made her way to the front door.

Corky went down Herbee Place and on to Bonner Street. To get to Liverpool Street Station he should have turned left, but when he glanced in that direction he saw a large policeman, helmeted head lowered against the driving rain, turning ponderously towards him. He looked to the right and saw no one, so set off at a brisk run, trying to hold the carpet bag away from his legs, though without much success. As yet, the hunt for himself had not begun. Once on to Old Ford Road, wet as a drowned rat already, Corky stopped a minute to consider. Only one person in the whole world knew where he was heading and that was Mrs

111

Perkin, but suppose the police used their common sense? If Mrs Perkin mentioned a railway station, it would naturally be Liverpool Street, and though he was sure that, for her own sake and that of her son, she would never give him away, mistakes do happen. He might get to Liverpool Street Station, by either hopping on a bus or slogging on in the rain, and find a welcoming committee of grinning coppers, eager to carry him to prison, or to Borstal, whichever was the worse.

On the other hand, he knew the way to Euston Station extremely well because there were several small shops in the area from which Wilf had both bought and sold. Yes, he could make his way there easily. By the time he was on Old Ford Road, however, the rain had begun to defeat him and when a bus swished up beside him, its destination board proclaiming that it went to Euston, he jumped aboard gladly. The bus was already crammed with wet and depressed passengers so he had to remain on the platform, and sat down on his wet carpet bag before he remembered the food inside and hastily stood up again. He paid his penny and in no time, it seemed, was descending into the rain once more. He marched, resolutely, under the great arch into the sooty station, keeping a weather eye out for policemen, but saw no one in uniform, save for porters and other railway officials. There was a short queue at the ticket office and he joined it, his mind still full of the events of the day. Every time he thought about Mrs Perkin and Herbee Place, his chest tightened and he felt a horrible hollow feeling inside. She had been so good to him! He knew that she had used him for her own ends but knew, also, that a genuine liking had grown up between them. The two of them had shared many little jokes, and she had been concerned for his welfare, had appreciated his good points, and had been interested in how he spent each moment of his day. He had striven to please her and she, in her turn, had striven to please him. She had cooked his favourite food, introduced him to many new dishes, and had talked to him of the old days, when she was a girl. He had told her about the orphanage, about their rare treats, the visits to the Isle of Dogs to play football on the old Millwall ground, and the constant comings and goings on the docks, which the boys watched eagerly whenever the opportunity came their way and which was the reason, Corky supposed, that nine out of ten of the boys wanted to go to sea as soon as they were old enough.

Edging gradually forward, Corky thought about Wilf's shop and the treasure chest of wonderful things he had grown accustomed to whilst he was with the Perkins. When he lived in the orphanage, he had never heard the word 'antiques', let alone seen one. His life had been full of deal tables, scratched and kicked door panels, and narrow iron cots with thin straw mattresses. Ugliness had surrounded him and he had not even known these things were ugly because he had had nothing with which to compare them. Now, he knew the beauty of old, well-polished furniture which had been made with such loving attention that men paid large sums to possess it. He appreciated the delicacy of the porcelain figures in the china cabinets – his mind gave an uneasy wriggle at the thought of china cabinets – and he had even begun to be able to tell the good from the bad. A Dresden shepherdess with each finger crowned by a tiny, perfect nail might look, at first sight, similar to the fake, but the Perkins, and now Corky himself, could tell the difference all right.

Then there were people. You might say the Perkins were ordinary people, perhaps not even very nice people, but they had liked Corky, had found him useful, amusing, and pleasant to be with; so different from his former gaolers – he thought of them as gaolers now – the men and women who had ruled his life with an iron rod. He remembered angry faces, and indifferent ones, but never interested or sympathetic expressions, though he did remember that the reporter who had first given him the idea of escape had been both interested and sympathetic. However, all that was behind him now. When he had left Redwood Grange, he had known nothing about normal family life. Now, thanks to Mrs Perkin, he knew that it was a wonderful thing, something he would not willingly do without. Wherever he ended up, he would find himself a family, and when he did so . . .

'Next! C'mon, boy, don't stare at me like a

landed fish with your gob wide open. Where d'you want to go?'

It was the official, staring at him through the glass of the little ticket window, and drumming his fingers impatiently upon his stout wooden counter. Corky gulped. What a fool he was! He had simply stood in the queue, letting his mind wander, without the vaguest idea of where the trains went, let alone where he himself would like to go. Without thinking twice, he heard his own voice saying: 'Single to Liverpool Street, mister,' and realised, with horror, that this was just what he did *not* want. Besides, he doubted that it was possible to get a train from one London station to another.

The official, however, did not seem at all surprised. 'One single to Liverpool Lime Street,' he said, sorting out a ticket. 'Next one's the five fifty, platform three. I take it you're a half. That'll be . . .' He named a sum and pushed a pink square of cardboard nearer the window, though he kept one finger on it whilst Corky opened his carpet bag, got out the little wash leather purse with the cord round its neck that Mrs Perkin had given him for his savings, and fished out the requisite sum. Only then did the official shove the ticket under the glass and take the money, calling 'Next' as he did so. Corky moved hastily away from the window, shoving his purse right to the bottom of the carpet bag before closing it firmly once more. Then he gazed around him at the vast concourse, the hurrying people and the big clock. It was a quarter past five. Assuming the man in the ticket office meant that the train left at 5.50, he had plenty of time to find the right platform and make sure he really would not end up at Liverpool Street Station. It would mean asking questions and Corky did not wish to leave a trail for the rozzers to follow, but he thought he was probably safe enough here amongst such an enormous number of people.

He looked around carefully, saw a fat little woman with curly white hair sitting on a bench, and went and sat next to her. The old woman was eating a sandwich so Corky opened his bag once more and produced an apple. After a couple of bites, he turned to his companion. 'Excuse me, missus, but I've been told by my uncle to buy a ticket for a place called Liverpool Lime Street. He's going to meet me there. Is that – that far from here?'

'Well, it'll take about four hours on the train; dunno if you'd call that near or far,' the woman said equably. 'I'm going to Liverpool myself, though I'm only staying there one night. Then it's on the ferry bound for Dublin and a whole week's holiday with me daughter.'

'O-o-o-oh!' Corky said, on a long sigh. What a fool he was! Mrs Perkin had talked and talked about Liverpool, and her life there before her parents' death, after which she had been sent to an orphanage. She had talked of the docks and the great ships, and the thousands of Irish people who had come across to the city at the time of the potato famine. She had told him of the great River Mersey and the huge buildings which lined its banks and were paid for, she had said disapprovingly, by money from blackbirding, which was the local name for the slave trade. He even remembered her mentioning Liverpool Lime Street, the station from which she had set out when she had run away to find the Perkin family.

He turned and beamed at the old woman. 'My uncle says he'll meet the train but I weren't able to tell him which one I'd be catching, so I'll mebbe book myself into lodgings for the night and then make my way to – to . . .' His mind searched desperately for a street name and caught, thankfully, at one Mrs Perkin had mentioned. '. . . St Domingo Road, where me uncle and aunt live.'

He hoped he had not chosen a road so near the station that lodgings would be out of the question, but the old woman merely said: 'I dunno nothing about St Domingo Street, or Road, or whatever, but I know there's decent lodging houses down by the docks. Only, I dunno whether they'd take a kid by hisself.' She looked at him narrowly. 'They might think you was runnin' away; you aren't, are you?'

'No indeed; I'm going to visit my aunt and uncle so I can look after my young cousins – they've half a dozen kids – because the family is moving to a bigger house,' Corky said, improvising wildly. 'You know what it's like, missus; as you get more kids, you need more space. I'm from a big family myself, so I know all about living cramped up. And another thing: I'm keen to go to sea as a cabin boy as soon as I'm old enough, and my Aunt Aggie told me Liverpool had a lot of transatlantic liners what needs a good many cabin boys, so when my aunt and uncle don't need me any more I'll see if I can get myself a job.'

Almost shocked by the number of lies he had told in such a short time, Corky decided to investigate the contents of his carpet bag. He dared not open the purse's drawstring neck with so many people milling about, but on the pretext of extracting a cheese sandwich from its newspaper wrapping he managed to have a good feel round the outside of the purse and decided – oh joy – that it contained at least one banknote, and possibly two. Dear Mrs Perkin!

Despite his brave words to the old woman sitting next to him, he had no idea what he would do when he reached Liverpool, but with real money in his possession he should be able to afford a bed in a cheap lodging house until he found work of some description. It was a pity he was small for his age – he blamed this on the home and the poor quality of the food they were given – but during his stay with the Perkin family he had learned that a strong boy, not afraid of hard work, could make himself enough money to get by . . . and there was always the hope of a job as cabin boy aboard a big liner.

Presently, the old woman got to her feet and picked up her suitcase. 'Train's in; we might as well get ourselves a seat,' she said. Corky tried to take the case from her but she hung on grimly. 'No, no, we'd best each manage our own,' she said. 'You hang on to that there bag of yours an' all, 'cos all big stations is full of thieves.'

Corky understood from this that she trusted no one and, on reflection, thought her sensible. He, too, must remember that everything he possessed was in the carpet bag. If he found a lodging house, he would pull the bag into bed with him and sleep curled round it, for without it he would be lost indeed.

The oddly assorted couple went straight to platform three – the old woman knew the way – climbed aboard the train and settled themselves comfortably in a No Smoking carriage. The old woman advised Corky to put his bag under the seat where he could feel its comforting bulk against his calves.

The carriage began to fill up and then, as the train pulled out of the station, Corky felt his eyelids begin to droop, for it had been both an exciting and a tiring day. At first he struggled against sleep, but then it occurred to him that his new friend, whose name was Mrs Arbuthnot, might well wish to continue their conversation and he was not sure he would be able to remember, as he grew sleepier, with which particular lies he had regaled her. He had told her, feeling extremely guilty, that he was Cyril Samuels, had claimed to be the eldest of a large family, had said he was on his way to visit relatives who lived in . . . oh lor, the name of the street had completely escaped him. Hastily, he let his head loll forward and gave what he hoped was a small but convincing snore. He would feign sleep; it would be a good deal safer than falling into conversation once more.

Presently, he opened one eye a slit and glanced through his lashes at his companion. She, too, seemed to have given way to slumber so it would probably be safe enough to sit up and begin to look around him, even to watch the passing scene, for he had managed to get the corner seat. But he decided he would just close his eyes for a minute whilst the train chugged through the sprawling city suburbs; he would wake up properly once they were in the countryside. But he was tired, most dreadfully tired . . .

Corky slept.

He awoke when the train drew into a busy station and half opened his eyes. Mrs Arbuthnot was pushing her suitcase back beneath the seat, having abstracted some item of food from its depths. She looked a little flushed, doubtless from the effort of getting the suitcase out without waking him, but she sat back in her seat and began to eat the sandwich which she held in one hand. It looked good, and for a moment Corky was tempted to ferret in his carpet bag, for he had plenty of sandwiches still left in there himself, and seeing the old woman eating so enthusiastically had made him hungry. But even as the thought entered his head, the train began to move once more, and the swaying movement, as well as the soft, rhythmic clatter of the wheels, soon had him sleeping soundly once more. He awoke because someone was shaking his shoulder. It was Mrs Arbuthnot. Her hair stood wildly on end and her crumpled little face was pink, so Corky guessed that she, too, must have slept, though she was now wide awake.

'C'mon, young feller; you've no time to lose if you're going to get to a lodging house before they're all full of sailors and such,' she said, pushing him ahead of her on to the platform. 'I won't go with you, 'cos I always lodge with the same fambly, but I can put you on the right road.' She seized his arm and Corky, grasping his carpet bag, though still dazed with sleep, almost had to run to keep up with her. He saw a policeman standing on the platform and his heart missed a beat, then he remembered that he was far from the Perkins and Herbee Place and straightened his shoulders; no copper was going to be on the lookout for him here, not yet at any rate.

Outside the station, night had definitely fallen, and though the gas lamps were lit and there were plenty of people jostling along the pavement Corky felt extremely uneasy. He had never ventured up London's West End so had seen none of the big shops, office blocks and hotels which abounded there, and the authorities at Redwood Grange had never taken the boys to see St Paul's, Westminster Abbey or the Houses of Parliament, so Corky was astonished at the size and magnificence of the huge building opposite the station, which he afterwards found was called St George's Hall. He was also amazed by the numbers of elegantly dressed ladies who strolled up and down the pavements, occasionally accosting, or being accosted by, passing men. They were very beautiful, but something about the way they looked at him was worrying and he was glad when his companion hustled him past them, pointed to a street on the opposite side of the road and told him that he must go down there to reach the docks and the lodging houses she had mentioned.

'I can't come with you, 'cos I'm late already,' she said hurriedly, giving him a push which nearly sent him under the wheels of a passing lorry. 'Off you go, young feller-me-lad. You've got enough for a night's lodgings at any one of them places down by the docks. Take care now.'

Corky began to cross the busy road, frowning a little. What had she meant? He had not discussed his finances with her but supposed she had simply guessed that he must have sufficient money for a night's lodging. He gained the opposite pavement and gazed down the road she had indicated. Suddenly, he found himself feeling distinctly lost and alone. He turned to stare after the old woman but she had disappeared completely and he realised that though she had talked of lodgings where she always stayed when she visited the city, she had neither named her landlady nor mentioned a street, far less a number. Still, she was an old lady – no, a nice old lady – who had done everything she could to help him. She had simply forgotten to tell him where she was staying or perhaps had not considered it necessary. Why should he need to know, after all? He had told her he was going to visit relatives and then look for a job. The fact that she had mentioned his money meant nothing, nothing at all. It was just a guess, and a pretty wild one, too, since he knew very well that his money would buy him a good deal more than one night's lodging.

He told himself that all this should have eased his mind, but somehow it did not, and when he saw, to his left, a pleasant-looking public garden surrounded by sandstone walls, he glanced round hastily, found himself alone and unobserved, and shinned over the wall. He dropped on to the grass and looked around him; there was a bench nearby and he sat down on it and then, feeling that he was being a great fool for everyone knew that white-haired old women meant young boys nothing but good, he plunged his hands inside the carpet bag. The first thing he noticed was that his packets of sandwiches felt considerably smaller than they should have done. He pulled them out, then counted the contents. He had eaten one of each on the platform, which should have left five of each. Instead, there were now two ham sandwiches and four cheese ones. Corky's heart started to thump uneasily as his fingers rooted through his small personal possessions to the very bottom of the bag where, to his immense relief, he found the wash leather purse, strings drawn tight. His heart immediately slowed to a more normal pace but he drew the purse forth, telling himself that Mrs Arbuthnot was welcome to the sandwiches, which he would have happily shared with her had he been awake to do so. The money, of course, was a different matter, but there was still money in the purse . . . however, he must check. He untied the little bow, inserted both forefingers and stretched the neck of the purse wide open. Then he looked inside and his heart began to thump quickly once more. There were no notes, nor was there the gleam of silver. In fact, the small purse was half filled with copper: pennies, ha'pennies and even farthings.

He could not believe it at first. He spread his spare shirt out on the bench and tipped the contents of the purse out upon it. There was a lamp quite near the bench and it illumined only copper, yet he knew that there had been no copper at all in the purse when he had set out, unless Mrs Perkin had put some in, as well as the notes which he had felt, crackling crisply, when he had explored the purse earlier. Of course he had not looked inside, not with so many people about, but he had known the feel of banknotes, though of course he could not tell whether they were ten shilling or pound ones. Then it occurred to him that the old woman might have decided to give him a tip. She might have fished the purse out, emptied the contents into his carpet bag – clearly not realising their worth – and filled it up with the collection of copper it now contained.

Feverishly, Corky's hands explored every corner, every crack and crevice of the carpet bag, and found nothing, save for his clothing, copies of *Chips* and *Film Fun*, two of the three apples and the chunk of fruit cake which Mrs Perkin had pressed upon him. Wild with despair, yet with hope still not dead, Corky tipped the coppers carefully back into the purse, tied its drawstring neck and then upended the carpet bag on to the bench until it was as empty as a bass drum. It was only then that he was able to acknowledge that he had been duped as though he were no more than two years old, by a crafty woman who must have taken his measure from the moment she had seen him in Euston Station.

Corky began pushing his possessions back into the carpet bag, hissing maledictions between clenched teeth. Now he realised why she had advised him to put his bag beneath the seat instead of up on the string rack above their heads. She would not have been able to get his bag down – she was a small woman – without drawing attention to what she was doing whereas, because it was beneath the seat, all she had had to do was bend down, unclick the clasps and pretend to be helping herself to a sandwich. Dimly, he now remembered hearing her telling someone that this young fellow was her nephew, and the two of them were travelling up to Liverpool to look after the children of a sick relative. At the time, he had thought how wonderfully kind she was, pretending that they were together so no one would suspect him of being a runaway. Now, of course, he knew better. She was as cunning as a fox, as crooked as – as Wilf Perkin, and as mean as it was possible to be, for she must have known he was alone in the world and dependent upon the money in the small purse. He was working up a good rage towards Mrs Arbuthnot – only her name was probably Crippen, he thought nastily – when he remembered all the lies he had told. He had said he was going to relatives who needed him, would only want lodgings for one night until he could reach his uncle's home, had a family back in London who had supported him, giving him his train fare with their blessing so that, when his uncle and aunt no longer needed him, he might seek his fortune among the transatlantic liners.

Corky finished his packing but kept the sandwiches beside him on the bench. Sighing, he reminded himself of what he had been told so often at Redwood Grange: liars never prosper. Well, he had proved the old saying true tonight. Mrs Arbuthnot was doubtless a nasty old woman, a thief and a liar, but she had not known she was robbing a friendless orphan boy of his only means of support. Anyway, it would teach him not to go round trusting everyone he met, and in the meanwhile he would eat his sandwiches and then kip down on the bench for what was left of the night. Fortunately, the weather was clement, and he told himself that by the time morning came he would have worked out a plan. Presently, having eaten both the ham sandwiches, he returned the cheese ones to the carpet bag and, using his luggage as a pillow, curled up on the bench. It was hard and the carpet bag was not soft either, but Corky had been through a great deal that day. Very soon, he slept.

Chapter Five

Wandering along in the sunshine, Dot felt at peace with the world. Passing Mr Rathbone's shop she smiled to herself, for the previous day she and Aunt Myrtle had done the messages together and her aunt had announced her intention of visiting Rathbone's. 'Now that Mr Rathbone and your uncle are on good terms, like, I'll see if I can get some meat a bit cheaper,' she had said. 'You go on up to the greengrocer's and buy a stone of spuds, a large cabbage and a turnip or two.' Dot had groaned a bit at the thought of lugging all that weight about but when Aunt Myrtle had said, amicably enough, that if Dot preferred it they would swap over and she would get the vegetables, Dot had said at once that she would rather leave things as they were, since Mr Gaulton, the greengrocer, would very likely give her a plum or a small red apple, whereas Mr Rathbone only handed out abuse and clips round the ear.

Her aunt had laughed and gone off quite happily into Mr Rathbone's shop, apparently believing that because he had been drinking with her husband he would treat her like a valued customer. And when Dot and her aunt met up again, she told her niece that this had indeed been the case. 'I axed for a nice lean piece of pork and said I'd be obliged if he'd throw in some bones for stock and let me have half a pound of calves' liver to make a nice rich stew. He pulled a sort of face, but went over and got everything I'd asked him for, wrapped it all up in newspaper, shoved it into me bag, give me a bit of a wink and only charged me a few bob for the lot. But I reckon I'd best call on him myself in future, so's we get stuff cheap because, as you say, he don't like kids and might not know you were me niece.'

'Well, I'm blowed,' Dot had said. 'I never would have thought it. Still, if he's a pal of Uncle Rupe's then I s'pose that accounts for it.'

'I dunno as they're pals exactly,' Aunt Myrtle had said, giving the newspaper parcel an affectionate pat. 'Rupe's working for him after he finishes in the factory.'

'Oh? What does he do?' Dot had asked, as the two turned towards Lavender Court.

'He does a deal o' heavy lifting, taking stuff from the back room into the shop,' Aunt Myrtle had said, 'and he goes wi' Mr Rathbone in the van, to fetch carcasses from the slaughterhouse in St Andrews Street. It's heavy work, but reg'lar, and he gets a fair wage, he says.'

'Oh, I see,' Dot had said vaguely. She could not have cared less what her uncle did for Mr Rathbone so long as she, herself, was never expected to visit the butcher's shop; and it looked as though she was not going to be asked to beard Mr Rathbone in his den after all. Feeling as though a great weight had been lifted from her shoulders, Dot turned her mind to Sunday dinner. Aunt Myrtle was not a good or inventive cook but she did know how to do a Sunday roast; and Dot's mouth watered at the thought of a big joint of roast pork, with apple sauce on the side and lots of crispy roast potatoes.

But right now, perhaps because her worry about shopping at Rathbone's had been lifted, Dot was wandering, idly, in the direction of the churchyard. It had been several weeks since she had last visited her little friend Rhiannon, and so long as she did not behave suspiciously, there was no reason why she should not do so now. After all, she had played in the churchyard long before the burglary, so no one would think it suspicious if she continued to do so, provided she did not show too marked an interest in little Rhiannon's grave.

It was a sunny August day and the streets were full of children like herself, enjoying the freedom of the school holidays yet not quite knowing how best to employ their time. Normally, Dot would have been with Fizz, but he had gone off to visit an uncle who ran a gentlemen's outfitters in Southport and gave Fizz a holiday by the sea in exchange for working as a delivery boy, whilst the young fellow who usually did the job took his own holiday. So here was Dot, carefully kicking a round pebble along the pavement, to the annoyance of passers-by, and wishing that she had had the fore-thought to get some bread and jam from Aunt Myrtle's pantry before she left home, or to visit the vegetable market on Cazneau Street to see if she might nick some fades. It was not that she was hungry, exactly, but shoved down the front of her faded cotton dress was an old copy of the *Sunbeam* comic paper and Dot belonged to the school of thought which believed that reading and eating go together.

However, she continued on her way. It would be nice and cool in the churchyard, she told herself, and she could lie on the grass beneath the old yew tree which flourished in one corner, read her comic and perhaps even take a quick look at the little grave to make sure that it had not been disturbed. Not that she had the slightest fear of this happening, she reminded herself. Indeed, it was quite difficult to pick out the tiny gravestone now that the grass had grown so high but, nevertheless, she did like to check. Also, if she were honest with herself, she had been consumed with longing for some while now to take another look at the necklace. The trouble was, she had only seen it once, on the day she'd first buried it, and that had been at night. It had not been possible to see the beautiful green colour of the stones and Dot felt obscurely cheated. She had risked a great deal for that necklace, yet the only time she dared disinter it would be at night, when she could not see its beauty properly.

But it was no good repining and presently she reached the churchyard, climbed the crumbling wall and glanced around her, giving a small sigh of satisfaction as she did so because for her this was an enchanted spot. The churchyard was old and neglected and had run completely wild. Flowers which you never saw in the parks and gardens of the city flourished here, and last summer Dot had decided that she would discover what each bloom was called and write it down in a notebook. There was a nature book in school and this was some help, but she soon realised that she would need something more detailed in order to list all the wild and wonderful flowers which grew there.

To make such a list had been a good idea but she had been unable to find a notebook or an old exercise book in which to begin, so somehow the project had come to nothing. But now, settling herself comfortably in the long grass, with her back against *Agnes, beloved wife of James and mother of Algernon, Philip and Susanna, who departed this life on 17 August 1779: Rest in Peace*, Dot decided that she really must have another go. It would please her teacher, Miss Spellman, and it would give her a good excuse for visiting the churchyard whenever she felt like it. Next time someone pays me a penny for doin' their messages, I'll spend it on a notebook and then I can start, Dot told herself, fishing the *Sunbeam* out of the bosom of her dress and flattening it out against her knees. As she did so, she glanced cautiously around her. The church-yard wall was not particularly high but trees grew close against it, and though a good many people passed along the pavement Dot had noticed before that they never so much as glanced towards the churchyard. Probably most of them did not even know it was there. It was strange that children did not frequent such a marvellous playground, but a couple of years earlier, when she had brought Phyllis with her and proposed a game of hide and seek, her friend had been both shocked and horrified. 'Don't you know there's a murderer what's buried in that churchyard? I thought all the kids knowed that,' Phyllis had told her. 'They say he comes alive and so do all the little kids he murdered, and they wail round the churchyard and in and out of the ruined church. I wouldn't play there for a hundred pound, honest to God I wouldn't.'

'But – but not in the daytime, surely?' Dot had said. 'I've been here often and often an' I've never seen no one – unless you count the odd cat, mousing among the ruins, and the birds an' squirrels.'

'Well, it ain't only the ghosts; my mum says there's subsi – subsi . . . I can't remember the name of it, but it's when the earth sorts of falls away, leavin' great gaping holes. She says that's why the church were abandoned, years ago, an' that's why no one goes there any more.' She had looked at Dot with round-eyed distress. 'We mustn't play there, Dotty. The church could fall right down any day, crushin' you flat, or the earth might swallow you up.'

Even then, Dot had been so familiar with the churchyard that she could have poured scorn on Phyllis's fears, but she had not done so. If fear of ghosts and the ruined building kept kids away from this delectable spot, then who was she to say it was all lies and risk her favourite playground being overrun? So she had meekly agreed not to suggest playing there again and instead she and Phyllis had trekked down to the canal and sat on the bank, paddling their feet in the water and watching the boys swimming and splashing in the Scaldy.

Naturally, after Phyllis's revelations, Dot had scoured the churchyard for signs of the subsidence which Phyllis had mentioned and had found nothing. To be sure, some of the older graves had caved in and others were lopsided, but it was easy to see that this had happened many years ago and was no longer a threat. The ruined church was another matter; ivy-clad and sinister, the great sandstone blocks still standing did look dangerous and common sense had kept Dot well clear of the building, despite knowing nothing of its ghostly reputation. So she had continued to enjoy what she now thought of as her own private place and had never even brought Fizz here, because he was such a gossip and would undoubtedly tell everyone in his class – everyone in his school, probably – that the churchyard was an excellent place to play, which would completely ruin it so far as Dot was concerned.

Now, having glanced carefully around her, Dot pushed the comic paper back into her dress and set off in the direction of Rhiannon's little grave. The birds seemed to be kicking up more of a din than usual and she supposed that there was a cat somewhere about, but when she reached the shade under the yew she received a considerable shock. Sitting cross-legged beside the little grave was a small girl. She wore a crisp, pink dress, with a matching pink ribbon tying her abundant brown curls back from her face, and she was carefully setting out the contents of a small box on the flattened grass before the little tombstone. As she did so, she was chatting cheerfully away in a high, clear little voice and Dot crouched almost double before she crept slowly forward, hoping that the child's companion was not a grown-up who might ask awkward questions.

'One for you, one for me, and three for the little ghosts,' the small child was saying. As she spoke, she was arranging what Dot recognised as a doll's tea service on the grass. Dot caught her breath; it was the sort of thing she had seen in the windows of expensive toy shops, but had never actually handled. This was one very lucky little girl! Dot suddenly realised that the child had no companions, except imaginary ones, with whom she was playing tea parties, for she had picked some of the wild flowers and was placing a few blossoms in each small cup and plate. Presently, the child sat back on her heels and picked up the nearest cup, pretending to drink from it.

Dot must have made some movement at this point for the child jumped, then turned round. Seeing Dot, she smiled a welcome, though Dot could not help noticing that she looked a trifle anxious. She held out one of the cups, upon which reposed a poppy and a cornflower. 'Hello,' she said cheerfully. 'Have you come to my tea party? Are you a ghost? I met a girl in the street who told me not to play in the churchyard or the ghosts would get me, but you're the only person I've see'd. And you don't look much like a ghost to me.'

'Well, I'm not – a ghost, I mean,' Dot said, gravely taking the delicate little cup and sitting down beside the small girl. 'Are you all by yourself? I heard you talking as I came up, but I couldn't see anyone else.'

The little girl stared at her, her eyes rounding. 'Course I'm not by myself,' she said indignantly. 'I never go anywhere without my friend Marietta. Can't you see her? She's got long golden hair, done in two plaits just like yours, and she's wearing a pink party dress and pink ballet slippers. She's sitting right opposite me and she's smiling at you, so you'd better say hello,' she finished.

'Hello, Marietta, how very nice to meet you,' Dot said seriously. She turned to the little girl. 'Actually, I can't see Marietta, because you're the only one who can do that. But I know she's there because when I was little, like you, I had a best friend no one else could see. Her name was Jennifer Jane and I really loved her.'

The little girl beamed at her. 'Jennifer Jane's a lovely name, but then so is Marietta,' she said. 'What's your name? I'm Sadie O'Brien, and I'm five, and me and Marietta are running away from home because Nanny was cross. Marietta chalked on the new wallpaper in the dining room, so we got sent up to bed, only we sneaked out when no one was looking, with the tea set in its little case, and just ran off.'

'Oh, I see,' Dot said slowly. 'But your nanny will be ever so worried, Sadie, and you won't want to be here when it gets dark, just in case.'

'Oh, I shall go home at teatime,' Sadie said airily. 'Auntie Ethel and my cousin Lucy are coming to tea so there'll be red salmon and a great big salad, thin bread and butter and hard-boiled eggs cut in half. And afterwards, there'll be a sherry trifle for the grown-ups and red jelly for me and Marietta – and Lucy, of course.'

'Oh!' Dot said enviously. Red salmon was a luxury she had not even tasted. She had guessed, from Sadie's clothing and the doll's tea service, that Sadie had well-to-do parents; now she was sure of it. Dot's own feet were bare but Sadie wore short white socks and brown leather sandals on her feet, which proved that her parents were rich, for it was summertime and all the children Dot knew either went barefoot or wore shabby plimsolls in the school holidays. She looked, speculatively, at her small companion. 'Do you live near here? I've had quite a walk, but my legs are longer than yours.'

'I live at number four Shaw Street,' the little girl said glibly. 'What's *your* name and where do *you* live?'

'Oh, I live off Heyworth Street and me name's Dolly,' Dot said, with equal glibness. This little girl was a right tartar, probably her mammy's spoilt darling. Dot could just imagine her turning up in Lavender Court and telling everyone, including Aunt Myrtle and the cousins, that she had met Dot in the disused old churchyard, where they had played tea parties together. It seemed that she did not need to worry, however.

'Heyworth Street? Well, I don't know it but then I don't look up at street names when my mummy takes me shopping, 'cos I'm too busy looking in the windows,' Sadie said. 'I've got a tricycle – do you have a tricycle? – but I'm not allowed to ride it in the street until I'm six, but even then I 'spect Mummy will say "we'll see". My daddy's captain of a big huge ship though, and when he's home he takes me to the park – he carries my tricycle all the way, imagine that – and I ride and ride and ride, and tinkle my bell and have a grand time.'

Really rich people, Dot thought, awed, whilst replying that she did not have a tricycle but hoped to possess a bicycle one day. If Sadie was telling the truth and her father really was captain of a big liner, then she was a very lucky little girl indeed and Dot need feel no scruple about discouraging her from playing in the churchyard. She began at once, telling Sadie impressively that this really was a dangerous place, that the ground was undermined by old graves and could cave in any minute and that she, Dot, meant to find somewhere safer to play in future.

Sadie, however, did not seem at all impressed. 'Well, I'm going to play here,' she said firmly. 'At home, we've got a great big garden, with a lawn and flower beds, and a place where Mr Pritchard grows fruit and vegetables. But am I allowed to dig a little dig? No, I am not. Daddy bought me a wooden spade and a beautiful bucket with dolphins and fishes on when we went to Llandudno last year, but Mr Pritchard is an old beast and told me he'd tan my little hide for me if he caught me digging in his flower beds again.' She looked up at Dot, eyes limpid with mischief. 'So I'm going to have my own little garden, right here by this baby's tombstone. Next time I come, I'll bring my bucket and spade and I'll clear all the horrid grass away and dig and dig, and then I'll plant roses and big yellow daisies and geranymums and lilies . . .' She seemed to run out of flower names at this point and stopped, looking enquiringly at her companion. 'Isn't that a good idea? Wouldn't it be lovely for the little dead baby to have her own beautiful garden?'

Poor Dot was in a quandary. She thought that Sadie was a contrary young person so if she tried to pour water on the idea of a garden it would probably make her more determined than ever. But if she said it was a good idea, then Sadie would probably ask her to help and Dot's mind cringed away from what would happen then. Sadie would undoubtedly discover the necklace, but even if by some miracle she did not do so, the fact that someone had been digging would alert any chance person walking through the churchyard to the fact that something might have been hidden there.

'Well?' Sadie's expression was enquiring. 'It must be a baby 'cos of the tiny tombstone. Don't you think she'd like a pretty garden, Dolly?'

Dot made up her mind. Now that Sadie knew about the graveyard and had chosen to have her tea party upon little Rhiannon's grave, it was no longer a safe hiding place. She must come this very night and move the necklace to a better place. And in the meantime, she might as well go along with whatever Sadie said, since the two of them were unlikely to cross paths again, for Dot did not think she would dare re-inter the necklace anywhere in the churchyard, no matter how safe it seemed. Sadie was only small, but she lived in a posh area and had rich, and probably influential, parents. Dot had never come across such people, but something told her that the captain of a big liner could probably get away with things that an ordinary person could not. She was a bit vague as to how Captain O'Brien might be a danger to plain little Dot McCann, but there was no point in tempting fate. She would accompany Sadie to her front door and make certain that she was safely inside, then she would go home and have whatever meal Aunt Myrtle had provided and after that she would snug down on the sofa, and pretend to go to sleep. But when all the boys were home, and Uncle Rupert was snoring, either in the front parlour or in his own bed, she would sneak back to the churchyard and retrieve the necklace. She had not yet decided what to do with it but hoped that inspiration might come fairly quickly. She could easily dispose of it since weeks had elapsed since she had first hidden it, but she would not do so. Even her one glimpse of it, by starlight, had shown her that the necklace was more beautiful than anything she had ever dreamed of possessing. Insensibly, over the weeks that had passed, she had grown to think of it as her own, and knew now that she could not bear to part with it. It would be lovely to bring it home, to gloat over it in daylight, to put it round her neck and see, in the cracked bit of mirror above the sink, how it gleamed and sparkled, but Dot knew this was impossible. Once her aunt or uncle set eyes on it, the secret would be out and the questions would start. No, the necklace must be hidden once more; she would think of a good place whilst she walked Sadie O'Brien back to her posh home on Shaw Street.

It had been a warm and pleasant day but by the time Dot set off for the churchyard once more a nippy little wind had got up, though the starlit sky was black and clear above her. It was after midnight and the streets were deserted, but even so Dot kept close to the shadow cast by the houses and shops which lined the pavements, flitting along as silently as a shadow herself. Occasionally, a cat crossed her path and once she saw a large rat trundling across the road, which made her stop for a moment before continuing, resolutely, on her way. She was afraid of rats, had heard how they would turn on hunters when they were cornered, but told herself that they needed human habitation to thrive and were scarcely likely to inhabit the deserted graveyard. She also told herself that the only people liable to be on the streets at this hour were scuffers or thieves, and this made her extremely cautious, peering round corners to make sure the coast was clear and crossing the wide, deserted streets at a fast run. However, she reached the churchyard without seeing another human being, scrambled over the wall and dropped, gladly, into the sheltering trees. She took a quick look round but knew that, even if somebody was present, she was unlikely to see them in the faint starlight, half hidden, as they would be, by tombstones and the long, wild grass. However, movement was a real giveaway so she stood very still and watched. After a couple of minutes she decided that it was useless because the breeze tossed the branches of the trees and stirred amongst the grasses. But then an owl hooted and she saw its shape as it crossed from the ruined church to the old yew tree; she did not think the owl would have flown to the tree if someone had been hiding there, so she squared her shoulders and set off.

It was easy to pick out the small headstone, thanks to Sadie who had flattened the grass in order to have her tea party. Dot squatted down, cast one last look around her and then seized a handful of grass and heaved. The grass, dry as tinder, promptly broke and Dot realised that the earth, which had been soft and friable in March, was now hard as iron; she should have brought something to dig with, even if it was only an old fork, or the big spoon which Aunt Myrtle used when she dished up blind scouse.

Dot sat back on her heels and frowned. There must be something she could dig with. There were cracked and ruined urns . . . she got to her feet. Over the opposite side of the churchyard, hard up against the ruined church, there were a couple of box-like graves which were protected by rusty iron railings. She was pretty sure that the last time she had walked by, one at least of the railings had been loose. If she could just detach it . . .

To think was to act. Dot hurried across the churchyard, jumping over fallen headstones and skirting patches of bramble. There were nettles, too, which she did her best to avoid, but soon enough she found what she was searching for. It was only half of a railing and it was rusty and rotten, but it ended in a sharp spike and Dot knew that it was as near ideal as she would get for the task in hand. She picked it up and banged it against the nearest headstone to rid it of as much rust as possible, wincing at the noise she had made, but comforting herself with the recollection that most kids would think the hollow booming was made by ghosts and that scuffers, no matter how keen, would be unlikely to investigate since it meant climbing over the wall and scuffers had their dignity – as well as their uniform – to consider. Besides, she knew that a number of animals lived here and supposed that any one of them, scuttling through the ruined church, might dislodge a fallen slate, or brick, or rotten branch, causing a noise similar to that which she had just made.

Holding the broken railing like a sword, she slashed at a patch of nettles and with considerable satisfaction saw them keel sideways; she had brushed against them on her way to the old graves and now, she thought, they were paying for the stings which even now patched her skinny legs. She contemplated having a go at the brambles as well – a branch had scratched her from knee to ankle – but decided against it. She was fond of blackberries and in a few weeks there would be rich pickings; but not, of course, if she laid about her with her spiked railing.

She reached Rhiannon's grave without further incident and began to tear and claw away at the weeds and grass until she had a couple of feet of bare earth. Then she picked up her spike and began to batter it into the earth, using a large stone which had once been part of a grave coping. She wanted the spike to go down deeper than the burial place of her necklace; with a bit of luck she might bring it up as soon as she began to lever the railing, for she had not forgotten that the necklace lay a hand's length from the gravestone and in direct line with the initial letter of the child's name.

She wished she could have pushed the railing into the ground soundlessly, but she could not avoid the thump, thump of the stone. However, the wind was gusting now in the trees and she was pretty sure that no one, beside herself, could hear it, so she continued to thump until the railing was eight inches into the earth. Then she seized it and began to pull sideways.

Within a very few moments, she realised that she had, indeed, struck lucky. A large clod of earth shot into the air, with a curl of dried grass at its base, and Dot remembered how she had folded the necklace in the grass before burying it. Triumphantly, she plunged her hand into the hole, scarcely able to believe her luck, for she had expected to make several attempts before finding her treasure. Her fingers closed round the stones and she drew the necklace forth, seeing the glitter of it even in the faint starlight. With a satisfied sigh, Dot sank back on her heels and eyed her booty lovingly. 'Well, I managed to find you without too much trouble, but what the devil I'm going to do with you now I honestly don't know.'

'If you've no use for it, you might as well hand it to me.'

The voice, husky and menacing, almost stopped Dot's heart. She whipped round, knowing that the speaker was close, but not knowing whether it was male, female or ghastly apparition, for all her self-confidence had fled and she was sure she was about to be both robbed and killed or, if it was an apparition, frightened to death, which would come to the same thing in the end. The figure stood behind her and seemed immensely tall. She looked up and up until she saw, in the moonlight, a dark face, grinning down at her.

'Well? Don't just gawp at me, tell me what all this is abaht, and what you're doin' diggin' up jewels in the middle of the night? You're a bit on the young side to be a grave robber, ain't you? And besides, how did you know which grave to rob?' He jerked his chin at Rhiannon's small head-stone. 'This here's a baby's grave and babies don't usually get buried with all their worldly posses-sions. Come to think, it's only ancient Egyptians what have jewels stuck in their tombs, ain't it?'

Dot nodded dumbly, and as she did so the full awfulness of the situation overcame her. She had begun to say that she wasn't robbing anyone, that the necklace was hers, when she burst into tears. It was all too much. She had been so careful not to be seen climbing over the wall; she had had to work extremely hard to dig the necklace out; and here was this boy – she could see he was a boy now, probably only a couple of years older than herself – walking up as cool as you please and obviously going to rob her, even if he stopped short of murder.

'Hey, what have I said? For Gawd's sake, girl, stop makin' that awful noise unless you want to bring the law down on our ears. Look, I ain't gonna do you no harm an' I don't mean to steal your necklace, or whatever it is, because I'm in enough trouble on my own account, without adding thievery to my sins.' He knelt on the crushed grass and put a consoling arm round Dot's heaving shoulders. 'Now just you stop cryin' like a bleedin' fountain and tell me what's been goin' on.'

Dot gave an enormous sniff, then wiped away her tears with the heels of both hands, and looked both long and hard at the boy in the faint starlight. She decided that he had a nice face, not particularly handsome, but kind, and his expression was rueful, as though he had suddenly realised how much he had frightened her, how close she had come to hysteria at the sound of his voice, coming suddenly out of the dark, when she had believed herself alone. Dot opened her mouth to speak, to begin to explain, then suddenly changed her mind. 'It's – it's a really long story and I don't know who you are or how you come here and – and if you were to tell someone else about my necklace, then I could be k-killed,' she said, in a strained and wobbly voice. 'Do you live near here? I live with me aunt in one of the courts off Heyworth Street, but if you tell me where you live I'll swear on me own life that I'll come round to your house in the morning and explain.'

The boy grinned again but shook his head. 'That won't do, 'cos I don't live anywhere proper at present,' he said. 'Truth to tell, I'd snug meself down in an old shed, close up agin the boundary wall of this churchyard. It's so overgrown I were lucky to find it; it's pretty tumbledown – covered with creepers an' that – but it suits me fine. I were actually sleeping in there when I were woken up by someone banging something on a gravestone, but if you want to come back to my shed we can exchange stories there; only it's got to be you first,' he added firmly.

Dot stared at him. She thought she knew the ruined church and the graveyard pretty well, but she had never come across a shed. However, she realised that despite their short – and strange – acquaintance, she already trusted him, felt that he was the sort of person who would keep his word. So when he rose and pulled her to her feet, she followed him meekly, stuffing the necklace into the pocket of her skirt, and clutching the back of his jacket, though he was a good deal less careful around nettles and brambles than she had been – no doubt because of his boots – and ploughed across the churchyard with little regard for his companion's bare feet.

They reached the corner of the graveyard, which was, as the boy had said, just a wide tangle of saplings, creepers and low bushes, and, to Dot's surprise, there was the small, tumbledown wooden shed he had described, so overgrown by trees and bushes that it was almost invisible. The boy pushed the door wide and ushered her in, then produced a box of matches, struck one and lit a candle wedged in the neck of a bottle. Then he pulled the door shut behind them and sat down on an upturned wooden box, waving Dot hospitably to another one. 'I've been using this place to sleep in ever since my money was stolen from me when I first arrived in the city,' he told her. 'I've managed to feed myself so I've not starved, but I need to be getting a job soon, 'cos this shed ain't weatherproof – he pointed at the sagging roof through which Dot could see the stars – 'and when winter comes I'll have to move into lodgings or get some sort of proper roof over my head. I might make this place weatherproof, I suppose, and go on living here, but if I do I reckon someone will realise it's occupied and I'll wake up one morning to find a couple o' rozzers on my doorstep.'

'Rozzers?' Dot's tone was puzzled.

'Coppers. Policemen I s'pose you'd call them.'

Dot laughed. 'Scuffers, you mean,' she said. 'You'll have to learn to talk proper if you're going to stay in Liverpool for long.'

The two grinned at one another. Already Dot felt that they were friends as the boy produced a battered tin mug and a bottle of water from a shelf at the back of the shed. 'Want a drink before you start talkin'? And there's some apples 'n' all. Are you hungry?'

Dot accepted the drink of water gratefully, but

refused an apple. 'It's a long story. It started back in March when some pals and meself were playing relievio and I decided to hide in old Butcher Rathbone's dustbin . . .'

She told the story quickly and well, though she had to stop several times to explain herself more fully, for she had realised as soon as this boy opened his mouth that he was not a Scouser. When he had queried what she meant by relievio and she had explained, he told her that in London, where he came from, the game was known as Rescue.

At the end of her recital, her companion was round-eyed. 'What a bleedin' adventure,' he breathed. 'An' that's the very necklace – the one that would give it all away if the coppers got their hands on it? Let's have another butcher's then.'

'Butcher's?'

The boy laughed. 'It's Cockney rhyming slang – butcher's hook – look,' he said laconically. 'I mean, can I have another look at the necklace, please?'

He said it in an ultra-posh voice to make her laugh, and Dot could not help doing so as she produced the necklace and handed it to him. He held it up; it looked brilliant in the candlelight, the faceted green stones reflecting a million points of light, the gold links gleaming and the diamonds set between each green stone sparkling with all the colours of the rainbow when they caught the light.

'It's bleedin' beautiful,' the boy said reverently, handing the necklace back and watching as Dot wrapped it carefully in a clean piece of rag. 'It oughtn't to be buried; can't you think of somewhere to hide it where you can take a look at it every now and then?'

Dot shook her head. 'Too dangerous,' she said decidedly. 'Can you think of a good hiding place? Because we're going to have to hide it before daylight. I told you I thought one of the men had recognised me, but I didn't tell you I thought someone had tried to push me in front of a train. Me pal said it were just the crowd surging forward, but – but I'm not so sure.'

As she spoke she realised how completely she trusted this boy whose name she did not even know.

'We'll think of somewhere safe,' the boy said, and, as though he had read her thoughts, he added: 'My name's John Cochrane, but everyone calls me Corky, and some while ago I ran away from the Redwood Grange Orphanage for Boys in the East End of London. And my story is damn nearly as strange as yours, 'cos you ain't the only one what fell in with thieves . . . an' mine's a long story an' all, so pin back your lugs and listen hard, young . . . what's your name?'

'I'm Dorothy McCann, but everyone calls me Dot,' Dot said. She held out a hand. 'How d'you do, Corky? D'you know, I'm real glad I met you. I've never dared tell a soul about the necklace and what happened that night, but now I've told you I feel . . . I feel lighter, somehow, and not nearly as frightened.'

'I know what you mean,' Corky said. 'I've not

spoke to a soul since I arrived in Liverpool, 'cept to buy things. It's grand to have a pal, someone I can really trust. Now listen, 'cos I'm goin' to start right at the beginning when this here reporter chap came to Redwood Grange, 'cos he were writing a series of articles for some big paper – the *Herald*, or the *News Chronicle*, I think it was – about how orphanages were run in different parts of the country. I can't remember his name . . . but he were ever such a nice feller.'

Corky's story had Dot staring at him, round-eyed. 'Ain't that the oddest coincidence?' she breathed, when Corky had reached the end of his tale. 'You and me both getting tangled up wi' crooks, without doing anything wrong ourselves. But at least you've left your troubles behind you, Corky. I wonder – I wonder if I ought to run away an' all? Only I don't know how I'd go on 'cos I'm too young to work an' though me uncle hates me, Aunt Myrtle does her best. I do have a roof over me head an' grub on the table once or twice a day. An' I tell myself that if I keep me head down I'll be all right. But where should we hide the necklace?'

'Somewhere where no one don't go,' Corky said, without hesitation. 'The church, if you're right and no one visits no more. There's bound to be a loose stone or a bit of a cupboard, or somewhere where we could stow it away and know we could find it immediately if we wanted to. Diggin' around in the graves is all very well, but you leave traces, you can't help it.'

'Ye-es, but the church really is dangerous,' Dot pointed out dubiously. 'Some of them big arch things have fallen down, an' there's beams an' rubble an' stuff all over. Wouldn't this shed be safer?'

Corky laughed. 'No it wouldn't, 'cos if a tramp spotted it he'd come in, same as I did, an' make himself at home,' he pointed out. 'As for the church being dangerous, that makes it the best hiding place of all. No one won't go poking about in there in case it comes down on their heads. Besides, I've another idea which may mean we only need to hide the necklace for a bit. Want to hear it? The other idea, I mean.'

'Course I does,' Dot said eagerly. 'Fire away, Corky.'

Corky, however, said he thought they ought to hide the necklace first, so the two of them walked, cat quiet, across to the ruined church. Dot felt horribly nervous and soon realised that there were unexpected snags to Corky's suggestion. Inside the shelter of the ruined walls – the roof had long gone and the windows gaped, empty of even a trace of glass – brambles and nettles had grown up until it was just about impossible to push through them. What was more, had they done so, they could not have failed to leave a pathway showing exactly where they had gone. However, whilst she was still staring in dismay, Corky cautiously lifted a great curtain of ivy and pointed to one of the stones, smaller than the rest. 'I'll wiggle that half out – well, right out, really – and we'll push the necklace inside, as far as it will go, then we'll replace the stone,' he said. 'No one will think of lifting the ivy, far less moving a stone, so it'll be safe enough. Is that all right by you?'

'Yes, I suppose so,' Dot said, rather doubtfully. 'I wish we could have found somewhere – somewhere easier, so I could have got it out from time to time to – to make sure it was safe, like. Still, I reckon you're right. It's best that it's well hidden and I'm sure no one would dream of coming even this far inside the church, it's too perishin' dangerous.'

'You hold the ivy up whilst I get the stone out,' Corky said, and in fact it proved to be the work of a moment to do just that. Dot watched sadly as the necklace slithered to the back of the crevice and Corky pushed the stone into its original position. As he did so, Dot became aware of a creepy sort of feeling between her shoulder blades. Suddenly convinced that someone was watching them, she swung round but could see nothing except the ivy and creeper-clad walls of the church, and the masses of brambles and nettles which grew in their shelter. She opened her mouth to share her fears with Corky, then noticed a shape perched high in an empty window embrasure and let her breath go – she had not realised she was holding it – in a long sigh of relief. It was an owl, or some other night bird, watching her with huge curious eyes whilst it turned its head from side to side, the better to see what they were about.

Gently, Dot touched Corky's arm. 'We're being watched,' she whispered. 'Is it an owl, Corky?'

Corky followed the direction of her pointing finger, but even as he looked the bird took off on silent wings and disappeared into the churchyard. Corky smiled; she could see the flash of his teeth, even in the dark. 'You didn't half give me a fright,' he said reproachfully. 'But yes, you was right, it were an owl. Don't you go scaring me like that again, young Dot.'

Dot, glancing uneasily around her as she dropped the curtain of ivy back into position, promised that she would not. And because of her promise, she did not mention that the feeling of being watched persisted. But as she told Corky, she really did think they had the ideal hiding place. The stone was triangular – obviously at some stage a corner had been knocked off one of the big square blocks from which the church had been constructed – and fitted back into place exactly, as though there were nothing behind it at all. The two grinned at one another. 'That's all right,' Corky said, brushing the stone dust off his hand and moving out of the ruined church. 'And now I'll tell you my idea; well I will when we're back in the shed, at any rate.'

They were entering the shed again when Dot glanced up at the sky and gave a gasp. The stars were no longer visible, and towards the east there was a line of brightness along the horizon. It was pretty clear that morning was about to arrive and she had no desire to be seen entering the house by some early worker or, worse, by a member of the Brewster family. She jerked Corky's arm and pointed to the east. 'Corky, it's nearly morning! I've gorra go . . . how about you coming with me part of the way? I'll show you where I live an' we can talk as we go.'

Corky agreed, and the two of them scrambled over the wall and set off along the street. Oddly, the street seemed even darker than the churchyard, which was a bonus. Very few people were about, and those that were were intent on their own business and did not give the youngsters more than a passing glance. Presently, Dot nudged her companion. 'Well? What's this plan of yours?' she asked curiously. 'I hope you ain't goin' to suggest we bring in the scuffers or tell someone like a teacher, 'cos I dare not, an' that's the truth. Remember, Corky, one o' them fellers thought nothing of beatin' an old man over the head, so I reckon he'd do the same to me – and you, if he knew you had anything to do with it – and I aren't prepared to take the risk.'

Corky grinned indulgently and gave her shoulder the lightest of light punches. 'I'm not mad, you know,' he said reprovingly. 'Rozzers – coppers – scuffers don't always believe kids and some of them, where I come from at any rate, are pretty quick to pocket anything valuable that comes their way. No, what I want you to do, later in the day, is to take me to that shop, the jewellers, I mean. It hasn't closed down or anything, has it?'

Dot cast her mind back to when she had last visited Church Street. At the time, she had been far too nervous even to walk on the same side of the street as Mitchell & Grieves, but she had cast a couple of covert glances at the shop as she passed and she was pretty sure it had been open for business. She said as much and Corky nodded in a satisfied way. 'Good. Hasn't it occurred to you that the necklace really belongs to whoever now owns that shop? 'Cos it does, you know. You've been thinking that in a way it belonged to the thieves and because they chucked it in the bin it's more or less yours; ain't that right?'

After a few moments' hard thought, Dot nodded reluctantly. She realised she had begun to think of the necklace as practically hers; 'finders keepers' was a common cry amongst the kids at school, but of course Corky was absolutely right. No matter how you looked at it, the necklace really did belong to Mitchell & Grieves. However, there was one point she would have to make. 'Only old Mr Grieves is dead, killed by the 'orrible Ollie,' she pointed out. 'And Mr Mitchell . . . well, it said in the paper Mr Mitchell started the business back in the 1850s an' he's been dead years and years. So where does that leave us?'

'Dunno. But mebbe there's a son, or a nephew even. The old feller must have left the shop to someone 'cos if that wasn't the case – if there were no relatives, I mean – then I'm pretty sure it would have closed down. But anyway, I think we should reconnoitre tomorrow, find out as much as we can. And then, if there is a young Mr Grieves in the shop, we could work out some way of getting the necklace back to him and – and if he seemed an easy sort of fellow to talk to, like, we could go into the shop and you could tell him your story. I reckon he'd be likelier to believe you than the coppers would, especially since you'd have evidence.'

'Evidence? Oh, you mean the necklace. All right, we'll do it your way.' By now, they had reached the entrance to Lavender Court and Dot drew Corky to a halt and lowered her voice. 'I'm going in now, and you'd best get back to the churchyard before it begins to get really light. But can you meet me here tomorrow morning at, say, eleven o'clock?'

She expected an immediate affirmative but Corky shook his head. 'No chance. I'm pretty well wore out an' I reckon I'll go back to the shed and sleep the clock round. Let's meet at three in the afternoon; I'll be meself again by then.'

Dot agreed, rather wistfully; she knew her own chances of snatching more than three or four hours' sleep were slight indeed and she watched Corky lope off along Heyworth Street with real envy. How she wished she could accompany him, but it would not do. Her aunt must never know she had been out half the night, particularly now that her uncle had grown so friendly with Butcher Rathbone. You could never tell with grown-ups, and if it got to Archie Rathbone's ears that she was in the habit of prowling the streets after dark, he might put two and two together and her goose would be properly cooked. So Dot went quickly and quietly across the court and in through the door of No. 6. The door swung shut without a sound and she flitted along to the kitchen to find everything exactly as she had left it. She took off her cotton dress, then wriggled on to the sofa, pulling the thin blanket up around her ears, and was soon asleep.

Chapter Six

'I say! And that's the very shop, where it all happened? It's like an adventure story in *Chums*. They used to get that at Redwood Grange – only one copy, mind – and I can tell you it's a grand read. You ever come across it?'

'I've seen it, but it don't matter, Corky. What matters is why we're here,' Dot said impatiently. 'I reckon we'd best go and look in the window, pretend we're lookin' at the rings and that, only really we'll try and see who's standing behind the counter. And we won't go in, or ask questions, even if the feller behind the counter looks real friendly, because kids don't go into jewellers' shops, do they? But there's one of them places what sells newspapers and cigarettes quite near ... we could ask there.'

'And there were a super toy shop a few yards back,' Corky said wistfully. 'The one with the Hornby train in the window, and the rails and the station ... cor, if I were rich I'd buy the lot.'

'Yes, I dare say, but you ain't rich,' Dot said roundly. She had seen the wistful look in her companion's eyes and sympathised but felt they should keep their attention on the matter in hand.

First, they must discover who now owned the shop, and next, whether he was the sort of person to believe the rather wild story they had to tell. They did not mean to confide in someone who would grab them by the ears and march them to the nearest police station, so they had to investigate the new owner of the shop as thoroughly as possible before making their move. They could go into the toy shop, wander round and then, if there was a young and friendly assistant, ask a few questions without giving too much away, and they could do the same in the newsagent's further along the road. But first, they would look in the window.

They stopped before the brilliant display and gazed earnestly. Diamonds, sapphires and emeralds, rubies, amethysts and topaz glittered back at them, while gold chains were displayed on a higher shelf. Dot was so taken up with the jewellery that she forgot to look through into the shop. She tugged Corky's arm, pointing out the cream velvet oval, now empty, upon which the emerald necklace had once been displayed. 'I dunno why they've not put anything in its place, 'cos it spoils the look of the window—' she was beginning, when Corky cut across her.

'There's a *girl* sitting behind the counter,' he said. 'We never thought of a *girl*. But she can't be the owner, girls don't own shops. I suppose she's just a sales assistant. Can you see her? She's rare pretty . . . oh, cripes, she's cryin'. There's tears fairly pourin' down her cheeks . . .'

Dot craned her neck to take a look herself, then realised that Corky was no longer at her side. Bold as brass, he had pushed the door open – the bell above it gave an alarmed tinkle – and walked into the shop. Dot tried to grab him, to remind him that they had agreed not to go inside, but it was too late so she followed him. Corky went slap-bang up to the counter, leaned across it and gave the girl's shoulder a little shake. 'What's the matter, miss? You been given the old heave-ho?' he enquired genially. 'Don't worry, there's other jobs. Why, I'm sure you could do anything. Me and my pal, we've see'd cards in the windows of several shops what need sales assistants. Or – or do you work on commission and is business bad? Only there were a robbery here, weren't there? An' I suppose the boss is havin' a bit of a struggle to make up the loss. That right?'

Dot expected the young woman to tell them, roundly, to get out of the shop and mind their own business, but instead she rubbed vigorously at her reddened eyes and then looked up at them and gave Corky a tremulous smile. Dot saw that she was very pretty, with curly dark hair pulled back from her face, big dark eyes and a clear, pale complexion. She really was quite young, probably no more than eighteen or nineteen, which almost certainly meant that she was a sales assistant after all. If Corky were right, and she was crying because she had been dismissed, then she might be quite eager to tell them all about her boss.

The young woman leaned forward. 'I *am* the boss and that's why I was crying,' she said, in a small voice. 'I was an art student before Grandpa died, but he left me the shop in his will. It's very kind of you to show concern, but – but there's nothing anyone can do. It – it isn't just the robbery ... oh, dear. It isn't like me to give way, but I've been feeling so helpless.' She smiled from Corky to Dot, then stood up and spoke resolutely. 'Now run along, children; it's about time I did some work and stopped feeling sorry for myself.'

Dot would have left at this point, for though the girl was young she was still a grown-up and there was authority in her voice, but Corky was made of sterner stuff. 'Look, miss,' he said urgently, 'I know we're only kids – I'm fourteen and Dot here's a couple of years younger – but we're ... we're more involved than you think. For a start, we know where that necklace is – or we think we do, anyway,' he amended hastily, when Dot glared at him. He was ignoring all the careful plans they'd made but she realised he was right to do so. If they were ever going to get anywhere with this young woman, they had to gain her confidence, which meant letting her know that they were, as Corky had said, involved.

At Corky's words, the young woman's whole face changed. Colour bloomed in her cheeks and her eyes began to sparkle. 'You know where the emerald necklace is?' she gasped. 'Oh, I'd give anything to have the necklace back. My grandfather made it, you know. He was a jewellery designer, and it was his set piece, the piece you were judged on, and he always said it was the Grieves luck: that while we had it in the window we would do well and the business would thrive. He sent me to art college to learn to be a jewellery designer like him. He never meant me to work in the shop, but – but after he died . . .' Her voice wobbled into silence for a moment and Dot saw that she was fighting back tears. 'He and I were very close.' She looked enquiringly at Corky. 'But you said you know where the necklace is . . . ?'

Corky was beginning to reply when behind them the bell tinkled and the shop door was thrust open. Both children swung round and caught a glimpse of the man in the doorway. Astonishingly, for it was a warm day, he wore a large cap pulled down over his eyes and a scarf of some sort obscured the lower half of his face. He was clad in a long Burberry raincoat, very new and stiff, with the collar turned up. For one awful moment, Dot thought a second robbery was about to take place, but the man said gruffly: 'Sorry, didn't see you had customers,' and backed out of the shop, shutting the door behind him.

Dot stared after him; there had been something oddly familiar in the low, growling voice. Was it the voice she had heard when hidden in the dustbin? She turned back towards the young woman and saw that she had clenched her hands into fists and that her brows were drawn into a frown, but before she could ask who the man was Corky leaned across the counter and took hold of the woman's hand. 'What is it?' he said urgently. 'Who was that feller and why was he wearing a Burberry on such a fine day?'

The young woman sighed and came round the counter. She locked the door, swung the 'Open' sign round to read 'Closed' and beckoned to the children. 'I ought to introduce myself. My name is Emma Grieves and my grandpa and I lived in the flat above the shop, and now I live there by myself,' she said. 'If you're going to be able to talk freely, we'll have to go upstairs. Who are you, by the way?'

'I'm John Cochrane, known as Corky, and my pal is Dot McCann. How d'you do, Miss Grieves; nice to meet you.'

Emma Grieves laughed. 'We seem to have skipped most of the preliminaries,' she said cheerfully. 'Follow me.' She led them through what Dot guessed must be a stockroom, and ushered them up a flight of stairs, at the top of which was a small landing, flanked by four white-painted doors. Emma Grieves flung open the nearest to reveal a pleasant and modern kitchen. 'I often sit here – it overlooks the back so it's quieter. We'll have a cup of tea and a bun whilst you tell me just what you meant, down there,' she said, ushering them into the room.

'It's a long story . . .' Corky began, once they were settled with cups of tea and iced buns before them. 'But first of all, miss, I'd like to know what that feller wanted just now, the one in the Burberry.'

'Oh – oh, oh,' the young woman said. 'That's a long story, if you like, but – but can't you just give me a clue about my necklace first? You don't know how much it means to me.'

Corky and Dot exchanged glances, then Dot began to speak. 'Me and some pals were playing relievio around the entries and jiggers off Heyworth Street,' she began, and told the story as far as the part where the men had thrown the necklace into the bin and gone off. Here Miss Grieves interrupted her.

'Then *you've* got my necklace,' she breathed. 'Oh, Dot, if you've kept it safe for me, I can't thank you enough. Once it's back in the window . . . but I don't suppose I'll ever dare to put it back.'

'I think we'd much rather you didn't, for a while at any rate,' Dot said cautiously. 'You see, one of the men spotted me running out of the jigger – he saw me, we looked into each other's faces – and I reckon he meant to get the necklace for himself and that was why he was turning into the jigger when we met, head on. He must have seen the scuffer and changed his mind, and then, if they discovered it was missing next day, which I suppose they must have done, I reckon that Ollie – that was his name – must have guessed it was me who took it. So you see, Miss Grieves, if you suddenly let folk know you've got the necklace back, those two men may guess that you and me both know who did the robbery – and killed your grandpa – that night.'

'Yes, I understand that. And you must both call me Emma,' their new friend said, rather abstractedly. 'Look, I think you're right to be frightened of those men, Dot, because they've a lot to lose and such people are dangerous. But can I take it that you've hidden my necklace somewhere safe?'

Dot and Corky both nodded vigorously. 'Yes. No one will find it again except us,' Corky assured her. 'But Dot knows she was seen that night, and – and a few weeks afterwards, someone tried to push her under a train. That's why we've not took the necklace to the police. We're only a couple of kids and they might think we made the whole thing up, just to get Butcher Rathbone and his pal into trouble.'

Emma had been staring into her cup of tea as though it were a crystal ball, but at Corky's words her eyes snapped up to meet his. 'Butcher Rathbone?' she said in a puzzled voice. 'I know you said you were hiding in his yard, Dot, but you never said it was he who was talking to the one you called Ollie. Are you seriously trying to tell me that Archie Rathbone was one of the thieves?'

Dot hesitated. Now that it was put to her so bluntly, she realised that she had not caught so much as a glimpse of the butcher and did not know his voice, not really. But then she remembered details of the conversation, and anyway, no one but the butcher himself would have had the keys to his shop, or talked so confidently about setting fire to the contents of the dustbin next morning, before anyone else was about. She told Emma this, wondering why the young woman had sounded so surprised at the mention of Butcher Rathbone's name. When she had finished her explanation, Emma nodded slowly.

'Curiouser and curiouser,' she said. 'Now, I wonder where *my* story should rightly start? It can't be with the robbery, because when it happened I was visiting London on my grandfather's behalf, buying precious stones.'

'How about telling us how you come to know Mr Rathbone,' Dot said bluntly. 'He can't be your butcher, surely? Heyworth Street is a good way from here.'

'Mr Rathbone and my grandfather were both members of the Chamber of Trade,' Emma explained. 'And because he knew I'd inherited the shop and wasn't experienced in retail trade, he came round one evening, offering any help and advice that he could give. Amongst other things, he asked me if I'd been approached by – by someone, suggesting that, for a small sum to be paid weekly, they would see I wasn't robbed again. Apparently, there's a group of men who will make sure your premises aren't robbed provided you pay a small amount each week, like a sort of insurance policy. It seems they'd offered protection to my grandfather and he'd refused it, and look what happened to him, Mr Rathbone said. He also told me that a number of shops in Church Street had been robbed or broken into over the past couple of years, but that no one who paid for protection had any trouble. He had never been robbed and neither had any of the smaller shops in his area because, presumably, they all pay up. He advised me, most strongly, not to stand out against the practice and – and I said I'd pay.'

'But that's blackmail,' Dot protested. 'You should tell the scuffers, Emma, let them sort it out. Anyway, it were probably Mr Rathbone what did all the other burglaries – it's probably him that's behind this protection scheme, as well.'

'Protection racket; they're called protection rackets. Don't you ever watch gangster films?' Corky said, rather scornfully. 'But I bet you're right, Dot, I bet old Rathbone's behind it.' He turned back to Emma. 'So did you pay up, Miss . . . I mean, Emma? Oh! That man who came into the shop . . . ?'

Emma nodded wearily. 'Yes, he's the man who collects the money once a week, and he's always muffled up so I don't know who he is, only I don't think he's Mr Rathbone . . . well, I'm sure he's not. That Burberry is far too big for him and he's got bony wrists and horrible thin hands, like a spider; Mr Rathbone's a huge man, isn't he?' She looked hopefully from Dot's face to Corky's. 'Mr Rathbone was so *nice*! I mean he told me it would be in my own interest to pay, he said they'd never ask for more than I could afford . . . he said all the traders pay up, though of course no one would admit to it, but he realised that because of the burglary I might be short of ready cash . . . he offered me a loan, honest to God he did, but I said I'd manage somehow.' She sniffed, then fished a handkerchief out from her sleeve and blew her nose vigorously. 'The fact is, I scarcely know which way to turn. Everyone assumes I'm just waiting for the insurance company to pay me back for the stolen goods but – but Grandfather was getting a bit vague and – and I heard today that he never paid his last premium, so the insurance has lapsed and I won't get a penny, so I really am in a bit of a hole. What's more, my grandfather's bank account has been frozen until probate has been granted, so I'm dependent, at the moment, upon what goes through the till. Fortunately folks still come in for wedding rings or perhaps a gold bracelet. So I'm keeping my head above water – just about.'

The two children stared, first at Emma Grieves, and then at each other. Finally, Dot spoke. 'No wonder you were crying,' she said. 'Awful things have been happening to you at the worst possible time and you've got no one to turn to. So what do you want us to do? We want to help you but we don't want those men coming after us.'

'No, of course you don't, and I don't want it, either,' Emma said. 'I wish you'd actually seen Mr Rathbone, though, Dot, but you're pretty sure it was him, aren't you?'

Dot nodded emphatically. 'I'm as sure as can

be,' she said. 'And no matter how nice he was to you, Emma, he ain't nice to kids like me, I can tell you. He's quicker with a cuff than a kiss, as the saying goes, and that's another reason why I didn't want to go to the scuffers. No kids like Mr Rathbone an' I'm scared they might think I was simply getting back at him.' She looked hopefully at the older girl. 'But it's different for you, Emma; couldn't you pretend you'd gone into his back yard on some pretext and found the necklace hidden away there? Or you could say you wanted his advice and when you got into his shop you could slip the necklace under the counter and make out it must have been there all along. Then you could go to the scuffers, and though it would only be your word against his I'm sure they'd believe you.'

Emma looked doubtful. 'I couldn't possibly do that,' she said. 'No, we've got to think of some way of implicating the thieves without running too many risks ourselves. And to be honest, the man I really want to see being put behind bars is the one who killed my grandfather . . . Ollie, did you say his name was?'

'That's right,' Dot agreed. 'If only there was someone who could *really* advise us – a grown-up, I mean, someone we know isn't involved – but I can't think of anyone. I live with my aunt and uncle, but just lately me uncle's got real pally with old Rathbone, and he wouldn't be any good anyway; all he thinks of is getting a bellyful of ale every night and doing as little work as possible every day.'

Corky chuckled. 'What about a teacher at school, or a friend's mum or dad?' he asked. 'I don't come from these parts, but if I'd still been down south I'd have talked to that newspaper reporter I told you about.'

'Yes, but he ain't here, so a fat lot of use that 'ud be,' Dot said scornfully. 'As for teachers at school, most of 'em's old and stupid; they'd hand us over to the law or say it were none of our business, an' even if they didn't do that, they'd tell their pals and it would get round to old Rathbone in no time. No, I reckon the three of us are on our own. You won't say a word to anyone, will you, Emma? Not without discussing it with us first, at any rate? Because I don't fancy being bashed over the head till I'm dead.'

Emma agreed that such a fate was to be avoided at all costs and the conversation turned to future plans. 'Tell you what, we'll all of us spend tomorrow thinking hard what to do,' Dot said, 'and then we'll meet up again the day after. How's that for an idea?'

Corky said he supposed that something might occur to him, and Emma began to clear away the tea things, saying as she did so: 'Look, I'm not doubting the story you've told me, either Dot's end of it or yours, Corky. But so far I've taken everything on trust. You've not shown me the necklace, nor told me where it's hidden, and it is my property, after all. If it's in a really safe hiding place, as you say, I wouldn't dream of moving it because that might put all of us in danger, but I think it's only right that I should see it.'

Dot and Corky exchanged dubious glances. Dot was sure that if Emma set eyes on the necklace she would want to keep it, and though she supposed it might be as safe in the flat above the shop as it was in its present position, she also thought that Emma might be tempted, one day, to put it back in the window where she must feel it belonged. But she could scarcely say so; Emma was right, the necklace really was her property.

Dot was beginning to say, reluctantly, that she saw Emma's point of view when Corky cut in. 'You certainly do have a right to see it,' he said briskly. 'But remember, it's Dot's neck that's at risk if the perishin' thing is seen by the wrong people, not yours, Emma. I don't much want to bring it to the shop – I know Dot agrees with me there – but I suppose if you come to where we've hidden it, and promise to take a look but not to touch it, that would be all right.'

Emma laughed. 'Don't you trust me?' she asked.

There was a short pause whilst Corky and Dot exchanged dubious glances once more. Then Corky spoke, his voice serious. 'It ain't that, Emma, honest to God it ain't. But – but the necklace is the most beautiful thing me and Dot have ever seen. We know it's yourn, no one denies that, but if we were to show it to you and you simply took it off of us, there wouldn't be a thing we could do about it, would there? And it could put Dot in real danger.'

Emma nodded slowly. The laughter had faded from her face as Corky spoke, and when she replied, it was in a tone as serious as his. 'Right, I swear I won't even touch the necklace, though I admit I'd like to make sure it's undamaged and so on. Now, when can you take me to its hiding place?'

'Well, it'll have to be at night, because the sight of a grown-up lady climbing walls and poking about in – in tumbledown buildings would soon set tongues wagging if we tried it in daylight,' Dot said slowly. 'Tell you what, Emma, could you find up some old, dark clothing from somewhere? Then you won't look so con – conspicuous.'

Emma agreed that she had suitable garments and would wear them. She suggested that she should be taken to see the necklace that very night but Dot said she simply dared not escape from the house two nights running, adding that she doubted whether she would be able to wake up for she had only had three hours' or so sleep the night before. 'I think we ought to do as I said: spend all day tomorrow trying to work out what's best to do, then sleep on it, then meet the following day to pool our ideas. Then, if nothing else has occurred to us, we'll take you to see the necklace,' she concluded. 'After all, it's been about five months since the robbery, so a day or two more won't hurt.'

Emma agreed, though a trifle reluctantly. She was clearly dying to see the necklace, though Dot did not think she doubted them for one moment. And indeed, as she ushered them across the stock-room at the back of the shop, she thanked them fervently for coming to find her, and for sharing their knowledge with her.

She unlocked the heavy back door and they were about to set off across the small back yard when Corky thought of something and turned back. 'That feller, the one in the Burberry, will he come back tonight, after you've closed? And what are you going to do about it? I know it's tempting to say you won't pay, but . . .'

'I wouldn't dream of doing anything so fool-hardy. I'll pay up, the same as I did last time, but once we've sorted things out he won't get another penny and I'll go round and tell the other traders not to pay either. See you in the shop the day after tomorrow. And come late, say around six, so I can let you in and lock up immediately afterwards. Come to think of it, it would be better if you came to the back door, the one you're leaving by now.' There was a stout wooden door in the wall of the yard and she accompanied Dot and Corky over to it, opened it, and told them to turn left along the tiny jigger which would lead them on to Leigh and Tarleton Street. 'This door is never locked and there is a bell by the stockroom door which rings in the flat, so give it a good long push and I'll come down and let you in. Take care, both of you; see you the day after tomorrow, around six o'clock.'

As they turned on to Church Street once more,

Dot looked carefully round her, aware of Corky doing the same. The pavements were still busy with folk going to the theatre or the cinema, and others just enjoying the warm August evening, or making their way to pubs. A newsboy was shouting his wares and a large policeman was stolidly walking his beat and stopping now and then to exchange a remark with a passer-by, but there was no sign of the ferret-faced one, or of a man in a big cloth cap and a long Burberry. Satisfied that they had emerged without being spotted, Dot and Corky sauntered on their way.

Emma closed the back door and relocked it. Belatedly, she realised that she had no idea where either Dot or Corky lived, so could not get in touch with them if she needed to do so. However, she would be seeing them the day after tomorrow; surely nothing of importance could happen between now and then?

Having seen the children off, Emma went back up to the flat again and began half-heartedly to prepare her evening meal. She laid slices of ham upon a plate, added tomato, cucumber and lettuce, and buttered a round of bread. Then she looked at it without much enthusiasm. She told herself that on such a warm evening a salad was ideal, that a hot meal would simply have made the kitchen unbearable, and sat down, pulling her plate towards her. She began to eat, then threw down her knife and fork and jumped to her feet. This was absurd! She was beginning to feel that the shop and the flat were a trap from which she could not escape, so why not prove herself wrong and go out for a meal? She could, of course, go to one of the many cafés or dining rooms in the area, but thought it would be pleasanter to buy fish and chips and bring them back to the flat. At least she would be getting a breath of fresh air before going to bed.

Without giving herself time to think, she snatched her linen jacket off the peg on the back of the door and headed down the stairs. She had drawn the blinds across the shop windows when she had closed so the place was in semi-darkness, but she could have made her way across the floor blindfold, and did not switch on the light. Instead, she unlocked the shop door, pulled it towards her and slipped out into Church Street. She locked the door behind her, pushing the key deep into her jacket pocket, and was turning to make her way towards the fish and chip shop her grandfather had favoured when a voice spoke almost in her ear, making her jump. 'Good evenin', Miss Grieves. You all right? It ain't often I see you entertainin', but I saw a couple o' young limbs goin' into the shop earlier – I been keepin' me eye on this shop since the robbery. Friends, was they?' The speaker was a police constable. He had a round, ruddy face and a little black toothbrush moustache, and he reminded Emma of someone, though she could not think of whom. But he was touching his helmet and smiling kindly down at her, and she realised that he must be the policeman she had half noticed earlier, when the children had first entered the shop. So she smiled up at him, sure that honest concern was his only motive in addressing her.

'Oh, good evening, constable; how you startled me! I expect you saw my young cousins; I invited them for a cup of tea and a bun when they popped in to ask if I'd like to go round to my aunt's place for Sunday dinner. To tell you the truth, I get rather lonely. I miss my grandfather more than you can imagine.'

The policeman nodded solemnly. 'Aye, that were a dreadful thing,' he said. 'So them kids is related to you, is they? Well, ain't that nice?'

His big, many-chinned face broke into a smile, but caution made Emma say hastily: 'Well, to tell the truth, I've always called them my cousins, but they aren't actually blood relatives. I couldn't invite them to stay for a meal because their mother expected them home, and besides, I'd decided to treat myself to fish and chips this evening because it's far too hot to cook.'

'Aye, you're right there,' the constable said, falling into step beside her. 'There's nothin' I like better than a nice piece o' battered cod and a paper of chips, well salted and vinegared.' He sighed deeply. 'But I'm on duty for another four or five hours and then it'll be a cup of cocoa, a round of bread and jam, and me bed. Which shop are you bound for, missy? If it's on my beat, I'll walk along o' you, keep you company like.'

'I'm heading for Jones's fried fish shop on Elliot Street,' she said. She looked speculatively up at him. He seemed a friendly and reliable sort of bloke, and she badly needed a friend. Should she – could she – confide in him? But then she remembered that the only information she had to confide was not rightly hers at all. Dot and Corky had shared their secret with her and had taken it for granted that she would respect their confidence. It was a pity, because when it came right down to it, the police had as much interest as she herself in catching the wrongdoers, and this man was clearly well disposed towards her. She was still reminding herself that she had not actually promised to say nothing, though she knew, in her heart, that both Dot and Corky believed she had done so, when the police constable touched his helmet once more. 'Me way lies along Waterloo Place and Ranelagh Street; I have to keep me eye on Central Station and then I makes me way to Bold Street, checkin' the shops, makin' sure there's no one hangin' about, suspicious like,' he said. 'Enjoy your fish supper, missy, and think of me when you sprinkle the salt and vinegar.' He gave a rumbling laugh, in which Emma joined, and their ways parted.

Presently Emma, joining the queue at the fried fish shop, found that she was glad the constable had left her before she spilled the beans. No matter how trustworthy the man might seem, it would have been a mean trick to break her word, besides being fraught with all sorts of difficulties. Everyone in Liverpool knew everyone else, and quite a lot of them were actually related. The constable might well have been either a neighbour or a relative of Dot's, and might go round to the girl's house and demand that she show him the necklace. He might even suspect the child of involvement with the burglary; worse – and here, Emma's hair rose from the back of her neck with horror – he might be either a relative or a close friend of Butcher Rathbone, and take the story to him.

Emma reached the head of the queue and asked for a nice piece of haddock and two penn'orth of chips. As she waited for her order, she told herself, severely, that she must put all thoughts of confiding in anyone right out of her head; it was far too dangerous. Indeed, she had imagined that Dot had confided in Corky only because, from the moment he had opened his mouth, she had known he was not local. Emma herself had realised, within seconds of meeting him, that he was a Londoner.

'There you go, queen,' the shop assistant said, handing her a newspaper-wrapped parcel. Emma handed over her money, took the parcel and made her way out of the shop, heading for Church Street.

Back in the flat, she settled down at the kitchen table and really enjoyed the fish and chips, eating them straight from the newspaper and employing only her fingers, though she felt a trifle guilty for so doing. She could imagine her mother's disapproval, though her grandfather had always maintained that fish and chips on a plate was not to be compared with the same food eaten out of hot and vinegary newspaper. Also, it meant no washing-up. She turned the paper over; it was the *News Chronicle*, a national daily, not a publication which Emma usually read, though her grandfather had sometimes picked one up from the nearby newsagent's shop. She pushed it into the bin and carried her cocoa to her bedroom. She washed, undressed, put on her cool cotton nightgown, and slid between the sheets, telling herself that after such an exciting and eventful day she would doubtless fall asleep as soon as her head touched the pillow. She certainly hoped that this would be so, since she was most dreadfully tired and on the morrow had ten people coming to the shop to be interviewed for the post of sales assistant. Mr Humphreys, who had worked for her grandfather as long as Emma could remember, was retiring at the end of the month and was, consequently, only working part-time at present to accustom himself to the change which would shortly be upon him. He came in at ten o'clock in the morning and left at three in the afternoon, five days a week, and on Saturdays, which was their busiest day, he did not come in at all, so Emma was eager to find a replacement who would work a full day, six days a week, and rid her of the necessity of being constantly in the shop.

Unfortunately, the longed-for sleep would not come. The worries which had haunted her ever since her grandfather's death were all too present.

The man who came each week for her 'protection money' annoyed her, but he frightened her, too. There was something sinister in the long, bony wrists and the thin fingers, so matted with black hair that they made her think of giant spiders. The man, faceless but menacing, haunted her dreams – when she was able to sleep, that was – and now, thanks to the children, she had a worse worry on her mind. They might know where the necklace was, and this was a secret she was soon to share, but not one of them knew what best to do about it. Emma tossed and turned until the early hours. When at last light filtered through her curtains, and she should have been thinking about getting up, she fell deeply asleep, but bad dreams continued to haunt her. The children became little fiends, who taunted her with the necklace, waving it before her eyes but never letting her touch the glittering jewels. The policeman she had met that evening jeered at the story she told him and snatched her fish and chips from her hands, cramming the food into his mouth and threatening to throw her into prison for libelling his best friend. Even poor Mr Humphreys, who would not hurt a fly, became a monster in her dreams, reaching into the window and cramming his pockets with her precious rings, brooches and bracelets, whilst telling her that he had told the insurance company not to pay up, had said the emerald necklace – and everything else that was missing – had been cleverly made out of paste by her wicked old grandfather. Emma awoke with tears on her cheek.

As Emma had expected, the day was a busy one. All the prospective sales assistants attended for interview and, rather to her embarrassment, all of them were older than herself and more experienced in the retail trade. In the end, she chose a man for the full-time job, since she felt that she needed some sort of masculine support, and one of the older women on a part-time basis, to become full-time if, and when, Emma considered that she might return to her studies.

The young man – Mr Winterton – was in his mid-twenties, short, square and strong-looking. He would work nine till six, five days a week, and nine till one on early closing day, but she explained that there would be nights when he would work a good deal later, because books had to be balanced, stock ordered and cleaning and polishing carried out; work which could not always be fitted into a busy day.

Miss Snelling was a large, plain-featured woman in her late thirties, with dark hair pulled severely off her face and knotted in a tiny bun at the nape of her neck. Emma had chosen her because she had worked with fashion jewellery at one of the big department stores but wanted to have the opportunity to work with real gems rather than artificial ones. Emma liked her frank smile, but most of all she appreciated Miss Snelling's interest and the fact that the older woman was attending evening classes in order to learn more about the jewellery which she hoped she would be handling.

By six o'clock, Emma was so tired that she decided she would finish off the salad she'd prepared the previous evening and go straight to bed. She had kept both her new employees in the shop with her and Mr Humphreys until half an hour before closing time, so they could be shown the ropes and the stock.

When she was alone in the shop once more, having satisfied herself that everything was in order, Emma went over to lock the door and was annoyed, but not really surprised, to find it being pushed open by a large and hairy hand. She had guessed that the presence of her new employees had kept the protection man at bay and had half hoped he might have given up and gone home, but this was clearly not the case. He came right into the shop, shut the door and leaned against it. She saw that he had a large and bushy moustache and thick, bushy eyebrows and smiled to herself, for the moustache was a false one, as were the eyebrows, and neither had been put on with very much skill. 'Yes,' she said baldly, staring straight into his small, mud-brown eyes. 'What do you want? And if you think that moustache looks natural, you're quite wrong.'

The man grinned, a quick flash of rotten teeth. 'You knows very well what I wants,' he said gruffly. 'And don't be all night about it, because you've held me up considerable already.'

Emma turned back towards the counter. She had not taken a great deal of money that day, but did not mean to let the man see inside the till. When he would have followed her, she turned back at once, saying briskly: 'Stay where you are, please. I will pay you the sum I've been told is necessary to stop my shop from being broken into again, but that is all I'm prepared to do, and I won't do that if you come anywhere near the counter.'

The man hesitated, plainly considering whether he should defy her and take a look in the till, or perhaps even try to snatch some of the jewellery displayed, but he must have realised that this would lead to complications and stopped short. Emma went to the till, took out the money, crossed the shop and pushed it into his hand. 'There you are,' she said, shuddering a little as her fingers brushed against his. She reached for the door but he grabbed for the handle and let himself out, disappearing at a smart pace into the crowds on the pavement.

Emma watched him go, suddenly aware of a feeling of helplessness mixed with rage. Mr Rathbone had said that the money demanded would not change, but now that she had reason to believe the butcher to be a crook, she could not trust his word on anything. Once she had established herself in the Church Street shop, she meant to start introducing some of the beautiful hand-made jewellery her grandfather had specialised in. If the crooks realised that she was beginning to make a good profit, she imagined that they would want their share, and the thought both infuriated and terrified her. She really ought to go to the police, but she supposed she should have some sort of proof before she did so. It might be an idea to talk to other members of the Chamber of Trade, or even simply to other shopkeepers in the area who had already been robbed and were presumably paying protection money as she was. Mr Rathbone had told her, in the friendliest fashion, that anyone who went to the police would find themselves with a burned-out shop at worst or broken windows and doors at best, within hours of visiting the police station. Yet if she did nothing . . .

Emma had been standing on the pavement staring after the man in the long Burberry and was about to turn back into the shop when a young man came to a halt beside her, clearing his throat, and saying diffidently: 'Miss Grieves? Miss Emma Grieves? I called on you earlier but I was told you were interviewing staff and could not see me. I wonder if I might have a word?'

Emma sighed. She had never seen this young man before in her life and imagined that he was selling something. He was coatless and wearing a tweed sports jacket and grey trousers, with a trilby hat on the back of his head. He had a pleasant, open face, dark hair and eyes, and a nose which had been broken at some time or other. But no matter how pleasant he might look, Emma did not want to buy anything from anyone. She wanted to lock up the shop, clear the window, the till and the display shelves, and then eat her salad and go to bed to think over her problems in comfortable solitude. So she shook her head, saying frankly: 'No, I'm afraid you can't have a word, and whatever you're selling, I don't want any. Good evening.'

She would have returned to the shop, was already halfway over the threshold, when he put a detaining hand on her arm and a foot in a brown brogue walking shoe against the door. He spoke urgently, keeping his voice low. 'Don't go, Miss Grieves. I'm not selling anything. Look, can you just tell me why that fellow with the bushy moustache was visiting your shop?'

'Get your foot away from my door,' Emma said coldly. She tried to wrench her arm out of his grasp, but he hung on grimly. 'Let go of me at once or I'll – I'll yell for help and get a passer-by to fetch the police. As for questioning me about my customers, what the devil do you mean by it?'

The young man snorted and released her arm, but kept his foot just where it was. 'Are you trying to tell me that man was a customer?' he asked incredulously. 'An odd sort of customer who doesn't move away from the door, and takes something from you but gives you no money in return. Oh, come, Miss Grieves, I'm not an idiot, you know! I was waiting for you to close so that I could have a word with you, and as soon as I saw that fellow I guessed he was trouble. Look, if you'll just let me in for a moment, I can explain everything . . .'

Seeing that he had no intention of moving his foot, Emma pushed past him and took a deep breath, intending to shout for help, but this proved unnecessary. 'Awright, awright, you win, for the moment at least,' the young man said, stepping back. 'But if only you'd listen to me . . .'

But Emma scarcely heard. She shot back into the shop, slammed and locked the heavy glass door and then, heart hammering, went into the stockroom, closed the door and applied her eye to the judas, the peephole which her grandfather had caused to be made in the strong oak door. She watched the young man turn away, then raced up the stairs and shot into the living room which overlooked Church Street. Not until the tweed sports jacket was out of sight did she again return to the shop, by this time in a state of nervous tension so great that she could scarcely cash up for her shaking hands. How dared that wretched young man try to bully her into talking to him, she fumed, as she went methodically about the shop stacking the valuables inside the safe and sliding the takings in after them.

Because she had been upset, the work took longer than usual, and when she finally went up to the flat she was already far too tired to think logically about her problems. Instead, for the first time since she had inherited the shop, she considered selling it, though only for a moment. She knew her grandfather would have felt betrayed by such an act, but for once escape seemed a good deal easier than any attempt to tackle what was happening to her. She felt guilty, because no doubt Corky and Dot were racking their brains for a way to implicate the thieves and bring the murdering Ollie to justice, but, for her part, the day had been too full. Besides, this young man's interference could not be discounted. If he decided to tell the police, what then? Now that she thought about it, he might be a plain clothes policeman, but, as she began to eat the limp salad she had prepared the night before, she was able to discount this. Had he been a policeman, he would have produced some means of identification, and having revealed his identity would not have let her refuse him entry.

Not only was the salad limp, but the ham had dried out and was curling up at the edges. After two mouthfuls, Emma pushed the plate away and made herself a glass of lemonade. Sipping it, she wondered if she had been wise to turn the young man away. After all, a disinterested observer, someone without a shop to be burgled or premises to be burnt down, might be able to help in a way a fellow shopkeeper could not . . . perhaps she had been wrong to dismiss him without hearing what he had to say, but even at the time in the back of her mind there had lurked the suspicion that this might be just another trick. The young man might be part of a rival gang who wanted to take over from Spider Hands and Butcher Rathbone. Sighing, Emma crossed the room and went to the front window and peered out. Nobody lurked outside, or seemed to be taking the slightest notice of her shop. She sat down on the comfortable sofa in the living room and her tummy gave a deep, protesting rumble, informing her in no uncertain terms that it had missed lunch and supper and considered it her duty to send it down a meal at once. Emma reached for her book, telling herself that she would read for half an hour and then go straight to bed, but found she was unable to concentrate. After a mere ten minutes, she threw the book down and fetched her linen jacket.

Very soon she had left the flat behind and was sitting in Lyon's Corner House in Church Street, eating beans on toast with a fried egg on top, and drinking a cup of strong tea. The restaurant with its tiled floor and marble-topped tables was cooler than the flat had been, and Emma enjoyed her meal. As she emerged on to the pavement once more she contemplated going to one of the many local picture houses, but she knew that she was too tired to enjoy a cinema show and so, reluctantly, returned to the flat. Presently she was in bed where, despite her resolve to think things over, she fell rapidly asleep.

About the time Emma was climbing into bed, Dot was returning to Lavender Court, no closer to finding a solution to their problem than she had been when she left the house that morning. She was prepared to find she had missed the evening meal and had already decided that she would go round to Fizz's house and see if his mam would give her a cut off the loaf, or a couple of apples, so she skirted round the Brewster house and went straight to where Fizz was playing five stones with a red-headed, freckly boy from the next court. Fizz greeted her rather coldly. 'I dunno what's up wi' you, Dotty,' he said aggressively. 'You ain't been near nor by for a couple o' weeks, but the first time you miss your aunt's grub you're round here like a dose o' salts, tryin' to get my mam to feed you. Oh, by the way, this is me new bezzie, Alfie. Alfie, this here's Dotty McCann, what were me pal, once.'

Dot sniffed disdainfully, though she said hello to Alfie politely enough. It was often the way in school holidays; Fizz wanted to be one of the gang of lads from the courts and quite resented having to drag Dot around with him. Well, this time she wouldn't plead with him to let her join in; this time she had fish of her own to fry, and a pal of her own as well – two pals, if you could count a grown-up lady as a pal.

'Well? Don't tell me you haven't come round here after grub because I shan't believe you. And when you've ate me mam out of house and home, don't come round beggin' for a game of footy, 'cos we's off with the lads and youse can play girls' games – hopscotch and that – wi' Lizzie an' Mabel.'

'Well you're wrong, Mr Clever-bloody-Fizz, 'cos I ain't even *been* home yet,' Dot said loftily. 'I – I wondered if your mam wanted a message run, that's all.'

Fizz gave a derisive snort and started to call her names, but Dot had already turned on her heel and was making her way back towards the Brewster house. She felt rather guilty, for she knew very well that she had neglected Fizz and had meant to ask his mam for food. But she did not mean to let Fizz know it and besides, you could never tell with Aunt Myrtle. She was a bad cook and a poor provider; sometimes the evening meal was on the table at five, on other occasions at eight. If her uncle had come in late, having somehow managed to get himself a bit of extra money from somewhere, then they might be having fish and chips right now. Mouth watering in anticipation, Dot shot up the front steps, through the front door and into the kitchen. So vivid had been the picture of a table laden with fish and chips and surrounded by her cousins that it was quite a shock to find the room empty of all save Aunt Myrtle and the table cleared and bare. Dot closed the door slowly behind her, then sniffed the air. No, it was not imagination, she really could smell fried fish. She glanced, hopefully, at her aunt. 'Sorry I'm late, Aunt Myrtle,' she said, rather breathlessly. 'I – I were trying to get a job helping to deliver newspapers over on the other side of the city, but they said I were too young. Did you – did you have fish and chips for your suppers? I don't s'pose there's none left, eh?'

Her aunt had been sitting before the open window, sipping something from a large tin mug. She turned and scowled at her niece. 'No, there's nuthin' left,' she said. 'What d'you expect? Your uncle brung 'em in 'cos he'd had a good day, an' now he's gone off to the bleedin' pub wi' these new pals o' his. He said I could send one o' the lads round to the pub with a jug and he'd fill it with porter, only – only they's all gone off and you're late, as usual, and – and I'm feeling sickish so I reckon I don't want his bleedin' porter. I'll stick to tea.'

Dot stared rather helplessly across at her aunt. Aunt Myrtle was frequently bad-tempered, quicker with a blow than a kind word, but Dot could not remember her sounding so down and depressed before. She took a couple of steps towards the older woman and saw, for the first time, that there were what looked suspiciously like tears on her cheeks. Fearful of a rebuff, she patted her on the shoulder, saying awkwardly as she did so: 'What's up, Aunt Myrtle? It ain't like you to be so glum.'

For a moment her aunt said nothing, then she heaved a long sigh and spoke. 'I'm in the family way, that's what. After all this time . . . it's half a dozen years since I fell with Alan, so I thought I were safe. Things have been easier, what wi' Sammy working – though it's little enough o' his money I see – and your uncle bringin' in a bit more from the part-time job he's got hisself when he's not in the factory. But another perishin' baby . . . well, that would have been bad enough, but this afternoon I went up to Brougham Terrace, and – oh, I can't believe it!'

There was a long pause during which aunt and niece gazed at each other blankly. Then Dot spoke. 'Wharrever is it, Aunt Myrtle?' she enquired gently. 'I'll help you with the baby. I like babies.'

'Babies is right, babies is the word,' Aunt Myrtle said grimly. 'It's flamin' twins, that's wharrit is, and when I told your uncle, he – he *laughed*! And he's gone off to the pub to boast to everyone wharra fine feller he is, and how I'm to manage I just don't know.'

'I'll help,' Dot said again. Actually, she was almost as dismayed as her aunt at the thought of two babies in the cramped little house but she knew better than to say so. 'It won't be too bad with the pair of us at it, Aunt Myrtle. We can buy an old pram from one of the stores on Great Homer or the Scottie, and I'll be able to earn a bit more money doin' messages for the neighbours when I've got a great big pram to carry the stuff home in.'

Her aunt fished a piece of rag out of her sleeve and blew her nose. 'You! You won't be here by then,' she said mournfully. 'What d'you think I'm goin' to do wi' two babies, eh? There's no space for 'em in the boys' room and your uncle won't have 'em in with us, keepin' him awake half the night. No, they'll take your place in the kitchen and you'll go where you should ha' gone when your mam first dumped you on me, into a children's home.'

For a moment, Dot could only stare at her aunt. When she spoke, though she tried hard to control it, her voice quivered. 'You – you can't mean that, Auntie! Why, with two little babies you'll need all the help you can get, and I don't mind sharin' the kitchen with 'em. Or you could shift to somewhere bigger. Other folk do it, so why shouldn't you and Uncle Rupe?'

'Well, we will when there's a bit more money comin' in, but that don't mean to say I'm goin' to go on feedin' you,' her aunt said unkindly. 'Why should I? You ain't no child o' mine and your mam's long gone, like your dad. No, it's the children's home for you as soon as I can arrange it.'

Dot could see that, for the moment at least, her aunt was too upset to behave reasonably and was simply taking her frustration out on her niece. And oddly enough, her aunt's last remark gave Dot hope. She had not lived with her Auntie Myrtle for most of her life without getting to know her pretty well, and she was always intending to do this, that or the other but seldom got round to actually doing it. It'll be the same with the children's home; she'll mean to pack me off, keep plotting how she'll arrange it . . . and keep putting it off as a task which can be done another day, Dot decided. Besides, it was Uncle Rupert who resented Dot's presence; her aunt knew she was useful, must know in her heart that Dot would be a great help when the twins arrived. But it would not do to say so again, of course. Instead, she took the now empty tin mug from her aunt's hand and walked across to the fire, saying cheerfully as she did so:

'I'll make you another cup of tea, Aunt, and a jam butty if you'd like one. Then I'll do the washing-up and have a quick tidy round before I do the spuds for tomorrow night and lay the table for breakfast.'

'Oh, here's a change of face,' her aunt said dolefully. 'I've only got to mention a children's home and you decide to give me a hand. Well, it won't wash, young Dot; it's too little, too late, as they say. I've 'ad to lay the table meself and wash up the crocks for weeks, so you needn't think you can get round me by doin' a few little jobs. Still, I don't mind another cup o' tea.'

Dot was open-mouthed at the unfairness of this criticism. True, she had been steering clear of the house whenever she could but she still did a great many chores for her aunt, which was more than could be said for her cousins. When they 'forgot' to bring in water, it was Dot who lurched to and fro across the yard with the well-filled buckets. When they did not feel like chopping orange boxes for kindling, it was Dot who wielded the axe. When her aunt saw a sack of potatoes being sold off cheap, at the far end of Heyworth Street, it was Dot who humped it home, having to stop to rest every few yards and arriving at the court feeling more dead than alive. Why, once, when her aunt had bought a stone of wet and slippery plaice from the Charlotte Street fish market and had sent Lionel to help Dot carry it home, he had run off with friends when they were halfway along Shaw

Street, leaving Dot to wrestle with a wet and dripping – and still horribly wriggling – sack the rest of the way to Lavender Court. Fortunately, she remembered being told that pregnant women were often naggy and ill-tempered until they grew used to the idea of another child, so she spoke gently, pointing out that she usually did more than her fair share of the chores, as she handed her aunt the mug of well-sweetened tea. But it seemed Aunt Myrtle's mind was too full of her own grievances to listen to reason.

'Oh aye, you done your share from time to time, but not lately; lately, you've been off after your own pleasure from dawn till dusk,' her aunt said accusingly. 'An' that's always the way of it; you'll help while it suits you, then you'll sag off wi' your own pals and leave me, what's treated you like a daughter, to rot.'

Dot sighed but made no rejoinder. It was clearly useless to expect any sort of fairness when her aunt was in this mood. Better to leave the whole subject and hope that, as her time grew near, her aunt would realise the usefulness of a girl in a house full of boys and babies. She began to wash up the crocks, dried them on a thin tea towel and put them away. Then she peeled a mound of potatoes, slopped water over them from the nearest bucket, and began to lay the table for the next day's breakfast. She was now so hungry that her stomach rumblings almost drowned out the sound of her aunt's querulous voice, and presently Aunt Myrtle lumbered to her feet, announcing peevishly that she was off to bed. 'You can mek up the sofa any time you like, and get between the blankets,' she told her niece as she left the room. 'The fellers won't be in for a while yet.'

Sighing, Dot did all the chores still left, which included filling the buckets and damping down the fire, then got her blanket from the bottom of the dresser and prepared herself for bed. It was not until she had snuggled down that she remembered she had promised Corky and Emma that she would try to think of a plan to outwit the thieves. The trouble was, her own difficulties now loomed so large that robbery and murder, for the moment at least, took second place. But this would not do, Dot told herself. She tried to make herself concentrate, to think whom they could safely confide in. There must be someone who could tell them how to set a trap for the thieves which would not end in the exposure of herself, Corky and Emma as the people who had interfered in the doings of a well-known local figure – for Archie Rathbone was very well known, if not well liked.

But Dot's mind simply refused to do as she asked it and soon she fell asleep, to dream of children's homes, and other institutions, all night long.

Chapter Seven

Corky woke at sunrise, because a ray of light had fallen directly on to his face through one of the small broken windows of the hut. He sat up, rubbed his head and eyes vigorously, then reached for one of the withered apples he had nicked from a stall in St John's market the previous day. He had salved his conscience by telling himself that since the fruit had been dropped and rolled under the stall, it was unlikely that anyone would have bought it, and now he took a big bite out of the apple and got to his feet to peer out of the window at the day. The sky was blue, without a cloud in sight, and the sunshine fell warmly on his face. Because the weather had been good for days, he had slept in his underpants and now he dressed himself as he ate, and considered the day ahead. He and Dot were not meeting until five in the afternoon and then they were going round to Emma's flat, where they would discuss their plans. Corky had had several ideas which had seemed brilliant at the time, but now he was not too sure. He quite realised that he and the two girls might be disbelieved because Mr Rathbone was a grown man with considerable influence. Still, they did have the necklace, which was proof, of a sort, that Dot really had been hiding in the butcher's bin, and really had heard the two men discussing what they had done. The trouble was, neither Dot, Corky himself, nor Emma knew anything about the second man, apart from the fact that his name was Ollie. Dot had said that she thought she had seen him but Corky was doubtful about this. After all, all she had seen was a man turning into a back alley, and he might merely have been using it as a short cut to another street; the man into whose face Dot had stared was probably completely innocent, but even if he were not he could be anyone – a solicitor, a judge, even a headmaster. Corky thought that they should do everything in their power to discover his identity before they made a move, and this was what he intended to tell Emma and Dot when they met that evening. Since it was the school holidays, he and Dot were free to hang about in the vicinity of the butcher's shop without arousing suspicion, provided they were careful. He thought it unlikely that Ollie would visit the shop during trading hours, but in the evening, particularly after dusk, he might either go to the shop or arrange a mutually convenient meeting place where he and Mr Rathbone could discuss their affairs. Corky thought it would be easy enough to shadow Mr Rathbone, and once they knew the identity of his partner in crime they should be able to decide what best to do.

So when Corky was dressed and had eaten his

breakfast of bread and apples, he set out to make himself familiar with the butcher's shop and its vicinity. He would take a jolly good look at Archie Rathbone and his premises, spy out any good hiding places from which the shop could be constantly watched, and then see if he could find someone willing to share a newspaper round or let him run errands for them, so that he could earn some money.

Corky crossed the churchyard and slid over the wall at a point where overhanging branches obscured the bit of pavement on which he landed. Then he set off into the morning.

By the time Corky met up with Dot, he had a good deal to tell her. He had done as he intended and had 'cased the joint' beforehand, familiarising himself with the butcher's ugly face and figure so that he was now confident of recognising the man anywhere, as much by his ponderous gait as by his broad-lipped, beady-eyed face. Most of all, though, he was eager to tell Dot of an incident which had occurred earlier in the afternoon. They had met halfway along Heyworth Street, outside a confectioner's shop, and Corky had hurried into speech at once.

'Dot, something's happened, something not too good. I came back to the churchyard with a lump of bread and cheese a woman give me in one of the pubs. I got in over the wall, like we always does, and I were crossing towards the shed when something made me turn round, a – a feeling, sort of. And there was this little kid . . .'

Dot grinned. 'That'll be Sadie O'Brien; was she wearing a pink dress with a matching hair ribbon, and did she talk kind of posh?'

Corky grinned back, considerably relieved. 'Yes, she talked very posh, and her hair ribbon did match her dress, only it were blue . . . well, blue and white. And she had a little gardening set – real neat it was – and she'd dug quite a deep hole in one of the graves near the wall. She said she were looking for buried treasure and was certain she would find some because she had met a girl in here the other day who'd been searching for something, though she didn't know what.'

Dot groaned and dropped her head into her hands for a moment. 'Kids! Now whatever gave her the idea I was searching for anything? Come to think of it, I did try to stop her rooting around in the earth because then, of course, the necklace was actually buried there . . . where she was play-ing, I mean. Which grave was she digging in, do you know?'

Corky looked dubious. 'It were a baby's grave, a little tiny one. She explained that she had meant to plant flowers, only when she started to dig she found there was quite a deep hole, with straw and stuff in the bottom of it, and that made her sure something had been hidden there. She showed me the "straw and stuff" and it was dried grass really, but sort of curved round so that it did look like a bit of a nest. *Was* that where you buried the neck-lace, Dot?'

Dot groaned again and nodded, guiltily. 'Yes, it was – well, you saw me digging it out the first night we met, and I suppose you scared me so much that I completely forgot to take out the nest of grass I'd made for it.' She looked anxiously into Corky's face. 'You didn't let on you was living in the shed, did you? She's a nice little kid, but if you told her anything, anything at all, she might easily pass it on, even if only to her nanny. Oh lor, I s'pose she might have followed you. If she did, the fat's well and truly in the fire and you'll have to find somewhere else to kip down of a night.'

But Corky was shaking his head. 'It's all right, Dotty, don't get in a two and eight! She's only small; she couldn't possibly push her way through all them nettles and brambles and that in order to reach the shed. I asked her how she got in and she showed me.' He chuckled. 'She's so little and thin that she can squeeze through the side of them old iron railings by the gates, and the only places she can visit in the churchyard are the graves near the wall. Does she ever stop talking, do you suppose?'

Dot laughed with him. 'I doubt it; she's a gabby little blighter but a nice enough kid,' she said. 'Well, I don't think you need worry about young Sadie, not so long as you don't meet her too often so she gets suspicious. Anything else to report?'

'Not exactly, though I've spent all the afternoon

getting to know old Rathbone and his shop, and the area round it. I went into the shop pretending I were looking for a delivery job – cripes, he's a nasty blighter, ain't he? I'd barely got the words out before he started shouting at me, telling me if he needed a delivery boy he'd bleedin' well put a notice in the window. I got out of there real fast before he could get round the counter, because the last thing I wanted was a clip round the ear. Besides, though I need to be able to recognise him, I don't want him to go recognising me, do I?'

'No, I suppose you don't,' Dot agreed. 'But why is it important that he shouldn't recognise you?'

'Well, I wasn't going to tell you until I could tell Emma at the same time, but the fact is, I think we ought to watch old Rathbone night and day, so that we can identify for certain the man you call Ollie. Once we know who he is, we'll know whether it's safe to inform on them, if you see what I mean.'

'I'm not sure that I do,' Dot said thoughtfully, after a longish pause. 'Why should it be safer to tell on him once we know who he is?'

'Oh, Dot, do use your head,' Corky begged. 'If your Ollie is someone really important, someone like a judge, or a headmaster or a solicitor, then it would be our word against his, and what chance would we have?'

'I know what you're saying, but surely no judge or solicitor, or even headmaster, would be friends with old Rathbone, let alone join him in a jewel robbery,' Dot pointed out. 'Still, I see what you mean. And now let's get round to Emma's place so we can pool all our ideas properly.'

They arrived at the back door of the jeweller's shop dead on six o'clock – they actually heard a nearby clock chime – and rang the bell. Emma answered it so quickly that they guessed she must have been already in the stockroom. She ushered them up the stairs, saying as she did so: 'I came up earlier and got us some tea. It's all laid out on the kitchen table so we can eat as we talk. Do you both like veal and ham pie?'

The children assured her that they did and Corky's eyes gleamed when Emma led them into the kitchen. The table must have groaned beneath the weight of food for, in addition to a very large wedge of veal and ham pie, there was a plate covered in thick slices of ham, a big bowl full of ripe tomatoes, and another of boiled new potatoes, as well as a dish of bread and butter and various smaller platters with such things as radishes, cress and spring onions arrayed upon them. In addition to all this bounty, there was a trifle, an apple pie and a jug of custard standing on the dresser, as well as a tall, green glass jug full of what looked like lemonade.

The youngsters stared at this feast and needed no encouragement to sit down and begin to help themselves. Emma poured the lemonade, then took a seat. She put some ham, a couple of potatoes and a large tomato on her plate but did not start eating at once. Instead, she looked questioningly from one guest to the other. 'Well? Any ideas?' Corky began to answer her, but since his mouth was full of potato and pie the result was less like speech than gurgling. Emma laughed. 'It's all right. Eat first and talk later had better be our motto. I've done my best to think up some scheme which would implicate the thieves, but the more I think of it, the more I realise that we can only point the finger at Archie Rathbone; I mean, it was his yard that you were hiding in, wasn't it, Dot? And the truth is, when it comes right down to it, I'm keener to have my grandfather's murderer caught than I am to see Archie Rathbone punished. You know what they say: once a man has committed the ultimate sin of murder, he'll kill again and again, because the penalty's the same – you can't hang a man more than once.'

Corky stared at her, ceasing to chew for a moment. What she said was true yet somehow it was almost shocking. The man Ollie had killed once and, if Dot was right, had made a spirited attempt to push her under a train. In a way, Ollie had nothing to lose. If he discovered that they meant to spill the beans, then he might very well make a clean sweep and kill Emma, Corky himself and little Dot as well. Now that he came to think of it, it wouldn't be that difficult; Ollie could take his time, pick them off one by one . . . They simply must discover the second man's identity before he could realise what they knew.

'Corky? You look rather grim. What are you

thinking about?' Emma's voice broke into his thoughts.

Corky put down his knife and fork. 'It was what you said,' he told her. 'I was telling Dot we ought to watch the butcher day and night until we discover just who this Ollie is. I know Dot thinks she saw him when she ran out of the back alley, but I'm not so sure, and if the man's a murderer, then he's far more of a danger than the butcher and, as you say, he'll lose nothing if he kills again. I think, Emma, once we know who he is, you ought to go to someone real high up in the police department, show them the necklace and explain how you've got hold of it. They'll believe you where they might not believe Dot or myself.'

'Yes, I think you're right,' Emma said, after a few moments of deep thought. 'Look, when we've finished our meal, you two can have a game of cards or something whilst I nip down and check that everything is as it should be in the shop. Then I'll wash up the crocks and tidy things away up here – I'll pack up the rest of the food so you can take it back to your hideout, Corky – and go and change into something a bit less conspicuous than my working suit and we'll make for wherever you've hidden the necklace. It should be getting dark by then, but I still think we'd best leave here one at a time, rather than in a group. Where shall we meet up?'

'Outside Lime Street Station,' Dot said promptly. 'There'll be a heap of folk around, there always are. And even then, we needn't actually walk with you, Emma, just in case someone's watching. Me and Corky will kind of stroll along together, because no one notices kids, and you can follow us. And we'll wash up whilst you go down to the shop, as a sort of thank you for the best tea we've ever been give,' she finished.

Emma smiled at her. 'Thanks, Dot,' she said. 'I suppose you've not had any bright ideas? I'm afraid I've not come up with anything constructive, but watching Rathbone's shop is a real brain-wave. We'll do it in shifts; you two will have to do daytime because I'm working, but I'll do evenings and some of the night as well.'

Corky looked at her doubtfully. She was wearing a grey pin-striped suit and a dazzlingly white blouse, and her feet were clad in black patent leather court shoes. He was thinking that she would stand out like a sore thumb when Dot reminded them both that, in fact, Corky was best placed to watch the shop after it grew dusk. 'The two of us will manage just fine,' she said tactfully. 'Ladies like you don't hang around Heyworth Street much and we'll be all right, honest to God we will.'

Emma laughed and pinched Dot's cheek. 'We'll discuss it later,' she said. 'I shan't be very long,' and she disappeared in the direction of the stairs.

Dot and Corky cleared the table and washed up, and Dot was tremendously impressed by the many conveniences of the small flat. There was a neat little gas heater over the sink, which provided hot water for washing up, and a tap which brought cold water so that Emma never had to fill buckets. Next door to the kitchen, there was a proper bathroom – a thing Dot had only heard about. Here was a white enamel bath with another heater over it and two big brass taps. There was a wash basin and a lavatory with a cistern above it and a long chain with a pear-shaped pull on the end. She called Corky through to admire the amenities but he was inclined to laugh at her. 'A big institution like a children's home has to have running water and flush WCs,' he said authoritatively. 'As for baths, you couldn't have kids carting hot water to fill a tub this size, so it's got to be laid on. Haven't you never been to the public baths?'

'No, but I've heard about them,' Dot said yearningly. 'Folks say they're grand, but a bath costs a lot so kids don't get took there. Don't I just wish I could have a bath right now!'

They heard Emma coming up the stairs and rejoined her in the kitchen. They had put away all the crocks and cutlery so the room presented a very tidy appearance. Emma glanced round, then dived into a sideboard and brought out a pile of comic papers and magazines. 'Read these while I change into something dark,' she said, and disappeared towards her bedroom.

She was gone rather longer than either Dot or Corky expected, and when the kitchen door opened at last Dot, who was facing it, gave a squawk. A young man stood before her. He was wearing a large cloth cap, pulled well down over his brows, a navy blue shirt, a dark brown jacket and black trousers. He wore wellington boots and a rather self-conscious grin and when he spoke Dot knew him at once – or her, rather, for it was Emma.

'My grandfather was a keen birdwatcher and fisherman,' Emma said, half apologetically. 'These are his fishing clothes. I think they'll do, don't you?'

'They's – they's grand; you gave me a right turn. I didn't know it were you until you spoke,' Dot said honestly. 'No one will ever recognise you in that lot, Emma. I bet you didn't, did you, Corky?'

'No, I never,' admitted Corky. 'Why, you've even dirtied your face and hands! But – but where's all your hair gone? I s'pose you've had to cut it off?'

Emma laughed and pulled off the cap, bending her head to show them how she had pinned her long, shining curls up into a knob on top of her head. 'So now do you see how I can help out with night shifts?' she asked. 'There's always young men going to or from boys' clubs or pubs. Will I pass muster?'

The youngsters agreed that she most certainly would, and presently they set off. Corky went first and Dot followed a few minutes later, but speedily caught up with her friend. She told him that she, too, wanted to dress like a boy when watching the butcher's shop and thought she might acquire the clothes from one of her cousins, provided they did not realise she had borrowed their things.

Corky said he could well imagine that his friend would feel a good deal safer in such a disguise but voiced the objection that her cousins would most certainly miss their clothing. Dot was inclined to argue, but when Corky pointed it out she could see that a disguise might well bring more trouble than it saved. If she returned from watching Rathbone's shop late at night and walked into the kitchen to find Uncle Rupert or her aunt within, she could always say she had nipped out to the privy. But if she were wearing her cousins' clothes . . . she shuddered at the thought. There would be a frightful row, she would be accused of theft . . . and then, the questions would start. She had tried to forget that her uncle and Butcher Rathbone were now friends, or at least drinking companions, but she must not put it out of her mind altogether. Uncle Rupert would only have to mention that his niece had returned home late at night, wearing his son's old shirt and kecks, and Archie Rathbone would begin to wonder.

So she agreed with Corky that the idea would have to be shelved for the time, at least, and at this point they slid under the drooping branches of the yew tree which overhung the pavement by the church wall, and Emma joined them. Dot and Corky, familiar with the wall, told Emma where to put her feet and watched, admiringly, as the girl climbed, neat as a cat, up the wall and dropped to the ground. They followed her immediately, and all three stood quite still for a moment, carefully quartering the churchyard with their eyes, though this was not easy because the moon was at the full and a breeze had sprung up, so that there seemed to be moving shadows everywhere. Dot saw a rat sitting on a tombstone, combing his whiskers, and the dark shape of a large bird perched on an over-hanging branch, and nudged Corky. 'It's all right,' she whispered. 'As soon as we move out of the shelter of the trees, that rat'll be off. I don't reckon there's anyone here but us. Unless someone's hiding in the church itself . . . and they ain't likely to do that 'cos of the state it's in. C'mon.'

With Corky leading, the three of them made their way round the churchyard and then across to the church itself. Dot envied Emma her long trousers when she was stung by a spiteful nettle, but soon enough they were within the walls of the church. At a nod from Corky, Dot carefully lifted the curtain of ivy and watched as Corky levered out the triangular piece of stone behind which they had hidden the necklace. 'Good hiding place, eh?' he whispered to Emma, handing the triangular stone to Dot and pushing his hand into the cavity. 'Hey, I can't feel . . . anyone got a torch? I must have pushed it further back than I thought.'

Dot was beginning to say that she had no torch when a small beam of light illuminated the wall. Emma said in a low voice: 'I brought one, just in case. Corky, if you'd get your hand out of the way . . .'

Corky obediently withdrew his hand and they all stared into the hole which he had opened up with such confidence; then the three of them straightened up and stood back, staring unbelievingly at the cavity. The necklace had gone.

'It's got to be there; no one else could possibly have taken it,' Corky said wildly. 'Dot, your hands are smaller than mine, you'll be able to feel right to the back. It simply *must* be there.'

Dot pushed her hand right into the gap but could feel nothing but smooth stone. She gazed up at Emma in the semi-darkness, seeing only the pale oval of her new friend's face, unable to guess what she was thinking. Emma was their friend and ally, and both Dot and Corky had realised that it was essential to convince her that their story was true. Now, the only proof they had was gone.

The three of them stared around the ruined church as though expecting to see whoever had stolen the necklace grinning at them, but all they saw were the ruined ivy-clad walls rearing towards the starlit sky, and the pointed arches of the empty windows. After a moment, Corky said loudly: 'I bet it were that bloody little kid! She's always poking around, pushing her nose in where it ain't wanted. I reckon she took it.'

But Dot shook her head. 'I doubt if she could even reach the hole, and anyway, we hid it at night, and she's only five. She would have been tucked

213

up in bed long since.' She turned to Emma. 'Oh, Emma, we did hide it there, honest to God we did. I never said nothing to Corky, but when we were hiding it I – I kept getting the feeling that someone was watching us. I thought it were imagination – or the owl what lives in the high bit of wall at the far end of the church – but perhaps we really were being watched, and whoever was watching came and took it – the necklace I mean – as soon as we'd left. You *must* believe us, Emma.'

Emma began to speak but Corky cut across her. 'It were imagination, you little idiot,' he said scornfully. 'I felt exactly the same and who wouldn't? We were hiding away stolen property what could have a man sent to the gallows. And it's a pretty creepy place, a ruined church at night. No, I reckon that kid followed the trail of trodden grasses over to the church. She could pile the fallen stones up, I suppose, to make her tall enough . . .' As he spoke, he took the triangle of stone and pushed it back into the cavity, then withdrew it again and peered inside once more as though he was expecting the necklace to reappear, Dot thought, with an inward grin.

She was about to say so, when Emma gave an exclamation. 'Don't worry, Dot, of course I believe you. I know what happened,' she said excitedly. 'It came to me when I saw Corky pushing the stone back into place. Didn't it occur to either of you that it fitted far too snugly? I mean, the emerald necklace is pretty substantial, it takes up quite a lot of room. I think that you put the necklace safely away, and when Corky pushed the piece of stone back it must have hit the necklace and pushed it even further into the wall. Dot, I know you've had a good feel around already, but you were feeling for the necklace, not for a little hole. Can you put your hand in again, queen, and see if there's some sort of gap at the back?'

This time, it was the work of an instant for Dot to thrust her hand into the crevice and to withdraw it again, nodding vigorously as she did so. 'There's a gap all right; it's only a couple of inches long and not even an inch high, I shouldn't think, but it's quite big enough for the necklace to have slithered through. Oh, thank the Lord! I couldn't help thinking that those men might have seen us, might have got the necklace back . . . and might be planning to kill us off so's we couldn't gab to the scuffers. Phew, wharra relief!'

Emma smiled at her, a flash of white teeth in the darkness, but Corky gave a moan of despair. 'Oh, but you haven't thought, Dot,' he said. 'We need that necklace, you know we do, and if Emma's right, we'll have to pull the perishin' wall down to get it back. It 'ud be dead dangerous because we'd likely bring the whole building on our heads if we started dismantling this wall.'

'Yes, you're right,' Dot said, much crestfallen. 'Still, at least we know where the necklace is, and if we can't get it, no one else can.' She turned to the older girl. 'What do you think we should do now, Emma?'

'I think we should all go home and get what sleep we can,' Emma said decidedly. 'There will be a simple way to get the necklace back, I'm sure of it, but standing shivering in a ruined church isn't going to bring ideas flocking, exactly. For instance, we could try hooking it out with a bit of bent wire, or – or something of that nature. But for now we'll have to concentrate on other things, such as working out who Rathbone's partner in crime can be – this chap we know only as Ollie. And watching Rathbone is one thing we meant to do anyway, necklace or no necklace, so we might as well get on with it. It would have been nice to have had definite proof in our hands, but remember, we've still got definite proof, we just can't reach it at the moment.'

'We don't know for certain that it hasn't been stolen, though,' Dot was beginning, but Emma took her hand and began to lead her out of the church, saying as she did so: 'Yes, dear little Dot, we do know for certain. Don't you understand? Corky pushed that piece of stone back into place, level with the rest of the wall; if there had been *anything* behind it, he wouldn't have been able to get the stone flush with the wall again, d'you see?'

Dot heaved a deep sigh of sheer, blissful relief. Emma was undoubtedly right. 'Oh, Emma, you are so clever,' she said joyfully. 'Why, if someone *was* watching – and I'm sure now that nobody was – they could only have done what we've just done – pulled the stone and found nothing behind it.

They would assume we'd taken the necklace away with us . . . and come to think of it, it was dark, so they wouldn't even have known what we were trying to hide.'

'And since there weren't anyone watching, all we've got to worry about is how we're going to fetch the necklace out when we need it,' Corky put in. 'Look, my shed is just round the corner and I'm dead tired; will you two girls get home safe if I leave you here?'

Dot and Emma assured him that they would be fine and set off for the wall. Dot found herself almost relieved to be back on the pavement once more for it was so late that no one was about, and she had realised, when Corky had spoken, that she was very tired indeed.

The two of them set off along the street. 'D'you want me to see you home?' Emma asked. 'I don't think anyone will interfere with you whilst we're together, but my way is probably quite different from yours.'

Dot decided that she would be better by herself, in fact, though she thanked Emma for her thoughtfulness. 'I keep in the shadow of the walls and dodge about a bit,' she explained. 'No, you go off, Emma, and we'll come round to your shop at six tomorrow evening, same as tonight.'

Emma turned away with a quiet word of farewell, then turned back. 'I know where Corky lives now,' she said, 'but what's your address, queen? Only I might need to get in touch with you urgently.'

'I live at six, Lavender Court, which is just off Heyworth Street,' Dot told her, 'only I ain't often at home. Still, once we get this rota worked out, you'll find me hoverin' outside Rathbone's most of the day, I expect.'

Emma nodded. 'I won't come round unless there's an emergency,' she promised. 'See you tomorrow evening, around six.'

Emma found her walk home through the dark streets by no means as trouble-free as she had expected. There were several drunks about, and since she had no desire for a confrontation she spent some while dodging in and out of alleys and keeping clear of any doorway in which a man – or sometimes a young couple – seemed to have taken up residence. At first, the street lighting was poor, but the nearer she got to the city centre the better it grew, which was a comfort. There were more people about as well, and she felt a good deal less conspicuous. Folk were hurrying away from cinemas and theatres and towards the many public houses whose welcoming lights streamed across the pavement on almost every corner.

Church Street, when she reached it, was not busy at all and she walked along it slowly, pretending to look in windows as she passed. She reached her own shop, went to hook out the keys from her pocket, and remembered that she had only brought the back door key. Drat, she thought crossly, and lingered in the doorway for a moment, wishing she had had the forethought to detach the front door key from the bunch before deciding it was too heavy to cart around all evening. But since she had not done so, she had no alternative but to retrace her steps and go down the jigger which led to the back of the shop. This, naturally, was unlit by gaslights, and after the brilliance of Church Street it looked very dark indeed; so dark that she hesitated before turning down it. Then she scolded herself. There could be nothing to fear, and unless she wanted to sleep on the pavement she had to go down it to reach her own little yard. Once inside, she would go up to the flat, make herself a hot drink, and go straight to bed.

Slightly reassured at the thought of such a peaceful end to what had been a rather exciting evening, she went softly along the jigger, checking the gates until she came to the one she knew to be her own. She opened it quietly, crossed the yard, fished out the key to the stockroom door and began to try to fumble it into the lock, but even as she did so, she heard the gate behind her creak. She turned round, thinking that she could not have latched it properly, and saw a dark figure coming towards her. She gave a squeak and tried harder to unlock the door, but even as the key turned the figure leapt upon her, bearing her to the ground, and a voice in her ear said: 'You nasty, thievin' little tyke! What d'you think you're doin', sneakin' around here in the dark? Breaking and entering can put you in prison for years, let me tell you.

And don't think I'll not inform the police, because that's exactly what I shall do.'

'Get off me,' Emma said, her voice rising. 'This is my own property and – and you're trespassing. How dare you attack me . . . I must be bruised all over. And as for informing the police, that's just what I shall do the minute you let me go.'

'Ah, but I'm not going to let you go,' her attacker said grimly, hanging on. 'As for this being your property, pull the other one, it's got bells on! I happen to know the owner and you aren't . . .'

Emma gave a convulsive wriggle and kicked out; she had temporarily forgotten her disguise and was about to explain when her foot caught the door of the stockroom, which she must have unlocked without realising it, and it swung inwards. The man gave a crow of triumph and hauled her over the threshold, then fumbled for the light switch. He turned it on and heaved Emma to her feet, saying breathlessly as he did so: 'The owner of this shop is a very pretty young lady, whom I happen to know very well indeed, and you are . . . you are . . .'

The words died in his throat. Emma had torn off the large ragged cap and was desperately struggling, one-handed, to unpin her hair. Her other arm was bent up her back in a most uncomfortable hold, but for a moment her attacker was so astonished that he did not release her and it was only when she hissed: 'See? How many thieves do you know with shoulder-length hair?' that he let her go.

The young man stepped back and she saw the colour creep up into his face, but he said stoutly: 'Miss Grieves! What the devil are you doing in that rig-out? I'm most awfully sorry, but you can't deny you were behaving very oddly. How was I expected to know . . . ?'

Emma, nursing her bruised wrist, glared at him. 'What business is it of yours if I decide to – to dress up as a man?' she asked. 'As for behaving in an odd manner, I was doing no such thing. And I recognise you, too. You're the interfering fellow who tried to ask questions about my customers the other day. Well, I wouldn't speak to you then and I don't see why I should speak to you now. You know I'm Miss Grieves, you know this is my property, so you can just take yourself off before I call the scuffers . . . the police, I mean.'

The young man grinned, ruefully, but made no attempt to leave the stockroom. 'Look, I'm most awfully sorry but you *were* behaving oddly,' he insisted. 'I'd been to the show at the Lyceum Theatre, and I was walking back along Church Street, meaning to go for a meal, when I saw this young fellow in your doorway, apparently trying to open the door. I knew it wasn't you . . . well, I thought it wasn't you . . . so naturally, when he went round the back, down that little alleyway, I followed him. Honestly, Miss Grieves, what else could I do? Your shop had been robbed and your grandfather killed, and, to be frank, I thought you'd suffered enough. That was why I tried to talk to you the other evening, only you wouldn't listen. So I thought, if I prevented another burglary, you might give me a chance to tell you what's been on my mind.'

Emma hesitated. He was right, of course: her behaviour must have looked very odd to anyone watching and he had plainly been doing his best to prevent her having to face an intruder. She remembered how rude she had been to him the first time they had met, not allowing him to explain who he was and what he wanted, so now she said, rather stiffly: 'I'm sorry, but so much has been happening . . . shall we start again? You tell me your name and occupation – I suppose you aren't a plain clothes policeman – and I'll listen to whatever you've got to say and maybe even answer some questions.'

'My name is Nick Randall and I'm a journalist on a national newspaper, the *News Chronicle*; what they call an investigative journalist, which means that I'm interested in the spate of burglaries which have taken place in the city over the past two years, though I happened upon the burglaries more or less by chance. I was writing a piece about delinquent boys and how they are used by criminals for their own ends. One of the boys is in prison for breaking and entering and, though he would give me no names, he did say that he had assisted in a number of burglaries by watching – for weeks, sometimes – to find out when premises were likely to be unattended, or acting as delivery boy and taking wax impressions of door keys, and so on. Only, when I tried to question the shopkeepers themselves, they seemed unwilling to tell me more than that they had been robbed. Then a little woman who owns a newsagent shop muttered that she wouldn't be robbed again, thank God, because she was paying the money, and I realised there must be a protection racket going on as well as the burglaries. They seemed to happen about one every six months, so one is due any time now. If I could discover who was next on the list and lie in wait for the thieves, I'd have the sort of story any reporter would give his eye teeth for.' He smiled very beguilingly at Emma. 'So though I'm not a policeman, I am on the side of law and order and want very much to help you and your fellow traders,' he ended.

Emma had been staring at him as he spoke and thought that she liked what she saw. He seemed straightforward and had not hesitated to give her his name, and that of his newspaper. 'Okay, Mr Randall, you're one of the good guys,' she said, rather wearily. 'Look, I'll tell you as much as I can, including why I'm dressed the way I am, but I think we should repair to my flat. I've got most awfully dirty, rolling about the yard, and you're looking a trifle dishevelled yourself, so you can wash in my kitchen sink and I'll do the same in the bathroom, and change back into my own clothes. Then we can talk properly, sitting on chairs facing each other and not with one of us wedging his foot against the other's door,' she finished, rather acidly.

The young man laughed. 'I'm sorry about that, but I was beginning to feel rather desperate,' he said, following her up the stairs. 'I wonder what happened to my trilby? I guess it must have fallen off when I, er, attacked you.'

'You can collect it as you leave,' Emma said grandly, ushering him along the short hallway and into the kitchen. 'I'll join you in here once I've cleaned up; could you put the kettle on so that we can have a hot drink?'

Having seen that Mr Randall was supplied with soap and towel, Emma left him and presently returned to the kitchen, feeling a good deal better in a blue cotton dress, with her hair thoroughly brushed and her face shining after a vigorous application of soap and water. Her guest was seated at the kitchen table but sprang to his feet as she entered the room. 'I've put the kettle on, Miss Grieves, and got down a couple of mugs, but I didn't like to go rooting in your pantry for a tea caddy, so I'm afraid you'll have to do the honours.'

'I shall make cocoa,' Emma said decidedly. 'I've no fresh milk left and I'm not keen on sweetened tea, but sweetened cocoa is fine.' She crossed to the pantry and came back into the room with a tin of Bournville cocoa in one hand and a tin of condensed milk in the other. She waved the cocoa at him. 'Is this all right for you? I find it easier to sleep after a cup of cocoa than if I've been drinking tea.'

She did not wait for a reply but made a paste of the cocoa powder in the two mugs which the young man had stood ready, added boiling water from the kettle, and poured in a generous helping of conny-onny. Then she pushed Mr Randall's drink across to him and sat down opposite, studying him once more across the rim of her mug. 'Well? Who's going to go first?'

'I think it had better be you, because everything I've learned has been from the newspaper files, which isn't the same as actually experiencing something,' Mr Randall said seriously. 'I've tried talking to the police but they seem to be a rather suspicious lot up here; at any rate, they weren't prepared to help me, and apart from the old lady in the newsagent's on Parker Street, none of the shopkeepers have told me much either. I don't believe the larger shops are paying protection money – most of them have increased their own security – but even so, the people I spoke to weren't particularly helpful. In fact, the only person who said he would keep in touch with me and do his best to pass on any interesting information was one of the coppers on the beat, and of course he may not even be on duty when the next robbery occurs. So since I've already told you most of what I know, I think it would be better if you started.'

'Yes, I can quite see that is sensible,' Emma said, and then found herself in a quandary. She could tell him as much as she knew herself about the burglary in her grandfather's shop, but that would be very little more than he had already read in the newspaper files. The rest of the information had all been gleaned through Dot and Corky and she knew that she could not possibly reveal anything about the youngsters until she had spoken to them. She trusted Nicholas Randall, was sure he was indeed the 'good guy' she had called him, but Dot and Corky might not agree. They might feel it was downright dangerous to tell a newspaper reporter anything – who knew what he might write in his column? – and if this proved to be so, then her hands would indeed be tied.

Whilst Emma wrestled with the problem, the silence had stretched, and when she told the reporter that most of what she had learned had been passed on to her by a couple of children he merely nodded impatiently. 'It doesn't matter; if you believed them, then I'm sure I shall too,' he said, clearly misunderstanding her reluctance to speak. 'After all, they aren't nearly as liable to lie as adults, you know.'

Emma sighed; this was going to be difficult. 'It isn't that, Mr Randall,' she said. 'The fact is, this really is rather a dangerous business and everything the kids told me was in the strictest confidence. They asked me to promise not to tell anyone else, not even the scuff— the police, I mean. So you see, I shall have to get their permission before I can pass on what they have told me.'

She thought she had outlined the situation rather neatly, but apparently Nicholas Randall did not agree. 'I don't see why you shouldn't tell me what you know, simply leaving out names and so on,' he said. 'And anyway, I'll promise not to say a word to anyone – swear on the Bible if you like – which ought to calm your fears. So go on, spill the beans.'

'I can't,' Emma wailed. 'All I can tell you is that the youngsters know the identity of one of the thieves and – and have proof of what happened on that night. Look, if you come into the shop tomorrow at one o'clock, when I take my lunch hour, I might have been able to get their permission to talk to you.'

Nicholas Randall stared at her through narrowed eyelids. 'You don't trust me,' he said aggressively. 'You're still angry because I attacked you just now. Look, give me their names and I'll go round to their homes and talk to them, then you won't have to be involved at all. I dare say I can persuade a couple of kids to tell me what they know, since they'll have no reason to dislike me.'

Emma could have screamed. She had no intention of telling Mr Randall the names of either Dot or Corky, nor did she mean to reveal Dot's address or Corky's whereabouts. What was more, she resented the implication that Mr Randall could solve the mystery – if mystery it was – without involving her. She felt he was trying to exclude her, no doubt assuming that a young woman would be more hindrance than help, and this made her absolutely furious. She was tempted to tell him that the entire crux of the matter lay in what a twelve-year-old girl had heard whilst hiding in a dustbin, but of course she could not do so. Instead, she said, icily: 'Please yourself, Mr Randall, but since I've no intention of telling you anything more until I've spoken to . . . my young friends, you can either do your own investigating, or come to the shop at one o'clock tomorrow.'

Mr Randall rose to his feet. 'And suppose I come and you've not managed to contact your "young friends", or say you've not managed to do so?' he asked suspiciously. 'What then, Miss High and Mighty Grieves?'

Emma was about to tell him to clear off and not bother her again when common sense came to her aid. They were both extremely tired and she supposed that she had handled the whole business pretty badly. She should have remembered from the start that she could tell Mr Randall nothing of importance until she had the permission of her fellow conspirators, so she could understand his frustration. Accordingly, she rose also, and put a hand gently on his arm. 'Look, Mr Randall, I'm really sorry, but if you were in my shoes, would you betray a confidence? I'm very sure you would not, and just because I'm a woman you shouldn't expect me to behave differently. And now that you've raised the matter, I've realised you may well be right; it may not be possible for me to contact the youngsters tomorrow morning. So shall we say that if you come round here at six o'clock tomorrow evening, we'll all be here, and the youngsters can decide for themselves if they're prepared to, er, spill the beans, as you put it. How does that suit you?'

The young man stared at her for a moment and she saw the anger gradually leave his dark eyes to be replaced by a rueful smile. 'Sorry, Miss Grieves; the fact is I'm fagged to death and driven almost mad by the lack of co-operation I've received from everyone I've questioned. I'll spend tomorrow having a good look at the city and relaxing, and then come back here at six o'clock. And do call me Nick, because if we're to be fellow investigators, then I mean to call you Emma, since Miss Grieves seems rather too formal for such a relationship,' he ended.

'Very well, Nick,' Emma said, glad that friendly relations appeared to have been resumed. She grinned at him. 'I'll have to come down to the stockroom with you so that I can lock up after you leave, so please don't assume this means I think you're going to run away with half my stock.'

Nicholas grinned back. 'It's all right, I've got over the hump and am in my usual sunny mood. And thanks, Emma, for being so understanding and not biting my head off.'

They reached the door and Emma unlocked it and held it open for him. She peered out into the yard and announced, with a smothered giggle, that she could see his trilby in the light which streamed out from the open doorway. 'But I'm afraid it must have got squashed flat as we rolled around,' she told him. 'I don't think it will ever be quite the same again. Good night, Mr Ra— I mean Nick; see you tomorrow evening.'

Nicholas Randall strode across the yard, only pausing to pick up his trilby which was, indeed, flat as a pancake. But trilbies are resilient and he punched it out, dusted it off, and told himself as he emerged into the jigger that it would be good as new after a good brushing. It was a pity he could not say the same of himself; it had taken him all his willpower not to limp as he crossed the yard, for he had cracked his knee on the cobbles when he had pounced on Emma and his elbow had come into sharp contact with the door jamb as the pair of them had lurched into the stock-room. He quite envied Emma who could, if she wished, have a nice hot bath before getting into a comfortable bed, for it was very different in his own case. When he had announced to the editor of the *News Chronicle* that he wanted to follow up a story in Liverpool, his boss had immediately said that they had a Liverpool stringer whose wife kept a lodging house in Virgil Street. He had written to the woman and received confirmation that she had a room which Mr Randall could use for the duration of his stay, so Nick had gone along there as soon as he arrived at Lime Street.

It wasn't a bad room but the Cartwrights were a rather unpleasant couple and Mrs Cartwright was an extremely poor cook. Lumpy porridge, burnt toast and tea so weak you could see the pattern on the bottom of the cup were served every morning for breakfast, and after one evening meal – a tiny piece of meat stewed to rags, unpeeled carrots and turnips, and potatoes so hard that he nearly broke his fork on one – Nicholas had decided to provide his own food. He bought a small white loaf, a pat of butter and some nice, ripe tomatoes, as well as a piece of strong cheese, and ate these in his room when he returned to it each evening. He knew this annoyed Mrs Cartwright, that she felt the implied criticism, but since the paper was paying for half board he felt she had no right to object. What Nick disliked most, however, was Mr Cartwright's blatant curiosity. The other man cross-questioned him as to his reason for being in Liverpool whenever they met and took umbrage when Nick told him as little as possible. Nick was pretty sure that the older man had not stopped at questions, either. His room had been searched and his small possessions turned over by prying and careless fingers, but since his door had no lock and he always kept his notebook upon his person, he said nothing to the Cartwrights about this invasion of his privacy. It annoyed him, of course it did, but he was newsman enough to realise that the stringer needed to be curious in order to do his own job. Despite his understanding, however, his dislike of the Cartwrights and their ménage grew. The bathroom, shared by two lodgers and the Cartwrights themselves, was seldom cleaned. There was stubble and shaving soap in the hand basin, several rings of dirt round the tub, and before one could release one's bath water it was necessary to hook out of the plughole the soapy wodge of matted hair which constantly blocked it.

When he arrived at his lodgings, he decided against a relaxing bath to soothe his bruises. There would be no hot water for a start, and anyway, he was too tired to go through the lengthy cleaning process which must take place before his ablutions. He would let himself in with his front door key, knowing that no matter how quietly he trod Mrs Cartwright would grumble that he had woken her when they met at breakfast, and Mr Cartwright would want to know what he had been doing out so late.

Nick's key grated in the lock despite his best efforts to turn it quietly; he thought, crossly, that Mrs Cartwright must tip a little water into the lock each day so that the rusty squeal of his key would always give him away. He entered the house, locking the door behind him and inhaling, distastefully, the nasty smell of cooked cabbage and fatty mutton which assailed his nostrils as soon as the door closed. He climbed the stairs, already aware that the second step from the top must be avoided since its creak was similar to the shriek of a hunting dinosaur. He reminded himself that he still had not greased the hinges of his bedroom door so when he opened it that, too, added its tinny squawk to the noise he had already made. He closed the door behind him and began to undress, throwing his clothes on to the straight-backed wooden chair, donning his pyjamas and climbing between the sheets. It was a hard bed and the pillows were lumpy, but Nick was so tired that he thought he could have slept on a clothes line. Oddly enough, however, sleep did not immediately come. Before his mind's eye floated the deliciously piquant face of Emma Grieves, and though his cracked knee and bruised elbow ached he imagined that he could still feel the soft and yielding tenderness of her body when he had rugby-tackled her and brought her crashing to the ground. Poor Emma had been the one underneath, so he could only guess, wincing, how she must be feeling now. He would buy her chocolates tomorrow and a big bunch of roses, though arnica and a mustard plaster might be more appropriate.

Smiling to himself, Nick slept at last, and dreamed of Emma, and of himself as a knight on a white horse who would rescue her from all her dragons.

Chapter Eight

Dot got back home without incident and was glad that the whole house was in darkness. She fished the key on its length of string up through the letter box and unlocked the door, letting herself into the silent house. The parlour door was tightly shut, but when she put her ear to it she could hear her uncle's tremendous snores and guessed that he was still celebrating the fact that he was about to become father to twins. It was a pity, because for several weeks he had returned to the house, if not sober as a judge, at least no more than a little merry, and neither Aunt Myrtle nor Dot had any objection to this. But if he was sleeping in the parlour – and snoring like a pneumatic drill – it must be because he had drunk a great deal and that was bad news for everyone, since drink cost money and drunks cost Aunt Myrtle her peace of mind. However, she went through to the kitchen without incident and found her sofa bed had been made up which was, she thought, Aunt Myrtle's way of apologising for the bad temper she had shown when she had told Dot about the twins. The fire had been banked down but the tin of cocoa stood on the table and there was still a cupful of hot water in the kettle, so she made herself a quick drink, then climbed on to the sofa and was soon fast asleep.

She was awoken next morning by the sound of her aunt riddling the fire and got out of bed at once to take the ash pan from her and to say she would empty it into the bin whilst her aunt made a cup of tea. Aunt Myrtle merely nodded, but when Dot returned to the house and slid the ash pan back into place, there were two cups of tea waiting on the table and her aunt smiled at her. 'You're norra bad girl, queen,' she said. 'I'm sorry I weren't too pleasant to you when I told you about the twins, but honest to God, Dot, I don't know how I'll manage.'

'I said I'd help,' Dot said, rather reproachfully, fetching the oats from the cupboard and starting to make the porridge. She decided it was time that she, too, apologised, because she knew very well she had been so wrapped up in the affair of the necklace that she had not helped Aunt Myrtle nearly as much as she usually did. 'And I did mean it, honest to God I did. I know I've been out an awful lot lately, but you know what it's like in the summer, Aunt Myrtle. Me and me pals have a game goin' ... I can't explain it exactly – it's sort of cops 'n' robbers – but I'll tell them today that I can't hang around with them like I've been doing.'

Aunt Myrtle, slicing bread, nodded briskly. 'Right; I've gorra list of messages as long as me arm, so you can start by doin' them. Then you can give me a hand in the house 'cos I means to try me hand at some proper cookin'.' She looked rather shyly across at her niece. 'When I were young, me mam never bought anything she could make herself – in the cookery line, I mean – and your mam was a dab hand at cakes and pies and so on. I've never bothered meself, but after I'd seen the doctor up at Brougham Terrace, he sent me along to see one of them interferin' social women. I were in a fair old state, knowing it were twins, like, but she sat me down an' gave me a cuppa tea and then she talked about money an' that. D'you know, queen, that I can make a great slab of fruit cake for a quarter the price they charge in the shops? And it ain't only cakes: puddens 'n' pies – even loaves of bread – are real cheap if you make 'em yourself. She went on a bit about baby clothes, said I could make them an' all, but I aren't goin' to do that, not wi' Paddy's market sellin' stuff so reasonable.'

Dot, stirring porridge, smiled at her aunt. She still had a vague memory of the little house in Copley Street and the delicious smells of cooking which wafted from the kitchen on her mother's baking days, but she felt obliged to point out that there was one large snag to her aunt's plans. 'Yes, I guess cooking pies and bread yourself is much cheaper and the pies and bread will be very much nicer,' she admitted. 'Me mam did all our baking, like you said, but she had an oven, Aunt Myrtle. I always thought she stopped cooking when we moved in with you because there was no oven.'

'Ah, but Deerings on the corner of Abbey and Heyworth Street only charges a few pence to bake any number of cakes 'n' pies,' her aunt said. 'Them social women have their uses; she told me almost all the bakers in the city will cook for you if you prepare the food, like. It's odd, ain't it, Dot? I've seen women – kids sometimes – leaving the court with half a dozen loaves on a baking tray, but it never occurred to me to do the same.' Again she glanced shyly at her niece. 'They – they give me recipes at Brougham Terrace, told me how to measure flour an' that wi'out a weighing machine, so I thought you an' me might have a go at some grub today. You can read the recipe out to me and do some mixing an' that and we'll see how we go on.'

'If we're going to bake, why don't you ask Li and Dick to do the messages, so we can get on with the cooking?' Dot asked craftily, thinking that this would halve the tasks her aunt wanted her to do, but the older woman shook her head and smiled rather grimly.

'No, that's no use, 'cos till we've got the flour an' that, we can't do no cookin' 'cos I've got nothin' to cook with,' she said. 'Besides, you know what the boys are like; once you let 'em out o' the house there's no knowin' when they'll deign to saunter back in again. It could be teatime, which wouldn't be much help, would it?'

Dot was beginning to agree when the kitchen

door opened and her uncle shambled into the room. He was red-eyed and grey-faced, and groaned as he slumped into a kitchen chair. Silently, Dot made him a mug of tea and handed it to him but he shuddered and pushed it away, saying in a hoarse voice that the smell of the tea made him want to puke. 'What I need is a hair of the dog,' he said huskily.

Dot looked baffled, but her aunt said resignedly: 'Awright, Rupe, but I'm warnin' you, if you start drinkin' heavy again, I'll be off, twins or no twins, and then you'll only have young Dot here to make your meals an' wash your clothes an' that.'

Her uncle gave a rude snort. 'If you ever try to leave me, Myrtle Brewster, I'll find you if you've gone to the ends of the earth an' I'll break both your bleedin' legs an' then your bleedin' neck,' he said aggressively. 'As for Dot, she won't be around. She'll be in a bleedin' orphanage where she belongs.'

'And then you'd have nobody but yourself to make your meals and wash your perishin' shirts,' Dot murmured, but she kept her voice so low that neither her aunt nor her uncle heard. Aloud, she said: 'Want some porridge, Uncle Rupe? Though I've heard it don't go too well with porter,' for her aunt was offering him a mug full of the dark, strong-smelling liquor from a bottle which she produced from one of the cupboards.

'I don't want no bleedin' porridge,' her uncle said. He reached for the dish which Dot had placed on the table and she waited for him to hurl it across the room, as was his custom when annoyed, but it seemed that her aunt's strictures must have included a ban on chucking food about because, though he picked up the plate of porridge, he banged it back on the table, snatched the mug of porter, and drained it. Then, without another word, he lurched to his feet and shambled out of the kitchen, grabbing his cap off the hook on the back door and cramming it down over his uncombed greasy hair as he did so.

With his departure the atmosphere in the kitchen eased and when, presently, the boys hurtled into the room, demanding breakfast, Aunt Myrtle served them porridge whilst Dot poured tea into their mugs as calmly as though Uncle Rupert's threats had never been made. After all, though Uncle Rupert might hate her, Aunt Myrtle knew her worth, knew she would have great difficulty managing without her. Dot realised that she was the cuckoo in the nest in some ways; she had been dumped on the Brewsters by her mother, overcrowding their small house and making things difficult. But she also knew that she really was useful and determined to be even more useful in the future since the thought of being sent to an orphanage truly dismayed her. So she bustled around the kitchen, telling herself that she must learn to cook, for this would make her truly indispensable.

Presently, her aunt handed her an ill-written list of messages. Dot ran an experienced eye down the list and saw that, though most of the shopping could be done on Heyworth Street, there were some things which were cheaper when bought at the stalls on the Scottie. She informed her aunt of this fact but so eager was Aunt Myrtle to try her hand at cooking that she said, airily, she would sooner Dot stuck to the Heyworth Street shops, even if it cost her a bit extra. 'After all, we'll be savin' a mint by bakin' for ourselves,' she said righteously. 'You go off, queen, an' get back as soon as you can.' She grinned at her niece. 'I got the extra money from your uncle last night when he were too bleedin' sozzled to know what he were givin' me. Ah well, it's in his own interests in the end, you might say.'

Dot agreed that this was true and hurried off, the big canvas marketing bag slung over one shoulder. She rushed round the shops buying everything on the list, though when she passed Rathbone's and looked about her for some sign of Corky she was disappointed. She racked her brains, but she was pretty sure she had not said she would do the morning shift today, and anyway, she thought it doubtful that the conspirators would meet when the butcher's shop was at its busiest.

She got home to find Aunt Myrtle had had to borrow a mixing bowl, a rolling pin and several baking tins from various neighbours, having realised, belatedly, that she could scarcely expect any baker to provide her with such things. She was all agog to start the work and Dot felt the same, so the two of them were soon peeling, chopping and slicing. The social lady had advised that they start with something simple yet appetising, and had suggested a meat and potato pie, which could be carried to the baker's for cooking, and an apple pudding which could be boiled up in a pan of water on their own kitchen fire.

The pudding was simmering over the flames and Dot was gingerly rolling out her very first attempt at pastry, when someone knocked on the front door. She raised flour-covered hands, glancing towards her aunt, who was sitting in the fireside chair, watching the bubbling pan as though she expected the pudding to take a flying leap out of the water, possibly shouting *Stop that! I'm supposed to simmer gently, not boil like a bleedin' turnip!* She thought her aunt might go to the door but this was clearly not the case, so she dusted the flour off her hands as best she could and set off rather grumpily down the hall.

When she opened it, however, she was glad she had done so, for Emma stood on the doorstep. She was looking extremely apprehensive, but the look cleared when she saw Dot. 'Oh, thank goodness,' she breathed. 'I wasn't sure I'd got the right number, though I remembered you'd said Lavender Court.'

Dot looked quickly over her shoulder. 'You were dead lucky to catch me in. I've been doing the messages all morning,' she informed her visitor.

'What would you have said if me aunt had come to the door? Still, that don't matter; what's up, Emma?'

'Something's happened which is really rather important. D'you remember I told you about—'

'Dot? Who's at the perishin' door? If it's someone sellin' something, tell 'em we don't want none an' get back here afore your pastry goes hard.'

'Shan't be a mo, Auntie,' Dot shouted. She turned back to Emma. 'Quick! Wharris it?'

'It's – it's a feller who wants to help us only we've got to talk first, before we make up our minds what to do,' Emma hissed. 'Can you come to the flat at a quarter to six? And can you get in touch with Corky, only I walked past Rathbone's and he wasn't there. I don't like to go to the church-yard in broad daylight, but I thought the pair of you were almost certain to meet before this evening, so—'

'Dot!' Aunt Myrtle's shout was accompanied by footsteps. Oh heck, she was coming to see for herself who was keeping her niece at the door for so long.

Dot said loudly: 'Yes, miss, thanks very much, I'll do me best,' and then closed the door firmly in Emma's astonished face and turned back to her aunt. 'It's all right, Aunt Myrtle; it were one of the shop ladies – I told you I'd been looking for work, didn't I? – saying she'd like me to do a delivery for her this evening. It's only the one, just to see whether I can manage, so I said I would; is that

242

all right? Only it means I'll have to leave here around five, so I'll probably miss me tea.'

'If we get this pie to the baker's, you can have a slice and a bit o' bread an' marge before you leave,' her aunt said grandly. 'What'll they pay you for deliverin'? Is it newspapers? They pays all right for deliverin' newspapers . . . oh, no, it can't be, not startin' that late in the evening.'

'No, it's – it's a dressmaker who wants stuff delivered when her customers are home from work,' Dot said, improvising wildly. 'I dunno what she pays yet – probably not much – but I said I'd have a go; I could do wi' some pocket money.'

'Aye, you're not the only one,' her aunt said, as they reached the kitchen once more. 'Now, gerron wi' that pastry so's I can line the tin an' tip the meat an' potatoes in.' She swiped at a large blue-bottle which was making passes at the cooked meat and potato, cooling in its pan. 'I suppose I'll have to buy some more fly papers; them I got last week is so thick with dead bodies that the live ones can't climb aboard, even if they wanted to.'

Despite Dot's best endeavours, it was after five o'clock before her aunt said she might go. The meat and potato pie had been delicious; Dot had received the promised slice and had praised it extravagantly before slipping out of the front door and making her way towards Rathbone's. She had hoped to find Corky there, but there was no sign of him and she was turning away and wondering whether she would have time to get to the ruined church and back to Emma's flat by a quarter to six when she heard her name called and turned to see Corky materialising, apparently out of thin air. He fell into step beside her, saying reproachfully: 'I thought you meant to come along and take a turn at the watching. I didn't bother to come this morning, but I arrived at one o'clock – he closes for his dinner – an' I've been there ever since. Fine one you are! Me belly thinks me throat's been cut an' me tongue's turned to leather 'cos I'm so thirsty, but I s'pose that's girls for you.'

Dot opened her mouth to protest, then changed her mind. It was the sort of thing boys always said without necessarily meaning it. 'I couldn't help it; me aunt's in the family way and it was her baking day. I couldn't get away till about five minutes ago and then I came straight here. Only where *were* you? Emma came round earlier – come to think, it must have been around one o'clock, because it was her dinner hour – and said she'd been up to Rathbone's looking for you. So I guess you weren't watching then, Mr Clever.'

'I were, but I were keepin' a lookout for you. I dare say a dozen smart young ladies like Emma might have walked past me, but I were lookin' for a red-headed scruff bag,' Corky said airily. 'As for where was I, you didn't think I were goin' to stand around on the pavement in full view of the shop, did you? From what you say old Rathbone's no fool; he'd soon start gettin' suspicious if I was there for an hour, let alone six.'

'Well, if you weren't on the pavement, where the devil were you?' Dot asked curiously. 'I didn't see you, but you saw me; how did you manage that?' She had decided to ignore the remark about a red-headed scruff bag; she would get her revenge for that later.

'If you look back, you'll see that there's a sort of tunnel down between two of the shops, a bit further away, and some empty dustbins standing beside it,' Corky informed her. 'You can see the shop from halfway down the tunnel, and of course you can see it really well if you're crouching amongst the dustbins. I was there for a bit, then when a queue formed outside the baker's I joined on the end of it, then I went an' played hopscotch at the end of the jigger with three girls. When you come by, I was talking to the newspaper boy who stands on the corner.'

'Oh,' Dot said, digesting this. 'Then if you've been going in an' out of shops, why didn't you buy yourself a bun an' a bottle of lemonade instead of blamin' me? Look, don't bother to answer that 'cos Emma came round to Lavender Court to ask us to be at the flat by a quarter to six. She couldn't tell me much – me aunt were hoverin' – but, apparently, she's found some feller she thinks might help . . .'

'Some feller!' Corky said scornfully. 'We don't want no feller interferin', we're in trouble enough as it is. I hopes she's not been an' gone an' told him anythin', because if she has . . .'

'Of *course* she hasn't. She promised,' Dot said indignantly. 'That's why she wants us to go round this evening, to discuss what she should do. She's nice is Emma, and she knows how dangerous it could be if old Rathbone or his mate found out we knew what they'd been up to. Us women aren't like men, you know, we don't jangle to all our mates just to show how big we are.'

Corky began an indignant denial then stopped short, grinning at Dot. 'Awright, awright, maybe I deserved that, you red-headed scruff bag,' he said genially. 'But let's get movin' or we shan't get to the flat by a quarter to six.'

As they walked, Dot told Corky her aunt's momentous news and how it would affect her. When she came to the bit about being sent to an orphanage, Corky whistled between his teeth. 'You don't want to end up in one of them,' he said positively. 'If I hadn't been in an orphanage, I'd have had a job, been independent, like. But they don't let you get work until you're at least sixteen when you're from an orphanage, because they say you haven't had no experience of ordinary life. And besides, you haven't got a real home with a mum and dad to see to your food and washing and that, so they have to find you a place in a YMCA or a hostel, and that ain't much fun, I'm tellin' you. So you stick to your aunt and uncle. Why, you'll be out and earnin' money in less than two years, and then you'll be able to pay them for your keep. So we'll have to arrange for you to do your watchin' of old Rathbone when your aunt and uncle don't need you.'

'Evenings will be best,' Dot said, very relieved that Corky could see the importance of keeping in with her aunt and uncle. 'That's when most of the work's finished for the day and me aunt can relax; me uncle's usually down the pub or off with his mates, or playin' pitch 'n' toss. Oh, an' I forgot to say, Uncle Rupe works for Rathbone sometimes, heaving carcasses and that kind of work. I don't know when he starts, or when he finishes for that matter. But he's usually out of the factory by four or five, so it'll be some time after that. Did you see him this evening?'

'I dunno who I saw, do I?' Corky said gloomily. 'What's he look like?'

'Well, he's got dark, greasy sort of hair and a nasty, mean face. He's quite tall and fairly thin, I suppose, only pretty strong-looking. Oh, I dunno, it's difficult to describe someone you hate so much because you only glance at him in passing.'

'It ain't a shop as many men use, it's mainly women,' Corky said thoughtfully, after a pause. 'I did notice one chap, though; does your uncle have a black moustache and rare bushy eyebrows?'

'No, of course he doesn't,' Dot said, giggling. 'I'm not completely mad, you know, Corky; if he'd had a black moustache, or even a grey one – or a snow-white one, for that matter – I think I'd have mentioned it. Never mind, I just thought I'd tell you that he works for old Rathbone now and then.'

'Right. Tell you what, Dot, if you were to come down in the early evening, you could point him out to me, only I don't really see that it matters. I mean, you don't think he was involved with the robberies, do you?'

Dot giggled again. 'It certainly wasn't him in the alley that night, and I reckon he's too stupid to be much help to anyone planning something they want kept secret. He might be all right when he was sober, but when he'd got a few drinks inside him he'd start boasting about what he'd done. Though, come to think of it, he hasn't been drinking the way he used to, except when Aunt Myrtle told him about the twins.'

'Right; then your uncle ain't important,' Corky said decidedly. 'And I'm bound to recognise him sooner or later because you say he does the heavy work in Rathbone's shop. And now tell me about this feller Emma thinks might help us. I'm sure you're right, and she hasn't told him anything yet, but for myself, I'd rather we tackled it alone.' Dot explained that Emma had not had a chance to tell her anything but the bare facts, not with Aunt Myrtle coming out into the hall to see what was keeping her niece from her work. She did say, however, that she was all in favour of getting another adult in to help.

Corky disagreed and a lively argument ensued. He was afraid that Emma might want to confide in someone who, unknown to her, was a pal of the butcher's, or might know the mysterious Ollie –

might even *be* the mysterious Ollie. 'So you see, we're best off trusting no one,' he said earnestly, as they turned into the jigger which led to the back of Mitchell & Grieves jeweller's shop. 'We really know so little about Rathbone and his pals, but we do know about this Chamber of Trade thing, and when folk get together like that they'll sometimes stand up for each other, even if they know it's wrong.'

'But we've got to trust *someone*,' Dot was saying worriedly, as they knocked on the stockroom door. 'It's not as if—'

Her words were cut off short as the door swung open, revealing Emma in a light green cotton dress, with white collar and cuffs, looking very spruce and cool. She smiled a greeting and led them up to the flat where she sat them down at the kitchen table, fetched glasses of lemonade and biscuits, then joined them. 'It's rather a long story, but I'll keep it as brief as I can because I want you to hear what happened before Mr Randall arrives,' Emma told them. 'It all began after our expedition to the churchyard. I walked home with no trouble but when I reached Church Street I forgot I'd only taken the back door key with me and went to the front of the shop . . .'

She had reached the point in her story where Mr Randall had told her that he was investigating the burglaries and would very much like her help when there was a loud ring of the bell. Emma jumped to her feet. 'Here he is now; don't forget, I've told him nothing and won't do so if you truly think he's unsafe. But remember, he's not a local man, so he can't possibly be in league with the thieves, and—' The bell sounded again and Emma waved a distracted hand at them and headed for the stairs.

'Hang on,' Corky called after her. 'We haven't decided what we're going to do yet and once he's seen us he'll know who we are and he could start following us around.'

'Don't be so silly,' Dot snapped. 'He doesn't know what we know or how we know it; if we don't trust him we'll just say we were in Church Street when the shop was robbed and saw two men running past. We can give him a false description, I suppose, if it makes you happier, but I think you're being real stupid, honest to God I do. We need help, you know we do; all we've done off our own bats is lose the perishin' necklace . . .'

She might have said more, but at this moment Emma pushed open the kitchen door and ushered a young man into the room. He was tall, with curly dark hair, very bright eyes and a determined chin. He grinned at them and Dot braced herself because he looked nice and she hated to think that Corky was going to refuse to co-operate. If they started off by telling the young man lies, giving him false names and pretending to know very little, then it would be almost impossible to retract and ask for his help if she and Emma outvoted Corky.

But the most extraordinary thing was happening. The young man had smiled at them both, but when his eyes met Corky's he looked puzzled for a moment, then exclaimed: 'Well, if it isn't the young feller-me-lad I last met at Redwood Grange! And what might you be doing here? I guess I advised you to get out of the orphanage as soon as you could, but I suppose I never thought you'd do it.' He turned to Emma. 'This young man and myself are well acquainted. I interviewed him, and a number of his pals, several months ago when I was writing an article for my newspaper.'

He grinned down at Corky and, to Dot's immense relief, Corky grinned back. 'Oh, mister, it's grand to see you, and Emma was right; you won't split on us. What did you say your name was?'

At this point, Emma introduced everyone and then they all took their places round the table. Corky was still marvelling over the strangeness, the coincidence, which had led himself and Nick Randall to choose the very same city and then to find themselves involved in the very same mystery. 'Not that you're involved in it yet,' he added, grinning at Nick. 'But I'm pretty sure you soon will be; what do you say, Emma? Dot?'

Emma looked round the table. 'Are we all in favour of asking Nick to help us?' she asked the two youngsters. 'If either of you disagree, then the meeting must break up here and now. Otherwise, I think we should start by telling Nick the whole story. Those in favour?' She raised her own hand in the time-honoured fashion but Dot and Corky were ahead of her and Dot could not help thinking how fortunate it was that Corky had already met Nick. She was sure there would have been trouble otherwise.

'There you are, a unanimous decision,' Emma said gravely. 'Get out your notebook, Nick, because it's quite a complicated story and it will help if you write things down. Dot, you'd better start because it's more your story than anyone's.'

'Oh, oh, oh, but *where* shall I start?' Dot said wildly. Her mind was still playing with various schemes for recapturing the necklace – a piece of bent wire, a fishing hook, a magnet on a string – and she felt that the story should really start with the burglary itself which, of course, she had not witnessed. She began to say as much when Emma interrupted her. 'Nick knows about the burglary from the newspaper files,' she said firmly. 'But you're the only one who knows what you overheard, queen, so just tell your story as it happened. Begin at the very beginning when you hopped into that dustbin. Corky can take over once you get to the bit where you and he met in the churchyard.'

Dot opened her mouth to start but Corky butted in. 'But what about my story, Emma?' he asked plaintively. 'I bet Nick's real interested in how I landed up here. Gee, I had some adventures on the way, Nick. I fell in with a right crooked crowd – they were antique dealers, only they were thieves really – and they used me to deliver stuff and take messages . . . oh, all sorts—'

'Shut *up*, Corky,' Emma and Dot said in unison and Emma added firmly: 'I'm sure your adventures were very interesting, Corky, but they have absolutely nothing to do with the jewellery theft or my grandfather's death, so just you pipe down and let Dot tell Nick how this whole business started.'

'Well, I were playing relievio with me pals . . .'

Dot told her story quickly and well and finished at the point when she and Corky met in the church-yard, so Corky told the next bit, up to the moment when they had seen Emma crying in the shop and had gone in to ask if they could help. Then Emma told about the protection racket and how she had paid up without demur at first, believing that the weekly sum would save the shop from a second burglary. 'Only now I'm beginning to wonder whether Butcher Rathbone said *anything* that wasn't a lie,' she admitted. 'And he told me that the sum I would be asked to pay would not vary. Only, my grandfather specialised in very expensive hand-crafted jewellery – originals, you know – and of course he charged very high prices for such work. I mean to follow in his footsteps, but if I do so I'm afraid the protection people will realise what's happening and demand bigger payments.'

Nick nodded. 'Yes, of course they will,' he agreed. 'Extortion's like that; the victim gets in deeper and deeper. But if we sort out Rathbone and his pal, the burglaries will stop and so, of course, will the protection racket. It's a pity about the necklace but we'll get that back, never fear.

And I agree with young Corky here that the most important thing is to identify Rathbone's partner in crime.' He turned to Dot. 'You believe they've already made one attempt to shut your mouth for good, don't you?' he enquired gently. 'You think someone recognised you on the underground platform and tried to push you under the train. But don't you think that's a bit unlikely? You see, there were no attempts before and there have been none after that one incident, and I know from my own experiences on the London Underground that when a train comes into the station, people push forward.' He looked questioningly at Dot. 'Do you still believe it was an attempt on your life?'

Dot hesitated. 'I wasn't even sure at the time,' she admitted. 'Like you said, no one's tried anything since. Oh, one thing I didn't say when I was telling you my bit of the story was that Mr Rathbone and a pal of his brought me Uncle Rupert home one night when he were drunk as a fish. I were pretendin' to be asleep on the sofa – the sofa's me bed now that I'm too old to share with my cousins – and if the feller with him was the one I ran into when I shot out of the jigger that night, you'd have thought he might have recognised me because I expect my hair was sticking out from under the blanket and people do notice red hair.'

Nick laughed. 'It's been five months since that feller saw you running out of the alley, so I think you're safe enough from being recognised now,' he said. 'But we're not going to take any chances.

We'll keep an eye on the butcher's shop but, if you ask me, the two men won't meet whilst the shop is open for business. Is there a Mrs Rathbone?'

'I don't think so. To tell you the truth, I doesn't often go in there because Aunt Myrtle reckons she does better visiting old Rathbone herself. I told you my uncle helps there sometimes with the heavy work and ever since he started doing it, old Rathbone gives me aunt special prices, which he wouldn't do if it were a kid, 'cos he don't like kids.'

'Hmmm,' Nick said thoughtfully. 'So he doesn't really know you, then? As I said, there's not much point in watching the shop during the day, but evenings are different. Is there a way up to the flat apart from through the shop?'

Dot nodded eagerly. 'Yes, course there is. Old Rathbone were letting his pal out through the back door when I were in his dustbin. Oh, lumme, we've not thought of that. We ought to be watching the back of the shop after closing time, then, rather than the front?'

Nick nodded gloomily. 'Yes, but we really ought to be watching both,' he said. 'And time is definitely not on our side because I reckon they'll be planning another burglary any minute now. But first of all, from what you've told me, Corky, you have taken up residence in what sounds like a ruined potting shed; am I right?'

Corky nodded and Dot guessed that he was half ashamed and half proud of the home he had found for himself.

'Well, the first thing we must do is regularise the situation,' Nick said. 'Is that all right by you, young man?'

Corky grinned across the table at him. 'I dunno if it's all right or not, because I dunno what you mean,' he said frankly. 'If you want me to get in touch with Redwood Grange to let them know I'm okay, I done that weeks ago. Just a postcard, you know, sayin' I'd got a job and was lodging with friendly folk who were taking good care of me. I didn't know then, of course, that Wilfred Perkin was a fence as well as an antique dealer. Still, even if I'd known, I wouldn't have told them; working for a receiver of stolen goods ain't exactly the sort of thing that the staff at Redwood Grange would think suitable for one of their boys.'

'Wilfred Perkin . . . Wilfred Perkin . . .' Nick said thoughtfully. 'That name sounds familiar. Probably because he's been up in court when I've been sitting in on another criminal case. But no, I wasn't going to suggest that you got in touch with the orphanage. How old are you, Corky? Fourteen? Fifteen?'

'I were fourteen in June,' Corky said, secretly gratified to be taken for older than he was. He had heard a great many visitors to the orphanage say that the Redwood Grange boys were young for their age. He had also heard such visitors remarking that the orphans were underfed and that growing boys needed three good meals a day and not just weak tea, bread and marge, and tiny helpings of stew. 'But what's that got to do with regular – regularising, eh, Nick?'

'Well, I'm in a fairly cheap lodging house, in a pretty horrid little room. There's a small boxroom into which the landlady has squeezed a bed. Since you're fourteen, I reckon you could easily get some sort of job which would help to pay whatever rent Mrs Cartwright charged. I'd see you were fed, and so on,' he added quickly, 'and living in the same house it would be a lot easier to arrange who would keep a watch on Rathbone's place. What do you think?'

Corky thought it was a very good idea. He had already realised that he could not stay in the ruined potting shed for very much longer because last night, when it had rained heavily, he and his possessions had got well and truly soaked. Fortunately, the morning had been sunny and he had hung his clothes and bedding on some of the bushes surrounding his hiding place, but he had felt uneasy; such a blatant display would make it obvious to anyone peering through the churchyard gates that someone, perhaps a tramp, was sleeping there. He felt it was only a matter of time before he had to move on and Nick's proposal was a happy one. He had slept in a confined space whilst he was with Mrs Perkin, and had no objection to the arrangement Nick was suggesting; in fact he realised that having a proper address would make getting a job very much easier. He had cruised up and down the area, asking various shopkeepers if they needed a delivery boy, or someone to assist them in their work, but guessed that his unwashed and crumpled appearance had been against him. Now, looking respectable, he might easily land himself an equally respectable job. But Nick was still looking at him enquiringly and he realised he had not yet answered his question. 'It's a grand idea and I'll do my very best to get a job so's I can pay my own way,' Corky said earnestly. 'I've been wondering if I could find myself another place to roost ever since I got soaked last night when it rained so hard, but you don't want to go letting your landlady know we's pals, do you? It might set someone thinking and that might set them talking.'

'You're a bright lad, you are,' Nick said admiringly. 'I'd not thought of that, but you're quite right. I got lodgings because Mr Cartwright is a stringer for the *News Chronicle* so my editor booked me in, thinking to do both of us a good turn. Now I wonder how we can get you into that boxroom without arousing suspicion.'

A silence fell while everyone thought furiously, and finally it was Dot who gave tongue. 'Corky can just say he's hunting for a room. He can say he's only just arrived in Liverpool and went into a corner shop to ask if they knew of a vacant room and they told him to try Virgil Street because a good few folk let rooms along there.'

Emma began to say that she felt really ashamed for not having offered him her spare room when Nick interrupted, clapping a hand to his forehead and then rolling his eyes. 'What a fool I am, and

Dot, you're a genius! I nipped into the corner shop for a packet of Players yesterday, and I actually saw a notice in the window advertising my room at the Cartwrights'. I suppose they leave the advert in permanently because I guess no one stays there longer than they have to. So all you've got to do, Corky, is tell Mrs C. you're interested in the room they've got to let. And, sure as eggs is eggs, she'll take you straight up to the boxroom and probably let you have it cheap. Well, that'll regularise the situation all right, and if you can get a job somewhere fairly near Rathbone's, then I reckon we're almost home and dry. You'll be able to keep a bit of an eye on the place during opening hours; we'll get young Dot here to watch the jigger in the evenings between closing time and say, ten o'clock, and Emma and myself will take it in turns to make sure we see anyone who goes in or out through the shop. Meanwhile, I shall bend my powerful brain to thinking of a way to reach that perishin' necklace.'

'I want to try a piece of bent wire,' Dot said eagerly. 'I thought of a magnet, but I don't think that would work, would it? But a piece of bent wire . . .'

'No, that wouldn't work,' Corky said, decidedly. 'Think about it. If you tried to push a piece of wire into that cavity, it would hit the outer wall and stop short. It would have to be a long piece of wire . . . oh, I'm no good at explaining, but you see what I mean?' He turned to Nick. 'Why wouldn't a magnet work, though.'

'Magnets work on ferrous metals, not on noble ones,' Nick said. 'I wonder about tunnelling from the outside, under the outer wall? I know you said if we tried to remove one of the stone blocks, the whole wall might come down on top of us, but if we tunnelled underneath . . .'

'We'll think of a way,' Emma said reassuringly. 'But for the time being, let's concentrate on finding out who Rathbone's partner is and when they plan the next burglary. After all, as Nick says, to catch them red-handed is the best way to prove that Dot's story is true. Now, Corky will have to spend another night in the churchyard because he's got to clear the place of all his stuff and, of course, he'll have to visit this Mrs Cartwright and make sure she will let him have the boxroom.' She walked over to the kitchen dresser and pulled open one of the drawers, fishing a shabby old leather purse from out of its depths. She returned to the table and placed a one pound note before Corky. 'There you are; you'll need to show Mrs Cartwright that you've got money because I expect she'll ask for a week's rent in advance; most landladies do. Tell you what, Corky, why don't you nip into my bathroom and run yourself a hot bath? If you push your clothes out into the hallway, I'll give everything a good brush and iron them, so you look presentable when you call on the Cartwrights.'

'I'll put some blacking on your boots,' Dot said eagerly. 'Me dad once said he could tell a man's cir – circumstances by the state of his boots.' To

Corky's amusement, everyone immediately looked down at their own feet. Emma wore neat high-heeled court shoes, Nick wore brown brogues, and Dot sported ancient black plimsolls with holes in both toes – they had belonged to Fizz a short while ago. Corky's own boots were strong and sturdy – the staff at Redwood Grange knew it was false economy to buy cheap footwear – but they were covered in dust and scuff marks. Dot was right, a bit of blacking and some elbow grease would improve them no end.

'A hot bath would be prime,' Corky said eagerly. 'You are good, Emma. I never thought how nice it was to be able to get clean all over until I moved into that perishin' shed and couldn't do more than give myself a cat's lick and a promise. I'll be as quick as I can and then, if you don't mind, Nick, I'll walk back to your lodgings with you. I've done my best to get to know the area, but I've never come across Virgil Street.'

Nick said that this was a good idea, adding that they could plot as they went, and Corky disappeared into the bathroom. When he emerged again, wrapped in a towel and very clean indeed, Nick handed him his clothes and ushered him into the living room to dress. 'Emma's making everyone a meal. I was going to suggest that you and I nipped into the Corner House but I guess it's not wise to be seen together in public at this stage. Walking along the street is different, but having a meal together . . . anyway, Emma's doing new potatoes and frying ham and eggs, and there's a lovely big trifle for afters.' He grinned at Corky. 'So I graciously said we'd be pleased to stay for a meal, because it doesn't do to disappoint a lady.'

'That sounds grand,' Corky said contentedly. When Nick had left, he went and sat in the chair by the window, half turning it so that, if anyone happened to look up, they would not see him dressing. Church Street was crowded, as it always was, though the shops had shut long ago. Corky eyed the people, telling himself that the smartly dressed ones were making their way to theatres and cinemas, others would be having a meal out, and the really ragged man, who was slouching along on the opposite pavement, was probably intending to entertain the cinema queues with juggling tricks, or something similar. He saw that the man had a mouth organ sticking out of his jacket pocket, and was congratulating himself that he had guessed correctly when he noticed something else. There was a doorway opposite, the doorway of an extremely expensive toy shop into the window of which he and Dot had often peered. Standing well back in the doorway was a man, and it seemed to Corky that he was staring straight up at the flat. It was difficult to make out much detail because the doorway was in deep shadow, but his unwavering gaze made Corky nervous and he drew well back from the window. Sitting on Emma's small sofa whilst he put on his socks and boots, he could still see the man's head, though he thought that he himself must be out of sight. He watched all the while he struggled into his things, and the man remained motionless. For a moment, Corky actually wondered if he was looking at a cigar store Indian, but then he remembered that the shop was a toy shop and did not sell tobacco. When he was fully dressed, he crossed the room idly, as though merely moving from one seat to another, and managed to take a really good look at the watcher just as a street lamp in the road outside flickered on. It must have surprised the man for he moved his head and Corky saw the glint of his eyes and the quick, involuntary withdrawal even deeper into the doorway.

Then there was a bang on the door behind him and it shot open. Dot's voice was querulous. 'I thought it were women what took hours and hours to dress, not fellers! The grub's on the table and it smells awful good, but Emma said we must wait for you, so just you get a move on, old Corky, 'cos me belly's flappin' against me backbone, and if I don't get outside o' that grub, I'll probably faint clean away.'

'I'm ready, I've been ready for ages,' Corky said untruthfully. 'But wait on, Dot, there's a feller in the doorway opposite, watchin' the flat. He's not took his beady eyes off of this window ever since I first spotted him. Take a look, see if you knows him.' Dot would have walked straight across to the window, but Corky pulled her back with a hand on her arm. 'Don't let him see you,' he hissed.

'Creep over on all fours with just your eyes above the level of the window sill. I don't recognise him but I'm pretty sure it ain't Rathbone. See what you think.'

Dot, grumbling mightily, did as she was told, and after a few moments of intense scrutiny she crawled back to where Corky was squatting on the carpet. 'I think you're right and there is somebody watching the flat from Venables' doorway,' she admitted. 'But Corky, it could be *anyone*; it could even be a feller waitin' to meet a girl, because fellers hate to be seen hangin' around, particularly if they think the girl's going to let them down.'

'He's too old to be meeting a girl,' Corky objected, then wondered why he had said such a thing. He would have said he could see almost nothing of the watcher, yet there was something about the man which made Corky sure he was nearer forty than twenty.

The pair of them were still squatting on the carpet and peering at the watcher when Nick appeared in the doorway. 'What the devil are you two playing at,' he said wrathfully. 'It's like ten green bottles; first Corky disappears into the living room and doesn't come out, then I send you, Dot, to fetch him, and neither of you reappear. And there's poor Emma trying to keep the potatoes hot and the eggs from going hard.'

Both Dot and Corky had turned to stare up at him, but as they scrambled to their feet Corky said urgently: 'We wasn't just messing about, honest to

God we wasn't. There's a feller opposite what's been watchin' the flat ever since I came in here. He's difficult to see but now that the street lamp's lit – hang on, don't just walk across or he'll spot you.'

Nick shook his head. 'No he won't, not with a street lamp blazing down on him and us in darkness. Which doorway did you say?'

Corky began to point it out, then stopped short. The man had gone, disappeared as completely as had the necklace. 'But he *was* there and he was watching the flat too, wasn't he, Dot?' Corky said frustratedly. 'I'm pretty sure it weren't old Rathbone – well, it wouldn't be – but it were a big man, and not a young one either, ain't that so, Dot?'

Dot agreed that it was but Nick, hustling them through to the kitchen, seemed neither impressed nor perturbed. 'He was probably waiting for his girlfriend,' he said cheerfully. 'Why should anyone watch the flat? From what Emma has told me, she only sits in the living room for an hour or so each evening, and the only other room which overlooks Church Street is her bedroom. Since no one knew we were spending the evening here, what good would watching the place do? The shop's been robbed, remember, and Emma pays protection money to stop the thieves striking again. So why should anyone waste their time watching her flat?'

Hearing it put like that, Corky began to think that perhaps he had been mistaken after all. Yet though he agreed with Nick that he must be letting his imagination run away with him, a nasty little niggle of doubt existed in his mind. There seemed no logical reason for anyone to watch the front of the premises, but perhaps the man had not fancied skulking in the narrow jigger. There was certainly nowhere to hide round the back of the shops. At this point in his musings, they entered the kitchen and Nick told Emma, briefly, what the youngsters had been doing. Emma's eyes rounded. 'You're probably right about the thieves not meaning to tackle my shop again,' she said, beginning to dish the food on to four large dinner plates. 'But suppose they really are planning another burglary? They haven't done every shop in Church Street by a long chalk, you know. Mr Dibden sells antiques – he's three doors away – and some of his stuff is extremely valuable. There's a little oil painting in the window, by someone fearfully famous, I can't remember his name, but I know the price tag is enormous. Perhaps he's watching Dibden's. I remember someone saying – was it you, Nick? – that thieves watch a property for weeks and weeks before robbing it. That way, they get to know the shopkeeper's habits and routine and can choose the best moment to carry out the burglary.'

Nick nodded. 'You might be right at that, Emma.' He sighed deeply. 'This whole situation is growing stickier and stickier. I think we'll have to keep our eyes peeled for anyone hanging about in Church Street both after the shops have closed and during opening hours, and quite frankly, I don't see how the four of us can do it.'

'Don't you worry about that, Nick,' Emma said at once. 'For a start, no one is going to hang about in the doorway of a shop which is open for business; that really would be suspicious. Someone might walk up and down, I suppose, but once they've been back and forth two or three times they're going to be pretty conspicuous, so I can keep an eye out from the shop for anyone doing that. After six, I'll keep popping back and forth between the living room and the kitchen. But I'm afraid it means you'll have to leave me off the rota for watching Rathbone's place.'

'Oh, that's all right,' Nick said easily. 'The three of us can manage that. Pass the sauce, please, Corky; if there's one thing I love it's nice new potatoes with a drop of Flag sauce on the top.'

By the time Corky returned to the churchyard, he had accompanied Nick almost all the way to his lodgings, and knew he would be able to find the house the next day without difficulty. He waited his moment to climb over the wall, and then began to pack his meagre belongings into his old carpet bag. Fortunately, it was another mild night, but even so, he did not pack his thin blanket. Instead he wrapped it round himself and curled up, choosing the corner which the early sun struck first. He had removed his outer clothing and laid it carefully on a cardboard box which he had been using as a sort of bedside table, then glanced around the shed, almost regretfully. This place had been good to him, in its way. If it hadn't been for the shed, he would never have met Dot; never have become involved in the exciting events which now occupied most of his waking thoughts. Worst of all, he and Nick Randall would have gone their separate ways, never knowing that the other was no more than a mile away.

I like Nick, Corky told himself drowsily, just before he fell asleep. I like all of 'em, Emma and Dot, and even that little Sadie. When we find who Rathbone's partner is, we'll be able to pounce; I bet our names will be in the newspapers, and our photographs too, and we'll be on the wireless because they'll be bound to want to interview us and hear how we done it – caught the bad guys, I mean. I'll have to think up a new name for myself else the staff at Redwood Grange will be up here like a dose of salts. I'll call myself Jones, or Brown, or something. It'll be grand to be famous!

And whilst he was still wondering what name he should call himself, he fell asleep, and slept till morning.

Chapter Nine

Dot made her way home in a leisurely fashion for she was in no particular hurry to get back to the house in Lavender Court. When she did get back, she walked straight into trouble. As she crossed the yard, Sammy and Lionel shot out of the kitchen, Sammy calling over his shoulder as he did so: 'I told you we'd gorra go. If our Li is goin' to get a job like mine when he's old enough, he's gorra take the Sat'day job and I told Mr Swithin we'd go round to his house for half past eight.'

There was a roar from the kitchen, then Aunt Myrtle's voice called plaintively: 'Now, fellers, be fair, it won't take you a minute . . .'

But it was too late; Sam and Lionel had vanished. Dot made her way into the kitchen rather apprehensively. She hated family rows and clearly there was one in progress at this very moment. Dick and Alan sat at the table looking scared as their parents bawled at one another, or rather Uncle Rupert bawled at Aunt Myrtle, who was crying steadily, tears dripping down her cheeks. Uncle Rupert looked dreadful, grey-faced and sickly, with eyes like red hot coals. Dot noticed that every now and then he would tremble violently, shaking so much that the mug in his hand spilled its contents on to the floor. There was a meal on the table, though no one seemed to be eating, and Dot recognised the pie she had helped to make, though there was very little of it left now.

'I tell you it was your fault; it weren't nothing to do with me,' Uncle Rupert kept repeating, stabbing a shaking finger at Aunt Myrtle. 'I been on the wagon – well, nearly on the wagon – for weeks now, 'cos bleedin' old Rathbone told me he wouldn't employ no drunks and the money he pays me makes up for the rotten little screw they call a wage at McCall's. But now I've lost that, thanks to you and your bleedin' twins, an' I don't mean to lose me job at Rathbone's, so you've gorra go round there an' tell 'im I've ate something bad an' won't be in for a day or two.' He turned furiously and noticed Dot for the first time. 'And where d'you think you've been, gaddin' off just when we need you?' he asked aggressively. 'I told your aunt she'd gorra get round to Rathbone's toot sweet, because there's a decent bit o' money hangs on the butcher not findin' out McCall's have give me me cards. But you're only a kid; Rathbone don't like kids. Dammit, Myrtle, you've gorra go.'

'I'd go if I could,' Aunt Myrtle wailed. She lifted up the hem of her long dark skirt to reveal an ankle swollen to the size of a football. 'If you hadn't give me a kick what's likely broke me ankle, then I'd ha' gone round all right, 'cos I need every penny you earn to keep everyone clothed and fed. But I can't so much as put this foot to the ground, so how do you 'spect me to stagger round to Rathbone's, answer me that? Anyway, I don't reckon McCall's will sack you just because you fell down the iron stairway; why should they? It ain't no skin off their noses, if you see what I mean. And they've seen you drunk afore, many a time.' She fished a rag out of her sleeve and blew her nose noisily but made no attempt to stem the tears.

Dot, sitting herself quietly down opposite her younger cousins, now saw that her uncle's forehead sported an enormous lump and realised that his shaking hands also had skinned knuckles and purplish abrasions. Knowing Uncle Rupert as she did, she guessed that he had probably blamed the firm for his fall, blustering that there had been a spillage on the iron staircase, or even that the stair was unsafe. It would be just like him and would be the very thing certain to put up the backs of the managerial staff at McCall's. She did think her aunt was right, though: the firm might threaten to sack him but surely they would not actually do so? Her uncle had been with them as long as she could remember and knew as much about rope making as any other employee.

'If you're determined to send someone round to the butcher's, then I suppose it had best be Dot,' Aunt Myrtle said, her voice still thick with tears. 'And how you can blame me because I'm expectin' your twins, I really don't know. Any road, you don't see me gettin' drunk and boastin' over the thought of two more mouths to feed. And it were you what kicked me ankle with your damn great boot, or are you goin' to pretend it were little Alan here?'

Uncle Rupert mumbled something and looked down at his feet. Dot hoped he had not kicked his wife on purpose and actually thought it unlikely. He was a violent man but more apt to use his fists than his boots, and anyway he looked too sick to start a punch-up. But at this point Aunt Myrtle turned to her and held out a hand. 'Dot, me love, you won't lerrus down, will you?' she said coaxingly. 'Mr Rathbone will be real angry if your uncle don't tell 'im he's sick, 'cos he'll want som'un else to hump carcasses up from the slaughterhouse. I don't say it'll be easy to find anyone by tomorrer evenin' but at least it should be possible.' She saw Dot's uneasy expression and added: 'I know you say he don't like kids but all you'd be doin' is givin' him a message. The shop'll be closed, but there's a door round the back an' if you give a good loud knock he'll come down from the flat. You can tell 'im that Mr Brewster has been sick as a dog after eatin' a meat pie from Snetterton's on the Scottie. Say he'll be back to work in two or three days an' say as how he's real sorry. Can you remember all that?'

'Of course I can,' Dot said indignantly. 'But it is true, Mr Rathbone don't like kids. How about if I took young Dick with me? Old Rathbone ain't so likely to clout first an' hear the message after if there's two of us.'

She thought that her aunt was about to agree, but Dick began to whimper and to say that he wouldn't go to Rathbone's not if it were ever so. 'Me ball bounced into the shop when Freddie an' I were playin' footy down Heyworth Street,' he whined. 'Well, it weren't a ball, it were a bundle o' rags, but the mean old bugger chucked it in his waste bin and wouldn't give it back, no matter how nicely we asked. So Freddie shouted he were a nasty old scumbag an' he chased us halfway down Heyworth Street. We were scared; he were still holdin' his cleaver.'

Dot began to argue her own case but at this point Uncle Rupert interrupted before she'd got more than two or three words out. 'I don't want Archie knowin' I've gorra kid what gives cheek an' acts like a hooligan,' he informed them, glaring savagely at Dick. He turned to Dot. 'Just you go round there right now an' tell 'im I'll see 'im in a couple o' days' time. An' no argufying from you, miss!' With that, he slumped down in a chair and began to sip from the mug in his hand which, Dot realised with considerable surprise, contained tea.

Aunt Myrtle tried to get to her feet, but groaned with pain. 'Off you go, queen,' she said, not unkindly. 'I dunno where you're goin' to sleep tonight, 'cos neither your uncle nor meself will be climbin' them stairs, I can tell you. Oh, I dare say you can sleep in our bed 'cos your Uncle Rupe will be in the parlour an' I'll tek your place down here.' She indicated Dot's sofa bed. 'See you later, chuck.'

Reluctantly, Dot left the house and made her way to the butcher's. She went first to the shop, thinking that if Mr Rathbone had stayed open late it would be easier to give him her message in front of a shop full of people. As her aunt had predicted, however, the 'closed' sign hung on the door and the window blinds were down. Dot knocked on the door, then pressed her nose to the glass, but all she could see was the empty window and a large bluebottle crawling up the pane. For a moment, she employed herself by following the bluebottle with one forefinger, hoping to scare it into flight, but it was either a very intelligent fly which realised she could not possibly get at it, or a very foolish one which did not have the sense to look through the glass. So she turned reluctantly away from the shop front and went towards the jigger.

Heyworth Street was a busy thoroughfare in daytime, but at this time of night there was very little traffic and it was mainly children who raced up and down the pavement and popped in and out of the few shops which were still open, their mothers having sent them on last-minute messages. Dot went down the jigger, looking rather apprehensively about her. It was the first time she had come along here since her hurried flight on the night of the burglary, and she was surprised to find that the place was quite clean and that the wall was too high, for the most part, to allow even a well-grown adult to look in the back yards of the shops. On her previous visit, she had scrambled over the wall which happened to be nearest to her when she feared to be caught by Fizz, but now she realised she could just as easily have gone through the gate. It was a pretty solid affair, more like a door than a gate, really, and it was unlocked. Dot guessed this was because, in summer, the dustmen would clear the bins every day. She let herself into the yard, noticing for the first time that the butcher had stencilled both the number of his shop and his own name in white upon the green paint of his gate. And I was in such a hurry to get hidden that I never even noticed, she thought with awe. If I had, I'd have gone one further along, because even then I knew old Rathbone was a wrong 'un. But I'm glad I did hop into old Rathbone's by mistake, otherwise I'd never have met Corky, or got to know Emma. And of course the mystery of the necklace would have remained a mystery, though I dare say I'd have been a whole lot safer.

She was thinking this as she crossed the yard and it made her rap rather timidly upon the heavy oak door, but after a moment or two her courage returned and she looked round for something to bang the door with, and realised that there was a bell-push on the left-hand door post. She pressed it and presently its shrill summons brought some-one heavily down the stairs and the door swung open. Mr Rathbone was chewing and he had removed his collar and unbuttoned his shirt. He had a large meat pie in one hand and did not look at all pleased to be disturbed. 'Whadda you want?' he growled. 'Bleedin' kids! It's been nothing but bleedin' kids all day. If you've knocked your bleedin' ball into my bleedin' back yard, you can say goodbye to it 'cos I won't have kids on me premises; if I've told you once, I've told you . . .'

He looked as if he were about to close the door and Dot spoke up hastily. 'It ain't nothing like that, mister. I've got a message from me uncle, Rupert Brewster.' She eyed the pie in the butcher's hand and hastily changed her story. 'Me aunt were give a basket of eggs from her sister what lives on the Wirral. She made a great big omelette for me uncle's tea, but there must have been a bad 'un amongst 'em, 'cos he's been sick as a dog. The chemist says it's food poisoning an' he's to stay in bed till he stops chuckin' up.'

The butcher looked distinctly displeased. 'What you're tryin' to say is, he's goin' to let me down,' he said. 'Food poisoning! Fellers these days gerra belly-ache an' say it's food poisoning. Well, you tell 'im he'd best be back before the weekend or he'll find himself without a job.'

Dot opened her mouth to say that it really was food poisoning, that he had been so ill that he had fallen down the stairs, but such embroidery was denied her. She had left the gate in the wall open so that, if the butcher got nasty, she could make a

276

quick getaway, but it must have swung partly closed again, for she heard the creak of its hinges and saw the butcher's eyes flicker to something – or someone – behind her. She turned, her heart jumping into her mouth, but then it lodged itself in its rightful place once more. The newcomer was not the weasel-faced man she had met on the night of the burglary, but a scuffer, tall and broad, with a jolly, rosy face. He did not seem to notice Dot but touched his helmet to the butcher, saying as he did so: 'Evenin', Mr Rathbone, sir. I noticed your gate were open as I come along the jigger so I thought I'd best pop in, make sure you didn't have no trouble. I know you complained up at the police station that there had been kids muckin' about with your bins, and I know you always keep your gate locked, so I thought I'd best step in and make sure everything was as it should be.'

He had not so much as glanced at Dot and she decided that this was an ideal moment to leave. Mr Rathbone was saying, in a grumbling voice, that as it happened the kid was just passing on a message from a feller he employed, and very inconvenient it was liable to be, so Dot turned and hurried out of the yard. The policeman began to reply – Dot did not hear what he said – but just as she let herself out through the gate, Archie Rathbone raised his voice. 'Hey, you, wharrever your name is! Come back here, I've not finished wi' you yet.'

But Dot was already scooting down the jigger as

fast as she could and had no intention whatsoever of returning to the butcher's yard. She now knew that he had actually gone to the police to make a complaint about kids meddling with his dustbins, though she was very sure that he would not have said that anything was missing – how could he? He could scarcely pretend to have thrown away one of his own valuables, so it must have been a general complaint, rather than a specific one.

Having discharged her errand, Dot returned home to find her uncle already snoring in the parlour, and her aunt trying to make herself a cup of tea, weeping copiously as she did so.

'I've given Mr Rathbone your message, Aunt Myrtle,' Dot said cheerfully, taking the teapot out of her aunt's hands. 'Just you sit down and let me pour you a nice cuppa. D'you fancy a piece of that cake we made earlier?'

Her aunt sank into the nearest chair and received the mug of tea gratefully. 'You're a good kid, Dot. What did old Rathbone say?'

'Nothing much. Well, he moaned a bit, and said it was inconvenient, and Uncle Rupe must be back by the weekend, that sort of thing. Oh, and when he came down to the door he were eatin' a meat pie, so I told him you'd made Uncle Rupe an omelette with eggs your sister had sent from the Wirral, and one of them must have been bad. I was going to say as me uncle had been so poorly that he'd fallen down the stairs in his weakness, only a scuffer arrived, so I made meself scarce.'

'You're a good girl,' Aunt Myrtle said again. 'A scuffer, eh? I 'spect it was Constable McNamara; they're quite pally, I believe. Mind you, the constable's a lot more popular than Archie Rathbone, but I believe they was at school together, which accounts for it.'

Dot cut her aunt a slice of cake and watched her eat it and drink the tea. Then she had to pretend to eat a piece herself though she was full to bursting, what with the slice of pie her aunt had given her before she left the house, and the enormous tea she had eaten before she left Emma's. After that, she got out the bedding for the couch and helped Aunt Myrtle to remove her outer garments and lie down. Only when her aunt was comfortably settled did she turn out the lamp and make for the stairs, reflecting that it would be odd to spend the night in the creaking old brass bedstead which took up most of the main bedroom. She took off her own outer clothing and climbed between the sheets. She had not drawn the curtains since it would be her task in the morning to get herself washed and dressed, to wake the boys and then get Aunt Myrtle ready for the day. She thought her aunt should go to Brougham Terrace, where they would at least provide her with crutches, because otherwise she was going to make the ankle worse by using it whenever she wanted to go to the door, or to use the privy which was at the far end of the court.

In addition, she would have to make the breakfast porridge, brew the tea, slice the bread, and do all the other small tasks which she usually shared with Aunt Myrtle. Sighing, she also realised, as she cuddled down, that she was very unlikely to be able to get away from the house whilst her aunt remained incapacitated. Evenings would not be so bad because Sammy and Li would be home, but past experience had taught her that they were slippery as eels when it came to helping out. She very much wanted to see Corky and tell him about her visit to Mr Rathbone. If he knew Rathbone had reported her presence to the police, this might affect how they watched his premises. She supposed she could wait until the food was on the table tomorrow evening and then make an excuse and nip round to the churchyard. Why, provided she was not seen climbing the wall, she could go there when she was supposed to be doing her aunt's messages. It was only then that she remembered: Corky would not be there. He would have done his packing and would be making his way to Nick's lodgings the next day, and for the life of her she could not remember the name of the street where Nick was staying, let alone the number of the house.

Dismayed, she shot up in bed, then sank down again. Of course, Emma would know, and even if she did not, Nick and Corky were bound to visit the shop in Church Street. They would want to know if Emma had seen anyone acting suspiciously in the road outside, and to share any information they themselves had garnered. And then there was the necklace; if Nick really meant to tunnel under the wall to find it, he would need all the help he could get. It was a pity she had not noted the address of Nick's lodgings but she would put that right in the days to come.

Satisfied, she began to let her thoughts wander aimlessly and was on the very verge of sleep when something so strange occurred to her that she shot up in bed once more, staring through the uncurtained window at the clouds scudding across the moon. *Why* had the butcher's back gate been open, when even the scuffer had remarked that he always kept it locked? The dustmen would have visited hours earlier, and Mr Rathbone himself had removed his striped apron and the starched collar of his shirt, so as far as he was concerned his working day had been over. She knew what shopkeepers were like from her friend Phyllis's mam. Once the shop was shut, they would do all the necessary tasks and then take themselves off to their own quarters. Either Mr Rathbone had left the gate unlocked by mistake, which seemed unlikely since he had said nothing about it when he found her on his doorstep, or he had left it unlocked because he was expecting a visitor.

A visitor! What a fool she had been not to have realised earlier that the unlocked back gate was important. If she had hung around at the mouth of the jigger, she was now sure she would have seen Ollie, and clearly enough to identify him too. Then she remembered that Corky might well have been keeping an eye on the premises, might have seen what she had missed. She really must come up with some excuse to leave Aunt Myrtle next day and find Corky and tell him everything that had happened, because although it was annoying that she had missed seeing the butcher's visitor earlier, they now had a very real clue. When Mr Rathbone expected someone to come calling after the shop was shut, he left the gate unlocked. After the caller had left, he would relock the gate; Dot remembered the rasp of the key turning in the lock when Ollie had left on the night of the burglary. So if Corky – or whoever was on watch – tried the door and found it locked, they would know that they need not wait; but if, on the other hand, it was unlocked, then their lookout would not be wasted.

Dot lay down again, but though she tried to compose herself her mind was full of racing thoughts and possibilities, and despite the comfort of being gloriously alone in a very large bed, it was a long while before she slept.

Corky had intended to go straight round to Virgil Street just in case Mrs Cartwright found another lodger for the little boxroom, but when he was sitting up in the shed and eating his breakfast of bread and jam he changed his mind. He wanted, above everything else, to seem like any other young lad who had come up from London in search of work and such a lad, he knew, was unlikely to look for lodgings until he had paid employment of some description. He would have liked to get work which would leave him a certain amount of freedom since it was plainly imperative to be able to keep an eye both on Church Street and on the butcher's premises but in August, with the schools shut, he imagined that local lads would already have bagged all the delivery jobs, especially if they owned bicycles. He had had quite a bright, idea though: he would suggest to a score of small shops that he might deliver for all of them whenever they sold something which was too heavy for a housewife to carry home unaided, and that way he would have a good deal of freedom, be able to pick and choose whether he would work or not, yet still have some money coming in.

Accordingly, he finished his breakfast, hefted his carpet bag on to one shoulder, and set off into the misty morning. He went straight to Heyworth Street and walked slowly along the pavement, eyeing each shop speculatively as he passed. There were an enormous variety of establishments: several fishmongers, butchers, bakeries, greengrocers, drapers, boot makers and the like and, of course, the inevitable corner shops, usually presided over by a motherly woman who sold just about everything. When he reached the pet shop he stopped to look longingly in the window; it would be lovely to work there, getting to know the fat rabbits in their cages, the parrot dancing on its perch and shouting for peanuts in a harsh croak, and the gloriously wriggling puppies which rolled and yapped in the window, too intent on the game they were enjoying with each other to notice a boy with his nose squashed to the glass. Reluctantly, Corky moved on and very soon came to the dairy. It was a large building, and even had it not been clearly labelled Corky would have known it was a dairy by the lowing of a cow and the farmyard smell which emanated from the passageway down the side of the premises. Milk has to be delivered and the man who drove the horse needed boys who could pop to each house to deliver the milk that had been ordered, Corky reminded himself. Whilst he was with Mrs Perkin, it had often been he who had been despatched with an enamel jug into which the milkman's boy would pour whatever quantity of milk Mrs Perkin wanted. Yes, dairies needed boys all right and the dairy was a possibility, as was the large Co-op a little further along. Corky knew there were frugal women in every community who shopped once a week at the Co-op, giving large orders to be taken home by the delivery boy.

He did not think any of the hairdressers, or barbers, would need a boy for any particular purpose and neither did he intend visiting boot makers, but bakers were a possibility. He had seen lads with heavy wickerwork trays on ropes round their necks going from door to door selling loaves, and though he did not much fancy the job he supposed that if all else failed he would have to have a go.

Having seen how the land lay, he decided to try half a dozen of the smaller shops first, including two fishmongers, three butchers and a greengrocer.

The first butcher was a cheery little man with a bulbous red nose and very few teeth, but his shop was crowded and he was clearly a favourite with his customers, all of whom kept shouting out to him as they waited patiently to be served. Corky decided he would like to work for Mr Speed but when he reached the counter and asked if there were any jobs going, such as delivery boy, Mr Speed shook his head. 'Me customers aren't the sort to buy a baron of beef,' he said regretfully. 'Come Christmas I'll need a lad, what wi' turkeys the size of hostriches and hams what are a quarter of a pig, just about, but in the summer me ladies come in, pick what they want, and carry it off. Sorry, young feller.'

The other butcher had a similar response and the first fishmonger said, rather sourly, that with half the kids in the neighbourhood owning stirring carts and happy to deliver anything and everything for a ha'penny or so, there was little point in his employing anyone. Corky had seen the stirring carts, which the local kids made from broken-down orange boxes and old pram wheels, and left the shop feeling truly dispirited. But he had still to try the bigger shops, which were probably the best bet of all.

He was heading for the dairy when someone hailed him and he heard footsteps pattering rapidly behind him. He turned and there was Dot, pink-faced and breathless. She clutched his arm and pulled him round to face the opposite direction. 'Corky, I'm that glad I found you. Let's nip down Minera Street where it's a bit quieter and we can talk. There's a good deal you ought to know . . . oh, and I've just realised I dunno your new address.'

'I haven't got one yet,' Corky said, rather ruefully, as they turned into the side street. 'I've been trying to get a job of some sort because if Mrs Cartwright asks me where I'm working – and she's bound to – then I want to be able to give her a straight answer. Only it ain't so easy to get work in the school holidays, not with every lad in Liverpool eager to earn a few pennies.'

'Ye-es, but you know you'll be lodging in the same house as Nick,' Dot pointed out. 'Just give me the address so's I can come and find you if there's important news to tell.'

'Yes, but I'm *tellin'* you: I've not been there yet and she could have let the room or simply not like the look of me,' Corky said, rather crossly. 'Then you'll go round there and ask for me and she won't know who the devil you're talking about.'

Dot glared at him. 'I'm not a complete idiot, you know,' she said reproachfully. 'I'll ask for Nick, of course. Now, will you kindly give me the address or do I have to knock you down, kneel on your chest and get it out of you that way?'

Corky sniggered. 'Some chance,' he said derisively. 'Still, if it'll make you happy, it's number twenty-five Virgil Street – between Great Homer and the Scottie, you know – and even if Mrs Cartwright can't give me a room, Nick reckons most of the houses along there have a lodger or two, so mebbe I'll end up in Virgil Street anyway, if not at number twenty-five.'

'Right,' Dot said. 'Now listen carefully, Corky, because what I'm going to tell you is really important and may well make it easier to keep an eye on old Rathbone.'

She began her story, but had only got as far as her uncle not wanting to lose his job with Rathbone when Corky interrupted her. 'That means he's a worker short, if only for a couple of days,' he said excitedly. 'I won't let on I know but I'll ask him if there's any way I can help and mebbe he'll let me do your uncle's job, just till he's fit again,' he added hastily.

Dot pulled a doubtful face. 'Me uncle shifts carcasses at the slaughterhouse, puts them into Mr Rathbone's van and unloads them t'other end into his cold store,' she said. 'I think it's grown man's work, Corky, because no matter how strong you are, you haven't got the height. A big carcass . . . well, it 'ud drag on the ground, wouldn't it?'

Corky gave the matter some thought, then nodded. 'I guess you're right, but there's no harm in trying,' he pointed out. 'Maybe he'll fetch the carcasses himself and leave me to mind the shop or tidy up, you never know.'

'True,' Dot said. 'Look, I've gorra gerra move on because I left me aunt sittin' in a queue outside the doctor's surgery in Brougham Terrace. I reckon it'll be an hour or more before she's seen, but there's messages to get done 'n' all, so don't interrupt no more, just let me tell you about last night.'

Corky listened in silence, but when the story was done he clapped Dot on the back and told her she was a real bright spark. 'You're dead right that the unlocked gate is a real giveaway,' he told her. 'It'll make watching the place a whole lot easier. But why d'you think that there copper weren't the feller he were waitin' for?'

'Oh, because he was surprised when the scuffer walked across the yard and joined us; his eyes really rounded,' Dot said. 'And besides, the constable only came in because he saw the gate was open. And he said about Mr Rathbone making a complaint at the station . . .'

'Well I think it's odd,' Corky said obstinately. 'Your aunt said they were real pally, if it was this McNamara, so why shouldn't old Rathbone have been waiting for him? And why did he call you back? Have you stopped to ask yourself that?'

'I dunno, but I expect he'd got some sort of message for Uncle Rupe,' Dot said vaguely. 'But does it matter, Corky? What I feel cross with meself over is not hanging around to see if ferret-faced Ollie turned up.'

'Well, no use crying over spilt milk,' Corky said, as they returned to Heyworth Street. 'I've got a couple more places to try – Rathbone's and that baker's over there – an' then I'll go to the dairy and the Co-op. Surely someone could do with a lad to fetch and carry for them? Come to that, I'm not fussy. I'll do anything to earn enough money to pay my lodgings and keep me fed. Oh, I know Nick said he'd do it, but I'd far rather be independent.'

'Yes, o' course you would; but I'd best get back to Brougham Terrace before me aunt gets suspicious; I can pick up a bag of spuds an' half a pound of scrag ends on me way,' Dot said. 'Good luck with the job hunt!'

Dot watched as Corky disappeared into Rathbone's shop. She contemplated following him, for now Mr Rathbone knew that she was Uncle Rupe's niece he might well sell her the scrag cheap – if he wasn't still furious with Uncle Rupe, that was – but some inner caution advised her against such a move. He was bound to recognise her all right and might well also remember that he had shouted at her to return the previous evening, and she had not done so. She could of course claim that she had not heard, but she had no wish to become a messenger between her uncle and his part-time employer; no, it would be wiser to visit the next butcher she passed on her way back to Brougham Terrace.

So when Dot rejoined her aunt it was with a full shopping bag and Aunt Myrtle, sitting on one of the long wooden benches, gave a sigh of relief at the sight of her. 'I were getting real worried, queen,' she said reproachfully. 'I know I've got that old walking stick what you borrowed from Mr Hardy up the road, but I don't trust meself to walk more'n a few paces without your shoulder to lean on, and I'm in next.' Even as she spoke, the surgery door opened and a large, red-faced woman emerged. Aunt Myrtle got to her feet and grabbed Dot's skinny little shoulder. 'In we goes,' she said bracingly. 'Keep it nice 'n' steady so's I don't go slippin'. I couldn't do wi' a broken leg as well as a sprained ankle.'

Because the clinic on Brougham Terrace could not supply the crutches her aunt needed, she was given a doctor's letter and advised to go to the nearby hospital. Dot sighed wearily, knowing that such a walk, in her aunt's condition, would be a trying one, but fortunately the doctor realised it as well. 'Wait on the bench until you're called, and the pair of you can get a ride in the ambulance,' he said. 'We don't want you giving birth to that baby before your time, do we?' Aunt Myrtle agreed fervently that this would not do at all, and was grateful for the offer of an ambulance ride. But poor Dot sighed with frustration, knowing that the major part of the day would have passed before she got her aunt safely home again. And she was right. The pair of them staggered into the house at half past six that evening to find that, as usual, the boys had returned and were sitting round the table making no attempt to get a meal started. They had eaten every crumb of the cake Dot had made the day before, but had not even bothered to bring in water, let alone make up the fire, which was little more than a handful of glowing embers in the grate. Aunt Myrtle seldom reproached the boys for their laziness, but today was the exception. She glared at her sons, then tipped Dick out of her favourite fireside chair and slumped into it herself, before addressing them. 'Sammy, fetch the coal in an' make up that fire. Lionel, fill the water buckets. And you two young 'uns can go into the parlour and ask your da what he's up to, lyin' there all day doin' nothin' while Dot an' meself have got the messages and queued for hours at Brougham Terrace and the hospital to get me some crutches so's I can move around the house.'

Dick and Alan stared at their mother resentfully. 'Dad's not there – in the parlour, I mean,' Dick said sulkily. 'He went out, oh, ages ago. He sent Li round to Morris's on Heyworth Street for eighteen penn'orth of chips and a couple o' pieces o' battered cod.' He sighed reminiscently, licking his lips. 'It were grand, to have fish 'n' chips for us dinners. Our dad said he needed a decent meal to gerris courage up – he were real cross you'd gone out, Mam – and as soon as he ate all the grub and drunk a big mug o' tea, he went off.'

'Oh my Gawd,' Aunt Myrtle said, dropping her head into her hands. 'Don't say he's gone to the boozer!'

Little Alan, who had not spoken so far, trundled

across the room and patted his mother's hand consolingly. 'He ain't gone to the boozer. He said he were going to the rope works to see if he could get his bleedin' job back, an' then he were goin' to the butcher's, 'cos he said he felt well enough to work tonight if he took it slow an' easy. So don't cry, our Mam.'

Aunt Myrtle raised her head from her hands, blew her nose resoundingly on a piece of rag produced from her sleeve, and gave her youngest a trembly smile. 'You're a good little feller,' she said huskily. She turned to Dot. 'Get scrubbin' them spuds, queen, while I find up something to go with 'em. Scrag's all very well but it needs to be cooked for hours. Tell you what, Rupert lashed out at dinnertime so I'll take some cash from the tea caddy on the mantel and when Sammy's made up the fire he can go an' buy some bacon and half a dozen eggs from the Co-op. Though why I should give the boys bacon and eggs when they've already fed their faces wi' fish 'n' chips, I can't imagine,' she ended, a trifle bitterly.

As soon as Sammy returned, he made up the fire, using the poker to lift the glowing coals so that a draught might hasten the process. Then he took the money his mother offered and set off. Dot, scrubbing potatoes at the sink, thought wistfully that it would be nice if her aunt always made the boys do their share, and though she said nothing Aunt Myrtle appeared to have divined her thoughts, for she said abruptly: 'Me lads is gettin' a taste of what's to come, because when the twins is born they're goin' to take up all my time and almost all of yours, as well. That means the boys are going to have to change their ways, like it or not.'

Dot grinned but vouchsafed no reply, secretly doubting that her aunt would really make the boys do their share. But when she had scrubbed the last potato and peeled the last carrot, and put them all into the big iron pan, her aunt bade Lionel carry it over to the fire for her. 'You've twice the strength of a girl, Lionel Brewster, and it's time you learned to use it on something beside your own pleasure,' she said, rather obscurely. 'When the twins come . . .'

Lionel turned to stare at her. 'Twins? What twins?' he said aggressively. 'You're always talkin' about having too many mouths to feed an' now you're takin' in twins. Honest to God, Mam, have you gone mad?'

Aunt Myrtle's eyes widened. 'I am expectin' twin babies,' she said, speaking very slowly and clearly. 'Surely you must have realised that, Lionel?'

It appeared that Lionel had not and nor had the other boys. 'Twins! So that's what our dad were on about,' Lionel said. 'I knew there were a baby comin' because you'd gone so fat, but I didn't know it were twins.' He sighed deeply. 'No wonder Dad's takin' to drinkin' again. One baby's bad enough, but two . . .'

'That's quite enough of that,' Dot said briskly, terrified that her aunt would burst into tears once more. She got on quite well with Lionel, who was only a year older than herself, though he was both taller and broader. 'Lay the table, will you, Li? Your mam's going to need a good deal of help till she can use her leg again.'

Chapter Ten

Nick had been delighted when he got back to his lodgings to find himself being introduced to Corky, though for some reason the lad had decided to use a different name: he was calling himself Kenny Johnson. Kenny was sufficiently like Corky for his young friend to answer when he was so addressed, though after such a considerable lapse of time, Nick privately thought the change to be unnecessary. The authorities would scarcely look for him in Liverpool anyway, since he had no connection with the city.

Usually, Nick avoided Mrs Cartwright's evening meal, but tonight he and Corky had agreed to 'eat in', so to speak, in order that they might get to know one another officially. The meal was poor and plain, as usual – a meat and potato pie with only faint traces of meat and pastry so hard that you could have paved the street with it – but Corky gobbled his portion cheerfully, ate his share of the spotted potatoes and watery cabbage, and finished up with Mrs Cartwright's rice pudding: a treat which Nick usually managed to avoid by claiming to be unable to eat another mouthful.

During the meal, which was shared with the

Cartwrights and their other two lodgers, Mr Cartwright questioned Corky closely without getting very much satisfaction, though Corky did tell him that he was working for the Co-op on Heyworth Street as delivery boy and stockroom assistant. When Mr Cartwright questioned him further, however, he simply said he had only arrived in the city from London early that morning, and knew almost nothing about the area he would be covering. 'But they've give me a plan what I'm to learn by heart, so's I can deliver without making a muck of it,' he said glibly. 'I'll be all right; I were a delivery boy in central London for two years, and there weren't no complaints from me boss. When I told him I wanted to come up north, he wrote me a grand reference, so I 'spect that's how I got the job. I were in the Co-op in London too,' he added.

Nick hoped his young friend was not over-egging the pudding, but the reply seemed to satisfy Mr Cartwright, though he looked rather suspiciously at Corky, saying belligerently: 'How old is you, then? If you've been workin' two years . . .'

'Oh, I'm goin' on sixteen, but I'm small for me age, like me dad,' Corky said promptly. 'Me dad's only five foot two, but he's rare powerful. He's been all sorts, a seaman, a navvy . . .'

Nick saw Mr Cartwright's mouth open and feared that he was about to ask why Corky should have left home to work in Liverpool since he had family in London, but at this point one of the lodgers broke in with a story about what had happened at his workplace that day and Nick pushed back his chair and got to his feet. 'I'm off for a walk down to the docks. There's a ship down there which only came in today. I like to chat to the seamen because they've always got a story or two to tell, and you never know . . .' He turned to Corky. 'Want to come along, Kenny?'

Corky agreed, and two minutes later the pair of them were walking briskly down towards the docks. 'We'd better go and take a look at the shipping, since old Cartwright is so nosy – and so afraid of missing something – that he'll likely follow us,' Nick remarked. 'But he won't get near enough to hear what we're saying so you might as well tell me: are you really working at the Co-op?'

'I am, but only three days a week,' Corky said. 'As for stockroom assistant . . . well, I may be asked to help out in the stockroom but it's not a permanent job, like. And since there's no evening work, I'll still be able to keep an eye on Rathbone's. I tried for a job there too, but the old tartar wouldn't give me the time of day.'

'I'm hoping it won't be necessary for very much longer,' Nick said. 'I may have to hire some sort of equipment to prevent the wall coming down when I start tunnelling underneath it, but if we can get the necklace we may be able to use it to lure Rathbone's accomplice into the open. Or of course, we may see this Ollie for ourselves whilst we're watching the premises after closing time.'

'I'm not sure as I see why it's so important to know this Ollie feller,' Corky said, after a thoughtful pause. 'After all, you and Emma both believe Dot's story, and you know the necklace is where we say it is, so why shouldn't someone else?'

'Because we can't prove anything as matters stand and because Ollie could be the brains behind the robberies, and not old Rathbone; he might be a person of considerable authority, someone whose word might be preferred to that of a stranger like myself, and a young girl like Emma, to say nothing of two kids. Why, even Mr Rathbone is a respected member of the Chamber of Trade. There are a great many people who are going to find it difficult to believe he's a crook.'

Corky nodded. 'I see what you mean,' he said. 'Then shouldn't we be making our way to Heyworth Street right now? Oh, I haven't told you, but I met Dot earlier . . .'

He told Dot's story of her visit to the butcher's yard, and Nick nodded. 'I see; then if the door's unlocked, we'll know Rathbone's expecting a visitor, and if it isn't we can go home. And from what you say, Dot won't be able to watch this evening, not if her aunt's on crutches. So we'll "skip a lecky" as they say in these parts and go and check on the gate right now. Since we don't want to be seen together too much, I'll hang around there for a bit, and you take yourself off back to Virgil Street.'

'I think you ought to go and see Emma and let her know what's been happening; see if anyone suspicious has been hanging round that antique place,' Corky said. 'I'll go and try Rathbone's back gate. Remember, now I'm workin' at the Co-op, I'll be up and down Heyworth Street and in and out the jiggers, and they won't take no more notice of me than if I were a fly on the wall.'

Nick had been longing for an excuse to go back and see Emma again, and seized upon this suggestion eagerly. He and Corky walked to the nearest tram stop and he gave Corky his penny fare before striding off towards Church Street. He told himself, severely, that his desire to be with Emma had nothing to do with her pretty looks, nor even with her bright intelligence. No, it was because they were the only two adults involved in this affair and, as such, needed to talk occasionally without the youngsters being present.

He reached Church Street, more anxious than ever to see Emma once more.

Emma heard the bell and hurried downstairs. She opened the door cautiously and was delighted to see Nick's friendly face beaming at her. He followed her up the stairs and into the kitchen, where she had been piling the dishes from her evening meal into the sink. Now, she told him to sit down and put the kettle on the stove. She was about to light the flame and to offer Nick a cup of tea when he spoke.

'Look, Emma, we've got an awful lot to talk about but quite frankly, on such a hot evening, I'd rather do it in the open air. You see, Corky told me Dot made a discovery last evening which may make things easier. Is there a park round here or somewhere we might go and talk? Only you've been stuck in the shop all day and it can't be good for you. I know you said you'd watch for anyone acting suspiciously, but you can't spend your life peering out through the window. Anyway, once it's dusk and the street lamps come on, a lurker would be too obvious.'

The wireless had been playing softly, but Emma turned it off at once and smiled at him. 'I'd absolutely love to get away for an hour or two, if you think it's all right,' she admitted. 'And what's more, I'm on quite good terms with several of the constables on the beat. If one of the nice ones is on duty, I could just mention that I'd noticed some-one acting suspiciously last night, hovering in the doorway of Venables' toy shop.' She frowned thoughtfully, then her face cleared. 'Tell you what, why don't we have a real outing? We could go to Prince's Park on the tram and have a look at the aviary. There's a café there where we can get a cup of tea, if it's open, and it's just like the country there, honest it is. Then you can tell me what's been happening and we can get as much fresh air as you like because the park's so huge.'

Nick agreed enthusiastically to this and presently the two of them were strolling along Church Street in the direction of the tram stop. Nick, highly daring, had just taken Emma's arm when she suddenly broke away from him. 'There's Mr McNamara – Constable McNamara I mean – about to turn the corner ahead,' she said rapidly. 'I'll just nip over and have a word. You go on; I'll catch you up.'

Emma flitted ahead and caught Constable McNamara up without too much difficulty, for the policeman was moving ponderously. She began to tell him about the stranger in the doorway opposite her shop. The policeman listened to what she had to say, then nodded his large round head gravely, though with a lurking twinkle in his bright little eyes. 'Don't you worry yourself, Miss Grieves, I'll keep an eye on anyone loitering near your premises,' he said earnestly, giving her a fatherly smile as he spoke. 'But I doubt if you're in danger of being robbed again 'cos that ain't the way the criminal mind works, by and large. And, you know, it's not only lovers who lurk in doorways; policemen do as well. I weren't on duty meself last night, but one of my colleagues might have been keeping an eye on someone and a doorway is easy to dodge into if you keep well to the back. You can see without being seen, if you understand me.'

Emma thanked the constable, bade him good night, and rejoined Nick, a trifle breathless but well satisfied with the encounter. She tucked her arm into Nick's as they reached the tram stop. 'That's relieved my mind quite a lot,' she said. 'Mr McNamara assured me that he'd keep an eye on the shop, though he wasn't particularly worried about the fellow in the doorway; actually said it might have been a policeman! Apparently, they dodge into doorways when they're keeping an eye out for trouble, so we were probably anxious for no real reason. Now, if there is anything going on, anything planned I mean, then at least I've alerted the local scuffers. I'd hate to think of Mr Dibden being badly hurt, perhaps even killed, the way my grandfather was.'

They climbed aboard the tram and were soon descending and making their way to the park. They found a seat overlooking the lake and settled themselves, then Emma turned to her companion. 'Business first, pleasure afterwards,' she said gaily. 'Fire ahead then, Nick; tell me what's been happening.'

Nick began to explain to Emma about Butcher Rathbone's locked – or unlocked – back gate. Emma nodded her understanding, so Nick went on to explain how he meant to make some sort of prop to hold up the church wall whilst he burrowed beneath it to recover the necklace. Emma looked doubtful. 'It's too dangerous,' she said after some thought. 'There must be a way to get the wretched necklace back, if only we could think of it. But right now, surely it's more important to discover who Ollie is. He murdered my grandfather, so no matter if he's the mayor of Liverpool, he's got to pay the price.'

'I quite agree, and that's why we've got to put

a stop to it as soon as we possibly can,' Nick said. 'I do believe we're getting near him. If only Dot had thought of it last night, I'm sure she would have seen him and perhaps even been able to identify him,' Nick said regretfully. 'And now her aunt's not only expecting twins, but also on crutches because of a sprained ankle, which makes her very reliant on Dot.'

When they left their seat and began to explore the park, they were delighted to find a small fun fair had set up its rides and stalls under some trees. Nick took Emma's hand casually, almost absent-mindedly, and she felt the heat begin to rise in her cheeks. He started to play with her fingers, admiring the delicate little ring she wore on the third finger of her right hand. 'It looks old; antique almost,' he said. 'And now I suppose you'll tell me it was made no more than a year ago and make me feel an ignorant fool.'

Emma laughed. 'No I shan't, because you're quite right. When my grandfather met the woman who was to become my grandmother, he said he knew at once that she was the only girl for him and that they would marry one day. He was apprenticed to a goldsmith at the time and he saved up every penny he could spare to buy gold and tiny sapphire chips. He worked on the ring whenever he was not actually doing anything for Mr Mitchell, and when he asked my grandmother to marry him he slipped the ring on her finger and told her the story of how he had started to think about it the very first time he had asked her out. Isn't that romantic?' She smiled up at him. 'Gran always wore it. As my grandfather grew more and more successful he wanted to make her something larger and more elaborate, but she would never let him. When she died, she left it to me in her will and it's never been off my finger since, except once, when I decided to have it made a little smaller so that it didn't slip round and risk catching on something as I worked.'

'That's a lovely story,' Nick said seriously. 'My grandfather died some years ago but my grandmother is still very much alive and I'm extremely fond of her. She lives with my parents in a villa on Linden Park Road in Tunbridge Wells, just off the Pantiles, and keeps house for them because they both work.' He answered Emma's enquiring look with a grin. 'I know it's unusual, but my mother and father are both doctors. They have a surgery built on to the house and share the practice with my brother, Geoffrey, who's also a doctor. Of course he doesn't live in the house any more, because he married Penelope three years ago and they bought a house a bit further up the hill so he's not too far away. They have a small daughter who's almost eighteen months old. Penny used to act as receptionist, but of course she can't do that any more now she's got little Annabelle.'

'Gracious!' Emma said, trying to take in this potted history of the Randall family; she thought they sounded fascinating. 'How do the patients know which Randall they're going to get? And didn't they want you to be a doctor, too?'

It was now Nick's turn to laugh. 'They're known as Dr Bernard, Dr Lavinia, and Dr Geoffrey, of course, and as for wanting me to practise medicine, it would have made the surgery somewhat crowded, don't you think? In fact, my parents are very modern and wanted us to choose our own careers. I expect they were thrilled when Geoff decided to do medicine, but I'm sure they were equally pleased when I took to journalism. They've always been very supportive and very loving to both of us. You'll like them.'

Emma's eyebrows shot up. 'Oh? Are they likely to come and visit you whilst you're in Liverpool, then?'

Nick shook his head. 'No, they're far too busy. But since I mean to start saving up for some gold and perhaps a nice little diamond, I dare say I might persuade you to come on a visit one of these days. Kent is a beautiful county, particularly at blossom time; you really should see it.'

Emma said nothing, but knew that the colour was rising in her face. If Nick meant what she thought he meant, then he really was serious. But I'm too young to start being serious, she told herself wildly, and knew she lied. Already, Nick was important to her, and he would grow more important as time passed. Love at first sight sounds like a fairy tale but I do believe it's happened to me, she told herself, and it's obviously happened to Nick if I read the signs aright.

Nick took her hand and squeezed her fingers gently, but held on firmly when she tried to pull away. 'What's the matter, Em? Don't you want to see Kent at blossom time?'

'I – I don't know what I want,' Emma said, still much flushed. 'You're going much too fast; we scarcely know one another. Why, we met for the first time less than a week ago.'

'Ah, but I'm only following Grandfather Grieves's example,' Nick pointed out. 'You've been studying jewellery design so you'll have to teach me how to make a little ring like that one. I could buy it,' he added thoughtfully, 'but it would be much more romantic to make it myself, don't you think?'

'I think you're being very silly,' Emma said primly. 'And now, if you please, I'd like to have a go on the hoop-la and talk about something different.'

Nick smiled and led her over to the hoop-la stall, beginning to tell her of the assignment he had been on when he had first met Corky. From this, the discussion led naturally to Dot, of whom Emma was clearly already very fond. 'The Brewster family work her far too hard and don't seem to realise how lucky they are to have her,' she observed, just as her hoop fell over a small yellow teddy bear. She gave a crow of delight as she claimed her prize.

'There's a merry-go-round,' she said, pointing.

'Do let's have a go on it, Nick! Oh, how I love a fair!'

He slipped a casual arm about her waist; she stiffened, then glanced up at him and relaxed. Why should she pretend an indifference which she did not feel? She liked him very much and, above all, felt both safe and comfortable in his company. 'You're obviously a fast worker, Nick Randall, and I wish I was a bit older and more experienced, but I'm not,' she said. 'I ought to warn you that I'm an old-fashioned girl and I don't believe in kissing on a first date, or in hugging, either, so perhaps you'd better take your arm back where it belongs.'

'I'm merely trying to keep us together and stop you from being jostled by the crowd,' Nick said.

Emma gave a small gurgle of amusement for the park was almost empty and the fair by no means crowded, but she made no further effort to distance herself from her companion. He gave her waist a tiny squeeze and, after a moment, she slid her arm round him, though she felt a little self-conscious as she did so.

'Oh, Emma, I'm so glad I decided to investigate the Church Street robberies, and so glad that dear little Dot let us into her secret, otherwise we might never have met. I know it's only been a short time – and I'm not a fast worker whatever you may think, I promise you – but an hour in your company was enough for me to realise you were someone special. As for not kissing on the first date – well, that's up to you. I'll let you set the pace, provided you realise that I'm serious and want—'

Emma put a hand up and placed it softly across his mouth. 'Be quiet,' she said scoldingly. 'I said earlier I wanted to change the subject and you're cheating by going back to it again. You know Dot said the other day that she was the cuckoo in the nest and that all the Brewsters, except Aunt Myrtle, were trying to push her out? I'm sure if they succeeded, they would soon realise their mistake, but if they do – push her out, I mean – then I'd be very happy to take her on. I've got a spare bedroom, and in the school holidays she could help in the shop as well as keeping the flat tidy and giving me a hand with messages and so on. I nearly told her the other day that she could come to me if her aunt kicked her out, but the fact is, what with expecting twin babies and having an injured ankle, her aunt's need is greater than mine right now. So for the time being the poor little cuckoo child had best put up with Lavender Court.'

'Yes, you're right. Except that I thought the cuckoo was the one who kicked the other birds out of the nest,' Nick pointed out. 'I fear you've got it wrong, darling Emma.'

Emma tutted. 'There you go again, saying things you oughtn't to say. As for the cuckoo chucking out the other birds, that depends which nest the mother leaves it in. Our poor little cuckoo child was left in a nest of vultures, and I don't see even the most determined cuckoo getting far against nestlings like those, dear Nick.'

Nick gave a little chortle and squeezed her again. 'You're making progress, Nick Randall,' he said. '*Softlee, softlee, catchee monkee* is an old saying but, I fancy, a true one. Would you like some fish and chips?' he asked wistfully. 'Mrs Cartwright's cooking is abominable and I'm empty as a drum right now.'

Emma peered ahead and saw a fish van, drawn up by the trees. 'I'd love some,' she admitted. 'It seems a long time since my supper, and that was only bread and cheese, and a slice of apple pie. Tell you what, we could buy the fish and chips and take them to the aviary to eat. There are seats there. Then we'll walk back and have a go on the merry-go-round and swing boats. What do you say, Nick?'

'I say hooray for Prince's Park,' Nick said, hurrying her towards the fried fish van. 'We're having a grand evening; it just gets better and better.'

By the time Emma and Nick left the park, Emma was so tired that she made no objection when Nick almost lifted her on to the tram and sat very close to her, an arm about her. She was happy to snuggle against him and lay her head in the hollow of his shoulder, for it seemed to her that they now knew each other as well as any two people could. They had whirled on the merry-go-round, rolled pennies down the chute, tried in vain to capture a prize with the automatic grab and had laughed and laughed in the hall of mirrors, moving back and forth so that one minute their heads were shaped like huge pears and their bodies reduced to doll size, whilst the next they were nine feet tall and thin as runner beans. Time had rushed past unnoticed by either of them, and only when they were soaring above the park in a swing boat had Emma glanced at her small wristwatch and realised it was getting late. The gas lamps were lit and she had promised herself an early night and was extremely tired. She had said as much to Nick, who had slowed the boat immediately and lifted her out of it.

And now here they were, heading for home as fast as the tram could carry them. When they disembarked, Emma told Nick she would be perfectly all right to walk home alone since it was only just after nine o'clock, but he scoffed at the idea and they strolled along comfortably together beneath the street lamps, Emma, at least, aware that their relationship had subtly changed. Nick had made it very clear that he was serious about her and she had admitted to similar feelings. Their first meetings had been unconventional, to say the least, but what did that matter, after all? The important thing was that they got on well, liked the same things and were growing increasingly fond of one another.

They reached the door of the stockroom and Emma unlocked it, inviting Nick in for a hot drink, but he shook his head, smiling gently down at her.

'No, I won't come in, Em, but thanks for the invitation, I really appreciate it,' he said softly. 'You're very tired and you've got to get up to open the shop tomorrow, and I've got a fair walk ahead of me.'

'I am very tired,' Emma admitted, stifling a yawn. 'Oh, we haven't arranged another meeting . . . but I'm always in the shop, so you can pop in any time. Good night, Nick, and thanks for a lovely evening.'

She was turning away when she found herself being seized and kissed. It was a light kiss, and as soon as he felt her pull away he stepped back, saying ruefully: 'Now tell me I shouldn't have done that! I know I said you could set the pace, Emma, but you're so beautiful . . . I just couldn't resist.'

Emma's heart was thudding and she could still feel the imprint of his lips on hers. She knew she should be outraged, tell him that he had overstepped the boundaries she had set, but instead she found herself smiling up at him. 'It's all right, Nick; I owe you a kiss for giving me such a nice time,' she said lightly. 'And – and to tell you the truth, it's the first time I've been kissed and I liked it.' Startled at her own boldness, she closed the door quickly and shot the bolts home, calling 'Good night and thanks again' as she did so. Then she ran up the stairs, hurried across the landing and hid behind the curtain in the living room, watching his tall, athletic figure stride away down Church Street.

She stayed there for a moment, simply gazing out into the lamplit street, and was about to turn away when another figure hove into view. It was Constable McNamara, treading his majestic beat, looking neither to right nor left but, she imagined, thinking wistfully of the cup of tea and corned beef sandwich which he would enjoy when he returned to the station to fill in his report on anything that had happened during the past few hours. She was tempted to open the window and hail him, but she knew that if she did so he would expect to be asked up for a drink or a chat, and she was far too tired, she decided. The constable often popped into the shop around elevenses time and always appreciated her home-made oatmeal biscuits, but he would have to give them a miss tonight.

Yawning, Emma made her way towards her bedroom, knowing that she would sleep well after such unaccustomed excitement and hoping that she might dream of Nick.

At around about the time when Nick and Emma were stepping out of the swing boat, Dot was helping her aunt to get ready for bed. She had actually managed – with assistance from Sammy – to get her up the stairs, and now she was sitting on the bed whilst Dot took off her shoes, rolled down the thick woollen stocking from her uninjured leg, and checked the softly swathed bandage round the sprained ankle. 'When your uncle comes in, tell 'im he's got to be rare careful not to kick if he's going to share me bed,' Aunt Myrtle instructed as Dot began to help her out of the threadbare shawl, loopy old cardigan and high-necked blouse. Dot marvelled that her aunt could wear such a quantity of clothing in the August heat and suggested, diffidently, that the following day she might try leaving off a couple of petticoats and her thick woollen stockings. Aunt Myrtle looked shocked. 'You won't hear me complainin' about the heat so don't you go suggestin' I walk around half naked,' she said. 'Mind, I'll be a lot easier once the twins is born, that I *don't* deny.' She cocked her head. 'Was that the front door? I just hope your uncle ain't been down the boozer.'

'I shouldn't think so. Alan said he'd gone to try and get his job back and then didn't he say he was going along to Rathbone's?'

'Oh aye, you're right. And besides, he said something about Rathbone threatening him with losing that job 'n' all if he got sozzled again,' her aunt said vaguely. 'That Rathbone's norra bad feller – well, if he were a bad feller, Mr McNamara wouldn't have nothing to do with him 'cos a scuffer has to be careful about the company he keeps. Ah, that sounds like your uncle comin' up the stairs now.'

It was. Uncle Rupert came into the room and took off his jacket, slinging it on to the washstand. He looked pleased with himself and even grinned at Dot before saying, triumphantly: 'Done it! I spoke to the manager at the factory, explained fellers had been buying me drinks 'cos me wife were expectin' twins, and after a bit he come round. He fined me half a week's wages, which were fair enough, 'cos I've missed two days' work already, and said if it ever happened again I'd be out on me ear, no question. He didn't say ear, either, but I knows me manners before ladies.' He gave his wife a wide gap-toothed leer, which Aunt Myrtle ignored.

'I'm glad you got your job back because it's reg'lar money and we'll need that wi' two extra mouths to feed,' she said. 'But old Rathbone pays well, and now you're working for him he'll sell me a decent bit o' meat for half the price I'd pay as an ordinary customer, and cheap food ain't to be sneezed at. So what happened when you went round this evening?'

'Oh, everything went fine, just fine, though the old bugger mightn't have been so easy if Ollie hadn't turned up. I don't say Ollie believed I'd not had a drop, but when I explained there were a patch of wet on the metal stairs, he told old Rathbone that anyone could fall down once. A' course, it were none of Ollie's business really, but he an' Rathbone are on good terms an' I s'pose Ollie's used to puttin' his oar in and bossin' people about, 'cos scuffers is like that.'

'Ollie? Scuffers?' Dot said, in a dazed voice. What on earth was her uncle going on about? But before he could answer – if he meant to do so – Aunt Myrtle spoke.

'And since when did you take to calling Mr McNamara Ollie?' she said severely. 'He's Mr McNamara, or Constable McNamara to folk like you and meself, Rupert Brewster. You don't want to go gettin' familiar; you ain't his pal, like old Rathbone.'

Uncle Rupert shuffled and looked self-conscious. 'I suppose you'd rather I called him George, 'cos that's his given name,' he said truculently. 'But all the scuffers at the station call him Ollie because he's so like old Oliver Hardy – you know, Stan and Ollie, off of the fillums.' He turned to Dot. 'If you've finished helping your aunt to undress, you can just clear out,' he said nastily. 'Oh aye, an' when I say clear out, I mean clear right out. Go round to that pal of yours – Fizz – an' if his mam won't have you it's the nearest orphanage for you, my girl.'

Dot went to sidle past him and he raised his hand, but before she could even flinch her aunt spoke, her normally quiet voice loud and angry. 'Leave her alone, Rupert. She's worth her weight in gold to me. I've telled you an' telled you, she's the only one what'll do a hand's turn in the house. The only one what gets me messages . . .'

But Dot, fleeing down the stairs, heard no more. She was still trying to assimilate the awful fact that Mr McNamara was Ollie and it was Ollie who had killed Emma's grandfather. Yet he was a policeman, an upholder of the law, a highly respected member of the community. Folks said you could trust Mr McNamara to take your side if you got into some sort of trouble. It was difficult to believe that the fat and friendly scuffer could deliberately hurt anyone, but then she remembered that Mr Grieves had been killed by repeated blows from what old Rathbone had called Ollie's stick – his truncheon, of course. Dot opened the kitchen door and began, automatically, to make herself a cup of cocoa and to fetch her bedding from the dresser drawer, but as she sipped the drink and began to undress, things became clearer in her mind. Rathbone's gate into the jigger had been unlocked and who had come in? It had been Ollie McNamara! Mr Rathbone's eyes had widened at the sight of him, not with surprise, but with warning. And when she had turned to leave and the two men had had a chance to exchange a word or two, the butcher had tried to call her back. Yet, since Ollie was not the ferret-faced man who had collided with her in the mouth of the jigger, then how . . .

Of course! The policeman who had grabbed her as she had jumped down from Rathbone's wall had shone a torch in her face. She had been unable to see him except as a dark, helmeted shape, but he had been able to see her, clear as clear, and he had a good reason for being in the jigger, the best reason of all, in fact. She had heard him arguing that the necklace should not be thrown away, so he must have been coming back to get it out of the bin, only he had forgotten that the gate had been locked behind him and he was far too fat and ungainly to scale the wall, as she had done. Yes, there was no doubt about it: Constable McNamara and the murdering Ollie were one and the same, and the sooner she could get to Emma and tell her what she had discovered, the better.

Dot sat up in bed, then slowly lay down again. If she went round to Emma's now, what guarantee could she have that she would be able to make herself heard? Why, Emma might have been in bed for hours, sound asleep. There must be some way of letting her know. Restlessly, she tossed and turned for a bit, then decided there was no point in telling Emma anything right now. It was not as if the older girl could take any action at this time of night. No, she would leave it until morning and then go round before breakfast and tell Emma everything. Satisfied that she was doing the right thing, she pulled her blankets up over her head and began to try to forget her troubles in sleep.

Emma had gone to bed as soon as she reached the flat and had dropped into a deep sleep straight away, but it had been nightmare-haunted and she woke in a cold sweat from quite the nastiest dream she had ever had. It had begun pleasantly enough. She and Nick were all dressed up, Nick in an evening suit and herself in a long, pale green dress, and Nick was fastening around her neck the emeralds which had, until so recently, graced the jeweller's window. They were standing in front of the mirror in Emma's bedroom, so that she was able to see the necklace, brilliantly green against her white skin, and Nick's reflected face as he smiled tenderly down at her. 'You must wear it to get married in,' he said, indicating the necklace. 'After all, you were the one who found it.' And suddenly Emma was no longer wearing the green gown but a beautiful white one and her hair was crowned with tiny rosebuds and yards and yards of veiling fell about her.

She looked the perfect bride, but even so, she was curious. 'Found it?' she echoed. 'Where did I find it? How did I get it? I don't remember . . . oh, I *can't* remember . . .'

Nick shook his head chidingly at her. 'You thought of a way to recover your lost treasure,' he said. 'You asked no one for help but nobly did it alone. I would have helped if I'd known but you were too proud to ask for assistance.' He was looking down at her and suddenly she saw that his face was sad, and there were tears in his dark eyes. 'So of course you were killed,' he said regretfully. 'And I wanted to marry you . . . marry you . . . marry you . . .'

Emma glanced at her reflection in the mirror and saw, to her horror, that it was growing pale and misty. She could actually see through it. She turned her face up to Nick, feeling tears in her own eyes. 'Did – did they kill me, as they killed my grandfather?' she quavered. 'I can't remember, but I don't want to be a ghost – I won't be! I don't care about the necklace. They can have it and welcome, so long as I can keep my life.'

Nick opened his mouth as if he were about to speak but Emma snatched at the necklace round her neck, trying to jerk free of it, and felt it begin to give just as the dream faded, and she woke, thoroughly frightened.

She sat up in bed, her heart still beating uncomfortably quickly, and swung her legs out on to the floor. She would go into the kitchen and get herself a hot drink and hope that when she returned to bed she would have broken the nightmare's spell and be able to sleep dreamlessly until morning. She padded, barefoot, into the kitchen, lit the gas under the kettle and glanced at the clock. It felt like midnight but she saw it was not in fact ten o'clock. The nightmare must have come almost as soon as she had got into bed. She began to ponder the dream once more. It had been a foolish, frightening fantasy, yet she was suddenly sure that it had meant something, was reminding her of something. In the dream, Nick had said she had recovered the necklace; how had she done so? Her only idea had been to use a magnet and, as Nick had said, a magnet will not attract the noble metals. Noble metals, Emma's mind mused. Gold, silver, and platinum. When she was small, she had owned a game of magnetic fishing, complete with tiny fishing rods from which one dangled a magnet on a piece of string over a variety of brightly coloured fish, each one with a tiny piece of metal in its mouth. The clasp! Emma knew very well that the strong clasp which opened and closed the necklace was not made of gold. The necklace had been made simply as a window display item, and originally it had had no clasp, nor needed any. But five or six years ago, her grandfather had put a metal clasp on the necklace when he had loaned it to an old friend who was going to a fancy dress ball as Queen Elizabeth. Emma was so excited that all thoughts of cocoa disappeared from her mind. Of course, there was a way to get the necklace back without tearing down any walls. She was almost sure the magnetic fishing game was still in the big cupboard in her bedroom, along with abandoned teddy bears, games of snakes and ladders and ludo and a collection of tattered children's classics, and she was certain that the small horseshoe-shaped magnets were quite strong enough to pull up the necklace.

Losing no time, Emma shot into the bedroom and pulled open the cupboard door. The fishing game was still there. Emma picked up the four small rods and returned to the kitchen, then rooted in a drawer for some strong twine. She detached the magnets from the fishing rods and tied them as securely as she could to a doubled length of twine. Then she searched for something at least as deep as the cavity wall, for she would be quite literally fishing for the necklace and would need something long and narrow as her own particular fishing rod. Not metal; that might prove complicated since the magnets would probably cling insistently to it and refuse to do the job for which they were intended. She found a long wooden spoon and knotted the twine securely to it; no fear of its slipping off as she fished, not with the wooden bowl of the spoon at the business end.

Having tested her home-made instrument over a collection of forks, she decided that it would do the job admirably. If she went right now, surely she would be safe enough? She would wear the black dress, stockings and coat which she had worn for her grandfather's funeral . . . or she could wear the outfit she had worn the night she had been tackled by Nick: her grandfather's black trousers and waistcoat and the old brown jacket which had proved such a good disguise before.

Thoughtfully, Emma swung open her wardrobe door and regarded the contents, then picked out her grandfather's clothes and began to put them on. Almost without realising it, she had decided to go now, right this moment. It would have been nice to have had a companion but not necessary, she decided, making her way back to the kitchen. She took an apple from the fruit bowl, then glanced at the kettle, which was beginning to steam. She really was thirsty and a drink would warm her right through, yet she realised she would be happier, for some reason, if her adventure took place without delay.

Having decided that she would leave at once, she turned off all the lights and made her way down the stairs and into the stockroom. She had tucked her fishing apparatus into the bosom of her jacket, and had pulled open the dresser drawer and taken out the torch she had used on her previous adventure. She had ensured that it was in good working order by flashing it around the kitchen, and had then put it into her trouser pocket, so that both her hands were free. Unlocking the back door, she went into the yard and heard a tiny tinkle as something fell from her person. Damn, Emma thought, plunging a hand into the pocket of her grandfather's trousers. There was a small hole in the corner of the right hand pocket through which, she supposed, a silver sixpence, or possibly even a farthing, had slipped. Thanking heaven that the hole was not large enough to let her trusty torch slide through, she glanced incuriously downwards, but could see nothing in the faint light from the cloudy sky. Shrugging, she turned to relock the door behind her, being careful to place the key in the trouser pocket without the hole, before setting off across the yard.

The gate which led from the yard to the jigger was always kept closed, though never locked. Emma opened it and chided herself for not having oiled the hinges, which positively screamed a protest as she swung it ajar. She had never noticed the noise before but supposed she must have taken it for granted during daylight hours, or perhaps the sound had been masked by the muffled din of people and traffic in Church Street itself. However, she decided not to close the gate again, but to leave it open for her return. Then, hunching her shoulders and pulling her grandfather's cap well down on her brow, she began to walk in the direction of the old churchyard.

An hour later, Emma left the churchyard with a spring in her step, so excited and triumphant that she could have sung aloud. It had all gone just as she had planned. She had reached her destination without seeing another soul and had clambered over the wall without any trouble. She had found the triangle of broken stone and pulled it out, though with some difficulty, and had produced her wooden spoon and the small cluster of magnets from their hiding place and thrust them into the crevice. At first, she had wondered if the string was too short, but a couple of jerks had brought the realisation that the wall on the other side was not smooth; the magnets must have rested on a ledge or protuberance of some sort. A couple of careful swings had freed them and presently she felt a tiny quiver of strain run from the spoon to her fingers and saw the twine tauten. Even then, it was not as easy as she had supposed because she had to pull the magnets – and therefore the necklace – up at an unnatural angle, but she managed it at last.

And there it was, sparkling in the torchlight, her grandfather's emerald necklace and the proof that Nick had said was essential for Dot's story to be believed. Emma had tucked the necklace reverently into the inside breast pocket of her grandfather's jacket, detached the magnets from her fishing rod and slid them into the pocket with the necklace. Then she had sat down on a large chunk of fallen masonry and eaten the apple, suddenly realising that she had been shaking like a leaf and needed a few moments to calm down.

Now, however, heading back towards Church Street, the nervous strain of fishing for the necklace had gone and she felt only pride in her achievement. She was sure that Nick would be really pleased with her; that Dot and Corky would applaud what she had done. They had all realised the importance of retrieving the necklace but she had been the only one with the knowledge which had enabled her to get it back. None of the others could possibly have known that the metal clasp was not gold or silver, that it would respond at once to the magnet so that it could be drawn up to safety. Nick had been talking of tunnelling under the wall to get the necklace back and that would have been a difficult as well as a dangerous undertaking so, naturally, he would be immensely pleased with her when she showed him her prize.

Dreamily, Emma began to compose the little speech she would make as soon as she saw Nick. She would not tell him at once that the necklace was in her possession; she would pretend that there was something quite ordinary in her pocket and would then produce the glittering object and wave it triumphantly before beginning to tell him how his remark about noble metals had set off a memory in her subconscious which had come into her dreams and then been acted upon.

There were few people about and Emma was halfway down Whitechapel and beginning to think longingly of her bed when a heavy hand fell on her shoulder, and a voice said in her ear: 'Hold on, lad! Just what are you doin' out at this time of night, eh? I seen you earlier on Church Street, actin' suspicious.'

Emma wriggled wildly but the man had changed his grip to her wrist and was forcing her arm up behind her back so painfully that she stopped struggling and gasped out a protest. 'Oh, please, I've done nothing wrong, honestly! I – I live in Church Street . . . I went to meet someone . . . it's not what it seems, really it's not.'

'Live on Church Street, a dirty little tyke like you! Why, I know everyone in these parts, 'cos it's on my beat, an' I don't recall seein' you until tonight. Now don't you go wriggling or I'll have to use me handcuffs and you won't like that.'

Emma turned her head to find herself staring into the round, and usually cheerful, face of Constable McNamara. She gave a gasp of relief. 'Oh, Mr McNamara, it's you. And of course, you wouldn't recognise me because of my clothing. I'm – I'm Emma Grieves.'

Constable McNamara swung her round without

letting go of her and peered, incredulously, into her face. 'Well, if you ain't a hard-faced young 'un to expect me to believe a handful of moonshine like that . . .' he began. Then, still without releasing her, he pulled off her cap with his free hand and watched, with considerable amazement, her dark curls cascading around her face. 'Well, I'll be damned,' he said softly. 'You really are Miss Grieves. But I think you'd better explain, my dear, because it's plain to me you're up to something and you've no kith or kin of your own to look after you now your grandpa's gone, which is why we've been told to keep an eye on your shop to make sure you don't have no more trouble.'

Telling herself that she had little choice now but to speak the truth, Emma produced the necklace from her inner pocket. 'I don't know whether you recognise this, Mr McNamara, but for as long as I can remember it has been the centrepiece of my grandfather's shop window. Then, as you know, it was stolen, along with a great many other things, all of them precious and valuable, but none quite as distinctive and unusual as the emerald necklace. I – I was told where the necklace was but we all thought it was not possible to get it back, only tonight I had a brainwave, so I went to the place where it had been hidden and managed to retrieve it.'

'We?' the constable said slowly. 'Hidden?' He pushed back his helmet with a beefy hand and scratched his head. 'I think you'd better start at the beginning, miss, and tell me the whole story.'

'It'll be a relief to tell someone in authority,' Emma admitted. 'But it's a long story, constable, and when you hear it I think you'll want to take action fairly quickly, so should we go back to your police station so that I can tell you there?'

Mr McNamara thought for a moment, then shook his head. 'No. Give me a rough idea as we walk along, because if your tale has anything to do with the robbery at your grandpa's shop, then I think we'll keep away from the station – for now at least. You needn't be afraid of being overheard, not at this time of night, and when you've told me your tale I'll know best what to do.'

Emma agreed that this seemed sensible and presently she found herself pouring the whole story into the constable's sympathetic ear. She was careful, however, not to name names, and when Mr McNamara protested that, in the end, she would have to tell all she knew and not just a part of it, she said that she would do so as soon as she could consult 'the others'.

When she had finished, the policeman stared down at his boots thoughtfully for some moments. 'I'm going to take you to someone I can trust. A magistrate,' he said. 'You say Mr Rathbone was one of the thieves, but the other is still unknown to you, so I think it a good deal safer that we confide in someone right outside this area. Fortunately, he don't live all that far away and won't mind being knocked up – well, he's used to it, to tell the truth. He lives in Brownlow Street, just past the infirmary. Now step lively, young woman, because the sooner your story's told to the right person, the sooner I can conduct you back to your bed.' He chuckled comfortably. 'And come to think of it, Mr Trigby-Smy won't take kindly to not being told the names of your confederates, so you might just as well tell me, you know.'

Emma did not mean to break faith. She thought she could simply give the magistrate false names, or just first names, come to that. She could always claim she did not know their surnames and promise to find out, thus giving herself time to get permission from Nick, Dot and Corky before giving any more away. She was uncomfortably aware that she was considered to have promised not to tell anyone anything, but she had been placed in an impossible position and really had had no choice.

As they walked through the city centre streets, Constable McNamara questioned her closely on all that had happened. Presently, they climbed Brownlow Hill and turned into one of the side streets. When they reached a railway bridge, the constable stopped and leaned against the high stone parapet, saying comfortably: 'Not far now, Miss Grieves. Mr Trigby-Smy is a professor and lives in a neat little house further along, close to his work at the university. Now one thing I disremember you telling me: you said as your young friend, what hid in the dustbin, suspicioned it were Mr Rathbone speaking because he'd shouted at her some time before when she'd gone into his butcher's shop. You also said she thought she were in the butcher's yard. Now that ain't proof, though I'm not disputin' she may well have been right. But what about t'other chap? You said nothing except that he were unknown to the gal, so I take it she didn't recognise the second man's voice?'

'No-o-o,' Emma admitted, then a sudden thought struck her. 'Oh, Mr McNamara, I believe I forgot to mention it, but Dot told me that Mr Rathbone called his companion Ollie, though I don't know if—'

At this point, from the railway lines beneath the bridge, Emma heard the rumble of an approaching train; it was coming fast, possibly an express on its way to some exciting, far-off destination. She half turned towards the sound, just as Constable McNamara stepped forward. Above the roar of the approaching train he shouted: 'Dot, did you say? Would that be the little red-headed gal . . . let me have another look at the necklace, Miss Grieves.'

Without thinking, Emma pulled the necklace from her inner pocket, but when the constable's hand shot out to take it she suddenly shrank back. Something was wrong; she did not like the glitter in his eyes and realised, with a stab of dismay, that as soon as she said the name Dot he had recognised it. She tried to pull her hand back, but the constable wrenched the necklace easily from her grasp and shoved it into his own pocket, and in almost the same movement he produced his truncheon and swung it at Emma's head, saying as he did so: 'You aren't going to get the better of Ollie McNamara, you stupid little bitch. Take that.'

And on the words, the truncheon connected with the side of her head. Emma felt the sickening thud, and even as the words he had used began to make sense, she dropped into deep and stifling darkness.

Chapter Eleven

As Emma slumped forward, Ollie McNamara grabbed her and lifted her up over his head, cursing as one of her shoes struck him in the eye. He knew she was unconscious – might already be dead – but he was taking no chances. Muscles cracking, he heaved her over the parapet just as the train, with a great burst of steam, clattered and roared under the bridge.

Ollie gave a satisfied sigh and slumped against the stonework for a moment, his chest still heaving. Wretched, clever little bitch! But she had done him a good turn; he and Archie had been desperate to get hold of this necklace because they believed that the red-haired kid had filched it from the bin and if she had, she might know more than was good for either of them. Well, now he had the necklace and he knew, for certain, that he and Archie had been right: the red-headed girl had been hiding somewhere nearby when Archie had tossed the necklace into the bin. Ollie had guessed as much the following day, had even realised – he ground his teeth – that he had actually had his hand on the kid the previous evening. He had said good night to Archie, and had gone off, or pretended to go off. In reality, he had hung around until he was pretty sure Archie would have gone to bed. Then he had gone down the jigger again, fully intending to take the necklace for himself and decide what to do with it later. Archie thought it was just paste; a beautiful and clever piece of work for window dressing. But he, Ollie, was not so sure; old man Grieves was well known in the trade for making and selling only the very best. Was it likely that the main item in his window was a mere bauble? Ollie did not think so, but even if it were, he had believed that it was safer in his possession than stuck in Rathbone's dustbin, perhaps to be discovered the very next day by some interferin' kid or by some nosy old tramp.

So he had gone back down the jigger, seen the kid lurking, and grabbed for her, demanding to know what she was doing there. Of course, he had had no inkling that she had been there earlier in the evening and had not been unduly worried when she had given him the slip. Afterwards, of course, when he and Archie had realised that the necklace had been stolen from the bin, he had begun to wonder, but when nothing happened he had dismissed the idea. The necklace had not appeared anywhere, so far as he knew, so he had told himself that it had probably been broken up and sold as separate stones by some enterprising person, perhaps even by Archie, for he knew his old friend to be as crooked as he was himself.

But now the game was in his own hands at last.

He had the necklace. The girl Emma was undoubtedly dead, for no one could survive an express train, and all its carriages, thundering across her unconscious body. In fact, with a bit of luck, Emma Grieves would be unrecognisable and it would take time to find out who she was. Grinning to himself, he repeated the little rhyme which had always made him smile. '*Oh, Mother dear, what is that mess that looks like strawberry jam? Hush, hush, my love, it is Papa, run over by a tram*.' Yes, that would certainly apply to clever Miss Grieves and very soon to that nasty little redhead, Dot what's-her-name. He'd already had one go, though he hadn't been particularly perturbed when it hadn't worked since, at the time, he had only suspicioned she might have taken the necklace. But he wouldn't make that mistake again. He knew she lived in Lavender Court, knew she was the niece of Rupert Brewster, who worked for Archie. He could pick her off at any time, and the beauty of it was that no one would ever suspect a policeman. He would say that he saw her slip and reached to grab her before she fell into the roadway. All the locals knew and liked him – he was the scuffer who handed out free clogs and kecks to kids who couldn't otherwise have afforded decent footwear and clothing. No one would suspect good old Ollie of deliberately harming a child.

He glanced towards the parapet of the bridge and sighed heavily. Despite his certainty, he would have to climb over the side wall and make his way down to the line just to check that the girl was truly dead and that there was nothing on her which would identify her.

By now, his breathing had steadied and he was about to walk across to the side wall when he saw someone approaching. He hesitated, and was glad he had done so when a voice hailed him. 'Evenin', Ollie! Not that it is evening, since it's well past midnight. What are you doin' in this neck of the woods?'

It was Constable Barrow, a man whom Ollie knew only slightly since he was much younger and patrolled a different part of the city. He was not in uniform but sauntered along with a checked cap on the back of his head and his fawn jacket unbuttoned.

'Mornin', Barrow, then,' Ollie said with all the joviality he could muster, and fell into step beside the other man. He creased his big comedian's face into a friendly grin, though he was secretly furious. Damned interferin' fellow! When the body was discovered next day, and the report went round the stations, it might occur to young Barrow that he had seen Constable McNamara loitering near the railway bridge, a good march from his own patch. What was more, though he was certain the girl must have been killed by the approaching train, he would have felt happier had he been able to examine the body. But it was too late now; it would look very odd indeed if he made some excuse and turned back towards the bridge. So he

continued to stroll along beside the other policeman, chatting idly.

But there was still the problem to tackle of why
he was here at all and Constable Barrow was looking at him enquiringly. Ollie's mind raced, then
came up with a perfect solution. 'I'm in this neck
o' the woods because I've been takin' an injured
person into the infirmary,' he said glibly. 'Then I
fancied a fag afore goin' back where I belong.' He
fished a squashed packet of Woodbines out of his
tunic pocket. 'Fancy joinin' me? Only, like a fool,
I forgot me matches, so unless you've gorra light
on you . . .'

As he spoke, Constable Barrow produced
matches and lighted both cigarettes.

'What are you doing down this way, Barrow?'
Ollie asked, as the two men crossed Dansie Street.
'I disremember where you live an' you plainly
aren't on duty.'

The younger man laughed. 'I been round at my
young lady's place. Earlier, we went to the flick-
ers, then back to her house for a cup of tea and a
sandwich. Usually, I catch a tram – I lodge on Mere
Lane, which is a fair walk – but there's no trams
this late.'

'You're right there, but one thing being a policeman does teach you, and that's how to walk
distances,' Ollie said. 'Grand night, ain't it?'

The two men carried on, chatting comfortably,
and by the time they parted Ollie was truly hope-
ful that young Barrow would never connect the

fat and friendly policeman with the mysterious death of Emma Grieves when she was found next day, crushed and broken, near the Brownlow Street bridge. After all, there were half a dozen bridges across the railway line in this part of the city, all pretty well identical; he should be safe enough.

Emma regained consciousness slowly and stupidly. She was lying on something horribly uncomfortable and was incapable of any sort of movement. Her eyelids felt so heavy she simply could not raise them, but gradually she was beginning to realise that she was in a moving vehicle of some description because every now and again her bed of nails seemed to shift and a whole new set of pains attacked her. Emma wanted to groan, to cry out, to beg for help, but as yet that was beyond her. Her head was thumping even more badly than the rest of her and, for the first time, a vague memory came into her mind. There had been a man, a cruel and vicious man, who had hit her with some sort of stick, or had it been the butt of a gun? She had been talking to him, had thought him pleasant enough . . . but at this point her thoughts broke down; her mind could take her no further. The immediate present was too horrible to allow her to consider the past. Some instinct told her to lie as still as she could and to wait until her eyes would open. Then she could look around her and perhaps she would know how she had come to be here.

The next thing she registered was the simply appalling noise and the realisation that most of it came from an engine of some description. Was she in a large lorry carrying stones to and from some quarry or other? But then she heard a whistle, so shrill that, had she had the strength, she would have clapped both hands over her ears, and with the whistle came realisation. It was a train's whistle, which meant she had somehow got aboard a train. Cautiously, without opening her eyes, she put out a wavering hand and felt the nails nearest her, which were not nails at all, but extremely sharp and unpleasant stones. Further investigations with one fumbling hand told her that these were very strange stones indeed. Her foggy mind recognised the shape, yet she could not . . . it was coal! And at once her eyelids jerked open. She was still not capable of any movement other than the slight one of her hand, but she saw the dark and star-speckled sky above her, with clouds scudding across it. So it was still night, then. She had no idea at what time the man had hit her over the head, but she knew it had been dark and common sense informed her that it must have been fairly late, or someone would surely have prevented the man from so mistreating her? But what had she done to deserve such treatment and how had she come to be lying in a truck full of coal? Even as the thought entered her head, the train ran over some points and Emma's head jerked on its uncomfortable pillow. Pain arrowed through her and the stars and the dark sky were blotted out by a deeper darkness.

The next time Emma regained consciousness, she tried to sit up and managed to do so for several moments before sinking back once more. She put a wavering hand weakly up to her face and was horrified to feel wet and sticky tracks running down from her forehead to her chin. Cautiously, her fingers continued to explore, then she snatched her hand away. It seemed she had received a wound on her brow which was still sluggishly bleeding. No wonder her head was throbbing, she thought, and then realised that there was a strong wind which caught at her hair when she sat up. Looking round her, she saw that the sides of the container in which she lay were clear of the coal for quite two or three feet, and with that realisation came another. She had somehow fallen, or been thrown, into the tender of a train, and whenever the coals shifted beneath her it was because the fireman was shovelling fuel into the engine's hungry maw.

But how the devil had she got here? She was still too weak to sit up for long but she did shift her position slightly and saw, with complete surprise, that she was wearing trousers. Trousers? Why on earth should she be wearing trousers? Her hand crept out, feebly checking the rest of her clothing. She felt a ragged jacket, obviously a man's, and a shirt, collarless, the top two buttons undone. She was disguised, then, as a ragged man, though a hand put gingerly to her head informed her that the checked cap she had worn was no longer in place. Checked cap! And on the thought, she remembered. She had dressed as a man before; she could recall it distinctly. Her grandfather had not been a large man and she had borrowed the clothes he wore when he went fishing or bird-watching. He would not mind; he was generous and she must have had a good reason for donning the disguise otherwise Grandpa would never have consented . . . and this thought brought others flooding in. Her grandfather was dead! Her dear grandfather, who had brought her up, paid for her schooling, sent her to college to perfect the skills he himself had taught her, had died and she had inherited the shop. No, he had not died, he had been cruelly murdered, and it had been the murderer who had stolen something precious from her and had attacked her with his . . . his . . .

But the effort of such concentrated thinking in her present horribly battered state was too much for Emma. Her heavy, heavy lids closed slowly over her eyes and she lapsed into the coma-like state from which she had so recently emerged.

It might have been hours, or perhaps only minutes, later that Emma came to herself for the third time to find that the train was no longer moving. Cautiously, she tried to sit up, and immediately every bone in her body screamed a protest whilst her head flooded out a drumbeat of pain and her many bruises ached alarmingly. But her brain, at least, was clear, and she was beginning to remember how she and Constable McNamara had walked across the city together in order to visit a magistrate, though she did not recall his name. Emma frowned. Constable McNamara; she had always liked and trusted him so why, when she thought about him now, did her spine prickle with fear and a feeling of disgust well up within her? They had been standing by the tall stone wall which hid the railway lines from passers-by; she had heard the rumble of a train approaching, had glanced towards the sound, as one would, and then . . . she had got it! The constable had called himself Ollie McNamara . . . Ollie, the man who had murdered her grandfather . . . as he had swung his truncheon at her unprotected head. Wincing at the memory, she tried to work out once more exactly what had happened, whilst clambering painfully to her knees so that she could peer over the side of the engine's tender. She saw that the train was standing in a very large and almost empty station. Nearby, a nameplate announced that the train had reached Crewe. Emma's mind gave a jerk. If this train had left Liverpool at midnight, then it was the London sleeper and unless she disembarked pretty promptly she would find herself carried on to Euston. Her mind still refused to recall everything that had happened that evening, but she knew she simply had to get back to Liverpool or something dreadful would happen. She hauled herself to her feet and swung, with great difficulty, over the side of the tender. The platform seemed a long way below and, for a moment, she hesitated, feeling her head begin to swim. Then she gritted her teeth and told herself that this was no time to baulk at a little jump. She clung to the side for a moment longer, then launched herself at the platform.

Landing was almost as painful as she had anticipated and she was unable to prevent herself from slumping forward on to her knees. She allowed herself a moment to recover, then clambered, dizzily, to her feet and looked along the platform. At the rear of the train, porters, she presumed, were hefting mail bags from huge trolleys into the guard's van. Emma began to stumble towards them and, as she did so, tried to rehearse what she would say. A murder attempt, which had ended in her being thrown, presumably, from the railway bridge. The knowledge which she now possessed and which must be passed on to the police. Oh, and the necklace! Suddenly, she remembered the emerald necklace, the way it had glinted in the gas light, the way Ollie's hand had shot out to snatch it from her . . . and she had told him that Dot was involved! Oh God, oh God, after all their care, she had let Dot's name escape her and he had known at once whom she meant. *The little red-headed gal*, he had said. And that had been hours ago, hours and hours.

At the other end of the platform, one of the

porters raised his head, saw her and pointed. Emma broke into a lurching, stumbling run towards them, then saw that their figures were dwindling and that in front of her yawned a great, black pit. She knew she must jump it or she would never tell anyone her story. But even as she gathered herself together for the leap, she knew she would never make it. Weakness brought her to her knees as the blackness swallowed her up.

Dot slept well, though towards morning nightmares haunted her in which Mr McNamara somehow managed to learn who had been hiding in the dustbin and came after her, sometimes with a raised truncheon, at other times with a beefy hand planted between her shoulder blades, ready to push her under the nearest tram. She had intended to go round to Church Street as soon as the shop opened, but when she woke she decided that this was not a good idea. She guessed, by the amount of light showing through the thin kitchen curtains, that it was probably no more than seven o'clock; by eight, the family would be stirring and her aunt would be most upset, not to say annoyed, if her little helper disappeared without so much as assisting her to dress.

It was a shame to wake Emma early but Dot could see no alternative. She got up quietly and pulled the kitchen curtains a little apart so that she could see the clock, which read half past six. Dot glanced at her sofa bed, a trifle wistfully, then scolded herself. The one thing which had stopped Nick and Emma from going to the authorities was that they did not know the identity of Mr Rathbone's partner – he who had actually murdered old Mr Grieves – but now that Dot herself knew, the sooner she passed this knowledge on, the better.

Accordingly, she sloshed water into the washing-up bowl and had a quick wash, then dressed and tiptoed across the kitchen and down the hall. Since Uncle Rupert had come in sober the previous evening, the front door was locked and bolted, seldom the case when he had had a few bevvies too many. It was rather annoying because bolts are not easy to draw back soundlessly. But Dot took her time and managed the task without any squeaks or clicks. She let herself out into the deliciously cool early morning and closed the door behind her with infinite care. Then she set off in the direction of Church Street.

It was rather nice walking along the dew-wet pavements and seeing so few people about; a milk-man on his round, factory workers heading for their places of employment and a few delivery vans made the streets seem almost empty when one considered how crowded they would be in a mere hour or so. She slid into the jigger which led to the back entrance of Emma's shop. She had been this way several times now and was surprised to find the back gate ajar. She did not think it was ever locked, but she knew that there was a bolt which Emma slid across, saying that it was enough to stop strangers from entering her premises, though anyone who knew about the bolt simply put a hand over the gate and slid it back.

This morning, however, the gate was not bolted and somehow this worried Dot. What did it mean? Had someone been snooping around the back premises? If so, did Emma know or was she still slumbering peacefully, unaware that there had been a prowler?

Asking herself these unanswerable questions, however, would not do any good, so Dot crossed the yard and rang the bell long and hard, reflecting that Emma had told her she was always up and about by seven o'clock, and it was past that now; Dot had heard a clock striking seven as she hurried along Whitechapel. Since there was no answer to her ring, she supposed that Emma might have slept in for once, or might be listening to the wireless, for she had remarked that they must ring persistently if her set was playing.

Dot raised her hand to ring the bell again, then paused to listen. No sound came from the flat above so she assumed that Emma must have overslept. Glancing round the yard, she saw the dustbin standing meekly by the back gate and took the tin lid off it; she might wake the whole neighbourhood but she dared not let Emma sleep on, not knowing the vital information which she, Dot, was here to pass on. She banged on the door with the dustbin lid and was quite shocked by the resultant clangour, but there was no response from

Emma's flat, though Dot saw a face appear at the window above Beasley's china shop, next door.

It was only at this point that the possibility occurred to Dot that there might be another explanation for the open gate than that of a prowler: someone could have come in through it, but someone could also have gone out. Dot stepped back and looked up at the windows which overlooked the yard. The curtains were still drawn across and Dot just knew that by this time in the morning Emma would have been in the kitchen making an early cup of tea, with the curtains drawn back and probably the window open as well. Even if her friend were ill, Dot was sure she would have staggered to the kitchen to make herself a drink, for Dot herself was regretting that she had not stopped in Lavender Court for long enough to have a cuppa; tea would have taken too long but she could have mixed conny-onny with water and slaked her thirst with that.

Still, it was too late for such regrets. Dot turned disconsolately away, and as she did so, an object on the paving stones caught her eye and she bent to pick it up. Odd! It was a small magnet, the sort children use. Dot shrugged and slipped it into her pocket, concluding that it had nothing to do with Emma's disappearance. Yet she had a vague feeling, in the back of her mind, that the little magnet did mean something. When was she last thinking about magnets . . . ?

Dot was actually going out through the back

gate when a voice hailed her from the other side of the wall. She glanced across and saw Mrs Beasley, her grey locks still confined in a hairnet and her body swathed in a shabby red dressing gown. 'Mornin', young 'un! You tryin' to make a delivery? Only I don't reckon Miss Grieves is at home. I heared her go off last night – it must have been after ten 'cos I heard the clock strike just before, I can tell you that much – because I were too hot to get to sleep and that gate of hers squawks like a soul in torment whenever it's opened or shut.' She chuckled. 'I thought to meself I'd have a word with her about applyin' a drop of oil because I'm a light sleeper and I guessed I'd be woke again – if I'd had the good luck to fall asleep, that was – when she came back in. Only she didn't – come back in, I mean – so I weren't disturbed after all.'

'Then where is she?' Dot said wildly. 'I can't believe Emma would stay out all night! Oh, I do hope nothing awful has happened to her.'

Mrs Beasley clucked consolingly. 'Happened to her? Now whatever could happen to a nice young lady like Miss Grieves? Oh, I know her grandpa were killed during that jewel robbery, but she's a sensible girl, that one; she ain't going to go round wi' diamonds in her pockets or gold round her neck, so no one ain't likely to bash her on the head and steal from her. No, no, likely she's met up with one of her friends from that college she went to, and stayed overnight rather than come home in the early hours. Don't you worrit yourself about Miss Grieves; she'll be back.'

Dot thanked her and wandered back down the jigger into Church Street, her mind whirling. She might have accepted Mrs Beasley's theory of an old friend from art school had it not been for the hour at which Emma had left her flat. At that time of night, Emma should surely have been tucked up in her bed and would scarcely have left it to meet a friend, no matter how close the two had once been. Dot cudgelled her brain as she set out for Virgil Street. The young reporter might be able to throw some light on Emma's whereabouts, but if not, he still needed to know that Constable McNamara was the dreaded Ollie.

Dot broke into a run, then slowed to a walk once more, glancing up at the chemist's clock as she passed it. It was a quarter to eight, so it was still early enough to catch Nick and Corky at their breakfast. The more she thought about it, the more she worried about Emma. The older girl had been very kind to her and Dot's sharp eyes had spotted, some time before, that Nick was growing very fond of Emma. Whether her friend returned his feelings, Dot was not so sure, but it seemed to her that few women would be able to resist Nick's rueful smile and the twinkle in those dark brown eyes. Emma might not be in love with him yet, but Dot was pretty sure she would soon succumb. And Dot could not forget that Emma liked and trusted the fat policeman, nor fail to remember the cruel blows which had ended old Mr Grieves's life. Her friend simply must be warned about Ollie's true identity before something dreadful happened.

In Emma's eyes, Constable McNamara was the comfortable local scuffer who popped into the shops along Church Street for a chat and a hot cup of tea on winter mornings, or a glass of ale in the summer. Folk trusted their local policeman and would not dream that such a person could ever turn his coat, let alone commit murder.

By now, Dot was approaching No. 25 Virgil Street and was beginning to rehearse in her head what she should say to Mr Cartwright, or his wife, should one of them answer the door. This proved unnecessary, however, for she spotted Nick and Corky coming towards her along the pavement, so deep in conversation that they didn't even see her until she spoke.

'Nick! Corky! Oh, you don't know how glad I am to see you! The most awful thing has happened and I'm worried sick about Emma.'

Nick had been smiling a welcome, but at her words he stopped short and grabbed her arm. 'Emma? What's happened to Emma? Oh my God, if she's hurt . . .' He shook Dot's shoulder quite roughly. 'What's happened, Dot? Tell me at once!'

'She's not in her flat and I can't tell you where she's gone, but honestly, Nick, I think you'd better hear the whole story,' Dot said quickly. 'I don't know whether there's any connection between the two . . . look, where can we go to talk?'

Nick thought for a moment and was still thinking when Corky chimed in. 'There's the playground; it's too early for the kids to be out so we can be pretty private there.'

He was right; the playground was deserted and the three of them sat down on a low wall whilst Dot started her tale. This time she was determined to tell it all right from the beginning, and started with her visit to the butcher's yard on behalf of Uncle Rupert, ignoring Nick's impatient reminder that they knew all about this already. Corky, perhaps knowing Dot better than Nick did, waved the young man to silence. 'Let Dot tell the tale her own way,' he said reprovingly. 'This way we'll get the full story without important bits being left out. Carry on, Dotty.'

Doggedly, Dot carried on, though she could understand Nick's eagerness to learn what had happened to Emma, and it was not long before Nick and Corky were in possession of all the facts. She even produced the small magnet from her pocket and showed it to them, though Nick waved this aside as irrelevant. 'It's just a kid's toy,' he said disgustedly. 'Tell me what Mrs Beasley said again.'

Dot was beginning to do so when Corky cut in. 'I reckon that magnet is important,' he said slowly. 'Shut up a minute, Nick, and you Dot, and let me think.'

'What's important is why Emma left the flat just after ten and still hadn't returned by eight this morning . . .' Nick said, glaring at Corky. 'As you say, Dot, Emma really liked and trusted that fat bounder, so it's possible she may have confided in him. He might have lured her into some quiet premises and locked her in . . . he might have injured her in some way . . . oh, there must be something we can do.'

Corky waved his hand. 'Shut up and listen,' he said brusquely. 'Do you remember when we were talking about getting the necklace back, someone suggested fishing for it with a magnet? Only you, Nick, reminded us that gold and silver and such don't respond to a magnet. Everyone accepted that and Emma obviously knew it was true. But don't you *see*? Several times, Emma has said that the necklace wasn't particularly valuable in itself because her grandfather made it when he was a young man only to show what he could do, and she thought it was really a fake. If it was, then surely there's a good chance that a magnet could have brought it up, so Emma must have gone out, in the middle of the night when there would be few people about, to fish for the necklace. What's more, I reckon she got it,' he ended triumphantly.

The other two gazed at him, awestruck. 'I reckon you're right,' Nick said, his voice sinking to a whisper. 'I reckon you're right, Corky, and that's where she went: to the ruined church, I mean. But she can't have got the necklace.'

'Why not?' Corky said belligerently, bristling. 'I think she must have got it and perhaps she's taken it to someone really important, because it's proof, isn't it?'

'She won't have got it because she dropped the magnet,' Nick said patiently, but Corky immediately interrupted him once more.

'Oh, Nick, didn't you reckernise that magnet? When I were a little kid at Redwood Grange, we had one of them magnetic fishing games. It has four little rods, each wi' a magnet on the end. I reckon she'd have shoved all four into her pocket in case one weren't strong enough to bring up the necklace. That's what I'd do if it were me. And I reckon she's got the necklace right now and is probably back at the flat already, waiting for the rest of us to turn up so's we can plan our next move.'

Immensely heartened by these words, the three of them jumped to their feet and began to make their way back towards Church Street.

Emma had still not returned to the flat. Nick, Corky and Dot had gone straight to the stockroom door, but they retraced their steps and went round to the front and into the shop, which was now open, to ask if Emma was available. They were not surprised to learn that no member of the staff had seen her that morning and that no note, or message, had been left to explain why she was not there. Mr Winterton said, rather deprecatingly, that he suspected Miss Grieves was giving them a chance to show that they could manage without her, and since she had entrusted him with a key to the premises the previous day this did not seem unlikely to the staff, who knew nothing of Emma's departure in the middle of the night.

Miss Snelling, however, did not seem too happy. 'If you'd be kind enough to go up to her flat, Mr Randall – or perhaps it might be better if Dot went – then we could just ascertain that she isn't ill and in need of assistance,' she suggested. 'I quite understand what Mr Winterton means, but Miss Grieves is a very conscientious employer and would have come down by now had she been able to do so. Mr Winterton does not have a key to the safe so we have been unable to dress the window properly, and Miss Grieves did not give either of us the yellow bag which contains the float, so I assume that is also in the safe.'

Dot agreed at once to go up to the flat but came down again shaking her head. 'She must have had an urgent call from someone, too urgent to allow her to do more than fly out of the house,' she said. 'Her handbag is still on the kitchen dresser and the grey jacket which she wears for every day is hanging in the wardrobe.' She smiled at Miss Snelling with forced cheerfulness. 'But no doubt the mystery will be cleared up in an hour or two, when she either sends a message or turns up herself.'

Once outside in Church Street, however, the three exchanged worried glances. 'In my opinion, Ollie McNamara got wind of what was going on – may even have seen her prowling the streets in the middle of the night – and has done something dastardly,' Nick said, his voice grim. 'Isn't it time we went to the authorities? After all, we know who the murderer is now.'

'We know it was Ollie, but we still don't have the necklace,' Dot pointed out. 'And suppose he's got Emma locked away somewhere? If he knows we've discovered his identity he might think it was worth bumping Emma off – I mean you can't be hung twice, can you – whereas if he still thinks we don't know . . .'

Corky broke in at this point. 'The first thing is to find Emma, and if that means following McNamara – Ollie, I mean – for days and days, then I'm willing,' he said. He turned to Nick. 'Tell me honestly, Nick, can we go to the rozzers without the necklace to prove Dot's story isn't just made up? Remember, McNamara isn't just any policeman, he's the local bobby on the beat, trusted by everyone, and he's in league with Rathbone, what's a respected citizen, a member of the Chamber of Commerce, a feller who probably contributes to the Police Fund and does all sorts for the community.'

Nick began to look thoughtful and Dot realised that he saw the point of Corky's argument. She would swear on the Bible that she had been in the dustbin and had heard the two men discussing the robbery. She had believed herself to be in Rathbone's yard and had later satisfied herself that it was so, but she had never actually seen Archie Rathbone talking to Ollie, and had certainly not identified the fat constable on that particular occasion. Without the necklace as proof, it was possible that the authorities would prefer to accept whatever story Archie and Ollie dreamed up, and would dismiss her as an over-imaginative troublemaker. And though Nick was a reliable grown-up, he was also a stranger and one who had connived with a runaway orphan from a London children's home when he should, by rights, have handed Corky back to the authorities.

Dot glanced, despairingly, first at Corky and then at Nick, and saw her own fears mirrored in their eyes. Corky said a bad word and Nick echoed it, then grinned ruefully at Dot. 'Until we get our hands on Emma, we'd best do as Corky suggests and simply follow Ollie everywhere,' he said. 'And that's Corky and myself, young Dot, because your place is with your aunt. You're fond of her, despite all you've said, and she truly needs you. What's more, you see if you can get anything out of your uncle since he's plainly involved in the whole affair.'

'But how are we to find Ollie for starters?' Corky asked, rather plaintively, as the three of them left the playground and headed for the city centre. 'He might not be on duty . . . well, he won't be, if he was working last night, and if he came across Emma he must have been working, wouldn't you say?'

Nick agreed that this must be so. 'Which means our best bet is to check up at the police station,' he said, after some thought. 'After all, there's no harm in asking for Mr McNamara, and come to think of it, we could make the excuse that Emma has gone missing and since he's the bobby on the beat he might easily know where she's gone. Only – only, as you know, I made a lot of enquiries of the police when I first came to Liverpool, hoping that they'd help me out regarding the robberies in Church Street, and they rather fobbed me off. So I think, Corky, it had better be you who asks about McNamara. Can you make up some reason for wanting to know where the old devil is?'

Corky nodded enthusiastically. 'I'll say I've got some information for him which I can't give to anyone else,' he said confidently. 'Of course, he might be in the police station and they might fetch him out, and if they do, I'll – I'll say that Emma's missing, hasn't come in to work. Then I'll say someone saw the two of them together last night so I thought he might be able to shed some light.'

'That's brilliant,' Dot said admiringly. 'You really are clever, Corky. That way, if he *did* see Emma last night he'll get the wind up and probably start to bluster and then you'll know that he really was on his beat last night and may even have spent some time in Emma's company.'

Nick nodded agreement. 'And after that, Corky my boy, you can stick around near the station if McNamara is inside it, or you can go over his beat and see if you can pick him up if he's not. Meanwhile, I'll go along to this churchyard – you'll have to tell me the way, Corky – and see if I can pick up any clues to Emma's whereabouts.'

Corky, however, shook his head. 'There's no point, Nick,' he said decisively. 'Since you've not been there before, you'd have the devil's own job to find the path we've beaten down from the churchyard wall into the ruined building itself, let alone the crevice. Tell you what, whilst I do my investigating at the police station you can hang around watching for McNamara, and I'll make my way to the churchyard later.' He turned to Dot. 'Don't you think that's the best idea, Dotty?'

Dot agreed and presently the three separated and Dot set off, at a determined lope, for Lavender Court.

By the time she reached the house, Dot was beginning to feel apprehensive. She could not believe that either the boys or her uncle would have helped her aunt to dress and get down the stairs, and she could imagine how furious Aunt Myrtle would be to find herself marooned in her stuffy bedroom on such a warm day. She would be furious with her niece and, off hand, Dot could not think of an excuse which would be acceptable to an angry aunt. The truth, unfortunately, could not be told so she had better say she had gone to Church Street to run an errand for a shopkeeper there but it had taken longer than she anticipated. It didn't sound very convincing even to Dot herself, but anyway, it would have to do.

Dot opened the front door without having to fish the key up through the letter box, however, so she knew someone was home. Her hand was actually upon the knob of the kitchen door when she heard a movement on the landing and, glancing up, saw her Uncle Rupert standing there. His hair was on end, his face was red and his brows were drawn together into a deep frown, though much to Dot's astonishment his face cleared as he caught sight of her. 'Dotty McCann, where the devil have you been?' he asked wrathfully. Dot began to speak but he cut across her words. 'Well, never mind, queen, you're here now and that's what matters. Your aunt's been took bad but every time I've tried to leave her to fetch help she wails and carries on so that I'm scared for me life to go down so much as three stairs, lerralone the whole flight. But now you're here, I reckon I'd best go for the doctor, or the nurse what lives in the next court, while you give an eye to your aunt.'

'Shall I bring her up a cup of tea?' Dot asked, still hovering at the foot of the stairs, but her uncle, thundering down towards her, shook his head.

'No time for that now. Just you get up and stay with her till I brings back help. Shan't be long.' And on the words, he ran towards the door without even bothering to grab a jacket or cap, and disappeared into the court.

Dot entered her aunt's room with some trepidation and this was not unfounded, for she found Aunt Myrtle lying on the bed looking most dreadfully ill. She was white as a sheet but big beads of sweat were running down her face and her eyes were rolling in a truly frightening manner. When she saw her niece, she tried to pull herself up in the bed, then collapsed back on her pillows once more, groaning loudly.

'Aunt Myrtle, whatever's the matter?' Dot asked wildly. 'Have you fallen again? Is your poor leg paining you?'

Aunt Myrtle heaved a long, shuddering sigh then began to try to pull herself up in the bed once more. 'No, I didn't fall. The babies is comin' three months before their time and there's nothin' I can do to stop 'em,' she muttered huskily. 'The pain is awful, chuck, far worse'n a normal birth. And Rupe was so proud o' fatherin' twins an' now I'm goin' to lose 'em, I know I am.'

Poor Dot felt helpless in the face of her aunt's plight. She knew that if Aunt Myrtle was truly in labour, there really was nothing that could be done. So she said, cheeringly: 'If you're right, Aunt Myrtle, then there's nothing anyone can do for the poor little babies, but the doctor or the nurse can help *you*. Uncle Rupe's gone to fetch one of 'em and once they're here they'll – they'll give you something to ease the pain. Now just you look on the bright side, because you said yourself that you had enough mouths to feed without adding two more.'

Aunt Myrtle, however, was not to be comforted. 'But I didn't mean it,' she wailed. 'Oh, I know I *said* it, said I didn't want no more kids, couldn't manage with 'em, but I didn't mean for God to go takin' 'em away.' She gasped and clutched her swollen stomach as another pain attacked her. 'It's a judgement on me, that's wharrit is, an' if I die, I reckon I'll burn in hell for wishin' harm on two little innocents.'

It seemed like hours to Dot before help arrived and, when it came, it was unexpected. The doctor had clearly taken Rupert's worries seriously and it was two ambulance men who burst into the room, carrying a stretcher between them. They reassured Aunt Myrtle and tried to get her on board the stretcher, but she pointed out that they would never get the thing round the angle of the stairs with her on it and, presently, Dot carried the stretcher down while the two ambulance men manhandled her aunt as far as the front door. Then they got her on to the stretcher, wrapped in coarse grey blankets, for she was still in her stained and ragged nightgown, and Dot accompanied her to the ambulance waiting at the entrance to the court. She would have turned away then, to return to the house and see what needed doing, but was stopped short by a wail from her aunt. 'Dot, Dot! Come along o' me, there's a good girl. I can't go into one of them hospital wards with no one of me own.' She turned to the ambulance men. 'Is it all right if me niece comes along, mister? Only if it ain't you can just take me back indoors again.'

The ambulance man beckoned Dot aboard. She climbed obediently in beside her aunt, and the vehicle set off at a fast pace. Everyone in the court must have seen them leave but no one, not even a police-man, would come searching for her in a hospital.

For it had occurred to her that Emma, if she had been captured, might well have accidentally given away more than she intended and Dot was already aware that both Rathbone and McNamara knew she lived with her aunt and uncle. They could not know that it had been she who had overheard their conversation on the night of the burglary, but she was pretty sure by now that McNamara would have put two and two together and realised that the child he had caught skulking in the jigger had been no other than Rupert Brewster's niece. He would have been stupid indeed not to also realise that she could easily have taken the necklace from the dustbin and, whatever their faults, she did not think either Archie Rathbone or Ollie McNamara was stupid.

The ambulance swerved wildly round a corner and came to a screeching stop. The back doors shot open and two stretcher bearers entered the vehi-cle. Hastily, Dot followed them into the enormous building, her mind divided now between her own troubles and those of her aunt. What would I do if I were Mr McNamara and suspected that some-one had overheard that conversation on the night of the burglary, she asked herself, and the answer came far too pat for her own liking: I would silence that listener by any means in my power, she thought grimly. Suppose I went to him and swore myself to secrecy? But she knew she couldn't do that – wouldn't do that. She had never known Emma's grandfather, never even met him, but she knew his reputation. He had been good, kind and generous and had taken her friend Emma in and brought her up. No, his killer should not go unpunished if she, Dot, could help it.

The ward, when she and her aunt entered it, was a long room with cold white walls and a brown linoleum floor. The stretcher bearers put her aunt down on one of the high white beds and a nurse swished the curtain closed, then gestured to Dot. 'The doctor will be wanting to examine your aunt, so he will,' she said, in a strong Irish accent. 'You go and wait in the corridor, alanna, and I'll call you when it's all right for you to come back to your auntie.'

Dot trudged obediently out of the ward and hung around the corridor, but presently the doors to the ward shot open and her aunt was carried out once more, the stretcher bearers almost running, though not quite. To Dot's dismay, she saw that there was blood on the edges of the stretcher and that her aunt's eyes were closed, and that she was breathing in small, shallow gasps. Dot would have followed the stretcher but the Irish nurse who had spoken to her earlier prevented her from doing so, with a hand on her arm. 'Your aunt's miscarrying,' she said briefly. 'I'll take you along to the waiting room, then come and call you when she's back on the ward. Where's your uncle?'

'I don't know,' Dot said helplessly. 'He left me

with Aunt Myrtle while he went for the doctor, and he hadn't arrived back by the time the ambulance appeared. Why, nurse? Is he needed here?'

The nurse shrugged. 'I don't suppose it's important,' she said. 'If he comes, I'll tell Reception to send him down to the waiting room. Come along now.'

Chapter Twelve

Corky stood at the long counter in the police station and stared furtively about him, but could see no one who looked even slightly like Dot's description of Constable McNamara. In fact, there was only one policeman behind the long desk and he was a sergeant, with a big spongy-looking nose, small bright eyes and an engaging grin which revealed that he had a front tooth missing and gave him, for some reason, the look of an innocent schoolboy. He was taking down the details of a lost purse from a fat, untidy woman with a bush of grey hair, who was wearing a voluminous black dress over which she had draped a ragged grey shawl. Corky recognised her as one of the flower sellers from Clayton Place and wondered how she could bear to wear a shawl on such a warm day. Corky edged closer, thinking that the woman could not be much longer, but the sergeant was a friendly man and continued to assure her that he would inform all the local policemen of her lost purse, as they came in to report for duty. 'I'm not saying as I have a fortune in there,' the woman said lugubriously, turning away from the desk. 'Folk don't buy flowers when it's this hot 'cos they soon withers and dies. I never thought I'd be grateful to say as I'd had a shocking bad day but I doubt there were more than a couple o' bob in the purse. No, it's the purse itself that I values. It's a big leather one with three compartments and a button-down flap-over and it were me mam's . . .'

'Yes, yes, I've written it all down, Mrs Williams,' the policeman said comfortingly. 'I don't suppose you'll ever see the cash again but I reckon the thief will just chuck the purse away as soon as he's took the money out and some sharp-eyed youngster will bring it in, hoping for a reward.' His gaze turned to Corky. 'I suppose you're not here to report the findin' of a large leather purse and to reap the reward of . . . ?' He looked hopefully towards his first customer.

'Tuppence,' Mrs Williams said firmly. 'I'll pay tuppence to anyone what brings in me purse; that's fair, ain't it?' And she, too, looked hopefully at Corky.

Feeling quite guilty, Corky replied humbly that he had not seen a purse but would certainly keep his eyes open. He did not add that, if the purse was so precious to her, a tuppenny reward seemed rather on the mean side. Poor old gal, trying to sell drooping roses to folk who just wanted to get home so that they could take off their hot and uncomfortable city clothing and relax.

Mrs Williams sighed and lumbered out and the sergeant turned his attention to his remaining customer. 'Well, young feller-me-lad,' he said jokingly. 'If you've not found the lady's purse, then how can I help you? Lost your little dawg? Mislaid your sister? Found your bag of gold at the end of the rainbow?'

Corky laughed dutifully. 'No, none of them things, mister,' he said. 'I'm lookin' for Constable McNamara; is he about?'

'Well he ain't in the station, that's for sure,' the sergeant said. He turned away from the counter and raised his voice. 'Jenkins! Where's Ollie this morning?'

A door behind the long counter opened and a head popped round it, a young head with a lot of curly light brown hair, and a mouth which was chewing vigorously. 'Who wants him?' the head enquired, spraying crumbs. He saw Corky and grinned in a friendly way. 'Oh, it's you, lad, is it? All the kids like old Ollie 'cos his tunic pockets is always full of aniseed balls and gobstoppers. He hands 'em out to any kid what looks hungry, so they say. Eh, wharritis to be a scuffer wi' a private income!'

'Private income?' Corky chirped up. 'Scuffers don't have private incomes, do they?'

The face grinned more broadly than ever. 'Not as a rule, worse luck,' he said cheerfully. 'But Ollie's an only child and a bachelor, and first his old man died and left him a right nice little cottage in the country, then his old uncle – his mam's elder brother – what didn't have no kids of his own, upped and died as well. He were real well-to-do and left every penny of it to lucky old Ollie. So no wonder he's always smiling and cheerful, and no wonder he give sweets to the kiddies.'

'Gosh,' Corky said, rather inadequately. So that was how Ollie explained his sudden affluence to his fellow officers. It was pretty clever when you came to think about it. Ollie could spend like a sailor and no one would ever ask where the money came from because they thought they knew. But, useful though the information was, it was not what he had come to seek. 'Well, I ain't after sweets, all the same,' he said, rather reproachfully. 'I just want to know where I can find Mr McNamara.'

'At home in bed, I guess,' the face announced. 'He were on a double shift last night, so he'll be off all day. Anything anyone else can do?'

'No thanks, I really want to speak to Mr McNamara,' Corky said. 'To tell you the truth, I was supposed to do a message for Miss Grieves, from the jeweller's shop in Church Street, only when I went in there she'd not come in to work and – and someone said they thought they'd seen her talkin' to the constable last evening, so I thought it were possible Mr McNamara might know where she'd gone.'

Both policemen shook their heads. 'No, I were on duty when Ollie signed off this morning and he said nothing to me,' the head said. 'Sorry, lad; can't help you.' With that he withdrew, closing the door behind him.

Corky moved away from the counter. He was halfway to the door when a thought struck him and he turned; the sergeant was writing laboriously in a large red ledger. "Scuse me, sarge,' Corky said respectfully. 'But I dunno where Mr McNamara lodges. Could you give me his address?'

The sergeant looked up, tapping his teeth thoughtfully with the pencil he held and staring rather too hard at Corky. 'Now just what would you be wantin' with Mr McNamara's address?' he said suspiciously. 'Scuffers needs their sleep and some time to theirselves – goodness knows, we get little enough of it – so you just scarper, young man. Mr McNamara will be in tomorrow, no doubt; you can talk to him then.'

'Fair enough,' Corky said cheerfully. It was a nuisance, but the reply had been the one he had expected and since it seemed likely that Mr McNamara would spend most of the day in bed there would be little point in lurking outside his lodgings. Besides, every kid in the neighbourhood would be able to pass on the constable's address.

Corky found Nick leaning against a lamp post, newspaper in hand, and told him what had happened in the police station. Nick nodded and folded his paper, tucking it under his arm. 'Well done. Tell you what, you say any kid in the neighbourhood can tell you McNamara's address. Go and get the information while I stroll along to Rathbone's – they could be keeping Emma there – then you can nip off to the churchyard and check for clues. I dare say you won't find any – clues, I mean – but at least we'll have tried; we've got to explore every avenue, as they say.'

'Right,' Corky said briskly. He went off and returned before Nick had walked a hundred yards to give him the address he wanted. 'Danby Street is just off Heyworth Street, not very far from Rathbone's shop,' he told his friend. 'So if you walk up and down there, casual like, then I'll find you easy enough when I've checked out the churchyard.'

Nick agreed to this and Corky set off at a fast run. He reached the churchyard wall, slithered over and was halfway across when he saw a small figure in a print dress, trowel in hand. She appeared to be digging in the same grave where he had first met Dot. Cursing silently to himself, Corky dropped on all fours and crawled towards the church along the path they had made, feeling extremely undignified. But better the loss of a bit of dignity, he told himself, than having a small child poking around.

He reached the shelter of the church's crumbling walls and stood up, trying to ignore the scratches and stings inflicted on him by the foliage he had crawled through, and was immediately rewarded. One glance was enough to tell him that someone had not only been here but had been successful, for the triangular piece of stone lay on the ground and Corky knew that, had the necklace still been in its hiding place, Emma would have pushed the stone back and lowered the curtain of ivy which was still hooked back against the rest of the wall.

Corky looked around him. Had Emma been surprised here by someone and taken captive? He did not think so. There were no signs of a struggle and Emma had not disturbed the tall grasses which grew inside the walls, but had woven her way between them as Corky himself had done. Had a stranger been present, he was sure there would have been an area of broken and trodden grass. He went over to the crevice and peered within. Because it was daylight he had no torch, but even so, he could see inside tolerably well. There was nothing. Then he noticed a long groove in the dust and, beside it, a sort of swirl. Grinning delightedly, he picked up the triangular piece of stone and wedged it back into place, then untangled the ivy and let that, too, return to its former position. The marks in the dust, slight though they were, had told him a good deal. The straight groove was where Emma had pushed some sort of stick into the crevice and the swirl simply must be the necklace, moving the dust as it was brought up from the depths.

Corky stepped back, dusting his hands; he had something to tell Nick now! He was sure it must have been Emma who had got the necklace from its hiding place, for had not Dot discovered one of the magnets from the fishing game outside Emma's back door? And she had not been attacked in the churchyard, so it was just possible that Rathbone and McNamara did not know even now who held the necklace. If this was so, he did not think they would have harmed Emma; they would hold on to her as a bargaining point. They would offer to release her in return for the necklace because, of course, they would think that that was the only thing which connected them to the robbery and subsequent murder. They could not possibly know that Dot had been hiding in the dustbin; that she would tell her story to the authorities just as soon as Emma was safe once more.

'What's you doing here, boy?'

Corky had heard of people jumping out of their skin but this was the first time it had happened to him and very unpleasant it was. His entire body prickled with shock, as though an electric current had been passed through it, and his sturdy Redwood Grange boots must, he felt, have been six inches from the earth. Heart hammering, he turned to confront the speaker. It was the small girl in the pink print dress; what had Dot told him her name was? Sadie.

'You don't oughta sneak up behind fellers,' Corky said reproachfully. 'What are *you* doing here, come to that?'

'Followin' you; only I didn't crawl an' make me knees all green and get stung by the nettles,' Sadie said, glancing scornfully at Corky's trousers. He looked down and saw that the kid was right: crawling had certainly done his clothing no favours, but if he let his things dry off, no doubt a good brushing would set all to rights. 'Go on, boy, what are you doing here?'

Corky shrugged rather helplessly. What gimlet eyes the kid had for a small child. But he did not intend to tell her what he had been doing, innocent though it had been. He said repressively: 'I were looking for a pal; I know she comes to the churchyard sometimes and I just wondered if she might have come in here. It's dangerous though; we neither of us should be in here, so let's get back out into the sunshine.' As they made their way out of what remained of the building, he added: 'Do you know Dot? She's the pal I were hopin' to meet here.'

'I know everyone who comes to the churchyard,' Sadie said complacently. 'I'm here often, I am. Dot hid things here, I know she did, so that's what I do. And she liked the little baby's grave in the corner over there . . .' She waved a small and grubby hand in the direction of Rhiannon's resting place. 'Were you going to surprise Dot, like I surprised you? Was that why you were crawling instead of walking upright?'

Corky seized on this thankfully. 'That's right. You're a clever kid, you are,' he said admiringly. 'Who else have you seen in the churchyard?'

By now, they were out in the sunlight once more, but Sadie did not answer him until they had reached the grave in which she had been so industriously digging. Corky saw that she had planted a number of rather weary-looking pansies on the tiny mound and had decorated the small stone with wreaths of ivy and some slightly overblown red roses. 'I say, you've made this rare pretty, young lady.'

Sadie beamed at him. 'Yes I have, haven't I?' she agreed. 'Now let me see, who've I seen in this churchyard? Well, there was Dot, she's really nice. She plays with me when she has time. And there's the old tramp what lives round the back of the church somewhere. Then there's the very, very old vicar, only he's got a key to the padlock and I hid when I saw him because he brung in that big fat policeman an' I don't like him, even though he'll give you a sweet if you ask.'

Corky felt the hair rise up on the nape of his neck. So Constable McNamara had been here! 'When was this, Sadie?' he asked, keeping his voice flat and unexcited with considerable difficulty. 'When did you last see the fat policeman? In here, I mean?'

Sadie flopped down on the grass and began to pat another pansy plant into place. 'I'm not sure ... a week, two weeks ago, I should think?' she said vaguely. 'They weren't here long and I think the old vicar was cross with the policeman 'cos I heard him say no thieves were likely to come rooting round in an empty churchyard and that there were no hiding places for lost treasure inside the church itself, 'cos all the – the 'terior had gone long since.'

'I see. And you've not seen anyone else? No shopkeepers? There's a butcher on Heyworth Street who's friendly with Constable McNamara – the fat policeman – I s'pose you've not seen him?'

Sadie shook her head positively; she was, thought Corky, a very positive child. 'No, no one else,' she assured him. 'And I come here most days.'

'Well, thanks very much, Sadie . . . you are Sadie, aren't you?' Corky said. 'Dot told me she'd met a very nice girl in the churchyard called Sadie, so I reckon she must have meant you.'

Sadie beamed at him. 'That's right, I'm Sadie,' she agreed. She looked at him hopefully. 'Daddy's gardener says you should always put young plants in with water, but I'd got nothing to carry it in and besides, the tap is miles away. I suppose . . . I suppose you'll be too busy to stay and give me a hand?'

Corky agreed that this was so but promised to come back another day. 'Though there's bound to be a change in the weather soon, and then the rain will do the job for you,' he told her. ''Bye, Sadie; see you soon.'

Elated with his discovery, Corky stood by the wall until no one was looking his way, then climbed over it and set off for his rendezvous with Nick.

Nick had spent an uneventful time strolling up and down Heyworth Street. He had actually turned into Danby Street a couple of times and checked McNamara's lodgings but there had been no sign of life there. The downstairs curtains were drawn back but the room he assumed to be what landladies referred to as 'the best front' had its heavy dark blue curtains drawn across and Nick guessed that this was where McNamara slept. As for the butcher's shop, it was very busy indeed with housewives buying their weekend joint and even the odd child or two entering, though a trifle apprehensively, with a list of messages for its parent.

When Corky came into view, Nick greeted him thankfully and steered him into the nearest café where they shared a pot of tea whilst Corky told Nick everything that had happened since they had parted. Nick listened attentively, then gave it as his opinion that Corky should take over the task of watching for McNamara whilst he, Nick, visited the office of the *Liverpool Echo*. 'I've been using it as a base since I came to Liverpool, and I know the people there pretty well. Believe me, if anything of interest occurs in the city, then the journalists from the *Echo* will be on to it like a pack of wolves,' he said. 'News is news and if you ask me, newspapers are likely to get hold of a good story even ahead of the police. If I go in and tell the fellows that the pretty young girl who inherited Mitchell & Grieves from her grandfather has gone missing in mysterious circumstances, then everyone, even old Cartwright, who's only a stringer for the *News Chronicle* after all, will be on the lookout. I don't know that I dare hint at police corruption at this stage, but when I do, I can tell you, nothing will stop journalists from trying to get the story. We always co-operate with the old bill when we can, though they don't always reciprocate, but in a case like this the press will be prepared to keep it under their hats until they've got the full story.'

Corky thought this a good idea, so as soon as the tea was finished Nick set out for the *Echo* offices on Victoria Street. He walked into the foyer and was amazed at his reception.

A tall, gangling young man, who had been talking to the reception clerk, turned at his entrance and slapped a hand to his forehead. 'He's here! Nick Randall, I mean. Don't cut them off,' he said urgently. 'Well, if that ain't a coincidence to end all coincidences. Nick, someone's been telephoning you for the past half-hour, wouldn't speak to anyone else . . . look, you'd better take it in the editor's office – he's at a meeting – because the girl on the switchboard said it sounded real urgent, and private too.'

Nick felt his heart give an enormous bound. For a moment, the nagging worry which had haunted him ever since he had heard of Emma's disappearance lifted. Was it she? Had she managed to escape from wherever they were holding her? Then he realised that she was unlikely to telephone for half an hour; she would surely have made her way either straight to the nearest police station, back to Church Street, or even round to his lodgings. His heart sank. It could be anyone on the other end of the line; it could even be bad news. As he ran up the stairs, two at a time, he tried to comfort himself with what Corky had learned. The boy was certain that Emma had the necklace, was equally sure that she would not have shown it to her captors, if captors they were. She might tell them that the necklace was hidden, Corky had said stoutly, that she had friends who knew of its whereabouts, and this could be used as a lever; *let me go and the necklace will be in your hands within the hour . . .* that sort of thing. But Nick could not banish the uncomfortable knowledge that Emma had trusted McNamara.

He pushed open the heavy oak door and hurried round the big mahogany desk, snatching for the phone as he sank into the editor's leather swivel chair. 'Hello?' he said breathlessly. 'Nick Randall here. Can I help you?'

Emma awoke to find herself in a strange and rather frightening world. Her eyelids were terribly heavy and she could not move so much as a muscle, so she lay just where she was and listened with all her might. She heard quiet footsteps, then rustling. A woman's voice spoke. Emma could not hear what she was saying but realised she was asking questions since, at the end of each sentence, her voice went up. Then there was a murmur, gruff and croaky, which Emma took to be a reply. Still scarcely conscious, she tried to move her hand and immediately remembered a good deal which, she thought fretfully, she would be happier forgetting. Mr McNamara had hit her on the head and, presumably, thrown her over the bridge, straight into the train's path, only he must have miscalculated and she had landed in a coal tender instead. After remembering that much, the rest was easy. She had left the train at Crewe, had been trying to run along the platform to get help when she must have swooned or fainted; at any rate, she could remember nothing more until she had muzzily awoken two or three minutes before. She was still trying to convince herself that it was safe – indeed, sensible – to open her eyes, when she realised that it was not only her ears which were passing messages to her brain, but her nose also. She smelt antiseptic, floor polish, and a certain something which reminded her of her stay in hospital at the age of eight, when her tonsils had been removed . . . chloroform? The smell of it was faint but hung about her and was sufficient to bring her eyes wearily open for a moment. Everything about her was dazzlingly white: ceiling, walls, everything. Even her arms, lying on the white coverlet, seemed drained of colour, but she managed to raise one and put it to her head. Gracious, her head seemed to be bound up in something . . . bandages!

Emma heard firm footsteps approaching up the ward and hastily shut her eyes again. She felt it was too soon to be able to answer questions and realised that questions were certainly going to be asked. Whoever had brought her into the hospital would be completely in the dark as to why she had come stumbling down the platform and collapsed . . .

'Miss? Wake up, my dear. You're quite safe now. You're in Crewe General Hospital, though I dare say you're feeling a bit sleepy and stupid – you had to have an anaesthetic so that the surgeon could stitch up your forehead. You've got a long, shallow cut just below your hairline which he felt simply must be sewn up, but don't worry, you'll soon feel much more like yourself. What's your name, luv?'

It seemed downright rude to continue to pretend she was still unconscious. Emma moved her head a little on the pillow and fluttered her eyelashes. 'I'm Emma Grieves,' she whispered, 'and – and someone tried to kill me.'

There was a startled hiss of indrawn breath and Emma opened her eyes a slit to find a large woman in a navy blue dress and a white cap staring down at her. 'Tried to murder you?' she said incredulously. Then her face cleared. 'That's a very nasty cut on your forehead, my dear, and you've got a bump like an egg behind your ear. What's more, you're barely out of the anaesthetic, so I dare say you're a trifle confused, but not to worry. The station staff thought you might have been stealing coal but they soon revised that opinion. After all, why climb into a tender which might whisk you away at any moment when there was so much fuel in the nearby coal yard?'

'How did they know I was in the tender?' Emma

whispered. Every sound seemed to reverberate off the walls and to hurt her throbbing head.

'One of the porters saw you climbing out . . . and besides, you were smothered in coal dust.' The woman chuckled. 'We had to bathe you from head to foot and wash your hair, of course, before we could admit you. You didn't regain consciousness but you were having – or seemed to be having – some horrible sort of dream. You begged someone, Mr McEvoy was it, not to hit you, not to take your necklace . . .'

'The necklace!' Emma had forgotten the necklace, forgotten that it was the main reason for the constable's attack. 'It was Mr McNamara, not Mr McEvoy,' she whispered huskily. 'And – and he *did* take the necklace, truly, nurse. He stole it and then swung his baton . . .'

The woman took Emma's hand gently in her own. 'You mean you really were attacked, it wasn't just a nightmare?' she asked incredulously. 'Why, you poor little thing. No wonder you were in such a state when you were brought in. We checked to see if you wore a wedding band, just in case you were Mrs McEvoy – I mean McNamara – and had been involved in what the police call a domestic, but you seemed much too young. Also, your voice was that of an educated person, even when you were only half conscious, and clearly very frightened.'

Emma gave a very, very small smile. Her face felt stiff and even smiling hurt, and her mouth was dry and parched. 'I'll tell you all I can, nurse,' she croaked, 'but could I have a drink, please? It hurts me to talk.'

'I'll send a nurse to get you a cup of tea, but in the meantime you can have a tiny sip of water,' the woman promised. She called down the ward and a round-faced, pink-cheeked girl in a green dress and white apron hurried up. 'Yes, matron?' she said.

'Fetch me a glass of water right now, nurse, and then go down into the kitchens and get a cup of tea with plenty of sugar for this patient, please,' the older woman said pleasantly. The girl hurried off and the matron turned back to Emma. 'They only gave you a whiff of anaesthetic when they stitched you up, otherwise I'd not dare risk a cup of tea in case your stomach rebelled. And now, my dear, I think I ought to telephone to the police station; this is too serious a matter to be ignored.'

Emma heaved herself up in the bed and spoke urgently. 'Oh, please . . . is there a telephone I can use? I don't have any money but I'll pay the hospital back . . . only I've friends who simply must be warned . . . they think Mr McNamara is an honest man . . . I simply must warn them.'

The matron looked undecided but at that point the little nurse scurried up with a glass of water which Emma sipped cautiously before trying to get herself out of bed. The matron watched, indecision playing on her face, but when Emma told her of the jewel robbery and of her grandfather's murder, she seemed to make up her mind. 'Fetch a wheelchair, nurse,' she said briskly. 'Take this patient along to Sister's office and stay with her while she uses the telephone. Then bring her back to bed and make sure she's comfortably settled.' She turned back to Emma. 'I'll go back to my own room and phone the police from there. If you haven't succeeded in reaching your friend by the time the police arrive, then I'm sure we'll do it for you.'

Emma asked the operator for the *Echo* office number, but was unlucky; Nick had not called in that day. She left an urgent message for him to ring the hospital and returned to her bed but, by now, she had remembered that McNamara knew of Dot's involvement in events and fretted so much that the little nurse wheeled her back to Sister's office three times.

'It's a good job for the pair of us that Sister has been called over to theatre, or we'd be in hot water, I can tell you,' she told Emma. 'But she might be back any minute so this is the last time I'm taking you to the telephone – until I get more instructions from Matron, of course.'

It proved, however, to be fourth time lucky and it was with a great surge of relief that Emma heard Nick's voice in her ear. 'Hello? Nick Randall here. Can I help you?'

'Oh, Nick, thank God!' Emma said, her voice breaking. 'It's me, Emma. I'm – I'm in Crewe hospital.'

'In hospital? In Crewe? Oh, Em, my darling. We've been worried sick. Are you all right?'

'I'm okay, just bruised and shaken up,' Emma said.

'Tell me what happened – was it McNamara?'

'Yes it was,' Emma said, 'and he knows Dot's involved. Nick, he tried to kill me and jolly nearly succeeded. But you must warn Dot because I think she's in dreadful danger. I – I didn't realise he was Ollie – did I tell you he was Ollie? – and I mentioned Dot's name . . . dear God, you've simply got to warn her, make her stay out of sight until McNamara's arrested. You see, I—'

'Hush, my love,' Nick said, his voice gentle. 'Let me get a word in edgeways! Dot knows that McNamara is Ollie and I'm pretty sure she knows she's in danger from him. But I'll find her and stick with her from now on, and so will Corky.'

'Oh, thank God,' Emma said. 'I can't go into much detail because I'm using the hospital telephone, but I'd got the necklace back and, like a fool, I showed it to McNamara. We were on Brownlow Street by the railway bridge and he asked me if he could see the necklace. Nick, I honestly thought he was a friend. He pretended he was taking me to see a magistrate so I could tell my story to someone in authority. I pulled the necklace out of my pocket and before I could do anything, he hit me over the head with his truncheon and tipped me over the railway bridge in the path of an express train. Only I landed in the coal tender so I expect he thinks I'm dead and no threat to him . . .'

'The evil, murdering swine,' Nick said between

clenched teeth. 'When I get my hands on him . . . but what happened to the necklace? Have you still got it?'

'Oh, didn't I say? He snatched it out of my hand, just before he hit me. I'm so sorry, Nick . . .'

To Emma's bewilderment Nick laughed, a triumphant sound. 'It's all right, love. In fact, it couldn't be better. Look, I can't explain now but just you get back to bed and relax. I'll sort everything out this end and then come for you. And whatever you do, don't worry.'

'I don't want to go back to bed, I feel much better,' Emma said, rather fretfully. 'The police are coming to interview me and it would be much nicer – much easier that is – if you were here to back up my story.'

'Be sensible, my love; the fact that you're in hospital should be sufficient proof that something's going on . . . look, I must go. You said yourself that it's important to take care of Dot and I've got this idea . . . Emma? Try to understand!'

Emma was about to reply indignantly that of course she understood when she turned her head to see a tall young policeman, accompanied by two others, entering the room. At the sight of the uniforms, Emma's heart gave an uncomfortable bound, then settled down as she saw that the policemen were strangers to her. On the other end of the line, Nick was still talking but she cut across his words. 'Sorry, Nick, but the police have arrived. See you later.' And with that, she put the receiver down firmly and turned to smile at the newcomers. 'Good morning, officers,' she said formally. 'I'm sorry I'm in my nightclothes – they aren't even mine – but when I tell you how I came to be here at all, you'll understand. It was like this . . .'

Dot was only in the waiting room for an hour before a nurse came to fetch her. 'Mrs Brewster's lost the babies,' she said briefly. 'She's far from well, weak and feverish, but she keeps saying she must speak to you, she has something terribly important to tell you. In fact, she's made so much noise and fuss that Sister told me to fetch you along though, as a rule, children aren't allowed on the maternity ward. I doubt they'll let you stay for more than ten minutes, but perhaps you'll be able to relieve your aunt's mind of whatever is troubling her in that time.'

Dot found her aunt in a small, curtained-off cubicle at the end of the ward. Her face was flushed and her eyes were unnaturally bright, but when she saw Dot she managed a small smile and relaxed against her pillows. 'I've lost me twins, queen,' she said huskily. 'I feel bad about it, a' course I do, but I reckon it were for the best. Money's that hard to come by and Sammy don't seem inclined to hand over any of his earnings; it's like getting blood out of a stone to prize so much as a bob a week out of him, and I dare say Lionel will be the same. But there's something I've been meaning to tell you – oh, for a long while, only I kept putting it off. You see, I'm ashamed, only now I know you've gorra find out 'cos if I snuffs it, no one won't ever tell you.'

Dot sat herself down on the edge of the bed and took her aunt's hot, damp hand in hers. 'It's all right, Auntie,' she said gently. 'If it'll ease you to tell me, then go ahead, but if you'd rather not, I reckon I'll understand.'

Her aunt grinned. It wasn't much of a grin but there was definitely mischief in it and it cheered Dot up considerably, because it made Aunt Myrtle seem more like herself. 'It all happened a long time ago,' her aunt said. 'It's a common enough story; God knows it happens all the time, I'm told. But it – it explains things, like; things that must ha' puzzled you.'

Dot said nothing. So many things puzzled her: why her mother had never returned, why her uncle disliked her so much, why her mother had left her in the first place. But she said nothing, allowing her aunt to take her time.

'Give me a sip of water, queen,' her aunt said, after a long pause. Dot complied, then stood the glass back on the bedside cabinet as her aunt began to speak. 'The truth is, chuck, that when I moved you an' your mam in wi' us, your Uncle Rupert... well, he took a considerable shine to your mam. She were young and very pretty, recently widowed and still heartbroken, if you ask me. Your dad were a fine chap and Letty couldn't think of anything, apart from him. I'm sure she never even noticed, at first, how Rupert hung about her. She had a job in a dress shop on the Scottie, and he'd hang around outside so's he could walk her home. On Sundays, he'd take her off for a bus ride or a long walk in the country, telling me it was to distract her mind from her troubles, which no doubt it did, though not in the way he intended. Often your mam insisted on taking you along and I do believe it was that, originally, which set your uncle agin you.'

'I don't remember any of that,' Dot said, rather helplessly, when her aunt had been staring down at her hands for some moments. 'But if that were all, Aunt Myrtle . . .'

'Well, it weren't,' Aunt Myrtle said, her voice trembling. 'Everything fell apart when Rupert tried – tried to make love to her. He – he followed her into her room late one night – he had told me he was doing the late shift at the factory – and – and started gettin' . . . well, passionate. Your mam told me that she didn't want to wake you but she was scared for her life. There were a real struggle, for though your mam was young and strong, she weren't really a match for Rupert. Gawd knows where it might have ended if she'd not grabbed the chamber pot and broke it over his head. She knocked him cold and – and went.'

'Went? You mean left for ever?' Dot said, her voice small with shock. 'But – but what about all her things, and me? And what about you, Aunt Myrtle? You'd been good to her, I reckon.'

'Oh, she come back after a couple o' days, when

she judged your uncle would have recovered from the crack on the head and got back to work,' her aunt reassured her. 'I had a pretty good idea of what had happened, that same night. I went through to her room 'cos you was bawling your head off, and found Rupe unconscious on the floor, the bed streaked with blood and your mam missin'. When he came round, Rupert pretended he'd lost his memory, said an intruder must have crowned him with a stick or the butt of a gun. But he were terrified you'd seen more than you'd let on. He began to dislike you, good and proper, an' was always trying to get you into trouble, to persuade me to turn you out, put you in an orphanage.

'O' course, when your mam explained what had happened, I knew I ought to confront Rupert, kick him out, but . . . oh, dammit, Dotty, in those days I suppose I was still in love with him, and anyway, I had the boys to consider. I couldn't bring them up on me own without a wage comin' in. Your mam swore she'd never live under the same roof as Rupert, said she'd starve sooner. In fact, she didn't mean to stay in Liverpool in case Rupert found where she was, so she went to London. She meant to come and get you, but all her jobs were live-in – they had to be – so no place for a child, d'you see? She wrote regular for a whole year, but she never gave me an address, and then the letters just stopped coming. In her last letter, she'd said as she'd got a nasty dose of 'flu but would write again as soon as she was fit. She never did.'

There was a long silence, then Dot spoke. 'She died, didn't she? Otherwise, nothing would have stopped her getting in touch again,' she said flatly.

'I think you're right; she would have written if she'd been alive to do so. Remember, she never sent us her address so I couldn't find anything out for certain. I reckon she were afraid that Rupert would find out where she was and follow her. Me and your mam weren't just sisters, we were pals an' all. It took me a long time to forgive Rupert for what he did.'

'Thanks for telling me, Aunt Myrtle. I'm glad I know what happened; it explains a lot.'

'It's all right, chuck, but don't let it make you turn even more against your uncle, 'cos I'm goin' to speak to him when I get out of here. I'm goin' to tell him that unless he changes his ways, acts decent towards you, then I'll kick him out, wages or no wages. I've been weak not doin' something before but this has made me think. I ain't sayin' us Brewsters have treated you right, but at least we've fed and clothed you and I've kept you out of an orphanage. And now you'd best be goin', queen, 'cos I don't deny I'm fair worn to the bone.'

'I'll stay with you for a bit, Aunt,' Dot said softly, and was still sitting by the bed when her aunt began to snore gently.

Satisfied that she could now leave, Dot got to her feet and was making her way back along the hospital corridor when she came face to face with her uncle. He grabbed her arm, his face for once expressing concern, his usual malevolence missing. 'Dot! Where's your aunt? How is she? Is the kids awright?' he said hoarsely. 'The doc said he'd send an ambulance but he didn't say which hospital she would go to so I've been searchin' the city. But they said at the desk she were here.'

'She lost the babies,' Dot said briefly, carefully detaching her uncle's clutching fingers from her arm. 'She's sleeping right now but I expect she'll be glad to see you. Go in through the next lot of swing doors to your left, and she's in the little cubicle at the end.'

'Right,' her uncle said. 'And you'd best go straight back to Lavender Court and start getting something for us suppers. Need some money?'

Dot almost gaped. Her uncle often demanded that she run messages for him but had never offered her money before. He expected his wife to pay for all his needs, apart from those he purchased for himself. Dot, however, did not mean to go back to Lavender Court until she had found Corky and discovered what had happened to Emma, but it would not do to say so to Uncle Rupert. 'We can have fish and chips, so I won't need the money until this evening,' she told him. 'If you aren't home, I'll take the money from the tea caddy on the mantelpiece, all right?'

'Awright,' Uncle Rupert said, after a pause. Dot grinned to herself as she left him. She had seen from the expression on his face that Uncle Rupert did not at all like the thought of the rest of the family feasting on fish and chips if he was still tied to the hospital. Well, he would have to put up with it, she told herself, hurrying along the busy street, and anyway, she doubted that the hospital authorities would encourage him to hang around once he had greeted his wife and seen her comfortably settled. There was nothing he could do so he might as well go back to the factory. No doubt his boss would understand his absence when he explained that his wife had had a miscarriage, but they would not expect him to take more than an hour or two off work.

As she walked, Dot wondered where she should go first. Virgil Street was out of the question; neither Corky nor Nick would return there until they knew Emma was safe, and though she could go and hover outside the butcher's shop, she did not much fancy doing so. She was still convinced that Ollie, and now the butcher, suspected her involvement in their affairs and would do their best, by one means or another, to see that she did not talk. She could still remember vividly the sharp push between her shoulder blades which had nearly sent her under the train.

Finally, she decided to head for Church Street, and almost as soon as she reached it was fortunate enough to see Nick and Corky striding purposefully towards the shop. She shouted and they turned at once and came towards her. 'Well I'm damned; if you aren't the answer to a prayer, young Dot,' Nick said, beaming at her. 'We've just come from the *Echo* office; I've spoken to Emma and she's all right, though that swine McNamara did his best to add another victim to his list.'

Dot stared from one to the other. Corky nodded confirmation. 'That's right,' he agreed. 'She told Nick he threw her over a railway bridge into the path of an express train only he misjudged, or something, and she fell into the coal tender. We're going to fetch her – she's in Crewe – just as soon as Nick's seen McNamara safely locked away.'

'In Crewe?' Dot squeaked. 'That's miles away. Whatever's she doing in Crewe?'

Corky began to explain but Nick cut him short. 'You can tell Dot everything as we walk, but right now we're going to the police station,' he said firmly. 'I know we were afraid that we might confide in the very person who was Butcher Rathbone's confederate, but that was before we knew Ollie's true identity. Now I think we must act immediately, because I don't want Ollie and Rathbone to have a chance to put their heads together and concoct a tissue of lies which might be difficult to disprove. We know Ollie did a double shift last night, so he's still in bed, which means if we can convince the police to pick him up at once he won't have a chance to speak to Rathbone first. So step lively, young Dot.'

When Emma had begun to tell her story to the policemen who had come to the hospital, she had thought she might have difficulty convincing them, but as it happened one of the men – a detective sergeant – was familiar with the spate of burglaries which had taken place in central Liverpool over the past couple of years. He had talked to brother officers who had been involved and said that more than one of them had suspected either an inside job or someone in authority's turning a blind eye. He knew Constable McNamara slightly and said the fat policeman was known to accept bribes and did not seem at all surprised when Emma told her story, though when she got to her grandfather's death he whistled beneath his breath. 'I don't suppose he meant to kill the old man though,' he said, rather doubtfully. 'I read in the reports that both men were muffled to the eyebrows, so unless he thought the shop was empty and pushed aside his disguise, he had no reason to do anything other than stop Mr Grieves giving the alarm.'

Emma did not argue, but when she got to her own story, to how McNamara had treated her, and had added her inadvertent admission that Dot knew McNamara's true identity, the detective sergeant clearly changed his mind. 'If you're fit enough, miss, I think we ought to get you back to Liverpool,' he said. 'The man's a double murderer – or thinks he is – so he won't hesitate to silence your young friend, if he gets the opportunity.' He glanced at her doubtfully. 'Only we can't take you in a hospital dressing gown and the sister said the stuff you were wearing when you were admitted was just rags covered in coal dust, so it's been burnt. But I dare say one of the nurses will lend you something.'

Emma thought this an excellent idea. 'I am afraid for Dot,' she admitted. 'She told me once that someone had tried to push her in front of an underground train when she was taking a basket of laundry across to Birkenhead. Then, I thought she might have been mistaken, but now . . .'

'I'll go and get you something to wear,' the younger policeman said at once. 'And I'll organise the car, shall I, sarge? If we get a move on, we can be in Liverpool in an hour or so.'

When Nick, Corky and Dot arrived at the police station Nick immediately assumed control, asking to see the senior officer present and saying that it was a matter of considerable urgency. The desk sergeant remembered him and cocked a knowing eyebrow. 'Found out something about them burglaries, have you?' he asked, and when Nick nodded, he added: 'The chief inspector will want to know all about it, then.' He depressed a switch. 'Front desk here, sir. Will you ring me back when you're free? I think it's important.' He let the switch spring back and turned to Nick. 'But what's these two youngsters got to do with it, eh?' He grinned at Corky and Dot. 'A couple o' desperate characters if you ask me – oh aye, I can just see 'em wi' scarves wrapped round their faces and pistols in their hands.' He looked harder at Corky.

'I reckernise you, young feller-me-lad,' he said slowly. 'You were in earlier, askin' for Constable McNamara. Got anything to do with the case in question? 'Cos o' course, all them burglaries took place on Ollie's beat, or near by.'

Corky opened his mouth but Nick cut in before he could speak. 'That's right, sergeant,' he said cheerfully. 'I need Mr McNamara to corroborate what I've discovered; has he reported in for duty yet?'

The sergeant turned to gaze up at the big clock hanging on the wall behind him. 'Not yet; he's not due in till two o'clock,' he told them. The instrument at his elbow buzzed and he pushed down a switch. 'Mr McGovern, sir? The young reporter who were interested in the Church Street burglaries has got some information for you. Shall I send him up?'

The voice the other end barked what must have been an affirmative and Nick, Corky and Dot prepared to tell their story once more.

Dot had been dreading this moment because it was she, they had agreed, who would have to start the narrative. Once she began, however, the words simply tripped off her tongue and to her relief – and considerable surprise – Chief Inspector McGovern did not interrupt her once. He was a big, thick-set man in his forties, with close-cropped sandy hair, a neat sandy moustache, and very bright, very dark eyes. In repose, his face was severe, but when he smiled he looked both younger and friendlier. He smiled when Dot described her hasty descent into the dustbin, and from then on she found herself thinking of him as an ally, not an enemy. He did not frown when she said Archie Rathbone was much disliked by the neighbourhood children, and when she got to the bit she was most nervous of repeating – the involvement of Constable McNamara – he looked neither shocked nor disbelieving, but simply nodded gravely and Dot realised that, of course, he must have guessed the man's identity since he, and every other policeman in the Liverpool force, would have known the constable's nickname.

Nick took over when Dot finished her own part of the story. He told how they had been unable to fish up the necklace from its hiding place and how they had not even suspected that McNamara was Ollie. Then he told how Emma had dreamed up a scheme to get the necklace back and had actually done so and also what had happened to her, adding that she was in hospital in Crewe at this very moment, as a result of injuries sustained when Constable McNamara had thrown her over the railway bridge.

At this, the chief inspector nodded again. 'In fact, Miss Grieves is no longer in hospital,' he informed them. 'I had a telephone call from Crewe police station a short while ago, telling me that they were bringing a young lady – Miss Emma Grieves – to Liverpool in a police car, since she had information which they thought should be passed on to us as soon as possible. The detective who spoke to me said that of course he could not vouch for the truth of the accusations which had been made, but he thought we should hold a certain Constable McNamara in custody until the young lady had told us her story.'

Nick's eyebrows shot up, then drew together in a frown. This could ruin all his plans. 'Have you arrested him, sir?' he asked anxiously. 'If so, I'll have to rethink what I'd hoped to do.'

The chief inspector, however, shook his head. 'Without knowing the full story, I felt I could scarcely take such action,' he admitted. 'But I've got a young detective constable keeping an eye on McNamara's lodgings; if the feller comes out he's to follow him wherever he goes, and stick closer than glue.'

'Good,' Nick said, much relieved. 'The truth is, sir, that I've a plan which I think might very well work, but it's dependent upon Ollie – Mr McNamara, I mean – not being able to get to the butcher's shop before he's brought into the station, so if you wouldn't mind . . .' and Nick proceeded to outline his plan.

The policeman looked at his wristwatch, then got to his feet. 'I'll send someone at once, because if McNamara does intend to make for Rathbone's shop, he'll do so right away. I think you three had better stay here, because the sight of you would be bound to make him suspect trouble. I'll brief a responsible sergeant who will tell McNamara that we need him here to corroborate some evidence. The sergeant will dream up some story which will satisfy McNamara, don't you fear. I don't want him to suspect that the game's up until we've got him safely in the station.'

Nick and both children agreed that this was sensible and were taken to a quiet room at the back of the building, where they were supplied with tea and sandwiches and told that they would be called for in due course. The three of them sat around a large wooden table, trying to forget what lay ahead of them.

When Constable McNamara was ushered into the small interview room, he saw only Nick and smiled benignly at the younger man. 'Good afternoon, young gentleman; my chief's told me you're a newspaper reporter and need some information about a fire which occurred in the newspaper shop in Whitechapel and was thought to have been started deliberate,' he said, in his jolliest voice. He walked, ponderously, round the desk and sat in the swivel chair where an interviewing officer would sit. 'Now just you take your time, sir, and let me know exactly how I can help.'

Nick stared at him in stunned disbelief. Had someone made a mistake? This jolly, comical looking policeman could not possibly be the man who had bludgeoned old Mr Grieves to death and tried to kill Emma. But the moment the children were ushered into the room, accompanied by the chief inspector and two more policemen, he saw a change come over the comedian's face, saw the eyes glitter and the mouth tighten so that the lips almost disappeared, whilst the man's fat cheeks flushed scarlet and a vein began to throb at his temple. For a moment he looked every inch the villain Nick knew him to be, but then he controlled himself and his voice, when he spoke, was that of the friendly neighbourhood bobby on the beat. 'Ah, I see two of me young friends have come along to see what information they can give.' He looked at Dot. 'Now this young lady I *do* know 'cos I'm a friend of her uncle's; have been for many a long day. A bit fanciful is our Dot, a bit apt to make up stories. So what's on your mind today, little miss?' He turned to Nick, giving him what he no doubt thought to be a conspiratorial smile. 'You know what kids is like. I've give young Dot many a sherbet dab and heard many a fairy tale in return. Well, Dotty, what is it this time?'

Nick met Dot's eye and gave her a quick and secret wink. Dot immediately opened her eyes to their widest extent. 'Oh, nothing much, Mr McNamara,' she said sweetly. 'Only I think you ought to hand the necklace back; the emerald one what you took from Mitchell & Grieves' window the night old Mr Grieves were murdered.'

The constable's hand had reached almost instinctively towards his breast pocket, but he turned the movement so swiftly that it looked natural, and began to brush, thoughtfully, at his small moustache. 'Necklace?' he said, sounding completely baffled. 'What necklace is this? There were a heap o' necklaces taken . . . well, all sorts of jewellery as I recall. But you've gone and got it wrong, miss. I don't have none of them.' He chuckled but Nick saw beads of sweat break out on to his forehead. 'Why, that burglary were months ago. I dare say all the loot – now that's a good word, loot – has gone to every fence in the country by now.'

'Dot means the emerald necklace, Mr McNamara,' Nick said evenly. 'You must know, as well as I do, that a piece of jewellery so distinctive would scarcely be welcomed by a fence, and anyway, there are doubts as to the authenticity of the stones. But it was taken along with the rest of the jewellery and we have it on good authority that you are in possession of it.'

'I don't know on whose authority, but the feller's a liar,' McNamara said, his face reddening even further. 'I wouldn't touch no stolen property. I don't need to. I'm a man o' means, I am. Everyone knows I've come into a nice little estate on the Wirral, and a deal o' money as well. I don't need to go stealing necklaces and such.'

'And you didn't need to go walking with Miss Grieves last night, I suppose,' the chief inspector said, speaking for the first time. His voice was icy cold and when Nick looked at him, so were his eyes. 'But it's easy enough to disprove what the young lady has just said. Empty your pockets, constable.'

For a long moment, the two men stared at one another, but it was McNamara whose gaze faltered first. He lowered his head, then began, slowly, to empty his tunic pockets. A bag of striped humbugs, an enormous pocket handkerchief, a bunch of keys – he tried to cover them with the handkerchief, Nick noticed – a notebook and pencil. He laid the objects out on the table, then stared defiantly at the chief inspector. 'There you are, sir. No emerald necklace there, you see!'

'Your breast pocket, McNamara,' the chief inspector said mildly. 'Empty your breast pocket.'

The policeman's sausage-like fingers went slowly to his breast pocket. 'But it's empty, sir; I never keep nothing in me breast pocket because it makes me uniform bulge.' But when the two policemen stepped forward, threateningly, he fumbled in the pocket, then drew out, very slowly, the emerald necklace, staring at it as though he could not believe his eyes.

'Well – I'm – damned,' he said slowly. 'How the devil did that get there? Sir, as God's my judge I never knew it were in me pocket! I've never set eyes on the thing before . . .' He pointed wildly at the two policemen now standing one on either side of him. 'You've set me up, you buggers! I thought you jostled me when you came round the desk . . . you, Thompson, you've never liked me, always been jealous because I inherited money, and now you're trying to set me up, put me in the frame. Well, it won't work because I had nothing to do with that burglary. I were on duty; I've gorra cast iron alibi.'

'You were seen last night, Mr McNamara,' Nick said, his voice cold. 'You were seen on Brownlow Street, by the railway bridge. You were seen throwing something . . .'

Sweat was pouring down McNamara's face and he had seized the handkerchief and appeared to be trying to rend it in two. Nick thought, dispassionately, that he looked as guilty as hell and he did not yet know even a quarter of the evidence piled up against him. But the constable was not finished yet. 'Oh aye, I were on Brownlow Street last night,' he said, trying to speak evenly. 'I took a feller into the Infirmary, then walked up to the railway bridge to have a bit of a smoke. But I weren't the first one there – there were a young feller with curly brown hair and a girl, I didn't notice her pertickler – they were havin' a bit of a barney . . .'

At this moment, someone scratched on the door of the interview room. There was a tense silence, then the chief inspector said softly: 'Come in!' and the door began to open. As it swung wide, Emma stepped into the room. She was wearing a limp grey dress and her hair was loose around her blood-streaked face. She looked awful, frightening, and the navy blue cloak which she wore round her shoulders appeared to be blood-streaked.

Nick, despite the fact that he had planned this, gasped with shock and he saw Dot's hands fly to her mouth and Corky turn pale, but none of this compared with Constable McNamara's reaction. His big ruddy face turned yellow as cheese and his eyes bulged. He gave a strangled scream, then words burst from him, words which he was clearly unable to prevent from escaping his lips. 'You're dead, you're dead, you're dead!' he shrieked, in a voice totally unlike his own. 'You went under that bleedin' train – the midnight express – I know you did . . . I were there.'

'I know you were there,' Emma said calmly, as the policemen converged on their colleague and handcuffed him securely, before beginning to drag him from the interview room. 'You did your best to kill me, having already murdered my poor old grandfather when you stole the necklace; you needn't think you're going to wriggle out of this one.'

Struggling and swearing, alternately vowing that he had been framed, that he was completely innocent and that Emma was a lying jade, Mr McNamara was carried, almost bodily, from the room, and only then did Emma begin to cry as she cast herself into Nick's arms.

Chapter Thirteen

Much later that day Nick, Dot and Corky made their way towards Emma's flat in Church Street. Dot was looking forward to seeing her friend again and to hearing exactly what had happened, for Emma had not remained at the police station whilst the rest of them made their statements, since the chief inspector thought it was essential that she returned to bed and had some rest.

'This young lady, WPC Hetherington, will escort you back to your flat with another police constable and see you safely into bed. Then she'll make you a nice cup of tea and you will be able to rest whilst you sort out what you want to say in your statement,' the chief inspector had said kindly. Dot thought that he probably had a daughter of his own and knew how weary Emma must be feeling. 'I'm afraid it will have to be a pretty detailed statement, so if you'd rather leave it till tomorrow, Miss Hetherington will return in the morning. Is there someone at home who can be with you when the officers leave?'

'I have a sensible shop assistant, a Miss Snelling,' Emma had said wearily. 'I'm sure she'll come up and keep me company until I feel able to manage for myself.' She had glanced, hopefully, across at Dot. 'Dot, I know you've been taking care of your aunt, but – but could you possibly come round to the flat when you leave here? I've got a horrid sort of feeling that I shan't want to be alone tonight, and I can ask Miss Snelling to stay till closing time, but not after that.'

'Course I can,' Dot had said at once. 'Me aunt's in hospital; she'll be there for a week or more, I dare say, and to tell you the truth I'd rather be out of the way whilst my uncle and my cousins are at home on their own. Uncle Rupert blames me for everything bad that happens anyway, so he's bound to blame me for Aunt Myrtle losing the twins as well. I'd be glad to stay with you, Emma.'

Now, as the three of them turned into Church Street, Dot glanced across at Nick. 'Didn't Emma look terrible? It were an awful shock when she come into the room with her hair messed up and blood everywhere.'

'Tomato sauce,' Corky corrected her with a grin. 'But it looked just like blood, and having it all over her clothing and in her hair was a real clever touch. What made you think of it, Nick?'

'Well, it was Emma's own idea really,' Nick said. 'Apparently, the hospital had cleaned her up and had plaited her hair so that she looked like a little girl and not like Emma at all. With the bandage round her head, she could quite see old McNamara genuinely not recognising her and she knew that his first reaction must be one of total shock that she was still alive. So she unplaited her hair, took off the bandage and splashed a bit of tomato sauce around – she didn't mean to get it all over the cloak; it flew out when she shook the bottle – and I do think she looked pretty impressive.' He laughed. 'I think we were all pretty shocked at the sight of her, and McNamara gave himself away completely, of course.'

'Yes, it were a good wheeze,' Corky conceded. 'Even old Dot here went white as a sheet, and McNamara looked sick as a horse. I s'pose he thought she were a ghost, come back to haunt him for chucking her over that bridge.'

'Yes, I think that's exactly what he did believe,' Nick said. 'I wonder what they'll get out of old Rathbone? The chief inspector sent off four constables to bring him in. I think he means to confront him first with the necklace and then with McNamara . . . We'd best go in at the front, I suppose, since the stockroom door will be locked. No point in anyone having to thunder down the stairs when we can go in through the shop.' He turned to Dot. 'Are you sure you ought not to go home this evening though, Dot? Your aunt . . .'

'She's in hospital,' Dot reminded him. 'I did say, Nick. She had a miscarriage first thing this morning and Sister said they'd keep her in for at least a week and possibly longer. I dare say me cousins would like me to go home an' slave for them, but I don't mean to do it. They can bleedin' well find out what it's like to light a fire, cook a meal, wash their clothes and do the messages. It 'ud be different if me aunt were home, but she ain't.'

At this point, they entered Mitchell & Grieves and were sent upstairs by a smiling Miss Snelling. 'The police have left and the doctor's been,' she told them. 'I sent for him because I thought Miss Grieves was still looking very poorly, though she insisted that she was only tired. The doctor said she must stay in bed until she is stronger and left some tablets which he said would help ease the pain, but so far as I know she's not taken them yet. She went to sleep pretty soon after he left and she's asleep still, so I came downstairs to check that everything was all right here. You go on up and give me a shout if you need me.'

The three of them went straight to the kitchen. Dot put the kettle on the stove and lit the gas and Corky went and fetched a loaf of bread, some butter and a big piece of cheese from the pantry, whilst Nick went quietly out of the room, returning moments later to say that Emma was sleeping like a baby. He looked enquiringly at the food spread out on the table. 'What's this?'

'Grub,' Corky said, looking up from his self-imposed task of slicing the loaf. 'You know how generous Emma is – and we've had nothing to eat for ages. As soon as she wakes up, we'll feed her as well, and that'll make it all right, won't it?'

'Yes, I'm sure it will,' Nick said heartily, as Dot put a steaming mug of tea down in front of him. 'C'mon, everyone dig in and then we'll discuss what to do next. The chief inspector said I could have an exclusive so far as the paper's concerned, but I guess there are things you'd both rather I didn't write about, isn't that so?'

Dot and Corky exchanged somewhat guilty glances and Dot knew that Corky shared her own feeling that there were some things she would very much rather no one knew. For instance, she was pretty sure playing in the churchyard – and hiding a stolen necklace in the ruined church – were details better kept to themselves, and she did not want her uncle's part in the affair, innocent though it may have been, to become common knowledge – though the fact that she had hidden in Mr Rathbone's dustbin would obviously have to come into Nick's story.

'I guess you're right, Nick; there are some things which we don't want to see in the papers,' Corky agreed. 'I'm fourteen, but from what I've heard I'm under the control of the people at Redwood Grange until I'm sixteen. Can you use a made up name instead of my real one? Though I don't see why I have to come into it at all. I've been helping, but that's about it.'

'Tell you what, I'll type out my story tonight and then you and I will come round here tomorrow morning and I'll read it out to everyone,' Nick said. 'The chief inspector will want to make out a cast iron case against both men, Rathbone and McNamara, before he releases anything to the press, anyway.' He helped himself to a large cheese sandwich and spooned pickled onions on to his plate. Then, to Dot's surprise, he spooned them back into the jar. He caught her astonished look and a faint blush tinged his cheeks. 'I don't want to go breathing pickled onions all over Emma when she does wake up,' he said gruffly. 'I – I think I'll just pop back into her bedroom, make sure she's still asleep.'

A week later, things had become very much clearer. As arranged, Dot had moved in with Emma who, though very much better, still stayed in bed until noon and then ambled gently about the flat, but did not attempt to go outside. Dot had the little spare room and revelled in the luxury of wonderfully clean bedding and a bathroom in which she could take a daily bath. She had visited her aunt regularly in hospital, taking her small comforts such as a bunch of grapes, a bar of Nestlés chocolate and some scented soap. Her aunt had been grateful, though annoyed that Rupert and the boys were having to manage without Dot's help. However, she agreed, grudgingly, that it would probably do them good and make them appreciate Dot's presence when she returned to Lavender Court.

Dot did not tell her that she was unlikely ever to go back; she would wait, she decided, until her aunt was fully recovered before breaking what she now realised would be bad news. But she owed it to herself to take up Emma's offer of an apprenticeship in the jewellery trade and a home with her in the cheerful little flat, until one or other of them decided to move out.

Inadvertently, Dot had also cleared up another mystery. Emma had told the police about the man in the false beard and moustache, who had collected the weekly protection money, but had been unable to provide any real description, though she had said that his accent was a local one. She and Dot had been chatting idly one evening, over their supper, when Dot had said something which stopped Emma in her tracks. 'I'm glad I shan't ever have to go back to Lavender Court,' Dot had been saying, 'because I can't help being scared of Uncle Rupert. I keep imagining his hands, all covered with long black hair, gripping me round the throat. I don't wonder that me mam cut and run, though I can't help wishing she'd taken me with her. Wharrever's the matter, Em?'

Emma stared at her. 'Hairy hands?' she whispered. 'Is – is your uncle tall and skinny? Does he wear a brown raincoat which nearly reaches his ankles?'

'That's right,' Dot said, chewing a mouthful of salad and helping herself to another round of bread and butter. 'How d'you know, Emma? Oh, I suppose you've seen him in old Rathbone's yard, when he's been shifting carcasses.'

'No,' Emma said, no longer whispering. 'I – I rather think he's the man who called on me a couple of times to collect – well, to collect the protection money. You know, the money all the small traders paid each week to ensure that they weren't robbed again, and didn't have their windows broken or their stock ruined.'

'Golly,' Dot said inadequately, digesting this. 'So that was why Uncle Rupert went off after work each day and paid good money for that stupid coat. I did wonder why he had done so, because when he were humping carcasses old Rathbone gave him a filthy old boiler suit and a sort of rubber apron thing. Will he go to prison, Emma?'

'So far as I know, Archie Rathbone hasn't split on him,' Emma said. 'Nick said that Rathbone admitted he'd employed your Uncle Rupe but swore it was only to help move the carcasses and that he'd not taken him on until a couple of months after the last robbery. In fact, I don't know what's been said about protection money, but perhaps I ought to have a word with the police.'

To her own surprise, Dot leaned across the table and caught Emma's hand. 'Do you have to tell on Uncle Rupert?' she said urgently. 'I thought it would be grand if he were sent to prison, but now I'm not so sure. I – I don't mean to go back to Lavender Court, and without Uncle Rupert's wage poor Aunt Myrtle won't know which way to turn. The boys are no help, and – and . . .'

Emma smiled at her with real understanding. 'I don't think he would be sent to prison because, after all, he only did what he was employed to do: collect money from tradesmen who handed it over willingly. He could have believed the money was owed, I suppose, but I won't mention it, unless someone else is accused of course. Only – only if you don't mind, I think we ought to tell Nick and Corky, because one shouldn't keep secrets from friends.'

Dot agreed with alacrity; the close friendship between the four of them was the nicest thing that had ever happened to her and though at first she had been in daily dread that Corky's true identity would be discovered, despite Nick's sticking religiously to his promise not to name Corky in his article, this was one thing that no longer worried her. Earlier in the week, Nick and Corky had got on a train and gone back to Redwood Grange, where Nick had talked to the principal and then signed papers which allowed him to take care of Corky until he was old enough to fend for himself. Corky had told Dot, jubilantly, that the principal had not been too keen at first; in fact, he had been downright aggressive, saying that he did not mean to see a boy rewarded for ingratitude – that meant running away – and wickedness, which he supposed meant enjoying his freedom. Corky, however, had said bluntly that if he was returned to the Grange, he would make life hideous for everyone and would run away again at the first opportunity. 'I'll get a berth as a cabin boy and if I'm killed in a dockside brawl me pal Mr Randall will see that it's headline news on every paper in the country that you'd driven me to it,' he had threatened. 'What do you say to that, eh?'

Not unexpectedly, the principal had backed down and Corky had known that he was safe at last. After all, he would be fifteen in a few weeks; an age at which most boys were working anyway.

The two girls finished their meal and Dot carried the dishes over to the sink. She would have started to wash up but Emma, glancing at the clock on the mantelpiece, told her to go and get her coat. 'I'll wash up; I've got to start doing a bit more about the house,' she said. 'You go and visit your aunt and don't forget, sooner or later, you've got to pluck up your courage and tell her that you won't be returning to Lavender Court. After all, there's no guarantee that your uncle won't start trying to bully you again, and though you say your aunt finds you useful, she didn't do much to prevent his bad behaviour, did she? But she'll probably be released from hospital in a day or two, and I imagine when she goes home she'll need help. Whilst she thinks you're going back to Lavender Court, she won't make any attempt to find someone else to come in and I know you, young Dot. If you see she's in real trouble and she appeals to your better nature, you'll probably agree to help out for a few days and end up back in the old groove of doing everything while your uncle and cousins lounge around like lords, doing nothing.'

Dot assured her friend that she was not such a fool, but a couple of days later, when she visited the hospital, Aunt Myrtle was dressed and ready to leave and taking it completely for granted that Dot would return with her to Lavender Court and take up her abode in the kitchen once more. It was a difficult moment for Dot because though her aunt was very much better, she was still prone to attacks of weeping, and though she said, often and often, that she was better off without more children, Dot knew that she blamed herself for the miscarriage and for Uncle Rupe's disappointment, for he had certainly appeared to want the twins and had been cock-a-hoop to have fathered them at the age of fifty-six.

Dot waited until she and her aunt reached the kitchen of No. 6, Lavender Court. It was a dismal sight; the fire was long out and the room was chilly. Dirty dishes were piled up in the old clay sink and upon the wooden draining board, and the floor was covered in vegetable peelings, mildewed crusts and the caked mud from the men's boots. The room smelt horridly of decaying food, filth and mice, as well as the nasty, greasy smell from a sink which had not been used, by the look of it, for a couple of weeks or more. Aunt Myrtle looked around, then flopped into a chair, heaving a sigh. 'You'd best get going and clear up this filthy mess,' she said resignedly. 'I'd help only they told me at the hospital as I weren't to exert myself for at least a fortnight.' She glanced around her with an expression of distaste and Dot thought of the clean, disinfected ward, the nurses in their crisp, rustling uniforms, and the all-pervading warmth which came from the radiators and was not dependent upon an open fire. Poor Aunt Myrtle! It would have been bad enough in the old days, when she and her aunt had kept the kitchen as clean as they could, but after her protracted stay in hospital, the slovenliness of her husband and sons must have been hard to take.

Dot looked about her rather helplessly; where to start? Then she decided that she must light the fire because such refinements as a gas stove were unknown at No. 6, and if she was to clean the place thoroughly – and make her aunt a heartening cup of tea – hot water was essential. She said as much and Aunt Myrtle, eyes closed, nodded resignedly. 'I'm fair parched. I could murder a cup of tea,' she admitted. 'Get goin' then, young Dot.'

Though this remark was made quite cheerfully, Dot found herself bristling slightly. She could well see now what Emma had meant. If she came back here to live, no matter how sincerely Aunt Myrtle meant to change her ways, Dot would soon become the little skivvy again and the boys would take it for granted that she should do all the work, run all the messages, and cook and clean whilst they pursued their own interests and treated the house like a hotel.

However, this was not the time to say so. Dot fetched water from the tap at the end of the court, the buckets under the sink being empty, boiled a kettle, made her aunt a cup of tea and then, grimly, began the gargantuan task of cleaning the kitchen.

An hour later, she pushed the hair off her hot and sweaty face and went to examine the pantry. It contained a mouldy loaf of bread, an equally mouldy chunk of cheese, an almost empty tea caddy, the tin of condensed milk she had opened earlier, a flour bag which had split and must have got damp somehow since the flour inside was hard as concrete, and a blue bag with half a dozen sultanas sticking to the bottom. Dot returned to the kitchen. There was no need to ask what her cousins had been eating. Judging from the greasy papers she had found piled under the sink, it had been fish and chips, bought meat pies, bakers' cakes and anything else which did not need much effort to prepare. Well, if they could afford such things when she and her aunt were absent, they could bleedin' well go on affording them, she thought vengefully. She went across to the mantel-piece and picked up the tea caddy where her aunt kept the housekeeping money, but was not surprised to find it empty.

Dot cleared her throat and her aunt, who was noisily sipping her tea, raised her eyebrows. 'Wharrisit, queen? I dare say they've ate up all the food and took all me housekeepin' money, but if you nip out to one or two o' the shops on Heyworth Street and explain that I'm just out o' hospital, they'll give you tick till the end of the week.'

Dot pulled a face. 'What do you want me to buy then, Aunt?' she asked, rather suspiciously. 'I s'pose it'll be blind scouse, so that's a visit to the green-grocer, and then you'll want a screw o' tea and the same with sugar . . . that's the corner shop.'

· Her aunt stared at her incredulously. 'Blind scouse on me first night home? And you've not mentioned the pudding; Rupert do love a nice trea-cle puddin' an' so do me sons.' She began to tick items off on her fingers. 'You'll need flour, lard, some dripping when you go to the butcher's for the meat and some suet an' all. If you go to Mr Rathbone . . . oh, no, it'll have to be Henry Morgan, further up the street, but I'm sure he'll let you have lard, suet and scrag end . . . if you explain, that is. Then we'll want carrots, turnips and onions, an' half a stone o' spuds o' course, as well as a tin o' treacle for the puddin' and some Bird's custard powder. Oh, and you'd best nip into the dairy for a quart of milk.' She pulled a dissatisfied face. 'Your uncle will expect a jug o' porter on me first night back but I can't see the old feller at the Elephant giving tick to anyone.'

Dot stared at her aunt in disbelief. The older woman's reputation as a good payer was non-existent. She always sent Dot out to get messages with insufficient money and Dot had to plead and bargain and accept the cheapest of goods in order to fill her basket. As for providing her uncle and cousins with such a wonderful meal to celebrate their mother's return from hospital, Dot thought it was downright ridiculous. They could buy fish and chips again, or go hungry for all she cared.

She was tempted to say this to Aunt Myrtle, then decided not to bother. Instead, she left the house without another word – and without her aunt's big marketing basket either – returning after ten minutes or so with a screw of tea and one of sugar, and a small loaf which the nearby baker had given her for nothing since he said it was already going stale.

By the time she got back, her aunt was asleep and snoring gently, but she awoke when Dot closed the pantry door and rubbed her eyes, saying thickly: 'You were quick, chuck. Now if you'll just nip upstairs and do my room – an' the boys' room, o' course – you can start gettin' the meal ready when you come down. I dare say all the sheets will need washing, but you can leave the laundry till tomorrow, bein' as how it'll take you a while to prepare the food and a scouse is all the better for long, slow cookin'.'

Dot opened her mouth, then closed it again. She went upstairs and stripped the sheets, which were indeed dirty, from her aunt's bed, replacing them with the only other pair her aunt possessed. Then she took the chamber pot, which was full to the brim, and emptied it into the slop bucket under the washstand, clapping the lid on as quickly as she could to muffle the noxious smell. She hoped that, because the slop bucket was empty, it meant that Uncle Rupert had washed downstairs in the kitchen, but she thought it likelier that he had not washed at all. Without Aunt Myrtle chivvying him to do so, he had probably simply dressed and gone off to work each day, regardless of the state he was in. Dot put the slop bucket down on the landing and opened the door of the boys' room. The curtains were still drawn across the window and the stench of sweat, dirty clothing and bedding, and rancid hair oil, nearly knocked her backwards. She saw that both chamber pots were full – one had actually brimmed over on to the floorboards – and backed out hastily, closing the door firmly behind her. The boys' beds did not boast sheets but only blankets, and she guessed that the blankets would be riddled with bed bugs and fleas. All the housewives of the court waged a constant battle against such pests, and it was clear no battle had been waged in the boys' room since their mother had left.

Downstairs once more, she carried the slop bucket into the court, emptied it down the drain, rinsed it under the tap and went back indoors. She entered the kitchen, tight-lipped. 'I've done your room, Aunt Myrtle,' she said evenly. 'Uncle Rupert hadn't emptied his chamber pot for at least a week, so I've opened the window to get rid of the smell, but I won't go into the boys' room, norrif you paid me a hundred pounds. They can do it themselves; they're strong and healthy, and you know you said you were goin' to make 'em do more.'

'No point in bein' nasty, Dot, just because you're annoyed with the way your cousins left their room. Men aren't no good at housework; nor's boys, for that matter. So just you nip up an' clean the room for 'em, there's a good girl. I does it as a rule but I just ain't up to it, not yet.' She chuckled, giving Dot a sly glance under half-closed lids. 'I dare say all the bedding'll need a good wash 'cos the bed bugs won't have been treated to no Keating's Powder, nor disinfectant, while I've been away, but I'll let you off that for today; you can do the laundry tomorrer.'

Dot took a deep, steadying breath. It was the chuckle and the sly glance which had finally made up her mind for her. She knew her aunt had taken it for granted that she would traipse up and down Heyworth Street, getting shopkeepers to give her food for which she could not immediately pay, but she also expected her to enter the filthy, stinking pit which was the boys' room and could actually find the thought of Dot's tackling such a task amusing.

'No, Aunt Myrtle, I don't mean to do the boys' room and neither am I going to cook them a meal,' she said firmly. 'I did manage to get tea, sugar and a loaf of bread on tick, but I didn't try to get anything else. If you don't have any money, then you'd best make Sammy, or Uncle Rupert, go out and get fish and chips. After all, judging by the pong and the greasy newspapers under the sink, they've been pretty well living on the stuff since you and meself moved out.'

Her aunt bristled, the colour in her cheeks deepening to an angry red. 'Less o' that, young lady,' she said sharply. 'Don't you dare defy me, and

419

after all I've done for you, too. Why, your mam simply dumped you on me when you were no more'n five, but did I complain? Did I try to put you in an orphanage? No, 'cos I knew my duty: I fed you, clothed you . . .'

'You clothed me in what were little better than rags an' fed me the leavings from me cousins' meals,' Dot reminded her. 'You made me run your messages and do the housework even when it meant I gorrin trouble for saggin' off school. I had to buy me own second-hand plimsolls and then hide them away so's you wouldn't take them for Dick or Alan, an' though you wouldn't let me uncle send me to the orphanage, that wasn't because you loved me, or wanted the best for me, it was because I was too bleedin' useful.'

Her aunt stared at her, eyes fairly starting from her head, and Dot realised she had never expected the worm that was her niece to turn so decisively. She said feebly: 'It were only fair that you should help out now an' then. You're the only girl, and not my own get, at that. Why, when your uncle would ha' sent you away, I stood up agin 'im, which ain't easy.' Her voice changed to a wheedle. 'Now come along, Dotty, be a good girl an' get the boys' room redded up, then I'll see if I can find some money so's you can do the messages wi'out having to ask for tick. You an' me mustn't fall out; I were that fond o' your mam . . .'

'I'm not cleaning the boys' room and you can use the marketing money to buy the fish and chips,' Dot said firmly. She was extremely cross with her aunt for deceiving her and pretending there was no money in the house, for now she saw the older woman fumble in the kitchen dresser and produce from its dusty depths an old brown purse. When she opened it, Dot could see that it contained a great deal of cash.

'Me savings; even Rupert don't know about them,' her aunt said proudly. She fished around in the purse, producing two florins which she held out to Dot. 'Here you are, queen, get me messages and you can leave the boys' room till the veggies is cooking.' Then, when Dot made no move to take the money, she added sharply: 'Gerra move on, Dot, otherwise you really will find yourself knockin' at the door of the nearest orphanage.'

It was too much. If her aunt had made some attempt to show real affection for her niece, Dot might have remained for at least a couple of days. As it was, she shook her head sadly and turned towards the kitchen door. 'Goodbye, Aunt Myrtle,' she said cheerfully. 'I'll pop in from time to time to see how you're getting on but I don't mean to live in this house ever again.'

'Dot McCann, just you come back here,' her aunt shrieked. 'I'm a sick woman. They said at the hospital I weren't to exert meself. It's your duty to look after me until I'm well.'

Dot popped her head back round the door. 'No it ain't, it's the duty of your husband and your sons,' she said bluntly. 'If they can't manage, then

421

there's plenty o' girls what'll give a hand if they's paid to do so, but I'm not one o' them. See you sometime, Aunt Myrtle.'

She closed the door gently behind her and, with her aunt's wails echoing in her ears, made her way out of the house, across the court and into Heyworth Street. She felt wonderfully light, light as air, and though she kept telling herself that she should feel guilty – or, at the very least, distressed by her aunt's plight– she could not do so. If Aunt Myrtle had ever been truly fond of her, it might have been different, but that afternoon her aunt had made it clear as crystal that her niece was a useful tool and not a loved member of her family. So Dot fairly danced along the pavement, her feet tapping along to the tune she was singing in her head: *Ain't she sweet, see her walking down the street, well I ask you very confidentially, ain't she sweet?*

Presently, she found herself outside Rathbone's butcher's shop and stopped to look into the empty window. There was no meat on display, though a solitary bluebottle seemed oblivious of the fact and was buzzing hopefully round the large stainless steel trays. Dot knew that Mr Rathbone and Mr McNamara were both safely locked up in custody, where they would remain until their trial could commence. This would probably not be for several weeks, as Nick had told her that the police had to examine all the evidence very carefully before committing anyone to trial, although the chief inspector had told him that the outcome was not in doubt since a great deal of corroborative evidence had turned up. Tradesmen from Church Street, once they had been told that their oh so friendly scuffer on the beat had been involved in the robberies, had remembered something which had seemed neither relevant nor important at the time, but had tied McNamara in with the attacks on their own shops. He had wandered in and out during the day, chatting with the utmost geniality, his little eyes roving over everything: their stock, their precautions against theft, their tills and their young assistants. Some of the assistants had admitted that McNamara had befriended them, giving them the odd bob or two to visit a picture show, asking seemingly innocent questions about their time off, and that of their colleagues. Of course it had looked like friendly interest, the interest of a man whose job was to protect them against thieves. It was not until you twisted it round and looked at his questions from a more sinister point of view that you realised how clever – and how well placed – he had been to take up a life of crime.

Dot's nose was pressed against the window, and she was wondering who would take the butcher's shop on, when someone seized her arm. 'What are you moonin' about up here for? I went straight round to Church Street when I'd finished my deliveries and Emma's done a roast chicken, roast potatoes and all the trimmings, and she said you'd made an apple pie yesterday, so we're havin' that with custard for a pud. Only she were a bit worried like because she were afraid you'd let your aunt bamboozle you into returning to Lavender Court.' Corky, for it was he, peered anxiously into her face. 'You aren't going to do that, are you? You won't let our Emma down? Nick says she's only a kid really, for all we think her so grown up . . . but then he's twenty-eight, really old, so I s'pose what's grown up to you and me can seem like a kid to him.'

Dot, whose thoughts had been far away, managed to get the gist of this and replied readily. 'Go back to Lavender Court to live? Not for a hundred quid. Not for roast chicken and apple pie every night of me life! Still, I've settled me aunt in and cleaned up the kitchen an' her bedroom. It stank – me uncle had used the chamber pot for a week, I guess, an' never emptied it once, the filthy old bugger. Aunt Myrtle thought she could black-mail me into living there again, but then she went a step too far – threatened me with an orphanage if I didn't toe the line – so I told her to forget it. I tell you, Corky, I left the court and walked up Heyworth Street, an' I felt . . . oh, light as air, free as a bird, as though I'd left all me troubles with the Brewsters and was startin' me life anew.'

'Aye, I know what you mean,' Corky admitted. 'It were the way I felt when I first escaped from Redwood Grange, and then I felt it even more the other day, when Nick said he'd take me on and the principal agreed.' He grinned at Dot, and for the first time she noted the changes in him which only a few weeks of normal living had wrought. Oh, there were physical changes, of course. His hair had been allowed to grow a little longer, and curled, and his face had filled out. His shoulders were broader but she thought the main change was in his expression. His self-confidence showed in every movement. He gave his opinion freely, and though he still spoke with a strong London accent, he also spoke with authority.

'Well? Are you coming? Because if not, I'm telling you, I'll go by myself.'

Dot laughed and fell into step beside him. 'Of course I'm coming,' she said at once. 'Roast chicken, eh? Is Nick there already, or is he coming later?'

'He's probably already there by now,' Corky said, as they hurried along. 'He don't miss an opportunity to be with Emma, as I expect you've noticed. I reckon he's sweet on her. What do you say?'

Dot shrugged. 'He certainly likes her,' she conceded. 'He got in a rare old state when he thought McNamara might have killed her, but then I suppose anyone would. But, to tell you the truth, I don't know much about – about that sort of thing.'

'Nor do I really,' Corky admitted. 'But I know all about roast chicken and apple pie . . . c'mon!'

Ten minutes later, they arrived, breathless and panting, in Emma's kitchen. The air was redolent of roast chicken and Emma was setting out the food on four pretty china plates whilst Nick, with a flourish, carved the bird. Emma was dressed and was looking very much better, with colour in her cheeks and very nearly her old sprightliness in her step. All four of them laughed and joked their way through the meal, and when it was over Corky suggested that they should all play whist, or rummy, two card games which they had played a lot lately, since Emma had not been well enough – or simply had not wanted – to go out and about.

Nick, however, shook his head, and Dot noticed that faint colour rose in his cheeks. 'No, I've a better idea,' he said. 'I'm going to give you kids half a crown because I believe there's a good film showing at the Paramount Cinema on London Road. You'll be able to buy yourselves a box of chocolates and an ice cream in the interval, and still afford good seats. The film's a comedy; you'll enjoy that.'

'Gosh, it's ages since I've been to the cinema,' Corky said, whilst Dot beamed with happy anticipation. 'Thanks ever so much, Nick.'

'Yes, thanks ever so much,' Dot echoed gratefully. 'But why don't you and Emma come along as well? It would probably do you both good to get out, and it's nice to have a laugh now and then.'

Nick and Emma, however, declined the treat, though Dot was surprised and a little puzzled to see how pink Emma's cheeks grew as she stammered out that she and Nick meant to have a quiet evening at home, checking the books, for though Miss Snelling had meticulously filled them in, with notes as to prices received and what would need replacing, she, Emma, had not yet checked to make sure the figures were correct.

Dot happened to be looking at Corky as Emma spoke and wondered why he was winking so desperately. She was about to press the point when the penny dropped: Corky was trying to warn her that Emma and Nick wanted to be private for once. So she said, tactfully, that she quite understood and that she and Corky would probably not be home until well after ten o'clock. Then they left, Nick clattering down the stairs behind them to lock the stockroom door, telling them as he did so that he would remain at the flat until their return and would come downstairs to let them in as soon as they rang.

'I feel quite guilty,' Dot confessed, as they made their way towards the picture house. 'Ever since Emma's awful accident, I've not left her alone for one minute, except for visiting me aunt in hospital, and you've been around for most of the time as well. If you're right, and they really are sweet on one another, I expect they'll want to be alone. Courting couples always do, I'm told,' she finished.

'Well, I don't see why,' Corky objected. 'If they're courting, then they're going to get married, and married people spend all their lives together, without anybody interfering. I should think they'd be glad of a bit of company myself.'

'Ye-es, but then babies come along and they're never alone again,' Dot pointed out. 'When you think about it, why *do* people have children? They cost a deal of money, they eat a lot, they muck up even the tidiest house and they're the main cause of rows and fights between the mam and the dad. Oh, I know the women say it's drink what causes fights, but I reckon men wouldn't drink if they didn't have a house full of kids to keep. I tell you, Corky, I'm never going to get married, norrif it means having a tribe of perishin' kids round me ankles.'

Corky sniggered. 'You ain't sweet on anyone yet, so you don't know what it's all about,' he said. 'Now shut up, and join the queue, and keep my place while I go for some sweets. D'you really want chocolates? Only I'd rather spend my share on toffee and bull's-eyes, and perhaps a few sherbet lemons; they'll last right through the performance if we go easy.'

Dot agreed to this and presently the two of them settled themselves in their comfortable plush seats, with a bull's-eye bulging in each cheek, and looked up at the screen as the main feature began. But the two comical characters had scarcely appeared on the screen when Corky gasped, and then began choking violently as his bull's-eye went down the wrong way and appeared to lodge in his windpipe. Thoroughly alarmed by the strange wheezing noises coming from her friend, Dot thumped him vigorously between the shoulder blades. The bull's-eye shot out, scoring a direct hit on the head of the child in front, and Corky turned to his companion. Tears were streaming down his cheeks, but even in the dark Dot could see the grin on his face. 'I've remembered,' he croaked. 'I've remembered where I've seen Ollie McNamara before. C'mon, Dot, we've got to talk' – all around him, people were shushing – 'and we can't do it here.'

They hurried out of the darkened theatre, though Dot tried to prevent Corky actually leaving the building. They had been in the front row of the circle, a great treat, and as they descended the wide, luxuriously carpeted staircase, she pointed out that they might just as well talk here. 'No one won't interrupt us, and there's no one to hear what we say 'cos the doors is sound-proofed. And anyway, we can keep our voices down,' she told him. 'Then afterwards we can go back and watch the rest of the picture. The B film is a cowboy with Tom Mix; you won't want to miss that!'

Corky, however, was adamant and towed her out into the street. 'I've got to get straight to the police station,' he said breathlessly, pulling Dot along. 'We can talk as we go.'

'I don't see why . . .' Dot was beginning, but Corky just grinned at her and pulled her along faster than ever.

'No, of course you don't see why, because I haven't explained yet,' he said. 'Just shut up and listen for once, Dot McCann. D'you remember me telling you that when I lived in London, I worked for a feller who were a bit on the shady side, like? Well, he were a crook, what they call a fence, which means he bought stolen goods off of the thieves and then sold 'em on. D'you remember?'

Dot nodded. 'Wilf something or other,' she said. 'His mum were real good to you; I remember you told me that.'

'That's right. Well, I dunno whether I told you – I probably didn't 'cos it didn't seem important – but the very first time I met Wilf, something odd happened. I arrived at his back door when he were expecting customers, so he told me to wait in the darkened shop – it were all closed up – and to stay quiet while he conducted his business. He said his customers were really shy and wouldn't want to be seen, but the fact is, after about ten minutes in the dark shop I got a fright – it was only Mrs Perkin's cat, but I didn't know that – and I shot into the room where Wilf and his customers were sitting at a table. There was stuff all over the table – jewellery I think – but Wilf was so quick to come round and push me back into the shop that I scarcely noticed. There were two men; one of them had his back to me and never moved a muscle, so I dunno what he was like, but the one facing me was a big, beefy fellow, with a little toothbrush moustache. Even though I were in a bit of a state, I knew he reminded me of someone, but it weren't till just now, when Stan and Ollie come on to the screen, that I realised the customer looked just like

Oliver Hardy. And then, of course, everything clicked into place, neat as you please. It were McNamara what were doing business with old Wilf and I'm pretty well certain that the feller with his back to me was Butcher Rathbone.'

'Crumps, it's a small world,' Dot said reverently. 'But – but does it matter, Corky? I mean, we all know it was those two men who did the jewel robbery because of the necklace, and Mr Rathbone made no bones about saying it were Ollie who killed old Mr Grieves. Oh, I know McNamara tried to deny it, but when he found Emma was alive, he more or less confessed.'

'Yes, I know, but don't you *see*, Dot? There's been a big fuss because old Mr Grieves hadn't bothered to renew his insurance, so the insurance company won't pay out – well, you can't blame 'em – but if Wilf hasn't yet managed to sell the stuff on, the police can swoop. Emma can have the jewellery back and start restocking the shop, particularly now that she won't be paying protection money either.'

'I see,' Dot said. 'Won't Emma be delighted if she really does get all her stock back? She never grumbles or moans, but I know she's been worried about the shop, and she desperately wants to continue her training. I'm sure if she gets the jewellery back, she'll return to the college. But – but Corky, d'you think the police will believe you? It – it does seem such a strange coincidence.'

Corky considered this, a frown creasing his

brow. Then it cleared and he smiled. 'I'll ask to see the chief inspector,' he said. 'After all, coincidences do happen and it really would be wonderful to get Emma's stuff back, and I think we stand a chance because Wilf never sold stuff on quickly, but always hung on to it, sometimes for months and months, I reckon. I'm pretty sure that was why McNamara and Rathbone travelled all the way down to London when I bet they could have got rid of the stuff much nearer home. Local fences want a quick profit, I expect, whereas Wilf had a well established and well thought of antique shop and could afford to wait until he could get a higher price.'

Corky was in luck; the chief inspector was not at the station, but the friendly desk sergeant who had dealt with Corky on his very first visit was on duty. Corky told his story with Dot standing by, and the police sergeant immediately asked him the exact date and time when he had first visited Mr Perkin's shop. Fortunately, Corky remembered without too much trouble, whereupon the sergeant went over to a filing cabinet and produced a large ledger which he spread out on the counter. 'If Constable McNamara was on duty at that time then we'll know where we are at once,' he explained. 'But if he weren't . . . aha!'

'He wasn't on duty, was he?' Corky asked, seeing a smile spread across the sergeant's face. Despite his jolly appearance and occasional bouts of generosity, it had soon become clear to Corky that McNamara was not popular with his fellow police officers; was, in fact, much disliked, and from the smile on the sergeant's face it was pretty clear to Corky that here was someone who had taken Ollie's measure long since.

'On duty? No, he was on a forty-eight, which means he didn't have to sign on here for two whole days,' the sergeant said, closing the book. 'Now that ain't proof he were in London – there's really only one feller who could prove that – so just you sit quiet, you youngsters, while I make a few telephone calls.'

Corky and Dot went and sat on one of the long benches, expecting to be there some time, but, in fact, it took less than an hour to establish what the sergeant wanted to know. He made several telephone calls, some quite long ones, but then he came back to them, smiling broadly. 'Your former employer is at present a guest of His Majesty the King, remanded in custody pending his trial. All his property has been frozen; in other words, the shop's been closed down and everything has been seized, pending the outcome of the case. I explained to my colleague down south that we've a witness to some of Wilf's nefarious dealings and he made a suggestion which I think will help. If Wilf agrees to turn King's Evidence and identify the two men who brought a supply of very fine jewellery on to his premises, then the court might agree to impose a lighter sentence. Naturally, Wilf will insist the men lied to him, said the jewellery was their own property and so on, but even so, I think he will admit to having bought from these men before, which will tie them in with all the other burglaries.' He beamed at Corky. 'A pretty satisfactory result, wouldn't you say?'

Epilogue
Llandudno, 1929

'Well, Mrs Randall, how does it feel to be a married lady?'

The short April evening was drawing to a close, and across the sea the sinking sun cut a flaming path. Emma and Nick were sitting on a bench at the top of the Great Orme, looking out across the miles of glistening wet sand, the great stretch of the bay and the purple mountains in the distance. Emma heaved a deep sigh and snuggled her head into the soft hollow where Nick's neck and shoulder met. 'I've only been a married lady for a couple of days,' she reminded him. 'But so far it's been – oh, glorious! I'm so glad we decided to marry now, and not to wait until I had finished my course at college. And I'm glad to be going back to a place of our own. I know it's only a small terraced house, but I love it already. And Miss Snelling was delighted to move into the flat above the shop, to keep Dot company. I think the two of them will get on very well despite the age difference. In fact, everything has worked out pretty satisfactorily, wouldn't you say?'

'I would,' Nick said. 'We've been pretty lucky all round. And thanks to Corky, you got the stolen jewellery back. He's a good lad and a good deal happier lodging with his pal Herbie's family than he was with the Cartwrights. He enjoys working for the *Echo* as a messenger boy as well, and hopes to be a reporter one day.' He squeezed Emma's hand. 'And doesn't the emerald necklace look grand back in the shop window? Only we ought to stop calling it the emerald necklace.'

Emma chuckled. 'I always knew the stones in the necklace couldn't possibly have been real emeralds,' she reminded him. 'I said so over and over, but I don't think anyone really believed me, though when you remember my grandfather made it as a sort of test piece when he was only in his early twenties ... well, it couldn't possibly have contained precious stones. Mr Mitchell had suggested that they should make something really striking as a window display item, and that's exactly what my grandfather did.'

'But he used real gold,' Nick pointed out. 'It is real gold, isn't it, apart from the clasp?'

Emma chuckled. 'Yes, but it's only plate,' she admitted. 'Not that it matters. It's just so wonderful to see it in pride of place in our window once more.'

'That's right. And now we can close the whole episode and get on with our new lives,' Nick said contentedly. 'Oh, Emma, I'm the happiest man alive!'

KATIE FLYNN

No Silver Spoon

Set in Liverpool in the 1920s, this is a heart-warming tale of triumph over adversity, from the *Sunday Times* bestselling saga author.

Dympna Byrnes lives a simple life with her family on the Connemara coast. She adores her father Micheál, and does her best to help her family by working hard and expecting little.

But beneath the surface there are hidden secrets. Dympna's mother idolises her clever eldest son, yet her attitude to Dympna is puzzling. So when her family find themselves in desperate need of money, it is Dympna who crosses the water to Liverpool to seek a better life.

Immersed in the bustling streets of Liverpool, Dympna's circumstances begin to improve. But it is a chance encounter with orphaned, half-starved Jimmy Ruddock that sets her on an extraordinary path she never could have predicted . . .

arrow books

Hitler's war is reaching out to affect every
member of the Neylor family.

Val Neylor, driving an ambulance through the blazing heart
of London, is in an impossible position, for the man she
loves is a fighter pilot with the Luftwaffe. And Jenny, whose
husband Simon is flying Spitfires, finds herself working
as a landgirl on a Devon farm.

Cara, by contrast, develops her social life, and Maudie, in
the WAAF, falls in love with two men at once . . . And Tina,
matriarch of the family, loves them all, scolds them all, and
tries to understand the new generation growing up in
the troubled times of war.

**A warm and moving family saga set in Britain caught
in the torment of the Second World War.**